HUGS AND QUICHES

A Heating Up the Kitchen Novel

CANDACE HARPER

Content Notes

Hugs and Quiches is a high heat romance novel, which means that it contains explicit sexual content. This sex takes place between two cisgender women, both with and without the use of sex toys.

In order to ensure a good reading experience for everyone wanting to read this, I've included these content notes. Please take them into account when reading so that you can avoid anything that will trigger you or otherwise harm your mental health.

If you don't want to read these notes, you can skip to Chapter One with this link. Do what feels best for you and your reading experience.

Sexual:

Masturbation with a wand toy, oral and manual sex between two cisgender women

Non-Sexual:

Discussion of an emotionally and physically abusive marriage, declined marriage proposal, description of small injuries sustained during cooking, descriptions of blood and minor gore, discussion of parent with cancer, parental death from cancer (off page, minor character), discussion of diets, diet culture, appearance of an abusive spouse, threat of interpartner violence

If you see something in this book that you think should be noted in future books, please send me an email at contact@candaceharperauthor.com

Chapter One

AMELIA

I didn't need to look at the clock mounted on the copper hood of the stove to know that Janet was late. For the third time this week. With a sigh, I pulled out the tin foil and covered the baking sheet that held the herb crusted rack of lamb. It wouldn't be as crispy as it would have been if it were served on time, but at least it would be edible without reheating it. I'd give Janet another twenty minutes before I gave up and ate by myself. Again.

I looked around. The white granite counters of the kitchen were fairly tidy, thanks to my years of practicing mise en place, but there was still plenty of dishes for me to fill my time with. Rolling up the sleeves of my floral blouse, I picked up the bowl I'd used to mix the herbs and breadcrumbs for dinner and got to work.

Washing dishes was a chore that I had always found cathartic. With each dish cleaned and placed into the drying rack, my mind felt a little less stuck in the anger that always washed over me when she was late. By the time I finished the last of the dishes, I felt significantly more like myself or the person I aimed to be.

I heard the soft rumble of tires pulling into the driveway and paused, looking out the window to see her black sedan's headlights turn off. Her long, lithe figure stepped out of the car with a briefcase that I could already tell was way too full, even in the dim evening light. I wiped my hands on my apron and made my way to the door to greet her.

I stood next to the industrial hall tree and fiddled with the applique cherries that formed the waistband of my apron until the door swung in and she stepped in, humming a lilting tune. She lifted her briefcase off of her shoulder and turned to hang it on one of the coat hooks. Her eyes caught mine and she smiled.

"Oh, hey babe! I didn't know you were there! Hang on a second."

I waited. Janet swept me into her arms the instant her arms were free of her overflowing briefcase, spinning me around with a laugh. The sound warmed my heart and washed away a little more of the anger that had been lingering in my heart. Something good must have happened, and maybe that would explain why she was late.

"Babe, I had the best day today. You aren't going to believe what happened!" Her voice was exultant.

I smiled back at her and pressed a kiss to her cheek. "What kind of best day? Are we talking a really good wine or are we going big for champagne?"

"Champagne, for sure," she chirped exultantly.

I loved it when Janet got like this, when she was so excited about something that she could barely stand still.

"Did you already make dinner? It smells great in here."

She was right. I'd found a new recipe for herb crusted rack of lamb that looked—and smelled—delicious. I could only hope the taste would live up to my expectations, even after sitting for twenty minutes longer than it really should have. She was a very picky eater, which was both fun and difficult when it came to new foods.

Luckily, I was a highly trained chef who worked in one of the finest French restaurants in the state. I knew a few good work-arounds for a variety of food allergies, sensitivities, and preferences. It was good practice to actually use that knowledge every once in a while.

"Go and get changed and I'll pop a bottle of bubbly," I told her, shoving her gently in the direction of our bedroom. She laughed again and kept going, pulling off her suit jacket and throwing it over her shoulder as she went. I watched her go, then went back to the kitchen where the rack of lamb was still covered in foil. It really did smell good, I thought with pride, even if the herb crust was probably soggy by now. Opening the wine fridge, I pulled out one of the bottles we'd been saving for a special occasion.

She sauntered back into the kitchen as I turned around and my mouth went dry. She was wearing one of her barely buttoned nightgowns and absolutely nothing else. She was beautiful, from her pin-straight blonde hair and high cheekbones to the toned calves that she loved to show off in her favorite pencil skirts, but all I could focus on was the single button that held the long shirt together, right below her perfect tits.

"Hey, my eyes are up here," she teased, circling the tip of her finger around the button in a way that reminded me of the way she loved to tease me in bed. It really *must* have been a good day if she was teasing me

3

like this. Normally, she was as short and to the point with flirting as she was at work.

"I, uh…" She stopped my mouth with a kiss that had my knees turning into jelly. It was warm and passionate and, somehow, she was smiling through it. I didn't know what had caused this, but I would absolutely take it.

She pressed her body against mine, then backed away ever so slightly.

"That bottle is *cold*," she giggled against my mouth. "You got it open yet?"

I'd honestly forgotten I was still holding the bubbly. Pulling it out from between our bodies, I set it on the kitchen island. We could both see that I hadn't, but honestly, how could I focus on anything other than her right now?

"I've got everything I need right here." To emphasize the point, I wrapped one arm around her waist and used the other to pull her face back down to my level and kiss her.

"Mm…" she moaned, pulling back slightly. "But don't you want to know what it is exactly that we're celebrating?"

"Oh, I definitely do," I murmured, shivering when she trailed a finger down my spine. "I wasn't about to let this mood go to waste, though."

She laughed throatily and picked up the bottle, twisting it open with a practiced hand. The pop startled me, even as I watched it happen, just because we were so close together. "This'll make it even better. Got any guesses on what my news is?"

"You won your case?" She had been in court for weeks fighting through a divorce that had turned entirely too ugly, but she hadn't given me many of the details.

"I did!" she crowed triumphantly, holding the bottle in the air. "But! That ain't the big news! Keep guessing!"

I tried to think about what else her news could be, but I couldn't focus with her chest heaving with every breath, bringing her boobs closer and closer. It was hypnotizing in the most erotic way possible. I loved it more than I could even think in that moment. Judging by the wicked grin on her face, she knew it.

"I got the official word today that I will be offered the chance to be a partner at the firm next month. Which, of course, I intend to accept."

"Oh my god!" I squealed. "Janet, that's amazing! Congratulations!"

She had known that she was under consideration, but she had only worked at the firm for four years. From what I knew of lawyers—which was, admittedly, very little, all of it gleaned from conversations with Janet— that path usually took much, much longer.

I had assumed her being considered for the position was a formality since she had an extremely high win rate on the cases she took on. Apparently, that had not been the case.

They must have seen exactly what I did every day— Janet was a marvel. An extremely hardworking, brilliant, and entirely too beautiful marvel of a woman.

Well, hopefully not that last part, I thought territorially. Not that she would have any interest in them anyway. Her bosses were mostly older, married, straight men who had no business thinking much of anything about her looks. I just couldn't get over how thrilled I was for her.

"That is just... huge, Janet. I'm so excited for you. I don't even know what else to say." I laughed self-consciously, tucking a strand of my hair behind my ear.

She looked down at me with a smile stretching from ear to ear. "I've got an idea. Say you'll marry me."

Suddenly, the room felt as if everything had screeched to a halt. I had to be hearing things. There was no way she had just proposed to me.

"W-what?" I stammered. "What did you just say?"

Her smile faltered just a little, but she kept her eyes on me. "Marry me, Amelia. I don't have a ring or anything, but I want to spend the rest of my life coming home to eat your great cooking every night and working towards building a great life for us."

I took a step back. Something about what she had said was not sitting right with me, but I wasn't sure exactly what. I hadn't thought about what being married to Janet would look like. I had moved in with her more out of practicality than romanticism, and even that hadn't really worked. We barely saw each other on weeks when I worked the dinner service or she had a case to prepare for. Lately, with her being under consideration for partner, there had been more and more late nights—even when she'd promised to come home early and join me for dinner on my nights off.

With that thought, it was like a lightbulb went off above my head. That's what was bothering me. I had an entire refrigerator full of proof of the promises she'd broken and a heart full of hurt from the ensuing arguments we'd had without a satisfying resolution. Even tonight, she'd been twenty minutes late, I remembered.

Chewing the inside of my lip, I thought hard, trying to come up with ways to say what I needed to without hurting her any more than I had to.

"Janet…I can't marry you. Not now."

Her face fell for just an instant before she pulled it back into a neutral expression. I knew her well enough to

6

know from the set of her jaw and the way her eyes hardened that she was hiding pain and a little bit of anger. Hopefully she knew me well enough to know that I was feeling those same things, even as I said things that I knew would break her heart.

"What do you mean, not now? When will you want to marry me?" She was using her courtroom voice, the one that hid all of her emotions. Not from me, though.

"I don't know, Janet. What would our married life look like? You're going to be so much busier when you're officially a partner, but we barely see each other as it is." My voice was even, despite the lump in my throat. "What happens when I get promoted at the restaurant and have to work the dinner shift on a regular basis? I'm not gonna be home to cook you dinner every night, and I'm certainly not going to do that if you aren't even going to do me the courtesy of coming home when you said you would."

"Babe, this case has been hell. You know I'm not like this all the time. Nothing in my life is as important to me as you."

"No, I don't know that," I retorted, confused as to how she had thought that all of the arguments we'd had over the last few months could have been construed as me being happy enough in this relationship to marry her. "You haven't *shown* me that, at all. Every time a choice comes up between me and work, you take work."

"What, so you don't want me to take pride in being great at what I do?" She set the bottle of champagne down on the counter and buttoned her nightgown over her breasts, celebration forgotten. "Why shouldn't I be proud of the fact that I made partner at a law firm at thirty-two?"

"That is not what I said and you know it, Janet. I

love that you are a great lawyer. I love that you are passionate about it. I love seeing you succeed in your career. But you don't put that same passion into making sure that you spend time with me or the successes I have in my career. I thought moving in together would make it easier for us to spend time together, but it didn't. I feel like I moved into this house and you expect me to be a fifties housewife, happy to attend to you at any hour no matter what. And it's not working for me."

There was a beat of silence between us as she took in my words. She let her face show the emotions she was feeling, and the hurt washed over me anew.

"Is that really how you feel? Is that how I've made you feel?" Her courtroom voice was gone, replaced by a much smaller, quavering one that I had never heard before. I hated that I had been the one to make her use it, but nothing I had said was untrue. Being honest about my feelings didn't stop my heart from breaking when I saw tears rolling down her face.

I didn't speak, not trusting my voice to work. I simply nodded, feeling tears fill my own eyes.

"If that's how I make you feel, then maybe…maybe we should take a break from this and see if we're really meant to be together at all."

She turned and walked away from me. The tears spilled down my cheeks as I stood in the kitchen listening to the click of her heels on the hardwoods. It was the quietest death knell I had ever heard, but it was unmistakable. Our relationship was over.

I stood there until the door of our—her—bedroom closed behind her, then wiped my face. I had to pull myself together enough to find somewhere to go. My options were fairly limited. It was early—only seven o'clock on a Friday—so most of my friends would still be working the dinner service.

Shit. Dinner, I remembered. The lamb was surely cool by now, if it wasn't completely cold. I'd have to re-fry the crust if I wanted to eat it, and I couldn't very well do that here. And, damn, I was hungry. Maybe that wasn't something I should have been focused on in the aftermath of a breakup, but it was true.

Without letting myself think or feel too hard, I pulled out one of my Pyrex bowls, packaged up a serving of roasted spring vegetables, and laid the rack of lamb on top, bone side down. Hopefully, that would help keep it from soaking in the juice from the vegetables.

I left the rest of the food where it was. I didn't know if Janet would eat it, but the option was there if she wanted it. What she chose to do from here was none of my business. In more ways than one, I thought sadly. I untied my apron and placed it on the counter next to the cooling rack. Picking up my food with one hand, I pulled my phone out of my pocket with the other and scrolled through my contacts. My heart sank as I realized that there was really only one place I could go and be sure I was welcome.

Well, I thought to myself, I guess there's nothing to be done but to get going. And so, I did.

———

I woke up on my parents' sofa to two pairs of eyes staring down at me. Blinking rapidly, the faces around them swam into focus and I recognized my parents. My mother's thin, owl-ish face stood several inches above my father's round, bearded one, but both showed confusion and concern. *Shit.*

"This is not a flattering angle for either of you," I croaked.

My father laughed, his rich tenor filling the room. "You aren't looking too good from up here either, starling."

I could only imagine what they saw. I hadn't packed a bag when I'd left the house, so I'd slept in the only thing I'd left in my closet that wasn't a formal gown—a Disney t-shirt, that a relative had purchased for me years before, that was still way too big for me. The skin of my arms and legs was marked from how hard I had sunk into the leather cushions, and my hair was basically guaranteed to be an absolute mess. I also had a major crick in my neck, which I supposed was to be expected.

I cleared my throat. "Fair point. What time is it?"

"Nearly noon."

"Oh."

"Amelia, what are you doing here? This is, well, it's highly unusual, to say the least. Is everything all right?"

"I really don't wanna talk about it, Mom. I haven't even had my coffee yet. I just…needed someplace to stay." I could hear the whine in my voice. My mother pursed her lips, a gesture of frustration I was very familiar with.

She wanted to say something else, but Dad jumped in. "Of course, you're always welcome. You just surprised us, is all. It's not like you to just show up here late at night when we aren't home."

I blinked at them. "In what universe is 8:00 p.m. late at night on a Friday? You guys asked me to look after the house, anyway."

They had been out of town for one of their educators' conferences. I couldn't quite remember where this one had been—Charleston, maybe? Or was it Miami? It didn't really matter, I knew.

Dad shook his head at me. "Well, since you're here, why don't you join us for lunch? We were going to try that new place; the Laotian one. I've heard great things."

The mere mention of food had my stomach rumbling. It had been a long time since I had reheated the rack of lamb and roasted veggies and scarfed them down in near silence, even if I had been asleep for most of it.

"If you're sure I won't be intruding, I'd like that."

"Of course not," Mother chirped. "Just make sure you brush your hair first. The couch did you absolutely no favors."

"Thanks, Mother. I might have forgotten, having never gotten myself ready to be in public before," I said dryly. She just raised her eyebrows at me. Sighing, I ran a hand through it and winced when my fingers hit a snarl. "Give me twenty minutes and I can be presentable."

Without saying anything, Dad nodded and reached a hand out to Mother. She took it, allowing him to lead her away. As they walked towards their bedroom, I groaned. Lunch was going to be excruciating.

———

I was able to fill most of the drive to the restaurant with lighthearted chatter about their trip, but once we entered the restaurant, it was clear that nothing was off the table. The scent of Laotian style pho and red coconut curry wafted through the open windows of the brick building while small groups of people sat and ate. Dried bamboo wrapped in twinkle lights decorated the upper half of the walls and ceiling, casting warm light over the tables, making for a very welcoming atmosphere. Or at least it would have been, had I not been watched over like a baby bird who was learning to fly.

We were walked to our table and handed menus by a young Asian woman, then left to our own devices to decide what we wanted.

Mother kept peeking over the top of her menu at me, then trading glances with my father before looking back at the menu. After fifteen minutes of pretending I hadn't noticed, I set down my own menu and scowled at her.

"Whatever is on your mind, just say it? You're not as sneaky as you think you are."

She twitched her long nose at me. "Amelia, I'm not sure what you mean."

"There's six options on the menu, Mother. There's no reason for you to be watching me as if I'm going to explode at the slightest touch."

"We're just worried about you," Dad cut in. "The last time you slept on our couch was the night you were laid off from that diner. Before that, it was when you bombed one of your mid-terms and were convinced you'd have to drop out of school."

Huh. I hadn't realized I was so predictable. It didn't entirely surprise me, though. I made a point of dealing with most problems on my own, but those two nights had been the worst of my adult life, last night included.

I opened my mouth to allay their worries with a joke but was cut off by the reappearance of the waitress. Without hesitation, I ordered the tom khem and summer rolls with a smile. My parents frowned at me but ordered their own meals; pho lao for him and duck larb for her. The waitress refilled our water glasses and walked away, leaving me at the mercy of my parents' hawk-like gazes.

I met Dad's deep blue eyes across the table and the

ability to joke it away drained out of me. I traced the knots in the light wood table with my fingers, just to have something to do with my hands while they waited for me to speak.

"So, Janet officially made partner yesterday."

They traded glances before Mother spoke hesitantly. "Well, that's wonderful?"

"Yeah. And she proposed."

Dad's gaze dropped to where my left hand sat on the table, obviously noting the lack of an engagement ring. He met my gaze again and raised a bushy eyebrow. With a shaking voice, I explained what had happened; what had been going on the last few months. By the time I finished, my mother had pressed her ruby red lips into a thin line. Dad reached across the table to me, his face unreadable.

"Oh, honey. I'm so sorry. We really liked her."

Yeah...me too." I picked up my glass with both hands, swirled it, and watched the ice cubes whirl into a tiny, contained hurricane.

"What... what do you need from us?" Mother's voice was quiet, but firm. Glancing up, I found her blue eyes looking at something over my shoulder. I turned to find the waitress had returned with our meals.

Without a word, she set down a wide, shallow bowl in front of me, full of deeply caramelized short ribs, julienned ginger, and a soft-boiled egg set atop a bed of rice. The scent of pork, mingling with the salty yet sweet braising liquid and the perfume of the jasmine rice, was divine.

Next she placed a platter of bowls in front of Dad; one deep bowl with an intricate terra cotta pattern that matched mine and a dozen small, white bowls with everything from chili pastes to mung bean sprouts to lime slices. It took up almost the entire length of the table, but Dad looked thrilled. Mother had a small smile on her lips as she looked down at her own plate filled with the warm meat salad and lettuce leaves for serving herself.

"I hope you enjoy your meals. I'll be back to check on you in just a few minutes."

We all dug in, leaving the discussion of my love life alone for a few minutes. I knew I wasn't off the hook, though. My parents didn't believe in letting things work out on their own.

"Mm, Jenny you've got to taste this. This broth is sublime." Dad held out his ceramic spoon to my mother, who took it with two long, dainty fingers. She sipped at it and made a pleased sound deep in her throat before handing the spoon back.

"Oh, that's wonderful. Here, try mine."

She filled a lettuce leaf with a scoop of her larb and passed it to him. He took it from her, bringing a blush to her cheeks when his fingers brushed hers. For a moment, I wondered if I had made a mistake by crashing on their couch last night instead of getting a hotel room or something. Maybe the hotel would have been a little less painful—emotionally and physically. The crick in my neck was something else, but it was nothing compared to the way my heart squeezed as I watched them together.

My parents' marriage was something I'd always hoped for in my own, much queerer fashion. They had always been desperately in love with each other, something they had never bothered to hide from me. Normally, it was great to see. Today, though, fresh from being slapped in the face with the failure of another relationship…well, it was a lot less great.

"Guy, is there something on my face?" Mother drawled, a small smile on her face.

"No, why?"

"Amelia is staring at us."

I snapped my eyes back to my own plate, embarrassed that I'd been caught.

"Ah, well, we have been very rude. We forgot to share our food with her."

In one smooth movement that one might have thought was planned, they each offered me something from their plates the way they had to each other. That brought a genuine grin to my face as I took the ceramic spoon with both hands and took a sip. They were right. There was something incredibly comforting about the savory beef broth, especially the hints of star anise, ginger, and cinnamon

"You know, Amelia, you should really learn how to cook this. I think it would be a hit at your restaurant," Mother declared.

"I'm not so sure about that, Mother," I laughed, taking the lettuce-wrapped larb from her.

"Well, why not? It's delicious!"

I chewed, delighting in the bursts of lime and lemongrass on my tongue as I chewed the salad.

"Well, for one thing, it would be cultural appropriation, which I try to avoid whenever possible. For another, we're an Italian restaurant. It's not exactly on brand for our menu."

She waved a hand at me in a way that I knew meant she was acknowledging my point and dismissing it. "You can still cook delicious food on your own, though. I think you should learn to make this for us. In fact, your father and I would be happy to be your test subjects while you're home."

My breath caught in my throat and I coughed hard a few times. "What?"

Dad spoke up between sips of soup while I regained my composure. "You are staying with us, right? At least until you have time to find someplace of your own."

"You want me to sleep on your couch for a month?"

I took a bite of my own lunch, thinking hard. I didn't relish the thought of moving back in with my parents, but the truth was that I hadn't quite thought that far ahead. But my father, being head of the Finance department at NC State and the man who helped me with my taxes every year, knew exactly what my financial situation was. I couldn't afford to drop two months' salary on a deposit, first and last months' rent, and still pay the rest of my bills at the drop of a hat. Really, I wouldn't have been able to do it even before that. I made a good living as a chef, but not a good enough one to live on my own in Raleigh.

"We have other rooms in the house, dear. Many of them have room for beds and clothes, even," she teased. I stuck my tongue out at her, and she laughed before she spoke again.

"Really, starling, you are more than welcome to come home. You don't have to make a decision right away, of course, but just know that you have the option."

They were both still watching me, so I smiled and nodded, even though I felt a little queasy at the thought of moving in again.

"I think I'll take you up on that. At least for a little while."

They beamed at me like I had just made their day, then tucked back into their meals. It was all worked out, so now they could eat without worrying. Maybe I could too.

———

Chapter Two

ZOE

BAKING AND DECORATING A BIRTHDAY CAKE FOR A two-year-old was an absolute waste of time, in my opinion. And yet, a two-tier cake covered in lavender ombré buttercream and piped flowers was exactly what I had just spent the last four hours making and would probably spend another two on it to perfect it before it was ready for the birthday party tomorrow.

Despite my personal opinions, the cake served two purposes. Well, three, really. Violet would be able to smash her grubby little hands into the top layer the way she loved to do. Mom and I would be able to eat the rest of it and then the photos and recipe would go onto the blog to hopefully draw a few more eyeballs to it. Standing at the kitchen counter, I continued piping flowers directly onto the cake.

It was good baking practice, at least, and would be some good evergreen content for the site—everyone loved babies and cake, after all. If I got lucky, Mom would be able to help me with getting video of the smash cake's usage, and I could put it up on Facebook and YouTube as well, I thought to myself. If I wasn't, well, pictures would have to do. But, God, I wished it was possible to finish all of this up while sitting down.

This morning, like most Saturday mornings, had been a busy one at the diner. While the tips would make the pinch of buying birthday presents a little easier, my feet ached something fierce. Probably because I had worked a double yesterday and a split shift the day before, I thought ruefully.

This week had gone from giving me plenty of time to get things done for the party but not enough money to do it the way I wanted, to having the money but not nearly enough time to get it all done. Really, that was my life in a nutshell these days. It wasn't the way I'd always imagined motherhood to be, but I wasn't going to let myself sit here and mope about it. My daughter would be home in a little less than an hour and I wanted to make the most of every minute I had before I had to be Mom, again, instead of just Zoe. I needed to take advantage of that. And besides, the cake was beautiful, even in its slightly unfinished state. Taking a deep breath, I tuned out most of the messy kitchen around me, focusing on the motions I made with the piping bag and the twangy country music that played on the radio behind me. After what could have been ten minutes or two hours, the screen door swung open and a tiny tornado toddled in with my harried mother right behind her.

A smile stretched across my tired face at the sight of them both. I set the piping bag down and turned so I was facing the door. I squatted and reached for my daughter. She ran as fast as her chunky legs would let her; the curly hair, that she got from me, bouncing with every step until she collided with my chest. It was amazing how much force a thirty-pound child could generate.

"How's my best girl? Did you have fun with Granny today?"

She nodded vigorously and I laughed. "Good. And did Granny have fun with Violet?"

Violet nodded some more as my mother shook her head and gave me a tired smile. I shot her a commiserating smile over my daughter's head, knowing exactly how exhausting she could be without trying.

"Vi, didn't you want to show Granny the new toy Ms. Elizabeth got you?"

"Yeah! I go get it!" She ran back to her room. As soon as her little footsteps were out of earshot, I stood with a groan.

"What did y'all wind up doing today? Do I owe you any money for what y'all did?" Mom shook her head. "Mom, I can pay for whatever."

"We just went to the park and played, and to the library for story time. She had a good day, for the most part, but she got real cranky around three." Mom shrugged. "Honestly, I was also cranky around three, so I guess I can't blame her. And you never owe me money for watching my favorite grandbaby, Zoe Beatrice."

There was no need to use my middle name, I thought grumpily. I raised an eyebrow, about to remind her that Violet was her *only* grandbaby and that I was perfectly capable of paying for her needs, when she toddled back into the room pushing a pony that was almost as tall as she was. I was kind of impressed; I hadn't thought she'd be able to push it out here on her own through the pile of the cheap carpet.

"Wow, look at that pony! Can you ride her?" Mom asked.

I jumped in before she could respond. "Not without Mama, right, baby?"

She nodded again, though she didn't look at either of us. Her hazel eyes, that were just like her father's, were laser focused on the pony. I knew she was about to try and climb it, despite having literally just acknowledged that she was only supposed to use it when I was helping her.

"Here, Violet, why don't I help you with that?" My mother crouched and helped steady my toddler as she climbed the tiny pony. That was my mother in a nutshell, doing everything she could to make my life easier, even when it meant that at fifty-three she was one of the primary caretakers for a toddler. It probably wasn't how she had planned to spend her aging years, but she would never let anyone think she had even the most mild of complaints about it.

As I looked down at the two of them, I was overwhelmed with love for my family. Maybe this wasn't what we'd planned, but I wouldn't have traded it for anything in that moment.

———

The party, if it could be called such, was in full swing. Two of the kids from Violet's regular library group had come over for a birthday play-date, and my home was a riot of sounds. Children's laughter mixed with the music from their toys as they played on the living room floor while their mothers' chatter drifted over them from the couch. It was wonderful. I let the sounds wash over me while I watched the girls play.

"I heard there's going to be a new cooking show on the Food Channel this fall," one of the women was saying. "It's supposed to be a competition like MasterChef or something but with early-career food people."

I glanced at the woman speaking, curious. She had long, dark hair that she kept in a low ponytail.

I was pretty sure her name was Jennifer, but not sure enough to use it. I knew her daughter's name was Daisy, but that was only because she'd had to stop her from putting a variety of things in her mouth that didn't belong there.

"Oh, that sounds like it'll be fun to watch. I bet that's something you'd be good at, Zoe." Patti grinned at me. I smiled back at her.

"I don't know about that," I demurred. "Most people mean actual professional chefs when they're talking about stuff like that. My little site doesn't put me anywhere close to the same level."

From behind us, my mother snorted derisively.

"Doesn't your site pay for like, half of your bills at this point?" Patti asked pointedly, echoing what I was sure Mom was thinking. She was right. It had grown almost as quickly as Violet had, earning me enough to cover its own costs and help make it possible to work part-time and still make it through most months.

"Even so, I've never worked in a professional kitchen. I never went to culinary school. That's what they mean when they say food professionals. Not someone like me."

"Wait, you've never done this professionally?" Jennifer—maybe Juniper?— asked. I looked at them, catching how Patti glanced sideways at her.

She blushed, apparently realizing how her words came across. "Oh, sorry, I didn't mean that as an insult.

It's just…everything you've made is absolutely delicious. I thought you were professionally trained."

"That's sweet of you, but nope. This is all from the school of Mom and the Food Channel."

"And quite a bit of natural talent," Mom added. "I bet you'd clean-up at that competition."

My mouth quirked into a one-sided smile. "You have to say that. You're my mother."

"She's right, though. I don't see why you shouldn't enter," Patti said. "I mean, Jennifer thought you were classically trained and she spends her work day dealing with fine dining at the hotel."

Ha! I knew her name after all, I thought triumphantly. Maybe my memory wasn't quite as shot as I'd thought it was. My triumph faded a little bit as I realized they were all looking at me, waiting for a reply.

"Y'all can't be serious," I snorted. "I can't go on a cooking show alongside people trained at the finest schools in the world. I'd be out before the beginning of the first challenge."

Mom opened her mouth to protest, but I cut her off with a wave of the hand. "Even if that wasn't the case, they film those things over several weeks. I can't afford to miss that much work or get that behind on blogging, not to mention someone would have to take care of Violet."

I watched as the reality sunk in for all of them the way it had for me before I'd even thought to dream of it. Their faces fell. Strangely, I wasn't as disappointed as they seemed to be. Sure, I'd love to be a famous chef just as much as anybody, but the fact was that it wasn't likely to happen. That was just the way it was. Being popular on my corner of the internet and being a good parent to my daughter was good enough for right now. And right now, I had to get back to doing the second part of that.

"Now, how about some birthday cake?"

———

By the time our party guests were gone, Violet, Mom, and I were all exhausted. All of the kids had begun to struggle about an hour after dinner, as they tended to do when they got tired. To be honest, I had been struggling too. I just had the grown-up skill of being better at hiding it. It had been a long time since I had spent so long with other adults that didn't require me to be working, but honestly, parties weren't that different than a shift for my relatively introverted brain.

Violet and I stood in the door, waving as Patti and Jennifer shepherded their half-asleep toddlers out the door, when I heard a sound I had been dreading. What started with a quick hitch in her breath devolved into huge, body wracking sobs and wailing by the time they reached their cars.

I sighed and scooped her up.

"Shhh," I soothed her, wiping her curls away from her forehead and pressing a kiss there. "It's okay, sweetie. I know you're tired. We just need to give you a quick bath and then you can go to bed."

"Not tired," she insisted between wails. "Want friends stay."

"They have to go home to their own beds, but you will get to see them again tomorrow."

Her eyes widened a little and I laughed. Of course, she'd forgotten. "I will?"

"Yes. Tomorrow you're going to the library with Granny, remember?"

"Oh yeah..." She yawned so wide that her head fell

back against my shoulder. Her eyes fluttered shut and I had to smile.

Maybe we could forgo the bath, just this once. She looked so peaceful that I didn't want to wake her, and a bath would do just that.

Instead, I walked as quickly and quietly as I could down the hallway to the bedroom that we shared. Luckily, she hadn't dirtied her clothes too badly, so she could sleep in her shirt with no issue.

With one hand, I pulled off her pants and floral underwear and let them drop to the floor. I picked up a pull-up diaper and slid it over her exposed bottom, just in case. I hoped she wouldn't have to use it, but since she had fallen asleep before her typical last trip to the bathroom, it was a precaution I needed to take. I was not emotionally prepared to do another load of laundry in the event of an accident.

That taken care of, I gently laid her in the bed. Her curls flattened against the pale pink pillowcase and I tucked the soft, white blanket over her.

"Happy birthday, Violet," I whispered, watching her sleep with her eyes wet. "I'm so glad I get to be your mom."

I watched her for just a moment longer before padding out of the room and closing the door as quietly as possible. Mama was watching from the hall, a small smile on her face as she leaned on the wall.

"I remember doing the exact same thing when you were her age," she whispered. "Passed out just like that while we were at your Aunt Andrea's for your birthday. You didn't wake up the whole drive home or during your bath. Your father and I had our best night's sleep in months that night."

My lips quirked up in a smile. Like my daughter, I

had never wanted to go to bed when I was younger, even into my pre-teens. If only I had known then just how much I'd miss those hours as an adult, I might have been more willing to spend the time on sleep. Unfortunately, even if I had, chances were that I would have easily used up all the banked hours over the last three years alone, if not before. That was how adulthood worked, at least as far as I could tell. But there was nothing I could do about that now. All that was left for the future was to see what I could do about making sure I got what I could now.

First, though, we had to make our way through the day's dishes and put the leftovers away. There wasn't much—Grammy's mac and cheese recipe was always a hit, and I had planned the portions nearly perfectly for the brussels sprouts and fried chicken. There was just enough for the three of us to have lunch tomorrow, which meant that was one meal that we didn't have to worry about for the next day.

"I'll wash, you dry," Mama told me as we finished packaging them up in relative quiet. I shoved the leftovers into the fridge and let it swing shut behind me. Taking my position next to the sink, I waited for the first dish to be ready for me.

"You know, I've been thinking about what Patti and Jennifer were saying." She handed me a plate, which I polished with the dishcloth and set in the dish drainer.

"What part of what they did?" I asked, my weariness clear in my voice. "We talked about a lot of things."

"That television show. *Cooking up the Kitchen* or whatever."

"Oh. *Heating Up the Kitchen*," I corrected her.

"Whatever." She flapped a hand at me but spoke

25

seriously. "I didn't like how quick you were to say you couldn't do it."

I blinked, surprised. I hadn't thought she would fight me on that decision. "Mama, what…"

"No, no. Let me talk." She paused, and I knew she was waiting to see if I would argue. I knew better, though. "I didn't like that your very first reaction to hearing about it was to say that you weren't qualified, and that even if you were, you wouldn't be able to go. You've been through a lot in your years, more than I ever had to deal with. I know that weighs heavily on you, and I know it's been hard for us to get our feet under us ever since you came back home. I'm not trying to downplay any of that. But, if that show was something you wanted to do, we would be able to figure out a way to make it happen."

Tears were welling in my eyes again. When they spilled, they made their way down my face onto the plates I was supposed to be drying.

"Mama, I can't go on television," I protested. "Those things film over several weeks. I can't leave you alone with Vi for that long."

"Yeah, you said all of that earlier, but honey, I raised you for two thirds of your life on my own. Once school starts back up, Violet will be in the preschool while I'm at work anyway. We could make it work."

"Okay, well, what about the money? I'd have to travel to wherever this audition is, and that'll be expensive. And if I get on the show, can you afford for me to be out of work for several weeks?"

"We'd get by," she protested. "It'd be tight, sure, but it's not as if our finances haven't been tight before. What do you think would happen if the diner fired you tomorrow?"

"I'd go and find another job," I answered promptly. "I'm very employable and I'm willing to do just about anything."

Mama handed me the last dish and pinched the bridge of her nose with soapy fingers. "You are the most stubborn woman I have ever met. You are willing to do anything for your family and everyone you care about, but when was the last time you took your own happiness into consideration?"

I stared at her, knowing my mouth was as far open as it could get without physically detaching itself from my body.

"Zoe, you are an amazing woman. You are a wonderful mother and an astonishing chef. I am proud to call you my daughter. But what I don't want you to do is sit around and wait for a great opportunity to come and pull you by the ear, because that isn't gonna happen."

"So, what, you want me to try things that I absolutely know I won't be accepted for? You don't even know if this is something I *want* to do, Mama!"

"Child, you are testing my nerves," she snapped back. "You have been watching cooking shows and learning from them ever since you were Violet's age. You've talked about your dream of being a chef since you were ten. Are you telling me you *don't* want to be on that show?"

With that question, all of the frustration leached out of me. It set my mind whirling, and when I spoke, it was with a quiet voice.

"I…I'm not sure."

My mother was the one person in the world who knew me as well as I knew myself. There were times that I wondered if perhaps she knew me better than myself.

As she spoke, I knew that this was probably one of those times.

"Then take some time and think about it," she urged. "If you genuinely don't want to do this, I'll accept it. But if you're just too scared of the unknown to try, then I'll be very disappointed."

With that, she swept out of the room, leaving me in the empty kitchen with my thoughts. I swallowed, trying to keep my emotions at bay as I pulled out my phone and searched *Heating Up the Kitchen* application.

It pulled up a dozen pages of results, but the only one I needed was down towards the bottom of the first page. With a shaking thumb, I pressed the *Cooking Network's* page to open it up. A gunmetal gray website loaded quickly, with four, square, blue and black designs that looked like the eyes of a lit gas stove imposed on it. A different word was written in a heavy, san serif, red font over each - Judges, About, Compete, and Schedule.

Before I could talk myself out of it, I clicked the first section. Another page loaded, this one designed to look like the inside of an oven. One thing was for sure, they were dedicated to the kitchen theme.

Most of the basic details were what Jennifer had mentioned earlier. *Heating Up the Kitchen* was designed for people who had some professional experience with food. One line stood out to me as if it had been bolded and italicized. Its definition of professional food workers specifically included those who ran food blogs and video channels.

My heart rose to my throat and, suddenly, I was holding back tears again. I couldn't believe it. After years of being told and feeling like I wasn't good enough to call myself a food professional, here this new competition was explicitly saying that I was.

With another press of my thumb, I emailed the link to the application to myself. I might not have been sure that I wanted to look into this competition before, but now I was glad I had. This might just be possible for me, if I could just figure out the details.

———

Chapter Three

AMELIA

I walked through the back door of the restaurant and breathed a deep sigh of relief. After three days of upheaval while I moved back into my childhood bedroom, I had been looking forward to the difficult, but simple work of running the kitchen through a dinner service. It was just barely noon, but there was plenty of work to do to prepare, and I was ready for it. In the kitchen, there would be no conversations asking how I was feeling or sidelong glances when they thought I wasn't looking. There I was, simply, the sous chef and we had work to focus on; the work of feeding picky customers. That, I could handle.

Like usual, I wasn't the first person in the kitchen. Miguel, one of our line cooks, had his hands deep in a bowl of green pasta dough. I walked over to him and breathed in, relishing the scent of the spinach, olive oil, and flour. Fresh pasta didn't have a particularly strong scent, but it was one that I had loved ever since I had made my first batch in culinary school. I had thought that I might get sick of it after working in a restaurant where 80 percent of our dishes were pasta based, but four years in, there was no sign of that actually happening. For that, I was grateful.

"You're a freak, you know that?" Miguel's lightly accented speech followed me as I walked to the pantry to store my purse. I grinned, shoving the bag into the back corner of the bottom shelf next to the extra bags of flour and grabbing my chef's coat from the back of the door.

"Takes one to know one, my friend." I clapped a hand on his shoulder and he tossed a smile back at me. "Did I miss anything fun while I was out?"

"Just your favorite customer, as always. He asked after you, specifically; swore you were the only one who knew how to cook his food properly."

I had to laugh. We had, had the same customer come in once a week for the last two years, always ordering the exact same thing: one braised lamb shank cooked overly well with unseasoned vegetables, nearly burnt potatoes, and extra gremolata on the side. Mr. Barnes was one of our best customers, but God help me, he was a pain in the ass. If we didn't realize it was his order, he was known to send it back until it was made to his standard.

"How does the waitstaff not know to tell us that it's his order by now? They certainly know they want to wait on him."

Most of the waitstaff was pretty good about making sure his order was put in correctly, especially since he was known to tip exceedingly well when it came out right on the first try.

"I think it was one of the new kids. She didn't know any better yet."

"You'd think they'd train her to take down an order

properly, though," I grumbled, measuring flour onto the counter for another batch of pasta dough. "He's a very specific customer."

"Ah, she will learn," he clucked as he wrapped his dough in plastic wrap and set it aside. Miguel was nicer than I was, I thought as I began to crack eggs into my own pile of flour. For some reason, the restaurant's owner hired a lot of college students for the front of the house who thought that being a waiter was much easier than working anywhere else. They quickly learned what a mistake that was. Most of them left almost as quickly as they'd been hired. Maybe this one wouldn't. Either way, it wasn't something I needed to worry about until Mr. Barnes came back in on Sunday night.

"Mr. Barnes will tell me about whatever you've left out, I'm sure."

"How could he not?" Miguel laughed. Mr. Barnes loved to come to the kitchen door and watch us work, all while telling us all the things we could do better. I always looked forward to the nights he came in, for reasons I couldn't quite form into words. I was fairly certain I was the only one who felt that way, but I didn't care. It was comforting in a way, though I wasn't really sure why. I wasn't going to look too hard at it, though. A little bit of joy never went amiss in this hard, fast-paced job.

Once I'd made three batches of pasta to add to Miguel's pile, I carried them all to the fridge to rest until the dinner service. These would make delicious ravioli for the evening, and there was plenty left to do, starting with portioning out the lamb shank. It was one of the most popular dishes we served, and with good reason.

My muscle memory took over as I cut the legs of lamb away from the shoulder joint and pulled the extraneous tissue and paper-thin membrane to expose the lean muscle that would become someone's delicious dinner.

Each leg of lamb was rubbed with salt, pepper, rosemary, and thyme and browned in our handmade lemon-infused olive oil until there was a good color on the meat. While the meat rested on a plate to the side, red wine, beef stock, tomato paste, and chicken stock were added to the pan to create a sauce that would flavor and tenderize the legs that we submerged in it. Then we put a lid on the pan and left it to simmer for a minimum of two hours until it was cooked to a perfect 145 degrees and tender as the night.

The lamb was the only thing that we didn't cook to order. It was a lengthy process, but I knew for sure that the beautiful result had brought more than a few customers coming back regularly—most of whom ate it the way we intended, unlike Mr. Barnes. For now, twelve of the meat lollipops were laid onto a sheet tray and slid onto a shelf in the refrigerator.

Before I could pull out the vegetables to chop for dinner, a voice I knew almost as well as my own came from behind me. I whirled around just in time to see him reaching out to grab me up in one of his infamous bear hugs.

"Hey," Chef Ian Marks boomed, drawing the word out for nearly ten seconds. "Look who finally came back to work."

At 6' 4", he was taller and bigger than me with lungs that allowed him to bring enough volume to put fire engines to shame. He was one of my favorite people in the whole world. Grinning, I stepped into his arms and wrapped my own around his barrel of a chest. He picked me up and swung me around like I was a scrawny child instead of a 6 foot tall, fat woman in her early thirties. Was it appropriate for work? Probably not, but I loved it.

"I was thinking about replacing you with one of the new kids out front," he said with a joking gleam in his eye when we separated from each other.

"You could try!" I stuck my tongue out at him and he laughed loudly. I couldn't resist joining in.

Ian was a great guy and an excellent boss. However, he was known for being really relaxed in every part of his life…except in his kitchen during a service. No one without at least a little experience would survive back here as a cook. Hell, even some of those who had plenty of experience had found him impossible to work with. The only people who lasted longer than a month were those with real backbones and a willingness to do the work. For our kitchen, they had proven pretty hard to find and keep.

"Seriously, though, kid. The kitchen's not the same without you."

"Aw, you're being nice," I demurred, nudging him with a shoulder. He raised one thick slab of an eyebrow as if to say that he never did that, then shook his head at me.

"You got a minute? I wanted to talk to you about something." His voice was serious, which made me nervous. I nodded and he gestured towards the small room that served as his office. When he started walking, I followed him.

We both squeezed between the desk and filing cabinet to enter the room. He took his seat behind the large mahogany desk, leaving me to sit in the sturdy, yet uncomfortable, armless chair in front of it. He shoved papers out of the way so that he could close the laptop he used to conduct all of the restaurant's business and study my face.

After nearly a minute of silence, I began to squirm under his gaze.

"You've been here for a long time. Almost five years, right?"

I nodded hesitantly. I had started as a kitchen porter right after I'd graduated through the different stations and up to my current position as sous chef. Culinary school taught you a lot of skills and gave you a lot of necessary experience, but there was nothing like walking into a kitchen job to realize just how much there was left for you to learn. I had been incredibly lucky. After six months in his kitchen, Ian had taken it upon himself to teach me almost everything that was important to running a restaurant; from how to ensure that a plate was perfect every single time, to how to create a menu that was manageable for a small staff, but still interesting enough that you wouldn't get sick of cooking it day after day.

He had set me up to be his perfect successor in the kitchen, even though I was pretty sure he had absolutely no interest in retiring anytime soon. He wasn't going to fire me, not after that warm welcome. There was nowhere he could promote me to, unless he took me out of the kitchen. God, I hoped that wasn't what was about to happen. He fixed me with his gaze and I had to stop myself from gulping.

"What's your five year plan?"

I blinked at him. "What?"

"Your five year plan. Where do you want your career to go?"

Staring at him, I tried to figure out why he was asking. I knew the answer, of course. I'd had every one of my life goals planned out for years, with time and space built in for contingencies. Of course, I'd hoped that I'd have a long term partner at this point, but given the events of the last week, that was something that was on the back burner. I wasn't about to start talking about that at work, though.

"I'd like to keep growing as a chef. You know I want to have my own place someday, and it would be nice to be able to prove that I have the experience and the skill to make that happen."

He nodded, still watching me carefully. When he spoke again, he asked another question. This one was even more unexpected than the previous one. "What are your opinions on reality TV?"

I stared at him, completely flabbergasted. "My opinions on *what?*"

He started digging around in the piles of paperwork and receipts until he found a thick gray folder and handed it to me. On the front was an embossed square logo that looked like a lit gas stove. At the center, an H and K were written in thick red text on either side of a blue arrow.

"*Heating Up the Kitchen?*" I read. "I've never heard of it."

"It's brand new. I got this in the mail, while you were out, and called around. Apparently a couple of my professors from the CIA have been part of the team planning the challenges. It sounds like it's gonna be pretty fun, honestly."

"And you're showing this to me because…?" I was still really confused. He rolled his eyes at me as if I was missing something that was blatantly obvious.

"I think you should try out for it."

"What are you talking about? You were *just* saying that the kitchen isn't the same without me."

"That's true. But Amelia, you can't be my sous chef forever. You know that as well as I do. Even if I wanted to, there's only so far I can take you in this industry as your boss." He rubbed a hand over the back of his neck but kept his attention on me. When I didn't say anything, he tapped the folder I still held.

"Look at the prize money for that. Half a million dollars, not to mention the notoriety and fame that comes with being on a popular television network, would go a long way to making it possible for you to go out and make your goals happen. Not to mention…I think you would do well at it."

I had to sit with that for a moment, flipping through the paperwork absentmindedly. I was flattered, if I were being honest with myself. But, as it always was with feelings, that wasn't the only one swirling around in my belly. So much had changed in the last week alone that I was a little scared to move towards yet another change. It just seemed so sudden. But at the same time, $500,000 was *a lot* of money. It would more than pay off my student loans and be enough for a down payment on a house of my own, if I didn't want to immediately open my own restaurant.

As if he sensed how conflicted I was, Ian waved at me. When I looked up, he spoke softly. "You don't have to make a decision now. I know you'll want to talk to Janet about it and figure out if it's something that works for you both. The deadline is next week, though, so I wouldn't take too long about it."

I grimaced, but before I could speak, Ian cut me off.

"It won't take you that long to do the application. It's only like three pages. It'll be fine."

Sighing, I corrected him. It might have been a little foolish to think I'd be able to keep it from him for long, anyway.

"The timing isn't the issue. Well, not the only one, anyway. Janet and I broke up. I took the extra time off because I was moving back in with my parents."

Now it was his turn to blink and stare. "Wow....that really sucks, Amelia."

I laughed mirthlessly. "It was the right thing to do. We...we weren't well suited, it turns out."

"Then I'm glad you figured that out." He paused, though it was clear he wasn't finished talking. When he continued, it was in a quiet voice.

"I'm glad she won't stand in your way anymore. Now you can focus on your career and finding someone who respects that. Someone who respects you."

A smile pulled at the corners of my mouth. I should have known he'd say something along those lines. He hadn't exactly made a secret of the fact that he didn't like Janet, though he never said as much outright.

Instead of telling me he disliked her, he had just banned her from the back of the house after a few of our fights had come into the kitchen a few too many times.

Maybe I should have taken that as a sign, but I hadn't. I had been so sure that we were right for each other that I had ignored tons of red flags. But that was the way of things. Hindsight would always be 20/20, whereas my actual sight was only that good with glasses I hated to wear.

"Thanks, boss. I hope I can find that person too. In the meantime, I'll think about whether this is right for me."

He smiled his toothy grin at me. "If you do decide to apply, use me as a reference. I'm sure I can come up with *something* decent to say about you. Now get back to work. We have a full service to prep for."

My smile turned into a full-blown grin. "Aye, aye, chef."

———

We had finished cleaning up the kitchen and locked up around midnight. My feet and back ached by the time I got home, but my mind was entirely abuzz with the residual energy of the dinner service—and thoughts of the hard decision ahead of me.

When I walked into the house, I was surprised to find the living room and kitchen lights at their full brightness. It wasn't like my parents to leave lights on when they had gone to bed, and they were both early risers.

Poking my head into the kitchen, I found Dad puttering around in flannel pants and a fluffy bathrobe. I had to smile a little as I watched him. He hummed a little song as he tidied, swinging his hips a little along as he walked. It was adorable.

When he turned in my direction and caught me watching, he blushed deep red. I grinned at him.

"You've still got moves, old man. Has Mother seen those?"

He laughed quietly. "Not tonight. She's been asleep for a while. I had some grading to get finished and lost track of time."

Something felt off about that. I ran through the calendar in my head. It was mid-July and they'd just gotten back from vacation. How did he have grading to do?

"I thought school didn't start back for another month. That's why you got to go on vacation, right?"

"The regular school year starts in a month," he said patiently. "The last summer mini-mester started on Monday, which I told you I was teaching. Remember?"

"Oh, right. Sorry." I scratched my head in embarrassment. I had forgotten.

Dad had been made the head of his department at North Carolina State three years ago and had been teaching the shorter, more intense classes every summer since. He said it was the least he could do to give the newer tenure track professors a break. They had enough work to do with the stresses of researching and getting articles ready for publication that they deserved the summers off from teaching since he had to work anyway.

"It's okay. You have a lot on your mind the last few days. I won't hold it against you. This time." He winked at me.

I grinned back sheepishly. Him being awake made a lot more sense now. It was a lot of work to teach—and grade—an entire semester's worth of finance classes in five weeks, and it always left him keyed up. Luckily, I also knew the secret to helping him get to sleep. It was something he had taught me a long time ago, when I started having the same insomnia issues during my first year as a chef.

"You know you're going to regret being up this late tomorrow morning," I reminded him. "How about I make us both some spiced milk?"

He smiled widely at me. "That would be wonderful, dear. I'll get the milk."

I set my bag on the table next to his laptop and slipped out of my shoes. Padding over to the cabinet, I searched for the various bottles and jars I needed. Two were easy to spot, being almost as tall as the inner shelf of the dark wood cabinet—one filled with whole vanilla pods while another held sticks of rolled cinnamon bark. The other two bottles were a little harder to find amidst the packed cabinet. Eventually, I found the whole cardamom pods and the cloves and set them on the counter. Last, I reached into the only box there and pulled out a tea bag. I placed four cloves and two cardamom pods in it and tied it shut. Pulling out one of the vanilla pods and a cinnamon stick, my recipe was almost complete. I turned to the stove and found my father already heating a pot of milk.

The sight was so familiar, it made my heart ache a little. Dad had made this for me a thousand times when I was younger. Whether it was anxiety over a test keeping me up or just a bad dream, nearly every bad night had been made just a little better by drinking this simple blend at my father's side.

Stepping over to join him, I sliced open the vanilla pod and dropped everything into the pot of milk. It took less than a minute for the scent of the spices to fill the kitchen. Just that smell eased my mind a little, and I realized that maybe Dad wasn't the only one who needed it tonight.

"How was your first night back at work?"

"It was…interesting," I told him, turning away to grab our mugs. There was a tradition to these things. His was tall and wide with the NC State wolf logo on it. Mine was shorter, wider and pinker, one of the ones that may as well have been a soup bowl.

"Good interesting or bad interesting?" He didn't even look at me as he stirred the milk. There was a trick to doing this correctly, and he had it down to a science. You had to stir it carefully; slow enough not to make it take forever to heat but fast enough to keep a skin from forming on the top. Then, just before serving, you add a teaspoon of honey and allow it to sweeten it all. It was tricky, but it was more than worth it.

"Interesting, interesting," I said unhelpfully. "I told Ian about Janet and me, and he seems to think that I should try out for a new cooking show."

That got him to look at me, though his stirring hand never faltered. "A cooking show? Aren't those usually for home cooks?"

I shrugged. "This one isn't. I haven't looked that hard into it, but a few of his professor friends from the CIA are helping to plan the challenges. He thinks I have a shot."

Dad snorted. "I will never not laugh at that acronym. What good is an acronym if you have to explain every time that no, you're a cook not a spy."

"Yeah, yeah, I know. Though, really, if you were a spy, it's good to have a cover story. Being a chef would make a pretty good one."

Now he rolled his eyes at me, then turned his attention back to the pot. Lifting the honey jar, he squeezed it gently and poured it into the pot.

"We should be just about ready, dear. Ready the ladle!"

Laughing quietly, I reached around him and pulled out the ladle that was pretty much solely used for this drink. Placing it into the pot, I pressed a kiss to his fuzzy cheek.

He made a happy sound as he ladled the spiced milk into the mugs. When both were full, he pushed mine over towards me. Without waiting, I lifted it in both hands and inhaled deeply. The spices with a hint of sweetness felt like they floated directly from the mug to my soul.

Dad took his first sip, closing his eyes in clear happiness. I smiled and took a sip myself.

"This was a wonderful idea. And so is auditioning for that show."

I choked on my drink, swallowing fast to keep from spraying it all over the kitchen.

"Dad! Did you have to wait till I'd taken a drink?"

He chortled, taking another sip before he spoke again. "I think you should audition for the show. If you want, that is."

For what seemed like the umpteenth time that night, I found myself staring at him and blinking. When he saw my face, he continued speaking with a newly serious expression.

"You've just had a big setback in your life. I know you never intended to move back in with us. You're an excellent chef, and you used to love competing against your classmates in school. In fact, your mother still raves about those cocktail onion, stuffed, deviled eggs you made for her department's open house."

That had been a good competition. My final semester, Mother had hired my culinary class to cater the sociology department's annual open house. They were famous for having great speakers and great food; something my mother has been determined to ensure continued under her tenure as dean of the college.

My classmates and I, under the strict watch of our professors, were tasked with coming up with the perfect menu of appetizers for the night. It had been a fierce competition; one that I had honestly loved being part of. I had forgotten about it until he had reminded me.

Glancing back at my bag, I could see the folder

peeking out. I turned back to my dad's serious face and felt my lips quirk into a real smile.

"Do you want to take a look at the paperwork with me?"

Dad grinned and waved me towards the kitchen table. "I thought you'd never ask! Step into my office."

Snorting a laugh, I grabbed the folder and sat down. "Okay, professor. Let's see if this is worth it."

———

———

Despite being more than fifty pages, the application actually wasn't terribly complicated. Nearly half of the paperwork in front of us was asking for biographical information—when I started cooking, what my family was like, my education, and experience in actual restaurants. On top of that, it asked for me to describe my goals for the future.

It made sense, in a way. When you watched those shows, every competitor had a really compelling story. It made sense. Good stories made for good television, and the more they knew about us, the more they'd be able to play us off of each other.

The second half of the paperwork was the more complicated one. It was asking for our top five dishes, complete with recipes and cooking techniques. It also asked us to choose the location where we'd like to audition. Trailing my finger down the list, I read each one out loud. It looked like the closest one was in Atlanta. Specifically, the event center in the Omni Hotel in the CNN Tower.

"You'd like the Omni Hotel. They have a great bistro there."

Dad and I both jumped in surprise at the sound of Mother's high pitched voice. We turned to see her standing in the doorway with a crooked smile on her thin face.

"Hey, hon. Did we wake you?"

She shook her head. "I just came down for a drink and found you two having a party without me."

I smiled as she walked over and pulled out a chair for herself. She sat as primly as ever and rested her chin on her hands.

"What's all this for, anyway?"

Dad and I filled her in on the competition with as many details as we could manage. She listened carefully, asking a question here and there to clarify something we'd said.

"Well, that is a whole lot to digest at…" She checked her watch, then continued drily. "Two in the morning. It sounds very exciting, though."

"Doesn't it?" Dad's voice was almost gleeful. Mom lifted her head from her hands and placed one of them on top of mine, the other over his. It was as comforting as the spiced milk.

"I guess there's just one question I have left to ask, and this one might be a little complicated."

I looked at her, curious.

"Do you actually want to compete on *Heating Up the Kitchen*?"

Suddenly, I realized that I knew what my answer was. Somewhere in the last hour, talking over recipes and competition possibilities with my dad, I had grown attached to the idea of being a part of this.

"I think I do."

My parents' matching grins lit up the kitchen. Mom squeezed my hand.

"Well, then tomorrow, we are going to start helping you test recipes for this application. And after that, you are going to win this thing."

My heart leaped as I grinned back at her. I liked the sound of that.

———

Chapter Four

ZOE

By the time I arrived at the hotel where the auditions were being held, my head ached almost as fiercely as my hands did. I'd spent most of the last hour gripping the steering wheel and watching the road as if my life depended on it—which it did.

I'd heard people complain about Atlanta traffic before, but this was like nothing I'd ever experienced before. More than once, a lane had ended mere yards after it had started, leaving me slamming on my breaks and praying that the people behind me were paying better attention than I was. Luckily, they mostly were. A few horns were honked, but honestly, I was just glad I had made it there more or less unscathed—and that Mama hadn't heard me cursing like I'd spent the last five years in the Navy. She'd have had me washing my mouth out with soap every minute I wasn't in the audition, if she had.

I glanced around the lobby and found myself wishing she could have been here with me, though. People in chef's coats were being shepherded from room to room by people in all black and headsets; all of them looking harried. Soon, I would be one of them, and the thought brought a lump to my throat. They all looked so official and chef-like, while I had just spent a little over six hours in a car, desperately needed a shower, and was more than a little rumpled. All I could think was that it would all have been just a little bit less terrifying with her by my side to remind me that I was here for exactly the same reason as every other potential contestant in the hotel.

All I had to do was check in, take a shower, pull my head together, and get downstairs in time for my audition in two hours. One step at a time, I reminded myself, and went to stand in line at the front desk. A curvy woman in a pink houndstooth wrap dress and kitten heels stood in front of me with a black rolling suitcase. Her luggage tag showed that she'd flown from Raleigh Durham International; probably the smarter travel choice from our shared starting point, if I was being honest with myself. Unfortunately, I just hadn't been able to justify the $150 it would have cost to get me here, especially on top of the hotel bill and food costs that I'd need to deal with while I was away from home. But I couldn't think about the money right now. I had committed to trying my damnedest at this audition, and making myself sick worrying about money would absolutely sabotage any chance of success I might have.

Instead, I kept my gaze fixed on the woman in front of me as the line slowly moved forward. As I stepped forward and got a closer look, I realized that the dress that wrapped her curves beautifully was not the baby pink houndstooth pattern that I'd thought it was. The pattern was actually made up of tiny cat face prints in the form of houndstooth. It was playful, yet professional. I loved it.

She must have felt my eyes on her because she flipped her wavy, light brown hair back over her shoulder and looked at me. When her smiling green eyes met mine, I could feel my cheeks heating. I wasn't entirely sure if I was embarrassed about getting caught staring or because she was just that stunning. She had bright apple cheeks and a perfect Cupid's bow mouth that quirked up at the corners as I blinked at her.

"See something you like?"

Her voice was light and flirty, making my heart race enough that I could stammer out a response. "I, um, I like your dress?"

That brought a real smile to her face, showing off a glowing smile behind her pomegranate lipstick. "Thanks! It has pockets!"

She stuck her hands in her pockets and showed off the most magical of additions to any woman's clothing. I grinned back at her while she looked me over. Her eyes snagged on the cast iron skillet handle sticking out of my backpack and she took a small step towards me.

"You're here for the audition? *For Heating Up the Kitchen?*"

"Um, yeah. I'm auditioning this afternoon," I replied, glancing over her shoulder. The check-in clerk was smiling, but I could see impatience on her face, so I nodded in her direction. "Lines moving."

The other woman stepped forward until she was a reasonable distance from the person in front of her, then turned back to me. "I'm Amelia from Chez Marc. I'm auditioning today too." She held out one hand to me and I shook it, feeling a shiver race up my arm at her firm, callused touch. Something about her was absolutely captivating, and I couldn't put my finger on it.

"Nice to meet you. I'm Zoe. I run, *Cooped Up with*

Zoe." I held my breath, waiting for her response, hoping beyond reason that she wouldn't be a jerk about it.

"That's a strange name for a restaurant." Amelia wrinkled her nose and I felt the smile on my face tighten, knowing what was about to happen. "It sounds more like a food blog or a television show."

"That's because it *is* a food blog," I said, maybe a little more sharply than was necessary. I held my breath, waiting to see what she would say next.

"Oh. Then that's a great name," she amended, blushing. Even with as annoyed as I was with the unfortunately stereotypical attitude, I couldn't help noticing just how pretty she was when she blushed.

"Thanks." My answer was short, but it warmed me a little that she'd bothered to hide it. Maybe she was pretty and wasn't an absolute jerk. That would be a nice combination.

She opened her mouth to say something else, but the check-in clerk interrupted. "Ma'am, if you could please step forward. I'm ready to check you in."

She pressed her lips together into a tight smile that was probably supposed to convey her apology, and I nodded. With a whirl of hair that sent a wave of light citrus-scented air towards me, she turned to the clerk and began going through the process. I took a deep breath and tried to compose myself again. I was here for a reason, and that didn't involve staring at pretty women or caring what they thought about how I made my living. Especially when they were someone who could, very easily, be a competitor.

When she finished checking in, she turned to me with a smile. "I'll see you at the auditions, I hope. Good luck!"

"You too," I said simply. With that, she turned and

walked towards the elevator, leaving me alone with the check-in clerk and my thoughts.

"Whenever you are ready, ma'am."

———

A shower, a couple ibuprofen, and a sandwich later, I finally felt almost all the way human again. It was amazing what a little basic self-care would do to revive a person, even if said person hadn't managed to get more than a few winks of sleep the night before.

A nap would have been even more helpful, but I was way too keyed up for that to be possible. Besides, I only had an hour between now and when I needed to be at the audition.

Instead of being exhausted like I should have been, I was itching to work on something. If I'd been at home, I could have edited photos or the latest video. I could have even tidied up Violet's toys. From the inside of this hotel room and without my computer, though, there was only so much that I could do. So, I did what any woman who made her living on the internet would do; I swiped my phone open and opened Facebook.

The blue and white app loaded quickly, showing I had ten plus notifications and two messages. I grimaced. One of the messages was guaranteed to be an older woman who had read every single post I'd ever written and insisted on pointing out every grammatical error and misplaced comma in each one. The other, I wasn't as sure about, but I wasn't going to check it right now. That was sure to get me heated, and I didn't have the extra energy for that.

Violet's birthday post had gone up while I was driving, which meant most of the notifications would be likes and well wishes. Hopefully. There were some very cute pictures of her alongside the cake, and who wouldn't love a cute toddler with cake all over their face? I know I did, even if I was incredibly biased.

Luckily, my commenters agreed. One woman said it was perfect for her daughter's upcoming birthday. I wondered what Amelia, the chef from before, would think about that, then shook my head. She didn't matter that much in the grand scheme of things. The post had a good number of likes and shares, which was a relief. Sometimes the more personal posts weren't quite as popular, but this one seemed to have hit the mark with my audience. I typed up quick replies to the more reasonable ones and liked them all freely, making sure everyone at least had their comment liked before I navigated away.

One of my cousins had tagged me in the comments of one of those flat lay food videos asking me to learn to make something they called a unicorn omelet. It looked disgusting, so I clicked the next notification; a post from another food blog I loved. It shared a recipe for smothered oxtail that looked more delicious than anything I had eaten in days. I'd have to check that out when I got home.

Before long, my alarm was going off. It was time for me to go and cook my heart out. Surprisingly, I felt ready.

Let's do this, I thought. Grabbing the cast iron skillet, I'd inherited from my grandmother, and taking a deep breath, I walked out of the room and towards the competition that could either take me to the next level or put me back to where I'd started.

———

Chapter Five

AMELIA

My heart pounded in my chest as I made my way through the sea of people in the lobby of the hotel. Signs pointed to a long hallway and then to a room on the left. Four other women stood outside the door to that room wearing everything from chef's coats and pants to what I was pretty sure was a designer pantsuit.

Seeing them made me feel a little better about the pocketed wrap dress I wore under my apron. I didn't like that I was the last one to arrive, though. I was twenty minutes early, but my parents had ingrained in me a need to be on time from a very young age. I could still hear my father's voice saying that fifteen minutes early is on time and on time is late. I breathed a sigh of relief and stepped into line behind the last woman in line. She turned to look at me and I froze.

It was Zoe, the woman I'd offended in the lobby, carrying the cast iron skillet I'd spotted in her backpack. She looked better now. Her chef whites were crisp and fresh on her slim form, and her brown curls had been pulled into a simple bun. I couldn't help but notice that despite the frown on her face as she glanced at me, she was beautiful.

"Hey, Zoe?"

She turned to look at me fully, and I got a whiff of the hotel's shampoo and body wash.

"I wanted to apologize for what I said earlier. Or, the way I said it, anyway."

Now the other women were looking at me, too, but Zoe's expression hadn't changed.

"There's absolutely nothing wrong with food blogs, and I shouldn't have implied that what you do is any less important than cooking in a restaurant. I was a jerk and I'm sorry."

Our section of the hallway was quiet for a moment before Zoe nodded, a wicked smile spreading across her face.

"I appreciate that. After all, we're both here to compete for the same title. And I came here to win."

"Well, I'm glad to hear we've already got some trash talking going on," a woman's voice commented from the front of the line. "That'll make for great television."

The women in front of me whirled around to see a red headed woman wearing black jeans, a paisley blouse, and a crocodile grin.

All of us stood stock-still as we waited to see what she would say next.

"Hello, competitors. I'm Angela May, executive producer of *Heating Up the Kitchen*. It's time for all of you to get cooking."

At Angela's gesture, we filed into the room in silence. It was a lot larger than I had anticipated from the outside, and a lot busier.

There were five separate, but identical, backdrops spread around the room. Each *Heating Up the Kitchen* branded backdrop had a stool in the foreground and a huge camera in front of it. *Heating Up the Kitchen* might have been a new show, but the set up was one that would be familiar to anyone who watched any cooking show— the confessional booths.

Like any competition, they wanted us to talk about what our background is, why we were there, and what we would do with the prize money.

Angela confirmed as much when we were all in the center of the room, pointing us each to a stool. A bored-looking kid, who couldn't be more than twenty, stood behind the one she directed me to. I grinned at him.

"Let's get this show on the road."

————

————

AMELIA

When we had all finished our introductory videos, all of us were just a little bit calmer. Something about saying why we were here and talking about our dreams helped me to focus on exactly what I was here to do—cook my ass off.

Angela led us to a room that had once been the hotel's event space. Instead of holding hundreds of people at company booths, a stage had been set up with five stunning kitchens against a black backdrop. Off to one side, there was a pantry that any chef would kill to enter. I couldn't even see all of it, but what I could see was a wall of spices of every color and a rainbow of a produce stand that was making my blood heat from the sheer beauty. I couldn't wait to get my hands on the ingredients I needed for my dish, but first, we had to go see our stations.

Just like with the individual video booths, Angela directed us each to one of the kitchens. The stations were a thing of beauty. Each one looked like all of the vital pieces of a commercial kitchen and packed it into two counter tops in five square feet of space. Every single appliance was made of stainless steel that looked as if it had never been cooked on or used. A set of knives rolled in thick black cloth was laid out on each of the gas stoves, just waiting to be used. I couldn't wait to see what was inside it.

Looking around, I found that Zoe was to my left, her eyes wide as she inspected the space around her. I wondered if she'd ever been in a kitchen like this or worked under conditions like this. Then I rolled my eyes. Of course, she hadn't. I hadn't ever worked under conditions like this. I'd wager that nobody in here had— that was the point.

Focus, I told myself. *Get yourself familiar with the kitchen so you don't get turned around when you need it.*

That was one of the first things they had taught us in culinary school after the basic cuts. Making sure that you are comfortable in whatever kitchen you're in is vital to getting your work done. I had not worked in the kitchen that I wasn't familiar with in several years, but I remembered the process well.

The kitchen was small, but it was put together in a way that made perfect sense. It was set up like a galley kitchen with two sets of stainless steel counters parallel to each other and a hanging rack of pots set between them. Inset into the counter was a set of drawers and a state-of-the-art gas range. I rifled through the drawers, nodding at the contents of each. The first drawer was full of wooden spoons and other cooking utensils. The second was full of small kitchen tools, including the metal mallet I would need for my stuffed pork loin. The final, largest drawer, was full of cutting boards. The rest of it was divided into two long shelves with a variety of equipment that the contestants might need: food processors, blenders, even the clear plastic deli containers that we used so often to store our measured out ingredients.

The back counter was similar but designed for prep work instead of cooking. There was a sink set into the top of the counter and an easy-to-open full-height drawer for the garbage. The rest were long shelves holding serving dishes for every kind of dish I could imagine. It felt excessive and yet not. With slightly shaky fingers, I unrolled the knife roll and wasn't surprised to find that they, too, were some of the finest knives. They were already sharpened.

They clearly hadn't spared a penny on this set up, which was weirdly anxiety-inducing. Would my dish be good enough? I shook my head. Ian believed in me, and the people producing this clearly did as well—at least enough to get to the audition stage. Any moment now, the judges would come out and the process would begin. Surely having something to focus on would help me to get past these nerves.

As if they read my mind, the camera crew stepped in front of us. Some of them turned their cameras towards us, while three of them turned away from us. I looked to see why and my breath caught in my throat.

Four figures walked towards us from the production area. One was clearly Angela, the producer from earlier, signaling to the crew. She got out of the way quickly until only a trio of people walked towards us. I didn't recognize any of them.

Two of the other women had been chatting with each other, but their voices petered off as the judges walked towards us. I looked at them, then off to where Zoe and the other contestants stood. All of them looked as nervous as I felt. At least I wouldn't be the only one shaking on camera. I looked back at the judges, trying to see if I could figure out who they were.

They were dressed well. One white man was tall and muscular and looked like an English teacher in a long-sleeved, coral shirt and a black, argyle, sweater-vest. On the other side of the trio was a much shorter, thinner, white man wearing a simple white collared shirt and a black sport coat that fit him beautifully. The third, splitting the space between them, was a thin, white woman in a pale gray, pencil skirt and high-necked, white, silk blouse. These had to be the judges.

When the judges reached us, all of their faces were as serious as their outfits.

"Hello, chefs," they said in unison. "Welcome to the auditions for the first ever season of *Heating Up the Kitchen*."

They paused and we all clapped politely. When we finished, the female judge continued on her own. Her voice was as high and controlled as the ice blonde bun on top of her head.

"I'm Chef Denise Lyons, executive chef and owner of Crane and head judge here."

I gasped. I may not have known the chef by sight, but I knew the restaurant. Crane was a restaurant in New York that had opened with a waiting list over a year long because of the magic that the chef worked with molecular gastronomy. I had never thought I'd meet her in person.

"I'm Chef Bryce Jackson. Some of you might

recognize me as a former member of the British Men's football team, but I'm not just here for my good looks." He winked. "I'm also the former executive chef of Il Piacere in Seattle."

Bryce looked at the other man who cracked a smile and scratched a finger at the dark brown bun tied at the base of his neck. His crooked smile emphasized the bump in his nose from where someone had clearly broken it before. Even I had to admit it was captivating, even if I had never had any interest in men.

"And I'm Chef Nathan Weston. I'm the owner of the Tosi family of restaurants, and I'm your last judge today. We're so glad to have the opportunity to eat your food today, here in Atlanta."

On one side of me, I could hear the other women whispering to each other again. Angela shushed them and I smiled. I could see why they were impressed. Both of these men were famous in and out of the restaurant industry—for their food and for their exploits in the bedroom.

Chef Lyons, on the other hand, kept her business to herself. I wasn't sure I'd read or seen anything about her personal life in all the years I'd been tracking powerful women in the industry I loved. To be fair, I couldn't blame her for that. Misogyny was common in the industry, as in most things in our modern society. She would never be able to get away with the things her male counterparts did without sacrificing her reputation.

One thing was for sure, the three judges standing in front of us weren't going to make things easy for us today or any day in the competition. If we got that far.

"You all aren't here to hear us introduce ourselves today," Chef Denise continued. "You're here to cook. So, here is how it's going to go. We have provided a fully stocked pantry and kitchen for you. You may use one utensil or piece of equipment from home, but every ingredient and all other equipment used must be provided. If you do not see something you need to do this in your drawer or on the shelves in front of you, speak now. Everything needs to stay off of the counters until after we start rolling, though."

Quickly I dug into the drawer, double checking that the mallet was there. It was, right next to the roll of twine I would need. I let go and the drawer slid slowly back into the unit.

The woman on the other side of Zoe asked for a ricer after a moment, and someone else wearing all black brought one forward and slid it into the drawer.

"All good?"

We nodded, and Denise continued. "You are required to make two plates. One plate will be for filming, the other is for tasting. These should be identical. You will have sixty minutes to shop for, prepare, cook, and plate those dishes, understand? When the buzzer goes off, that is it. You are done cooking. But you won't be done.

"Unlike what you most of you are used to, you won't be serving the dish immediately. The crew will get video of you standing behind your dish and then we will get down to business. We'll only taste the dishes from one cook at a time. Whatever is on the plate is what we will taste, so if you forgot an ingredient…well, it'll make for better television."

Her smile turned wicked and she winked dramatically, which surprised me. The expression seemed almost foreign on her severe face before she dropped back into the half smile that seemed to be her default.

"Now, does anyone have any questions?"

I didn't. I wanted to get started. Judging by the silence around me, everyone else had the same idea. When none of us answered, she nodded to Chef Bryce who grinned wolfishly.

"Everybody take a deep breath now before the cameras start rolling. Once we get started, there's no stopping. It's just you, the food, about a dozen cameras, and a good chunk of money on the line. No pressure!"

Chef Nathan laughed out loud. "With that heartwarming thought, your cook time starts... now."

Like a light, we were off to the pantry. I deftly wove my body between the other contestants to reach the pantry first, going through my list of ingredients in my head.

Without stopping, I grabbed a simple silver wire basket and got to grabbing. After weeks of testing my favorite recipes on Mom, Dad, and Ian, the overwhelming opinion was that my andouille cornbread stuffed pork roulade was the best choice for this audition.

It could be done within the time limit, even if they didn't have any pre-cooked cornbread on hand, though it would be a crunch. Luckily, they did have it; one that looked sweet, one that was labeled savory. I grabbed both, thinking it would be better to have too much than have too little, or to have grabbed the wrong one. Once the cooking process started, there would be almost no time to run back in here.

I opened the fridge with force, grabbing the andouille sausage, butter, chicken stock, and pork loin I would need while briefly enjoying the hint of frost coming from the industrial appliance. Next, I moved to the open-faced produce refrigerator.

Celery, green peppers, green onions, sage, jalapenos, garlic, onion, and celery, I recited in my head as I grabbed each item. Next up, seasonings. I found the shelf and knelt with a quiet groan. They had literally every spice known to man on this shelf, but I soon realized they were organized by region of origin. With that in mind, I found the various fragrant spices I needed to make my creole rub quickly and stuffed them into my basket.

I set the basket down on an empty counter and went over every ingredient I would need for the dish that would determine my future. Years of having to cook without lists or recipes had taught me that putting your hands on each ingredient was the perfect way to ensure that nothing got left out of the process. I had everything I needed from within the pantry, so now, it was time to cook for my life.

———

I ran back out to my station and unpacked my basket, tossing it into the single bare place on the shelf beneath the counter. I fell into a slight trance as I got myself organized. Before I knew it, Angela was calling that ten minutes had passed and I had measured out all of my spices into the small deli containers.

Next, I needed to crumble the cornbread. After I chose which one to use, that is. I cut open the bags with the largest knife and took a chunk of each. I went with the savory first and smiled. It was deliciously dry and still slightly sweet. It was just like something I would get from my grandmother.

Tasting the other bag, I shook my head. It was too sweet and far too dense, like it had been soaked in honey for hours. There was no way that it would soak up the stock and sausage flavor the way it needed to for my purposes. I threw the bag of sweet cornbread back into the basket and set the savory down on top of the bag it had come in. It was time to hunt down my tools.

Turning to the rack behind me, I pulled out the perfect saucepan, large enough to sauté the stuffing and vegetables in and then sear the pork roulade, but not so large that everything would dry out while it cooked. I put that on the stove and turned the gas on to a medium heat, then tossed in the butter. While it began to melt, I dug out a wooden cutting board that had clearly never seen a knife. That wouldn't last for long.

I started with the celery, trimming and chopping them swiftly, then the peppersa, then the onions. When I was done, the butter sizzled in the pan. I dropped my work in, then cleared the cutting board of the leaves, seeds, and skins. Moving on autopilot, I grabbed the fresh sage, shallots, and garlic I'd need to chop, and got to work. When I was done, I pulled out a sauce pan to ready the jus I would need to bring this meal together. I grabbed the chicken stock and poured what looked like three cups worth into the sauce pan, tossed in my chopped herbs, and cranked the gas to high heat. It would need almost the entire time to cook down into the beautiful sauce it needed to be, so it needed to start now. As it began to heat, I cranked in the salt and pepper.

Once I had that taken care of, I started on the beautiful pork loin. I needed to reshape it and make sure it was absolutely perfect before I stuffed it.

I kept feeling eyes on me, but with so many people and cameras around me, I couldn't tell whose they were. Instead of looking for them, I focused on my hands as I pounded the pork loin flat on top of the plastic wrap. Before long, I found the lens of a camera hovering right above my hands, which was distracting. I hoped it wouldn't catch the way they shook ever so slightly as I struggled to get the second piece of plastic wrap off of the roll.

"You're turning a little green there. You got a little bit of meal envy?" I jumped at Zoe's voice from the bench next to me. Her tone was teasing, and she was probably right about the tinge of my skin, but I had no idea what she was talking about.

I looked up at her, confused. She grinned at me and the camera moved away from my hands. He moved to point the camera at my face, and as he adjusted his lens, I breathed a sigh of relief. That meant that I got a better look at her ingredients. Mushrooms, sausage, celery, onions, and a bag of brioche buns sat on her board right next to three bone-in, double-cut, pork chops. While I watched, she flipped the chop on its side and sliced right between the ribs with a swift movement that told me she had done this before.

Another cameraman positioned himself in front of us, a few steps behind the other cameras, probably hoping for some good drama to spice up the auditions. I guessed he'd be able to get both of us in the frame from there, and figured I could give him a little something to work with.

"I've never been green with jealousy before. I doubt anything here will inspire it, either. Even if we are making similar dishes."

Even as I said it, I knew it wasn't true. Maybe I hadn't physically turned green, but I was jealous of her, in a way. I wasn't jealous of her food. No matter how similar they were, I was confident in my skills and what I was making. I was jealous of the confidence that exuded from her every movement, the way mine should have. As far as lies went, it was a pretty white one.

I was a great chef. I knew it. This meal was one that I had made a hundred times before. I could have done it with my eyes closed in my kitchen at home. So why was I so nervous?

A bead of sweat dripped into my eye and I grimaced. I wasn't in my home kitchen or even the restaurant. In addition to the heat of my own stovetop and oven, I had four other contestants on the stage with me cooking up a storm, and there were three cameras assigned to each contestant. Not to mention, the television lights above us were *hot*.

All of it put together gave new meaning to the show's title. I shook my head at myself. None of this was anywhere close to what I should have been focusing on— the food in front of me.

If this wasn't the best meal I'd ever cooked, it was very likely the end of my time on *Heating Up the Kitchen*. I'd be relegated to nothing more than part of the audition montage. I was not about to let that happen.

Taking a deep breath, I smelled all of the herbaceous goodness sautéing in butter on my stove. It was time to add the andouille sausage to the pan.

I turned back to my cutting board and picked up the sliced open sausages. The casing was no good to me, but it worked to help me crumble the meat into the pan one-handed. The sizzle when each piece hit the hot pan was invigorating, bringing me all the way back into the cooking process. I turned back to the pork loin and sprinkled it liberally with a creole seasoning that would work well with the seasonings in the sausage. I picked up the ends of my plastic wrap, twisting them until the pork loin was rolled tightly into almost the same shape it had been before I began. Tying both ends with a little twine, I set it on the cutting board to relearn the shape so that I could stuff it more easily once I finished cooking the stuffing, which I needed to get back to.

When I got back to the stove, I looked up at the clock and cursed. There were only twenty-two minutes left, and so much left to do. I had to finish this stuffing and get this pork in the pan, and fast, or I was going to be in trouble.

———

Chapter Six

ZOE

I slid my pork chop into the oven just as Denise's bright voice cut through the noise of the five kitchens.

"Fifteen minutes remaining!"

I cursed internally. How was time going by so quickly? The pork would be cooked, but it wouldn't have as much time to rest as it really needed. I knew I'd also have to rush to get my creamy spinach sauce done. There was no time to waste.

I swung back into action, chopping a bunch of spinach and tossing it into my Granny's cast iron pan, still piping hot on the stove. Full of drippings and spices, it was perfect for wilting the spinach and allowing it to absorb the flavors of the pancetta, mushrooms, and sage I'd stuffed the pork chop with. Add a little extra salt, pepper, and garlic and it would be perfectly seasoned. Then you just add a little bit of stock and a little bit of yogurt and let it all cook together, and it would become a deliciously light creamed spinach sauce that was sure to knock the judge's socks off.

Adding the last ingredients, I let the pot simmer and

breathed the scent in deeply. The double-cut, pork chop was different from the usual discount chops I used, but everything else about this dish was something I cooked regularly. Creamed spinach was the base of so many of my meals while I was pregnant, and it was still something that brought me comfort on bad days. I hoped that this staple of my cooking would bring me a little luck with the judges and turn my dish into a proper entree good enough to earn me a spot here.

When a timer went off, I jumped. I'd lost track of time again while I stirred, but that was okay. I looked around before I realized that it was coming from my own station, and my nerves fluttered back into full force. My time to cook my pork was up. If these pork chops were raw, I was doomed. If they were overcooked, the result would be the same. It had to be absolutely perfect or this trip would have been a total waste of my time, money, and energy. And I didn't have enough of any of them.

Kneeling to get to the oven, I found myself whispering a prayer. I had to get these out and let them rest as much as I could to help the juices set, but I also had to put my plate together. Closing my eyes, I pulled open the oven door and let the heat wash over me. When I opened my eyes, I found myself staring at two beautiful pork chops that smelled like heaven. I had been meticulous while I cleaned the bones and rendered the fat cap before I had done anything else to make sure that there wasn't anything unsightly on the food after it came out of the oven, and that there was some delicious fat to sear the pork chop and cook the greens in. It had been worth it, I thought as I looked at the chops.

I pulled them out quickly and set them on a cooling rack to let the juices set properly, whirling around to grab the plates I'd set out earlier. They were simple, deep, round, white plates with a small flower painted on one side. I'd loved them the instant I set eyes on them. They would easily allow me to place the pork chops so that the bones weren't pressed into the sides of the bowl or sticking up at the top like a childish illustration of a graveyard. I wanted to lay it out so the judges could see the stuffing just peeking out from the meat, with the bones angled with the incline of the plate, and the sauce underneath them. My Instagram followers had been practically salivating over it when I'd posted it, so I hoped that would give me just a little bit of an advantage over the other competitors.

Plating and staging food was a very different beast than cooking something delicious. Food could be extremely delicious, but it was also hard to make sure that it was plated well enough to look delicious on the plate. My years of blogging had to be helpful there, as long as the food was pretty to start with. And that, I had managed.

I opened a drawer and pulled out a large, metal spoon. I pressed it into the creamy spinach on the stove and watched as it descended into the mass of greens. It was a little bit mesmerizing, but I didn't have time to focus on that. I had to make sure that I got every element onto my plates in less than a minute.

Turning to my plates, I spooned the spinach onto one plate and then another. I used the bottom of the spoon to make a beautiful swoosh. Before the creamy mixture could spread across the rest of the plate, I spun on my heel and carefully placed a pork chop onto each plate, so the bones laid over the cream and the painted flower without touching either.

I wiped my forehead with my sleeve and looked around. The woman on the far side of me had made fresh pasta and was ladling some kind of seafood soup over it.

On the other side, Amelia was slicing her pork roulade into medallions. She looked focused as she laid three of them across the remainder of her stuffing on the plate. My heart sank. I had teased her earlier about having meal envy, but I couldn't help feeling a pang of it myself as I watched the stage lights glint off of her juicy, beautifully cooked pork.

I looked back down at my own plates as the timer went off and asked myself a simple question. Have I done enough to make it through? Will my cooking stand up to hers?

It was a question that I couldn't answer. It was entirely up to the judges based on nothing more than a pork chop and some spinach.

"Time is up! Hands off your plates!"

Almost as soon as Chef Denise called time, the set around us exploded into action. I hadn't thought it was possible to have even more people surround me in the small kitchen, but I soon found that wasn't true. There had been two cameras focused on me the whole time, but as the judges walked toward us in tandem, nearly a dozen more sprung out to film everything in the kitchen —us included. I tried not to let my discomfort show on my face, but I knew it would be clear in the way I shied away from the operators.

"Congratulations, competitors," Chef Bryce called in his warm baritone voice. "You have completed your first taste of *Heating Up the Kitchen*. Now, it is time for us to taste what you have made. Will the first contestant please step forward?"

A tall, sallow woman walked around her bench and picked up a plate that looked nearly empty from where I stood. The judges waved her forward and the judging began.

———

———

It felt like hours passed before I finally got to present my plate to the judges, but judging by the clock on the wall, it had only been about ten minutes. None of the other competitors had revealed their results as they walked back to their stations with their plates, not even with a smile or a shake of the head. That had me worried. Were the judges not telling us what they thought?

As I walked towards the judges' table, I was more nervous than ever. I also found that I was almost prouder of my dish the closer I got to the seated trio. It smelled delicious and looked great on the plate. I had cooked my heart out and I couldn't wait to see exactly what these famous chefs thought of my work.

I put on my video smile and placed the plate before the judges. Chef Nathan was the first to speak, a friendly smile on his face making him a little less intimidating than he had seemed earlier.

"Welcome, chef. Please introduce yourself and tell us about your dish."

I was proud that my voice barely shook as I did so. I kept it brief and professional, with just a little bit of charm in my description. The charm didn't seem to do any good with the judges, but that was fine. Maybe it would help me with the viewers, if I got that far.

"Do you cook this at home?" Chef Denise asked. Her voice was as crisp as her suit, but her eyes were kind as they flitted from the plate in front of them, to me, and back.

"I do, in a way. I'm a single mom, so double-cut pork chops and hen of the woods mushrooms are not common on my table. However, I do a regular pork chop dish like this fairly regularly."

"I can understand that," Chef Bryce said. "What made you change it up for this competition?"

"I wanted to do something that was a little more elevated than what I would normally make for myself, but I also wanted to stick to the flavors and techniques that I'm familiar with. It's exactly what I do when I'm coming up with new recipes for my food blog, and I wanted to showcase that today."

I bit my tongue to stop myself from continuing to blather. How many times had I just used the word "wanted"? I had practiced this over and over in front of the camera and with Mama. Taking a deep breath, I tried to calm myself down. The judges were watching me, carefully, as if waiting to see if I was finished. I smiled and Chef Denise nodded.

"Well, the plate you've put in front of us is beautiful. It looks like the risk you took was worth it. But, it's all down to the way this tastes. Let's dig in, shall we?"

I held my breath as Chef Denise picked up a steak knife in one hand and a fork in the other. Please let it be cooked, I prayed as she sliced into the pork chop. Please let it be cooked right.

When the slice came away, she showed it to the camera. The sauce from the mushroom stuffing mixed with the clear juices of the pork chop as it ran over the slightly pink sides, and I breathed a sigh of relief. It looked exactly like the medium rare I had aimed for, and judging by the looks on the judges faces, what they had been looking for as well.

She cut the pork into smaller pieces and pulled the knife back, allowing the judges on either side of her to take a piece. Each of them carefully swiped the pork and stuffing through the spinach to create the all-hailed "perfect bite" from the plate. Slow smiles spread across the male judges' faces as they chewed. I could have cried. It was exactly the confirmation I needed that my dish was as good as I hoped it would be. Maybe I had a chance at this after all.

They all schooled their faces before Chef Denise spoke again. "Chef Cooper, thank you for this meal. Please rejoin the other contestants while we taste the remaining dishes and make our decision."

The dismissal was not unkind, but it was clear. I thanked them and made my way back to my kitchen with my head held high, knowing I had done well.

When I got back to my station, the final contestant made her way up to the table. None of the rest of us said anything while we waited. Weirdly, I wasn't as nervous as I had been with the judges. I knew the cameras were on us all while we stood there, but their presence didn't bother me the way it seemed to bother two of the other women.

It didn't seem to bother Amelia, either. I had seen that she had been nervous during the cook time, but that was gone. She was calmly, methodically tidying up her kitchen. It annoyed me to watch her wipe down her counters like she was the only person in the room. She may have apologized for her earlier comment, but it still rankled. It was something I had heard over and over again when I'd applied for jobs in kitchens, and when

Jacob had learned what I was spending my time doing when I wasn't at work. It was something that I hated.

She caught my gaze and, for a moment, her pink lips pursed as if she wanted to say something. Once again, I was struck how pretty she was. That annoyed me too.

I knew the restaurant she worked for, though I'd never been. It was farm-to-table fine dining, almost gourmet, Italian food that both the *Raleigh News & Observer* and *Durham Herald's* food writers had raved about. There had been puff profiles of the chef owner on nearly every TV station and in the magazines. I didn't know much about her past, but from what I could see, I would have put money on the fact that she was the kind of person who had had everything handed to her.

I didn't have much time to think about it, though. The judges walked towards us a second time. This time, each of them held a small envelope roughly as wide as their hands. My pulse raced as I tried to figure out what was in it. Many cooking shows chose aprons or chefs hats for their chosen contestants, but the package was much too small to hold anything like that.

"Chefs, we'd like to thank you all for what you prepared for us today," Chef Nathan announced. "Each of you created something that told us more than a little bit about you, as well as showing off your skills, and it was a pleasure to taste. Unfortunately, not all of you can be part of the final competition. Chefs Andrew, Jamikah and Elliot please step forward."

My heart sank to the pit of my stomach as all of the chefs I didn't know stepped away from their kitchens, leaving Amelia and I behind. It had been foolish to think that someone like me could make it into a competition like this. Maybe I hadn't been creative enough or seasoned my food well enough. Before I could fall too deeply into a spiral of negativity, Chef Nathan spoke again.

"All three of you cooked some delicious dishes, but there were too many small errors in your dishes for us to bring you into the competition. Please gather any items you brought from home and head back out to the lobby."

The breath I hadn't realized I was holding whooshed out of me as they filed out. Did that mean...?

"Chef Cooper, Chef Hughes, congratulations. You both produced remarkable plates that we were thrilled to taste. You are officially invited to compete in the inaugural season of *Heating Up the Kitchen*."

———

Chapter Seven

AMELIA

THE FLIGHT TO NEW YORK WAS COMFORTABLE. I HAD taken similar ones many times before while I was a student at the Culinary Institute of America, but it had been a while. The feeling of excitement that thrummed through my bones, though, was something that had only been present for the very first flight I'd taken up the east coast. Before I had switched planes in Atlanta, I had tried to focus on the packet of papers they had mailed to all of the contestants, but it had soon become clear that, that was a lost cause. My focus was shot, and besides, there would certainly be time to unwind before we had to get started with the competition. They couldn't expect people to fly in from all over the country, then immediately cook up something amazing. It just wasn't realistic.

Instead of thinking about the competition, I spent the two hour flight eavesdropping and people watching. It wasn't a long enough flight for a nap and there were several conversations going on around me about family drama that was more exciting than anything my brain could have come up with while I slept. It was weirdly draining to listen to, even though it wasn't my drama. By the time I got off the plane, I was more than ready for a nap and a shower, but the universe soon showed me that it had other plans for me. As usual.

Standing at the baggage claim was a Latinx boy who couldn't be older than twenty holding up a sign with four last names on it: Rose, Leonard, Cooper, and Hughes. Two white women stood next to him. One of them was several inches taller than me, but I didn't know her. The other woman, however, had been with me for every step of this competition. Zoe. Of course, she would be here.

As I crossed the room, she turned to look at me and her interested brown eyes flattened with an emotion I couldn't name but knew wasn't a happy one. I looked away, grabbing my suitcase from the conveyor belt and ensuring I didn't run into anyone as I walked.

"Ms. Hughes?" The boy's voice was thickly accented in the way that only a born New Yorker's voice could be.

I hadn't gotten the chance to talk to her after the audition, and I still had no idea what to think about the way she'd trash talked me during the cook. Was she still upset about that stupid comment? I'd have to ask her later, because the last member of our party walked up to us at that moment. He was a short, thin, Black man with a shy smile and a pink floral suitcase.

"Are you all here for the cooking competition?" He stretched his vowels with a clear Midwestern accent, then laughed. "I don't see no food!"

We all laughed with him. I could already tell that I was going to like him. Our escort rolled his eyes while he folded his sign up and slid it into his messenger bag. Clearly, these hometown jokes didn't impress him.

"If you all have your things, there is a car waiting to

take us to the hotel where there will be lunch laid out for all of the contestants. Are you ready?"

I took stock of the bag I'd checked and the one I'd carried on and nodded. The others did the same and then the boy smiled.

"Follow me, then. The kitchen awaits."

———

———

The whole ride to the hotel, all I could think was that it felt great to be back in New York. I loved Raleigh, but there was nothing like the sheer amount of sound that came with being in the greatest city in the world. It was exhilarating in a way that nowhere else had ever been for me. It made me itch with a desire to do something—try a new recipe, meet a new person, hell, even go for a run.

Two of those things weren't gonna happen, but there were several people in this shuttle I hadn't met yet. Our party of four had been met by another group of people I didn't know. The boy who'd gathered us seemed to know the woman leading the other group, though.

Despite being full of people, the shuttle was fairly quiet. Most of the occupants were looking out the windows for any glimpse of the city's glitz and glamour. So far, all they had seen were a shit ton of cars and sound-blocking walls on the highway.

The only contestant not looking out the window was Zoe. She had her head buried in her phone and only looked up the few times the driver had slammed on the breaks and honked at someone driving recklessly. She sat in the middle seat in front of me, but kept her phone tilted at an angle so that no one around her would be able to read what was on it. It was weird.

I wanted to ask what she was up to. She could be texting a partner. She could be working on a blog post. She could even be texting her kid or whoever was taking care of her. There were too many possibilities and not enough information for me to guess. No one else in the car was paying me the least bit of attention, so when she twisted in her seat to stretch her back, I seized the opportunity.

"What are you working on so hard?"

She jumped, dropping her phone face down on her lap. When her eyes met mine, there was something that looked like fear in them.

"Sorry, I didn't mean to scare you."

She pressed her lips together and breathed in through her nose so deeply her nostrils flared. As she focused her attention on me, the scared look was replaced with the same flat, annoyed expression she had given me at the airport.

"Why do you need to know?"

I shrugged. "I don't need to know. I just want to. Everyone else is looking out the window like they're going to lose if they close their eyes, but not you. It's interesting."

Her eyes narrowed as she looked at me, apparently deciding whether she wanted to answer or not.

"I'm finishing up a blog post," she finally answered. "I thought I could get it done on the plane, but I was having issues connecting to the server, so I figured I'd use this time to work on it. Is that a problem?"

Oh, she was definitely not over my snide comment from the audition. I opened my mouth to say something but was interrupted by our driver slamming on the brakes, yet again. Both of our heads slammed forward and a thunk came from the floorboards.

"What was that? Did we hit something?" the white man sitting next to me asked in a frightened voice. He clutched the wire frames of his glasses so hard they were almost coming apart at the center.

"Nope. That was my phone. You'd know if we hit something." There was a little bit of a laugh in Zoe's voice as she looked at him. It was melodic in a way that I hadn't heard before. I wanted to hear it again. Instead, I heard the man's whiny voice.

"Sorry, I'm not used to driving this much. I'm from DC. I take the subway." He tittered a laugh, reminding me of a particularly annoying bird.

As soon as the driver let off the brakes, Zoe bent nearly in half to reach her phone from the floor. The tall, pin-up styled woman to her right shuffled in her seat for a moment, then Zoe sat back up with her phone in hand.

"Thanks," she said shyly. "I…I like your shoes."

The woman grinned and turned to face her. "Thanks! I got them on sale!"

Zoe's face lit up as if that was the best thing she'd ever heard. "Really? Where from? I'm Zoe, by the way."

"Nice to meetcha! I'm Shauna. I think I got them from the clearance rack at Ross. I should probably pretend I paid full price, but I don't really care."

Zoe laughed again, and I was transfixed by the sound. Shauna must have felt me watching them, because she turned to me with a smile that showed off her slightly too large front teeth.

"And who are you?" Her blue eyes were sparkling as she waited for me to answer.

"Oh, um, Amelia Hughes," I stammered.

"Well, it's good to meet you, too, Amelia Hughes. Even if you think we're a bunch of country hicks staring out the window at the city."

She winked, showing she was teasing, and I blushed.

"I didn't say that!"

"Naw, but it's what you meant. That's okay, though. I am a hick at heart. Where are y'all from?"

"North Carolina," Zoe and I said in unison. She turned to look at me, and I was struck with the full force of her smile for the first time. I didn't need to see myself in a mirror to know that the blush on my cheeks would be maroon by now. God, that was embarrassing.

"Oh, sweet. I'm from Georgia. I've never been to New York before. You think we'll get to do any exploring while we're here?"

"I would love to see the rest of the city," Zoe gushed. "I don't know, though. We'll probably be pretty busy."

"They can't keep us cooped up in a hotel the whole time, right?" That came from the nervous man. "Derrick Elliot, by the way."

"Hi, Derrick," we chorused, then laughed. It seemed like the rest of the van had become part of the conversation, now, turning towards us instead of facing the windows for the first time since we'd gotten on the road. Shauna noticed it, too, and turned her charming personality onto the man on the other side of Zoe. It was the man who'd been part of our group, who hadn't introduced himself.

"What do you think?" she asked the Black man from our group on the other side of the bench.

"Well, I don't know," he said slowly, tapping his chin. "I guess I wouldn't think they'd want us stuck inside the whole time, but Zoe's right. We might not have much energy for anything else, judging by the way these other TV shows carry on."

"I guess we'll just have to see when we get there, won't we," Shauna replied. "It'll be weird not doing a regular kitchen service every night, though."

"We won't be?" I felt the entire car's eyes on me as soon as the words left my mouth.

"Somebody didn't read the packet," Zoe sing-songed after a beat of silence.

Surely I wasn't the only one, I thought. Looking around, at least two other people looked as confused as I felt. Most of the car laughed, but I shrugged. It wasn't the end of the world.

"There'll be thirteen episodes, and we'll be doing a set of challenges that may or may not include a meal service in each one," Shauna explained.

Huh. There had to be more competitors on their way, then.

"I'm glad they're not all dinners, honestly. I've only ever worked one as a waitress," Zoe admitted.

"You've never worked the line? How did you get here, then?"

"I run a food blog." Zoe's tone was as short as her sentence.

"A successful one?" a Latinx man said from next to me.

When she turned, Zoe's face was so frosty it made my blood run cold, even though she wasn't even looking at me. A wave of shame swept over me as I remembered how rude I had been to her.

"I've been successful enough to make it here just the same as all of y'all, haven't I?"

The Black man just laughed a loud cackle that filled the interior of the car. "Oh, and you've got some fire in you too. Good. That'll help you get through your first one just fine. I'm Ellis, by the way."

She just nodded at him, but before anyone could speak, the driver interrupted.

"If anyone wants to see anything, now is your chance. We are entering Manhattan."

My companions gasped and I looked out the window. Sure enough, we were crossing the East River on the Queensboro Bridge. I wasn't surprised. Cable cars full of people crossed the zip lines above us as we traveled, with gulls flying through the crisscrossed bars that separated the bridge from the air. It wasn't quite as new now as it had been the first time I'd seen it, but it was still breathtaking.

By the time we made it into the city, all talk of the competition was replaced by squeals of delight and a run through of the stores and sights that we passed. Restaurants, hotels, yoga studios, even a Whole Foods brought a joyful noise to the van.

When we pulled up to the hotel, though, the entire car went silent. The Roosevelt Hotel's marquee held a banner that read, "Welcome, Heating Up the Kitchen Contestants," in big block letters. I took a deep breath.

This was really happening.

———

———

I had guessed that the hotel would be fancy, especially because it took up the better part of a city block, but even my immense Googling of the place hadn't prepared me for the sight of the interior. The Roosevelt Hotel's lobby was basically a fucking palace. It was *beautiful* with warm golden tiles, plush red carpets, and glittering crystal chandeliers.

"Whoa," a black woman said, beside me, her ombré black to blonde twists nearly glowing in the light. "We in the right place? This place is…"

We were absolutely in the right place, but I understood what she meant. It was overwhelming even before a warm male voice boomed out from the raised alcove that must hold the check-in desk.

"Hello, contestants!"

That was when I saw a cadre of cameras converging on us from all sides. Had they been there the whole time? I was sure they would catch me looking as wide eyed and ridiculous as I felt, but I didn't care.

"Welcome to New York!"

The trio judges began to walk down the stairs towards us, and my heart began to race. This was beginning right now, for real. I was here, in New York City. No one and nothing could take this away from me but my own skills in comparison to those of the people standing around me. That was both amazing and fucking terrifying.

When the judges reached us, I had to remind myself to keep breathing. I couldn't let myself pass out from nerves before the competition even began.

"I'm sure you are all tired after your journey, but it isn't over yet. You may have noticed that there are more people here than you'd expect."

He grinned wolfishly at us. Looking behind me, I realized he was right. Even with all the cameras, there were at least 30 people with luggage. No matter how you sliced it, that was way too many people to compete in a thirteen episode season. *How....?*

"None of you will be checking into your hotel rooms right now. We're going to put your skills to the test, first, to make sure that you can stand the heat of this kitchen."

Fuck.

———

Chapter Eight

ZOE

THE JUDGES LED US DOWN A FAR TOO GLAMOROUS hallway to a room that was much simpler. There were no chandeliers here, just two dark wooden shelves with wire doors formed to look like the *Heating Up the Kitchen* logo. If my heart weren't trying to pound its way out of my chest, I'd probably smile at their dedication to their branding. I should have thought that something like this would happen. Skills tests and immediate challenges had become incredibly popular on other reality cooking shows; why wouldn't the producers try something to kickstart this competition and get the audience invested in the show?

God, I wished they had warned us, though. If I had come all the way out here just to get sent home...I couldn't even let myself finish the thought. Just like I'd told everyone in the car, I had earned my spot here just the same way the rest of them had. If I had to prove it again? Well, I'd do just that, no matter what they threw at us.

"Please place your belongings in one of these

cubbies. We will lock it behind you to ensure its safety," a man in the hotel's uniform said simply. "Your phone must be one of these belongings, per the contract you signed with the network. You will be able to retrieve them once you have finished your part of the challenge."

One white woman looked like she wanted to argue, but another staffer was beside her in a blink with a brilliant smile and a soft offer of assistance that was apparently convincing enough. The rest of us just got on with putting our things away. Sure enough, one of the staffers locked each cabinet separately and gave us a small paper ticket that we would be able to swap for access to our belongings later.

Not having my phone with me would be weird, but also probably for the best. There was no way I could focus on the competition if I also had to worry about my phone ringing while they filmed. That had happened once during a job interview, and I never wanted to deal with that particular embarrassment again, if I could help it.

The judges and producers were waiting for us in the next room, and oh, what a room it was. When I stepped through the door, it was like something out of my subconscious. Whether it came from a dream or a nightmare remained to be seen, though. Looking down, I had to confirm that I was definitely wearing pants, so hopefully, I had a shot at this dream.

It was a long rectangular room that almost looked like a throne room from some medieval fantasy. On one side of the room, there was a set of clear double doors that showed off a pantry the size of my living room. As we passed by it, holographic flames shot up to block the room off. One of the women shrieked, but I peered past the faux flames into the room. It looked even more packed than the one from the audition, which was almost hard to even think. I'd never, even in my wildest dreams, seen a pantry so well stocked, but there was so much else to see that we had no choice but to keep moving. We walked past fifteen perfect kitchen sets, that probably each cost more than my mother's house, until we made it to the front of the room.

The closer we got, the more the butterflies fluttered in my stomach. The judges stood in the center of a raised stage wearing stark black, perfectly tailored suits with their arms behind their backs. They looked like they belonged on the set of Lucifer.

"Welcome to the kitchen, contestants," Chef Nathan's voice boomed. As he spoke, a circle of holographic flames encircled them, making them look even more devilish. If they had, had a set of horns and a curled tail, the image would have been complete.

"There are thirty of you standing in front of us today, but only fifteen spaces in the kitchen," Chef Denise said, her voice cool and crisp. "Half of you will be exiting the kitchen before you've cooked a single meal."

She paused just in time for all of us to gasp. I'd known there were too many people for the show, but to cut our number in half before we'd even unpacked? That was harsh.

However, I wasn't about to be one of them if I could help it. With a shake of my head, I refocused my attention on the judges.

"Now, there will be three parts to this first challenge," Chef Denise continued. "If at any point your work is not up to scratch, you will be eliminated immediately."

I sucked in a breath, but the judges did not wait for

us to react this time. She just kept talking, her voice and face serious.

"The first part will be all about your knife skills. You will be given onions, celery, carrots, and a selection of herbs that you must cut according to our instructions. As you work, we will walk through the aisles and judge your knife work."

"Once you have finished preparing your vegetables, you will be provided with a whole chicken and three different fish," Chef Bryce explained. "Each of them must be broken down to get the most portions out of each animal. Again, we will be judging your butchering throughout the process. Anyone who cannot perform to our standards will be eliminated."

"Those of you who remain will have the chance to cook for us. Yet again, this will be a test of your skills," Chef Nathan said. "You will cook eggs in five different preparations and steaks to three different temperatures."

I found myself nodding. All of those tasks were pretty reasonable. They were things that any line cook would know how to do. I might not be as experienced with breaking down fish, but I knew the basics. Given enough time, I was sure I could manage it.

"You will have half an hour to complete the first section, forty-five minutes to complete the second and one hour to complete the third."

Chef Denise's words nearly stopped my heart in its tracks. Judging by the silence around me, I wasn't the only one in shock. That would be a tall order, even for cooks with years of experience. For someone who was still in their first five years as a professional chef, or someone like me? It would be nearly impossible.

"Does anyone have any questions?"

I couldn't answer. The butterflies that had been

fluttering in my stomach felt like they had crawled into my throat, making it hard to swallow.

A few contestants asked questions, but I could hardly hear them until Amelia spoke. Something about her melodic soprano cut through the panic enough for me to hear her asking what kinds of fish we'd be breaking down. I looked up to see Denise offer her a sharp smile.

"Excellent question. You will be preparing ahi tuna, monkfish, and trout. Each of you should be familiar with at least two of these fish, but none of them are toxic or particularly difficult."

The only one I had ever worked with was trout, from when Jacob used to go fishing.

"Will there be a demonstration on how to break them down?" That question came from a Black woman with a slight Cuban accent. "I've never worked with monkfish before."

"We will show you how to break down each of the fish once we reach that stage of the competition. Are there any other questions?"

When no one else spoke, Nathan clapped his hands together.

"Perfect. Now that we've gone through the actual challenge, let's talk about the television show part of it. You've been assigned a cameraman who will lead you to your station. Once you are there, we'll continue."

The cameras got even closer, and I realized that I had forgotten they were there, despite them standing between the judges and the gaggle of contestants I was part of. I'd expected to be more aware of them, to be more anxious about my appearance, but apparently that wasn't an issue. At least, not yet.

A purple haired camera operator with a they/them

pin on her headband caught my eye and gestured me over.

"I'm Portia, and I'm in charge of you for as long as you're on the show," they said with a bright smile. "For now, you're going to be in the third row on the right. Stand behind the set of chef's knives right there and you'll be ready to go. Any questions?"

My mind was mostly blank, so I just shook my head. They winked at me and got into position across the countertop. I looked down and found a beautiful set of knives, waiting for me, with my name embroidered on the front of the roll.

My fingers trembled as I ran them over the stitches. I opened the latches to even more beautiful knives than the ones we had used during the audition. These were *really good* knives, the kind that were all hand-forged and designed to last for the length of a chef's career.

Why would they spend all this money on flights and knives if they are just gonna send half of us home? I wondered. They'd already spent more on just me than the monthly mortgage for my mom's house, and we hadn't even gotten started yet. They must be taking this seriously, I realized. Weirdly, that realization made me feel a little more grounded, despite the stage lights and being surrounded by people I didn't know.

A staffer wove through the rows of people and counters with a cart full of metal wire grocery baskets overflowing with produce. He placed one in front of each knife kit and kept moving until he reached me.

"Good luck," he whispered as he set down the basket. "I'm rooting for you."

It was a small moment, and I knew he was probably saying it to every contestant, but it warmed me to my core. There were people out there rooting for me, and I was going to crush it.

I glanced to my left and saw that Amelia had been given the spot on the other half of this row. I couldn't seem to shake her in this competition, but that was okay. I would show her, show all of the other competitors, exactly what I was made of.

———

The first challenge was turning out to be harder than I had expected. The cuts were fairly simple and to be expected. We had to dice onions, julienne carrots, brunoise celery, and chiffonade a selection of herbs.

The problem was the volume. There were roughly two pounds, each, of the vegetables, which added up to a metric ton of chopping to be done in not a lot of time.

The clock was ticking down past the halfway mark of the challenge. My hands had yet to stop moving for even an instant, even after I finished the onions and moved onto the carrots. It was a flurry of grabbing, chopping, or moving the vegetables into their designated containers. I was making good progress, until I heard Amelia make a joyful noise from her place on the bench and the clink of her chef knife hitting the board.

Tearing my eyes away from my pile of vegetation, I saw that her basket was completely empty. She was surrounded by clear plastic containers full of proof of her skill. It all looked perfect.

What she's doing doesn't impact you, I reminded myself while I pushed down a snarl.

I redoubled my effort, focusing on turning the carrot on my board into perfect, 1/8 inch matchsticks just in time for the judges to walk by.

"Nice work," one of the male judges said. When I glanced up, Chef Nathan was watching me work. Chef Denise was inspecting Amelia's chopping with a look of intense concentration. Eventually, she nodded in approval, and Amelia beamed.

The chef directly in front of her, the nervous man from the car, was not having as good of a time of it. He was sweating so hard I could see the paisley pattern on the undershirt he wore under a pale blue button down. The judges seemed to sense his nerves, because they formed a semi-circle around him to watch him work.

I couldn't see what he was doing, but it was clear from their body language that they were not impressed.

"Chef Elliot, stop working," Chef Denise announced clearly. His shoulders tightened, then sagged as he set his knife down. "Your time in the kitchen is over. Take your knives and go."

"Thank you for the opportunity," he told them before following their instructions. I tossed the last of the carrots into the bin and wiped my forehead with the back of my arm. Victory was within my grasp. All that was left was to brunoise this celery and chiffonade a few leaves of mint.

The brunoise was the most time consuming cut of them all, but luckily, celery was much easier for me to cut than carrots. It was significantly less likely to roll around as my knife rocked back and forth to julienne the celery, then stack it and do it again. Brunoising vegetables created the perfect eighth inch cubes that were perfect for the finest sauces and broths. I didn't usually bother with it at home, but I'd done my time practicing to make sure that I could do it.

As I worked my way through it, I heard the judges send at least three more people home. I didn't look to see who it was. All that was running through my head was the tick, tick, tick of the oversized clock and the steps I had to take.

Grab. Slice. Stack. Slice. Clear cutting board. Over and over until the basket was empty. I looked up at the clock and found there were two minutes remaining. Plenty of time. I grabbed the package of mint leaves and folded a few of them together into a parcel. Carefully, I sliced backward, turning them into thin strands that would be fine enough to garnish even the most gourmet dish. Over and over I repeated the action until, finally, my board was clear.

There were only a mere thirty seconds to spare, but I'd made it through the first challenge. My shoulders sagged with relief as I released my fingers from the death grip they held the knife in. I had done it.

———

Chapter Nine

AMELIA

Eight chefs had been cut by the end of the first challenge.

I was sweating by the time the staffer set the second basket on my bench. This one was longer, wider, and shallower than the first basket, with three paper-wrapped fish and a full chicken in a plastic tray on the top.

Next to me, I heard Zoe gasp slightly as her basket was set down. I didn't blame her. As a home cook, would she have broken down fish on her own before? I didn't think I had done anything other than trout before I'd gone to culinary school.

I wanted to ask, but the judges were talking again, explaining the rules of the challenge again, then walking all of us through the butchering process for each protein.

I was confident in my skills with seventy-five percent of this challenge. Thanks to culinary school and years of experience, I could break down a chicken in five minutes while blindfolded. At least, I could when I graduated. I hadn't done it in a few months, but I had done it so many times before I stopped that I was sure it would be like riding a bike.

Glancing at Zoe, I saw that her eyes were glued to the judges as they demonstrated the fish breakdown, her mouth slightly open. It was impressive. They were clear with their instructions and explaining why they did what they did. Every fish had its own quirks that you just kind of had to know.

I'd grown up working with trout my dad had caught, and it was a regular feature on our menu. Trout just had to be descaled before it was filleted and have its mud vein removed. Ahi tuna was a higher value protein that had been very popular in the kitchens I'd interned in.

The monkfish, however, was worrying me. I had never worked with it before. I might have eaten it once or twice on vacations, but it had never been on the menu at Ian's restaurant. He had known that we couldn't sell enough of it to justify the cost of shipping it in from the coast every week. It was also almost as large as the tuna they'd given us.

When Chef Nathan pulled the monkfish from its paper wrapping, I was astonished at how ugly the thing was. It was wide and flat like a smooth, scaleless angler fish mixed with an alligator. Its large, toothy mouth could have gobbled up any other fish in its path, as it likely had in life, and its tail reached almost to the end of the table the judges were working on.

"There are three areas you need to focus on with monkfish: the liver, the cheeks, and the tails. The liver should always come out first because it will cause you a lot of problems if you do it poorly."

Nathan's movements were quick and sure as he flipped the fish onto its back, showing how confident he was with the fish. His voice was clear as he walked us through the process of removing the liver.

"You want to hold onto these small fins with your non-dominant hand. With your fillet knife in the other, slice away all of the loose skin here, pulling upward with the knife until the liver is exposed. Now, *very* gently, grasp the liver and lift it until you can see the rest of the membranes and internals. Then cut those away and place the liver on the serving plate."

I heard soft gagging from behind me as he processed it and couldn't resist rolling my eyes.

One less person to worry about, I thought grimly. Whoever it was would need to get their guts under control and fast. Anyone who couldn't clean and butcher meat without retching wouldn't get very far in this line of work—or in this competition.

He flipped the fish back over so its now empty interior was on the board.

"Before you start removing the cheeks, you need to make sure that the fish's jaw has relaxed. If you don't, you'll shred the most delicate meat on this fish. You can tell it's relaxed by the way the mouth is open and your ability to move the skin."

He slid his finger into the corner of the mouth and made the fish smile grotesquely. Laughs burbled out from several of the cooks, including Zoe.

"Okay, back to business. You start at the edge of the eye socket and cut through the top of the mouth. This flesh is pretty flexible and gelatinous, so make sure to hold tight to it. When you've reached the side of the upper jaw, stop and let it go. Then, move to the inside edge of the cheek. As you start cutting, use the fingers of your other hand to lift the cheek away from the other muscle as you work. When you're done, lift it away and cut it. When it's free, lay it on the plate like so."

He laid the monkfish cheek out so it neatly encircled the liver.

"Last, it's time to turn the tails into steaks. You need to remove all of the skin and the membrane, and cut this meat into portions."

He sliced the tail into six even portions and placed them on the tray. I had to admit, the process may have been gruesome, but it did look beautiful when it was all laid out. I did my best to commit everything I'd just watched to memory, knowing I couldn't afford to mess this up.

"Now that each of these has been broken down, you have all been given all the instruction that we can give you. It is time to begin the challenge in five...four... three...two... one...*Begin.*"

The whole set burst into action. I grabbed the chicken first, placing it breast down and slicing through one wing joint and then the other. I moved them to the display plate they'd provided, shaped to look like the chicken's body.

With practiced movements, I flipped it over and sliced through the thigh joints, then popping the drumsticks out, setting it all in its place. I let my knife slide through the chicken breasts, separating them from the bone like they were made of butter.

Last but not least, I flip the carcass over and cut out the chicken oyster and laid it between the wings. The chicken was done, and the challenge had barely started.

Nothing was going to stop me from making it into the full competition, especially not three fish. I kept working, making sure that my cuts were as precise as they could be on the trout and the ahi tuna. Finally, all that remained was the monkfish. Time was running short, and there wasn't any to waste.

I grabbed the large, ugly fish and got to work. It took me a little longer than the other two fish had, but I made it through. Barely. There were just a few seconds to spare as I set down the last fillet of monkfish. When the timer went off, my whole body ached and my chest heaved. I already felt like I had just run a goddamn marathon, and there was still another 5k to go in the next challenge.

"Eighteen of you stand in front of us, but only fifteen people will have the chance to be the first ever winner of *Heating Up the Kitchen*," Chef Bryce announced. "Now, when I ask you this question, there is only one answer I want to hear. That should be, yes, chef."

We all took deep breaths and nodded. I guessed what was about to come before he spoke again.

"Are you ready?"

"Yes, Chef!"

———

———

We were all exhausted and starving by the time filming wrapped up. After the challenges were complete, we were pulled aside into confessional booths to do voiceovers for all of our footage, which took at least another hour.

Unfortunately, our time "on" wasn't over yet. The judges and the executive team were providing us with dinner and talking us through what the rest of the season would look like.

I was glad we would be getting more information than we'd had so far, but God, I would have killed to have gotten a nap in. I was *tired* and I could only imagine everyone else was, as well. The good thing about it was that at least this part wouldn't be filmed, so we could relax a little bit.

Only a little, though. It might not have been an official rule, but we all knew that we had to make a good impression on the judges if we wanted to do well in the competition. They were top-tier chefs who had a lot of influence in the industry, and that wasn't anything to sneeze at. Hopefully, that was something I could manage to do, or avoid making a bad impression, at the very least.

The producers sent us back to gather our belongings and then directed us to a dining room that was set up to look simple but was clearly made from things that had cost more than my parents had paid for my college education. We were all seated on one side of long, rectangular tables facing a five-person table that was raised slightly so we were at eye level with their plates.

Denise sat in the center of the raised table with one of the male judges on either side of her. All of them looked serious. Angela, the executive producer from the audition, sat at one end of the table. Another woman that I didn't recognize sat on the other end, but I loved her dress. It was a floor length, dark magenta wrap dress that brought out the beautiful warm undertones of her dark brown skin.

"Good evening, contestants," the woman I didn't recognize said. Her confident voice rang through the dining room. "I'm Sophie Estrelle, CEO of the *Cooking Network*, and I'm thrilled to be the first person to say this for real. Welcome to the competition."

We all laughed, clapping in the pause that she made sure to leave. Down the line, someone hooted with joy.

Even the judges smiled at that, though their smiles fell away quickly when they looked at each other. I wondered what that was about but didn't have much time to think about it.

"As you'll know from reading the intro packet we sent you, there is more to this competition than just cooking. If you regularly watch our shows, you'll know that reality television like this has more emphasis on the television part than the reality part," she explained. "The winner for every challenge will be based on your cooking skills, but we are going to need all of you to play up some of the interpersonal conflicts that are sure to happen during filming. For example,…Amelia Hughes and Zoe Cooper, raise your hands."

I blinked, wondering what I could have possibly done to get called up with Zoe. Looking down the line to where Zoe sat, she looked as confused as I felt. We both put our hands up and Angela stood to join Sophie on the dais.

"You two are going to feature in one of the earliest storylines," Angela informed us. "Based on your performances during your auditions and this first challenge, we are going to lean into the tension that already clearly exists between you."

I bit my lip, feeling my cheeks heat. It hadn't been that obvious that Zoe didn't like me, had it? It had to have been, otherwise they wouldn't be talking about it in front of everyone else.

"We want to play with the inherent differences between people of your backgrounds," Sophie took over again. "The self-taught food blogger versus the CIA trained rising star. That's an example of the storylines that we have pulled together for the season, all of which are dependent on how far each of you gets within the competition. We are very much looking forward to seeing how this turns out. For now, though, we'd like to serve you a dinner from Chef Nathan Weston's very own Tosi restaurant!"

We clapped again as a bevy of servers walked out with menus. As those were handed out, several gathered water glasses and placed them in front of us.

Finally, I thought. Grabbing the cup, I began to guzzle it down like there was no tomorrow. When I had drained it, I set it down and realized that everyone else was doing the same thing—including the judges. That was something.

The menu was a small one: two appetizers, two entrees, and two desserts. I ordered the lobster ravioli, beef wellington, and the molten chocolate cake, while the tiny, old, white woman next to me ordered the vegetarian option of the first two courses and decided against dessert. *Her loss*, I thought with a shake of my head.

"So, you're gonna be the big bad meanie of the season, huh?"

Her voice was high and breathy, with a thick New Jersey accent that grated at my ears.

"Looks like it. I swear I'm not that bad, though."

"Oh, I'm sure, honey." She winked at me. "I would bet money that I'm gonna be cast as the poor vegetarian that the judges think can't hang with the big kids. That's fine with me, though. I'll show 'em."

I grinned at her. I loved her confidence, even if I was pretty sure that a vegetarian had never won a single cooking show in the history of reality television. Too many of the challenges were based on dealing with proteins that you had to know how to cook.

"Hey, you never know. Maybe you'll get cast as the

supportive grandmother that everyone loves," I joked, and was rewarded with a cackle that would have fit in a Halloween store.

"I'm a great-grandma, baby. You can't demote me like that! But you'll all see. You can't start a vegan diner on the Jersey Shore without having guts of steel."

"That's what you do? That's awesome."

She grinned back at me. "Yes ma'am! My diner opened up last year and it's doing great. I'm trying to win me this money to expand to a second location."

"That's amazing. I'd say, I hope you win, but…" I trailed off and winked. She laughed, as did the black man on the other side of her.

"You all seem to be getting on like a house on fire. Mind if I join in?"

"If we say no, are you gonna sit there quietly all season?" I asked, honestly curious.

"Well, that sounds like it would be mighty boring," he laughed. "I didn't fly all the way out here from Minnesota to be lonely. I'm Ellis Leonard. It's nice to meet you both."

"Fern Maxwell," my seatmate answered. The name suited her.

"Amelia Hughes," I introduced myself. "I gotta tell you, I love your suitcase!"

"Thank you! My daughter picked it out."

Fern looked at me like I'd grown three heads, so I explained. "We rode in together from the airport, but I didn't get to talk to him."

A waiter refilled my glass, and I scooped it up with a grateful nod.

"Yeah, she was too busy flirting with that girl she's supposed to be fighting with."

I spluttered, almost choked on my water. "Excuse

me? I was not *flirting*. That was just talking cause everybody else was looking out the windows."

He raised one salt and pepper eyebrow at me. "Sure, honey. Keep telling yourself that."

I decided to ignore him. "So, how old is your daughter? She has good taste in suitcases."

"She's eleven going on thirty." He rolled his eyes, though his smile stayed wide. "Thinks she's the one that's supposed to make sure *I* leave the house well dressed and make new friends. And I let her. Mostly."

It was clear just how much he loved his daughter, even if you hadn't heard him.

"I'm sure she's very proud of you for getting to come out here."

"She's very excited for me. She's less excited about having to eat her mama's cooking until I come home."

Fern cackled again. "My husband said the same thing, except about our daughters are in charge of feeding him while I'm gone. That man could burn water, if I let him anywhere near my stove."

That made me laugh. It was what Dad had said about Mother before he had left to teach a semester in Germany. Luckily, I'd been in high school at the time. What I couldn't cook, she was more than capable of ordering in for the pair of us.

Before we could say much else, the first round of food arrived in front of us. My stomach growled audibly at the sight of the lobster ravioli swimming in a brown butter sage sauce. Beside me, Fern dug into her gnocchi with a lemon cream sauce, making happy noises all the while.

"I know that's right," Ellis laughed. He'd gotten the same as me. I glanced over and saw him murmuring a prayer over it. My gaze skittered back to my plate, leaving him to his private moment.

I picked up my fork and daintily stabbed a ravioli. I dragged it through the sauce and took a bite.

It was *divine.* The lobster filling would have melted in my mouth if it weren't wrapped in the perfectly al dente pasta. The nutty flavor of the brown butter sauce enhanced it all perfectly.

We ate in silence, finishing our appetizers just in time for the entree to come out. The gold-rimmed plate came out with two steaming medallions of beautiful pastry-prosciutto-mushroom-wrapped beef tenderloin in the center, with mashed potatoes and haricot vert surrounding them.

Fern's plate held a personal roasted tart that had been filled with thinly sliced carrots, eggplants, and cabbage in a circle around a scoop of mashed potatoes. It looked just as delicious as the food on my own plate, and I didn't even *like* eggplant.

It made me want to cry. I was pretty sure I had never cooked anything quite this perfectly, let alone dishes to fill a table. There were many reasons I was on this side of the table and not one of the judges, but for a moment, I wondered if maybe, just maybe, I was out of my league.

"This is a damn good meal," Ellis declared after devouring half of his wellington. "Chef, you wanna share your recipe?"

Chef Nathan grinned back at him, showing off the playboy grin I was familiar with from the gossip magazines. "You're a chef. Figure it out!"

Chef Denise rolled her eyes at him and dug back into her food with slightly more force than was necessary for the tenderloin. It looked like she didn't have any more patience for his charm than she would for a wrinkle in her impeccably tailored skirt.

I knew I still had a lot to learn, but that would help me to start out with my best foot forward with her, at least. That would be a start.

———

Immediately after the meal, Zoe and I were ushered into a room not much larger than your average bathroom to find Angela sitting in a leather armchair behind a dark wooden coffee table. Two other armchairs sat at an angle on the other side.

"Ladies, it's a pleasure to sit down and talk with you finally," Angela crowed, wrapping her hands around her crossed knees. "I'm thrilled that you made it through our surprise first challenge because we have big plans for the two of you!"

She was way too excited about this, her blue eyes almost glowing in her weirdly unwrinkled face.

"So we heard," Zoe said. Her voice wavered, as if she was uncertain, but it didn't show on her face. Her expression was flat, almost disinterested, as she seated herself in the chair closest to the door.

"Is that a problem for either of you?"

"No, ma'am," Zoe said, her posture tense as if she wanted to run out of the room. I just nodded.

"Good," Angela said breezily. "Now, when you interact with each other on screen, we want you to be as vicious as you want, short of starting any physical altercations. That would be a liability for the network."

I just stared at her. This woman had clearly lost the plot.

"With that in mind, if you have any particular

worries or things that will trigger you, now is a good time to say so. We don't want to cause any lasting damage…"

She paused for only a second before rolling on. "Let's see, we also need to know if either of you have any food allergies. We forgot to include it in the paperwork you filled out, but we can't have any allergic reactions on the show. That would be a liability for the network."

I was sensing a theme here. Once it was clear that Angela was actually going to wait for a response this time, Zoe spoke quietly.

"I don't have any food allergies. However, I need to know that people aren't going to touch me without permission. Especially if I'm expected to put up with yelling and screaming for this storyline. I don't…deal well with being touched when my emotions are high."

I was glad to have had this conversation. I could understand not wanting to be touched, especially by someone I already didn't like. It was much better to know beforehand than to accidentally do something that would have huge repercussions.

"I have no issue with that," I told both women. "I don't have any food allergies, and I don't have any triggers. But I'd like us to be friends off camera, or at least friendly."

"Well, we'll have to see about that." Zoe's voice was still flat, but it sounded just a little bit more normal.

"Just don't get too friendly," Angela joked. "I know you both identify as LGBTQ+ and that's completely fine, but we can't be having any sex in the dorms. That would be…"

"A liability for the network," we muttered in chorus. I would have smiled if it hadn't been such a ridiculous reminder.

"Yes, exactly!" Angela beamed, and I had to resist the urge to roll my eyes.

We were grown-ass adults. Whether we had sex or not was none of the network's business as long as it wasn't on camera. And if I was having sex while on camera, they'd have to be paying me a whole lot more than the big fat goose egg I'd signed on for in hopes of winning the money I'd need to start building my future in the industry.

Not to mention, Zoe didn't even like me as a person, let alone as a romantic partner.

But you might like her, part of my brain whispered. I shoved that thought away. There was no time for even a hint of a crush, especially since I wasn't sure I actually *did* have a crush. The human brain was far too susceptible. Maybe it only had the thought because Ellis had mentioned that he thought I was flirting, at dinner.

*Or maybe...*My thoughts were interrupted by Angela, yet again.

"If that's all you two have to say to each other and to me, then off you pop. Please send in the next two people in line, and make sure you are in your hotel rooms by eleven."

Zoe and I exchanged a glance, then shrugged. Apparently, we were done talking about this. It was weird that they were giving us a curfew, but honestly, I was too tired to fight it.

"That is the weirdest meeting I have ever had," Zoe muttered as she walked out of the room.

I couldn't agree more.

Chapter Ten

ZOE

AFTER TOSSING AND TURNING FOR MORE THAN AN HOUR, I finally had to accept the fact that there was no way in hell I was going to get to sleep anytime soon. I kept expecting Violet to crawl into bed with me, or to doze off and find her weight snuggled up behind me, but the only thing I felt was the anxiety from my performance over the course of the afternoon coursing through my veins still.

I had succeeded. I'd made it through every single skills test. Sure, it had been hard to finish everything within the time limit, but I've been a single mom for three years. Being on a time crunch was my norm. But anxiety had never been a reasonable mental illness, so there was no point in treating it reasonably.

Of course, learning that I'd be spending the next few weeks in a rivalry where anything goes wasn't helping at all.

The only things I'd ever found to help with my anxiety were my medications—already taken—and finding something to immerse myself in. And I knew just what I wanted to lose myself in right now.

I'd done a little bit of exploring in the hotel between dinner and our lights-out time and I had seen a set of rooms designated for the competitors. I'd poked my head in, but I hadn't been able to do quite as much inspection as I'd wanted. I was fairly certain I'd seen a couple of bookshelves in there, which was always a good sign. If I was right about the contents of those shelves, they would contain a selection of cookbooks. That would be just the thing to let me soak up knowledge, improve my skills a little, and whittle away the hours until my brain would allow me to fall asleep.

If I were at home, I could do some dishes or look for recipes online. Here, I had no dishes to work on, thanks to the delicious dinner the producers had provided. In addition, the rules stated that we were only allowed to use the internet for family or work emergencies. It made sense, I guess, since they didn't want us to leak the details of the show or anything, but it sucked. I hadn't been off the internet in this long since before I was married.

I had to do at least one blog post while I was here, which I'd had to get special permission to work on. There were all kinds of rules, including that any filming or photographs had to be approved by one of the producers. Those didn't matter, except that I'd have to work further in advance than I typically did at home. Which meant I had to do more research.

Cookbooks, in addition to being part of that research, would be the perfect thing to help silence the repetitive thoughts that sounded remarkably and horribly, like the things Jacob had said so often when we were married. My heart began to race, again, just from thinking his name. As if I might need to run and hide, the way I used to.

Cookbooks, I reminded myself as firmly as I could. I'm going to go read cookbooks. Not think about that jackass. He is not here. He can't hurt you.

My inner voice was about as firm as jello; the way it always was during my worst moments. With a deep breath, I pulled myself out of bed and grabbed my phone. My sleepwear, a too big t-shirt and a pair of cloth shorts, were presentable enough to be seen in. It might get cold, though. Thinking as quickly and as clearly as I could, I grabbed a sweater from the closet, then my phone and wallet from the dresser. I slid my feet into the flip flops I never traveled without and let my bedroom door close behind me with a click.

The suite was silent, though someone had left the hood light on over the stove. Maybe I wasn't the only one who couldn't sleep. I shrugged, hoping I wouldn't run into any of them. Most of them were nice enough, but I wanted to get as much peace and quiet as I could while I wasn't on set. I especially didn't want to see Amelia again. She was pretty, but in my current state, I didn't want to deal with any more of Amelia's condescension tonight, even if it was mostly for the cameras.

I shook my head. *Cookbooks. Exploring.* I reminded myself again, a little more firmly this time. I walked out of the suite and into the hallway, following the houndstooth pattern of the carpet all the way down the hallway to the suite of rooms. Beside the glass door etched with the show's logo, there was a small scanner, much like the ones required to reach this floor of the hotel. I swiped my wallet over it, hoping I wouldn't have to pull the key card out of my wallet. My hands shook a little from the sheer power of my anxiety and I didn't want to spend time picking up the pieces of my wallet right now. That wouldn't solve anything except to make me more anxious.

I breathed a sigh of relief when a small green light appeared on the panel. A lock I couldn't see clicked and the door popped inward ever so slightly. Very fancy, I thought as I pushed my way into the room. What I found inside took my breath away in the best possible way.

I had been right earlier when I guessed that there would be more bookshelves in here, but the other things in the room took my breath away. It had been split into two main spaces. Most of the room was dedicated to the books.

The sheer scale of the shelves I found was astonishing. It was like a one-wall library. They absolutely covered three of the walls from floor to ceiling with deep set bookshelves packed with cookbooks of all shapes and sizes. In the center of them sat a quartet of black leather armchairs and a light wood and glass coffee table that matched the bookshelves.

The final wall held a kitchen set up almost identically to the ones we had auditioned on, except there were no cabinets to be seen. Two rooms branched off of it where a normal kitchen would have held a refrigerator and a sink, covered with a swinging door. I guessed one of the rooms would hold the refrigerator and pantry. I wasn't sure what the second room would be until I poked my head in.

Sure enough, the first room was a pantry, like they'd provided at the audition, only with a few less cameras and more dishwashers. The room was set up with two sinks with dish drainers, a commercial dishwasher, and enough dishware to feed an army in one sitting. Above all of that were even more glass-fronted cabinets that held more equipment than I could have imagined having access to. There were sieves of all sizes, immersion blenders, food processors, and a variety of different types of pots and pans, and that was just what I recognized from a quick look. My hands itched to dig around in there and see what I could work with. The idea of serving people at the small table off to one side excited me to no end.

For the third, and hopefully last time tonight, I reminded myself that I was here to look at cookbooks. Not cooking, not equipment; the books. And what a selection there was. Striding back over to the shelves, I saw a few familiar names on the shelves, some new and some old. All of them full of knowledge that was mine for the taking; if only I would open them up.

Searching the shelves for something that struck my fancy tonight, I trailed my finger along their spines until I settled on a book that looked unread, from the chef/owner of a gourmet Ethiopian restaurant I had heard a lot about in the news. It was a hefty book. As my hands closed around the cover, I could feel my heart rate begin to even out into a healthier rhythm.

Settling into one of the armchairs that took up the center of the room, I did what I came here to do.

I read.

———

———

I didn't know how long I sat there reading and making notes of things I wanted to try; flavor combinations that I thought would accentuate some of the dishes that I already loved to cook.

Before Violet was born, I had spent a lot of time learning old recipes from my mostly black neighbors, so some of the flavors I'd been cooking with for the last few years were similar to the ones that this chef wrote about, but he did them in ways that were slightly different, and it sounded delicious. I couldn't wait to try them out.

My right hand cramped slightly around my phone, and I had to scroll a ways to reach the top of the notes page. Both of those were a sign that it had probably taken longer than I'd expected to read through the book, and that I had taken pretty thorough notes. I glanced at the top of the screen and grimaced. It was nearly 3:00 a.m. If I wanted to look like a living human, I needed to get to bed soon, but there was a small problem with that.

I was hungry.

Lucky for me, there was a fully stocked kitchen just across the room and I didn't even have to keep the volume down. No one was sleeping on the other side of the wall or had to get up early for work. I didn't even have to worry about the cost of the food I was making. Something that was still blowing my mind.

Everything was part of the show's expansive budget, and I knew exactly what I wanted to make.

One recipe in the book was for a breakfast that had sounded delicious. It was a breakfast bowl made from teff grains cooked in almond milk and spices that I would have normally used for sweets: cinnamon, cloves, and cardamom. The chef topped his with pears, pecans, and maple syrup or honey. It made a beautiful looking porridge that I could never have afforded to do at home, but it sounded fascinating and tasty enough that I really wanted to try it.

Determined and hungry, I opened the book to the recipe page and set it on the counter. Walking into the pantry, I began to search for everything I would need. The almond milk and butter were easy, as were the spices, pears, and pecans. The teff grains were the hard part. Everything on the grain shelf had been removed from the easily readable packages and re-bagged in clear plastic, which just seemed silly.

Now, instead of sifting through the labels, I had to find the tiny grains that matched the photos in the book. I growled, turning on my phone's flashlight for a little extra help seeing the contents of the bags. There were more types of grain here than my grocery store usually carried of everything put together. I knew from watching cooking shows that teff grew on a stalk like wheat, but that it was closer to the size of grits. I had never cooked with it, though. At least seven dollars a bag; it hadn't been feasible.

Finally, all the way at the back, I found the dark brown minuscule grains packed tightly in a small plastic bag. The writing had to be as small as the grains, because I could barely make out what the label said. It felt like enough for what I needed, though, so I grabbed it and added it to the pile. All that was left to grab were the toppings: a couple of pecans, a pear, and the maple syrup.

Gathering them all in my hands, I walked back out into the kitchen and promptly dropped it all on the floor with a shriek. The lights had turned themselves off while I was in the pantry, but someone else was standing in front of the stove.

The figure whirled around to face me, and I recognized her before she spoke.

"Shit! Who's there?"

Fucking Amelia. Of fucking course. The light flicked back on, and I groaned.

"God, can't you make noise when you come into a room? How long have you been standing there?"

She shrugged, as if she hadn't been just as surprised to see me.

"A few minutes, I guess? I didn't know you were back there. Need help cleaning up?"

"Nope," I said popping the last syllable. "I got it."

I squatted with a groan, gathering the items I'd scattered all over the floor. I put each of them on the counter as I grabbed them, trying to avoid getting up and down with my hands full.

"You sure?"

I had to resist the urge to growl as I looked back up at her. She held the pear in one hand and a pecan in the other. Of course, they had rolled over to her.

"Thanks," I gritted out. "Just set them on the counter."

She did so, then stood there. She tapped her fingernails on the counter as I gathered the rest of my ingredients. I could feel my heart rate rising with each click. Taking a deep breath, I realized that the air around me was full of her scent.

She must have just showered, I realized. For some reason, that brought a heat to my cheeks so intense I could almost feel it radiating off of the stainless steel countertop as I looked at my ingredients.

Stealing a glance at her, she was studying the book in front of her. Either Amelia legitimately didn't notice the flush or she was pretending not to. Either way, I wasn't going to bring it up. I just needed to cook, eat, and get my ass back to bed for what little rest I could manage.

I plunked my phone next to the cookbook and opened it to the notes I'd been taking.

"What are these?" Her finger hovered over my

phone screen, those immaculate nails pointing at the sans serif words. I blinked at her.

"Notes. What does it look like?"

"What do you need these for?" Her voice sounded bewildered. My response did too.

"To learn to cook new things. How do you learn things?"

She shrugged. "I just experiment with things I think would taste good together. I don't think I've ever taken notes on cooking things. At least, not since culinary school."

"To each their own, I guess." I was starting to get really annoyed with her. "Reading other recipes and taking notes is part of my process."

"But cooking shouldn't be like this; this cut and dry. It should be intuitive and creative, not based on a formula. Besides, you've cooked with this before. We all have."

I stared at her in shock. She couldn't seriously be this snotty all the time. The worst part was that I was almost positive that it was unintentional.

Her eyes were wide and her eyebrows had almost disappeared into her hairline, but there was a soft smile on her face as she watched me chop the pecans with a little more force than necessary.

"No, we all haven't," I reminded her. "Not all of us can afford to experiment with forty dollars' worth of ingredients per portion," I bit out. "The notes help me to cut down on the experimenting and develop recipes that are much more likely to be good when I actually do cook them."

"Whoa, why are you snapping at me? I just…"

"Do you hear yourself?" I interrupted. "They might have asked you to be a snob on set, but the cameras are off. It's the middle of the damn night. You don't have to act like this right now."

Now it was her turn to blink in surprise, as if she hadn't realized how I would respond. "I didn't mean to…"

I pinched my nose and breathed in deeply. "It doesn't matter what you meant, Amelia. I just want to cook my food, eat it, and go to bed. I don't mind sharing the kitchen, but if you're gonna be here, you have to either be nice or be quiet. I don't care which."

I felt like I was talking to Violet when she was at her worst. Amelia recognized the tone, clearly. If she had been a cat, her fur would have bristled at my words. She stalked into the pantry, and I got to work measuring the teff, spices, and almond milk into a rice cooker. Letting my anger go, I turned it on and then turned back to my pear.

She walked back out a moment later with a basket full of ingredients. One by one, she set them on the counter: a quart of heavy cream, a small bottle of red wine vinegar, two sticks of butter, three eggs, a round of Gruyere, a few thick slices of ham, a jar of Dijon mustard, and a head of spinach.

Without saying a word, she moved around the kitchen like a dancer, pulling out a food processor, a mixing bowl, and a whisk. She started measuring her dry ingredients into the food processor, then cubing the butter into it.

She looked up and caught me watching her. Raising an eyebrow, she met my gaze with anger clear in her gaze.

"Did you have something else to say? I thought you wanted nice or quiet."

I flushed, not sure if it was because I was

embarrassed to get caught or because the way the light reflected off of her angry, brown eyes was more beautiful than anything I'd ever seen. For some reason, that just made me angry all over again.

I opened my mouth to speak, and she began to blitz her food into a crumble, pouring a little bit of water into it at a time. When she stopped, I opened my mouth again, and she began to pulse it again until the crumbles began to form more of a dough.

So, she didn't want me to say anything else. That was fine. I let myself fall into the process of slicing the pear, the fast rise and fall of the knife helping me to find peace again, until the rice cooker beeped to signal completion.

I caught a glimpse of her wrapping half of her dough in plastic wrap as I moved to open the rice cooker. The hiss of steam released made her jump a little. It brought a slightly vicious smile to my face that I hid by pulling down a bowl and two glass storage containers to put away what I knew I wouldn't eat tonight.

Then I shook my head at myself, knowing I was taking this way too far. Sure, she was being rude, but there was no reason for me to be rude back to her. That was what I taught Violet was the golden rule. Maybe I should apologize, I thought.

One look at Amelia's face told me that she wasn't ready to talk to me, so I kept my mouth shut. And honestly, that was fine by me.

She left the room to put her pie crust in the fridge, and I portioned the nutty-smelling grains into their containers, lovingly adding the toppings until each was perfectly layered. I put the lid on them both and licked the serving spoon clean before tossing it into the rice cooker pot.

I nearly moaned with delight. It was just as delicious

as I'd hoped. The dark brown porridge looked almost like brown sugar, but it was soft and subtly spiced. The slices of pear so thin they almost looked like potato chips, and chopped pecans added sweetness and crunch in the perfect way. This might not be something I could afford to eat every day, but nothing was going to stop me from enjoying it while I had it in my hands. I pulled out another spoon and dug in with gusto, not bothering to hold back the sounds coming out of my mouth.

When I had finished the bowl, I looked up to find Amelia's eyes watching me as she whisked her ingredients together. There was still a trace of anger in the set of her mouth and the vigor with which she mixed, but there was something else on her face. Something that I couldn't quite identify.

That was when the smell of her ingredients hit me, now that there was nothing left in my hands to smell. In my head, I went over what she'd carried in: eggs, cheese, cream, vegetables, and pie dough. She must be making a quiche. That was brave of her. I knew my proportions for those like the back of my hand, but late night baking usually meant a lot of mistakes that meant inedible food.

I opened my mouth again to say something—I wasn't entirely sure what—but she turned away from me and started the search for a pie tin. Getting the hint, I took the tools of my meal to the other room. As I washed the dishes, I let myself enjoy the quiet of a contented stomach. I could apologize tomorrow, but for now, it was time to go to bed.

―――

Chapter Eleven

AMELIA

I SLEPT HORRIBLY THAT NIGHT. AFTER BEING UP LATE cooking and eating, I went back to my room and laid there in the silence going over everything that had happened in both of the kitchens I'd been in and thinking about what tomorrow's challenge would bring.

I hated how the conversation had gone between Zoe and me. It seemed like every time we spoke, I stuck my foot in my mouth and offended her. And we'd only spoken three times! It was like being back in middle school all over again, except with more rules.

I'd finally read through the packet while I waited for my quiches to bake, and they were ridiculous. I was glad to see that the warning about having sex while on the show was a rule for everyone, not just the queer contestants. That still rankled, even though there was no homophobia at its core.

When my first alarm went off, I barely felt alive enough to turn the alarm off. I groaned and slapped my phone screen until the beeping stopped. No matter how old or how much sleep I got, 8:00 a.m. was always going to be an atrocious time to be awake.

Rolling out of bed, I slipped on my favorite knee-length bathrobe and padded out to the suite area. Judging by the quiet all around me, no one else was awake. That was fine by me.

I had one task and one task only in mind—making coffee. One of my proudest accomplishments as a young chef was figuring out the perfect timing that would allow me to get clean and my pot of coffee to be brewed.

Now, at home, I'd usually be entirely nude and it would be closer to noon, but I could keep a little bit of my routine consistent. The coffee maker was a simple machine, and I got it going with ease. Before I left the kitchen, I pulled the quiche out of the shared fridge and set it on top of the preheating oven. Twenty minutes at 350 degrees would have the edges crisped and the insides warmed perfectly enough for me to share it around. That would be the perfect start to a day that was already looking to be rough.

———

———

When I got out of the shower, I was feeling a lot more human. I slid into a pair of black pants and sports bra, then stood in front of the closet and pondered what I wanted to wear on my first real day on set. Yesterday, I'd had no choice but to wear my travel clothes, but today, I was going to dress like the chef I had to prove I was.

I had a collection of chef coats in a variety of colors and patterns. Most of them had been custom made, since chef's coats were not designed with fat, well-endowed women in mind. The ones that were, were either a basic white, that was stained before I finished a single service, or so poorly designed that I looked like I weighed twice what I already did and tore if you looked at them funny.

I'd decided a long time ago that I wasn't going to deal with boring, ugly clothes, if I had any choice about it, so I had gone bold with my choices. The result was a collection of patterns and colors of all sorts; just the way I liked it.

After a little bit of Googling, I'd learned that smaller patterns tend to run together on screen, so I'd packed all of the brighter colors and larger patterns for on set. It was a veritable rainbow, but my favorite baby pink coat with a peter pan collar was calling my name today.

I grabbed it and slipped it off the hanger to reveal a simple, tagless, black t-shirt underneath it. Pulling them both on, I walked out into the suite to find that I am not the only one getting ready for the day.

A Black woman with beautiful natural twists leaned against the countertop with her eyes closed, a mug of coffee steaming in her hands. On the other side of the counter, facing away from me, was Zoe. Of course, we'd be in the same suite. And of course, she'd be wearing a sports bra and a pair of tight sleep shorts while she poured herself a cup of coffee. The sight, and the memory, of last night's conversation made my heart squeeze.

"I hope that coffee's strong," Fern's scratchy voice called from behind me. I turned to find her and Shauna walking towards me. "Not all of us can get up early and pin curl our hair every morning."

That was an obvious dig at Shauna, whose hair was curled as perfectly as if she'd walked out of a salon. The woman laughed, then swept her hair into a ponytail as she walked. The movement was graceful and, honestly, kind of mesmerizing.

I shook my head and grinned back at the older woman. "Almost strong enough to chew. We're all gonna need it today."

"Lord knows that's the truth," Zoe murmured.

I had gone straight to my room after dinner the night before, so I hadn't realized who else was in the suite with me. Apparently, these were the women I'd be spending the next few weeks with both on and off the set.

"Well, if everyone's drinking, we better get another pot going and get to know each other. I'm Amelia, by the way."

"I'm Zoe, and I've already got another pot on."

The Black woman raised a hand in a half-hearted wave. "I'm Jada. Thanks for the coffee."

I smiled and nodded as I made my way into the kitchen. Fern and Shauna introduced themselves as I put the two quiches into the oven and grabbed a cup for myself.

"Ooh, she makes coffee *and* she makes breakfast," Shauna squealed. "My husband would be thrilled. Whoever marries you will be a happy man."

The first sip of my coffee soured on my tongue at the remark. It felt too much like what Janet had expected of me, not that Shauna could have known that.

"A happy lady," I corrected her. "And no, she wouldn't be. I can't remember the last time I got home from work before 1:00 a.m. in the morning."

"I know that's right," Jada said, a slight Cuban lilt to her words. "I'm lucky my partner works nights or we'd never see each other. This is way too damn early, though."

"Amen to that," Fern declared. "I don't suppose that's vegan, is it?"

I shook my head. "Sorry. I didn't realize I'd be sharing it with you. Next time I make something, I'll be sure to keep you in mind.

"That's sweet of you. How about I do breakfast for tomorrow, if I survive today's challenge?"

I smiled. "Sounds great."

"Any guesses as to what today's challenge is going to be?" Zoe asked, her first unprompted remark since we'd gathered.

"My bet is on a team challenge," Shauna declared. "It doesn't make sense for us to do two solo challenges in a row when they have plot lines to get started."

I pondered that while I sipped my coffee. It made sense, but I really hoped she was wrong. I would love to get started with some real cooking and show the judges just how good I could be at whatever they decided to throw at us.

"I'm hoping for a solo challenge," Jada said, echoing my thoughts. "No offense, but I don't know any of y'all. What if I get stuck with people who are great at prep work and terrible at actually cooking? No thank you."

We all laughed at that. It was a completely valid fear. It didn't take long for the oven to beep and for all of us to dig into the quiche in relative quiet. We had just cleared our plates away when alarms went off on all of our phones. It was time to go.

———

———

The set was just as intimidating as it had been the night before, even though I had a little bit more of an idea of what was going to happen today.

Especially because the kitchen layout was completely different. Instead of fifteen different kitchens, they had been combined into three square formations that made each of them look like professional kitchens.

We all murmured to each other as we made our way to the front of the room to stand in front of the chefs.

"Being a professional chef takes a lot of different skills," Denise said, her voice ringing through the room. "Technique. Creativity. Consistency. And, last but certainly not least, communication. If you cannot talk to your teammates about what you are cooking and when it will be completed, you will struggle to complete a dinner service."

Beside me, Jada groaned.

"Now that all of you have shown that you have the technical skill to be a part of this kitchen, we'd like to see how well you can communicate, and how consistent you can be as a team. You are going to be serving brunch to the entire staff of the Roosevelt Hotel and our own crew. That's seventy-five people total, split into three groups."

Holy shit. That was a large group of people, even for three teams of five. Especially because none of us had worked together before. Hell, most of us hadn't even introduced ourselves to each other at this point.

"To make this easier for you, we've crafted a simple, but delicious, menu for you to serve today," Bryce explained. "Three main courses, three side dishes, and two drinks. Your main dishes will be eggs Florentine, chicken and waffles, and avocado toast, served with side options of a pina colada fruit salad, latkes, and cinnamon date pudding. The drinks you will be making are a hibiscus rose tea latte and black coffee."

That was going to be a lot of work, but it was doable with the right team.

"Since none of you have gotten to know each other yet, we are going to simplify the process of choosing teams by choosing for you. One of us will be part of your team to make sure that all the food that goes out is safe and up to the standard we require."

Now it was my turn to groan. Never had I ever seen a challenge like this go well this early on in a television show. This one definitely wasn't, since they were hoping to show off the drama between Zoe and me. This was going to be an adventure.

———

Chapter Twelve

ZOE

I felt like an imposter as I stood among the rest of the group, but I tried not to show it. Could they tell I'd barely slept? Or that this was only the second time I'd ever worn my chef's whites?

The judges divvied us up by suite assignments, which pleased me. The other women had seemed knowledgeable while we talked this morning. I already knew Amelia could cook, so even if the rest of them were terrible, I was pretty sure we could manage it.

"You will have half an hour to prep, and one hour to cook, before you must serve all twenty-five plates to your portion of the dining room. If your food is not plated at the end of the hour, you must send empty plates, and your diners cannot vote for you. The team that gets the most positive feedback from its diners will win the challenge."

I took a deep breath and fisted my hands behind my back to keep them from visibly shaking. I'd never cooked for this many people, and I was nervous.

You got accepted into this show the same as everyone else, I reminded myself. *Before yesterday, you'd never gotten on a plane before. This is all about trying new things.*

We were declared the yellow team and handed armbands to show our affiliation before being sent to stand in the middle kitchen. A line of five tickets hung from yellow thumbtacks on the plating pass like the world's most boring birthday party garland. The rest of our ingredients were spread out across the rest of the counters waiting to be dealt with.

"Now, everyone remember your roles to play. There are medics available should you need them, but please be careful," Bryce cautioned. "Last but not least...have fun! Begin working...now!"

The entire kitchen burst into action. Amelia gestured for all of us to gather around her in the center of the kitchen.

"Does anyone else have experience working a line?" she asked.

"I do," Fern and Jada chorused. Shauna and I shook our heads.

"Does anyone have a problem with me taking charge of this service?"

Now we all shook our heads. Amelia charged ahead, barking out orders like it was her career.

"Great. Fern, when we start cooking, I'd like you to take over the sides. Jada, I'd like you to take over the fried chicken. It's gonna need to be perfect. Shauna, you take over the drinks and Zoe, you take over the eggs Florentine. I'll take care of the avocado toast and plating. Sound good?"

We all nodded in unison. I could handle creamed spinach, an English muffin, and a poached egg.

"Let's go, yellow team! Let's get prepped! Keep me

updated on what you're all doing throughout the time, please."

The team rushed forward, grabbing the things we'd need for our individual dishes. I grabbed the bundles of baby spinach, garlic, and two onions and ran to the nearest sink. The small oval leaves had flecks of dirt on them, probably from when they'd been trimmed from their plant, and that wouldn't do anything to help the flavor of the creamed spinach.

As I rinsed, I planned my prep time. The onions needed to be finely chopped, the garlic needed to be minced, and I needed to grate some parmesan.

I couldn't start cooking the cream yet, because we still had way too much time. The poached eggs would take only a few minutes to cook, so as long as my space was ready, I'd be all set with time to help somebody else get their stuff ready.

"Amelia, how many eggs Florentine do we need? I don't want to make too much, since we're only serving twenty-five, and there's so much else on the menu."

I looked up and found her scooping the pits out of her avocados up at the pass.

"Uh, give me a second." She turned and started counting things off the ticket under her breath.

"We've got twelve orders of Florentine across the tickets and the recipe makes six portions, but I want you to make an extra batch just in case something goes wrong with one pot."

"Sounds good to me. I don't think we're gonna need it, though. I got my pin with creamed spinach," I reminded her.

"Well, if that's the case, then we'll have enough for lunch for ourselves afterward and everybody wins. Please just do it?"

I bristled. "I already said I would."

"Oh. Well… good," Amelia stammered, then seemed to collect herself. "If anyone finishes early, Fern's gonna need help getting her latkes and fruit salad prepped in time."

I nodded. "I'll move over there as soon as I have this set up."

She called out the rest of the orders: four avocado toast and nine chicken and waffles entrees.

We all went back to work and, for the next ten minutes, the kitchen was silent except for the chop of knives and the whir of the mixer. And then, I was done. My spinach was cleaned and trimmed, my onion and garlic was ready to go into the pan, and I had all of my spices set aside for all three pots of spinach.

I wiped my hands dry on my hips and moved down to where Fern stood next to the small refrigerator we'd been given access to. She was cutting banana after banana and dumping it into a mixing bowl, muttering to herself as she worked.

"Fern, what do you need me to work on?"

"Uh, fruit salad, please. I've got the strawberries and bananas done. Can you deal with the pineapple for me?"

"Yeah, how many do you need cut? Just one?"

"Uh, two. We need to juice one and include cut pieces of another."

Amelia looked over at me with annoyance clear on her face. She was slicing yet another bag of muffins, and I realized I'd forgotten to tell her what I was doing. Surely she could hear me, but it was better to be safe than sorry.

"Gotcha. Amelia, moving over to help Fern."

She flashed a smiled at me. "Sounds good. I'm finishing up slicing the muffins, then I'm gonna help Jada finish up. Shauna, you're awful quiet over there. How's it going?"

"I'm doing just fine," she said in a sing song voice. "Just mixing tea like it's my job over here."

"You sure you're good, Shauna?" I didn't know her well enough to tell whether there was a hint of bitterness there or if that was just the way she sounded when she was under the gun.

She turned her head, tossing her glistening curls and a smile over her shoulder. "I'm good. Really."

With a nod, I got to work cutting the pineapples into bite sized chunks. Fern and I talked a little about what had brought us here, which the cameras made sure to catch every second of.

I wondered how much of this footage would actually make it onto the screen. They had three teams working, and none of this was particularly dramatic.

As if the rest of the contestants could hear my thoughts, I heard an argument begin in the next kitchen over, and grinned.

"I guess Amelia and I aren't the only ones charged with bringing the drama this season," I murmured to Fern. She shook her head and laughed, and I joined her.

I tossed the chunks of pineapple in with the strawberries, leaving the other on my cutting board. "Any idea where the juicer is in all this?"

"I think it's under here," Shauna called over. Sure enough, I could see the tell-tale funnel of the appliance right next to her left leg.

I grabbed the appliance and moved it to where Fern and I had been set up. Amelia had joined her in my absence, cutting the potatoes into small enough pieces to fit into the food processor.

"Do either of you know how to work one of these?"

Fern looked at me with mild reproof, but I just shrugged. I'd never had the budget for fancy equipment. All I could tell about it was that it was heavy, like the expensive stand mixer I had had to leave behind when I'd taken Violet and ran.

Amelia plugged it in for me and showed me what to do. It turned out to be incredibly simple. You plug it in, flip a switch, ensure the tubs are in the right spot to catch the juice and the fibers, and shove the fruit in.

"So, I know this is probably a silly question, but…I need to make sure. Both of you know how to cook the things you're responsible for? I already asked Jada and she's all set on the fried chicken and waffles."

"What, are you gonna teach me how to make a latke?" her thickly accented voice dripped with sarcasm. "I may be vegan, but I'm still a sixty-year-old New Jersey Jew who runs a *diner*. I've been making latkes for more years than you've been alive. Why on earth would that be a silly question?"

I snorted as I watched Amelia's face redden with what I hoped was embarrassment.

"And, as I reminded you earlier, creamed spinach was part of the dish that got me into this competition. Or had you forgotten?"

Her color deepened with every word. I would have felt bad about the barb, but honestly, this was too much.

"Look, not everybody knows how to do everything. I just thought that, if there was a problem, I could run through it with you before it became a real problem."

I shoved the first piece of pineapple into the juicer, letting it shut out whatever else she said. She frowned at me, and I could see her saying that she wasn't done talking. I shoved another few chunks in, making it clear I was done listening to her. Amelia flung her hands in the air and walked over to Shauna.

"Do I know how to make latkes," Fern mocked under her breath.

"At least those require a little finesse," I groused. "She didn't think I could cream spinach and poach eggs."

She snorted, then moved back to squeeze the liquid out of the potatoes and onions in cheesecloth.

"All right, ladies! Ten minutes left! How are we doing?" I jumped at the sound of a male voice, looking up to find Chef Nathan and his playboy grin across the counter from us. His grin widened when he saw my shock, showing off slightly pointed canines and dimples that would have made me swoon if my heart hadn't been trying to beat its way out of my chest. Fern, however, wasn't fazed. She just shook her head at him with a smile.

"Chef, you oughta know better than to sneak up on a bunch of women wielding knives. You might wind up with a few more piercings than you came in with."

He leaned forward, placing his elbows on the counter and laying his head in his hands. "Ooh, what would you give me? Another ear piercing? You'd have to find room for it. I've been thinking about doing my septum."

At his antics, I had to smile. "My mama would say not to put any holes in that pretty face of yours when it's what pays the bills."

"And she would be right," Fern echoed with her cackle.

"You make a fair point," he sighed, straightening up. "You're also doing a great job with the fruit salad and latkes. How do you feel about cooking for twenty-five people all at once?"

"I've done this once a week for about twenty-five years. I wouldn't have minded a little extra prep time, but it'll get done. We've got a good team getting everything together, with none of that foolishness I hear happening in the other teams."

"So it seems! Well, I hope your service goes as smoothly as your preparations." He stole a grape from the fruit salad and popped it into his mouth before he walked away. It reminded me of Violet sneaking chocolate chips out of the bag when I made pancakes for us both.

Before I knew it, we were as prepared as we could be. Fern had set up her cup measure, fish spatula, and cooling rack for when she could start cooking. Her oil was in the pan just waiting for us to be allowed to turn the stove on.

I measured out my cream into deli containers, leaving them in the small refrigerator until it was time to work, and joined Amelia at the pass. She was setting out plates and planning everything out based on the tables they would eventually go to. She glanced from the clock to the plates and back to the clock again once every minute or so. There were only three minutes left, and she looked frazzled.

"What do you need me to do?"

"Um…" she looked around, pushing a lock of hair out of her face. "Can you wrap the silverware for me?"

"Yeah, I can do that." I picked up the basket of forks, knives, and cloth napkins and got to work. She offered me a grateful smile and my stomach flip flopped.

The feeling, one I'd always associated with crushes, surprised me almost more than the kindness I saw on her face. I hadn't felt anything like it since…

No. You're not thinking about crushes right now, I told

myself firmly. *It's just nerves about the challenge. That's all. You don't have a crush on her.*

I redoubled my focus on the silverware, trying to avoid thinking too hard about feelings. It was simple work.

Fork, spoon, knife, napkin. Wrap. Place on tray. Repeat.

Work I was used to from my time at the diner. It had long since proven its ability to take my mind off of nearly anything, and it didn't fail me this time.

However, it couldn't do everything. I didn't quite get all of the silverware put together before the timer went off. I wiped my forehead on the back of my arm. I hadn't noticed it while I worked, but I was sweating profusely. Had been for a while, if the dampness on the back of the sleeve of my chef's whites was any indication. But I had made it through the first part of the challenge, and that was no small feat. I couldn't help but be a little bit proud of myself.

———

Chapter Thirteen

AMELIA

THERE WAS A WAIT BETWEEN THE END OF OUR PREP TIME and beginning of the cook time. The crew had to put the final touches on in the dining room to make it filming friendly.

People milled about and their voices called out from every corner of the room, directing everyone and everything that might be relevant to the scene they wanted to show the viewers.

Unlike the room where all of us contestants had dined the night before, they had set up the room adjacent to us to be functional, rather than formal. Simple round folding tables were covered with the simple tablecloths I knew could be ordered in bulk from any restaurant supply store. They were in the primary colors that signified each of the three teams. Each table was then surrounded by five high-backed, black chairs, with black chargers placed on the tables in front of them.

The scrape of tables and chairs as they were moved around the room added to the general feeling of chaos in the room.

On the other side of the kitchens, the three judges stood on the dais surrounded by a semi-circle of camera operators. We couldn't hear what they were saying, but they were discussing something very animatedly.

———

By contrast, the kitchen I stood in was like a small oasis of calmness. There were still cameras focused on us, but we weren't working on anything. We were just…waiting. I tapped my fingers on the counter rhythmically while I watched the crew work. They were faster than I had expected them to be, clearly practiced at working quickly despite barely having worked together before.

The same thing could be said for my own team, I realized as I looked around the small yellow-accented kitchen. Despite my earlier stress about getting everything done in time, we were in really good shape.

I wished that I could see the other kitchens to see how far they had gotten in their preparations. It was probably good that I couldn't, as it would only fuel the stress and anxiety that came with competing.

It had already gotten the better of me once this morning. I had known the instant the words left my mouth that Fern and Zoe would be offended. Jada had eyed me askance when she answered too.

Hell, if someone had asked me that under any other circumstances, I would've let them know exactly what I thought of the question. It wasn't as if any of them had given me any reason for concern. I knew better than to treat chefs under my command like that. Especially when my command over them was tenuous at best like it was here. I also knew what I needed to do, at least for my own conscience, and there was no better time to do it.

"Hey, guys? Can I talk to you for a second?" My voice was quiet; hopefully quiet enough that the mics wouldn't pick up every word I said. The other women in the room heard me, though. Jada and Zoe traded a glance at my words, but they walked back toward me. Fern and Shauna crossed the room, and they came to where I stood at the pass.

"I owe you all an apology. I was an ass earlier when I asked if you knew what you were doing. I should have trusted all of y'all to tell me if you couldn't do what I assigned you, especially with a menu like this." It all came out in a rush, my words stumbling into each other like a pair of drunks. It apparently got the message across, though.

Jada smiled and nodded. It was already clear from our time together that she wasn't much for talking, which was fine. Shauna's smile and murmured thanks was gracious, even though I hadn't even spoken to her much during prep. Fern thanked me for the apology, but she still eyed me skeptically until she walked away with the others.

Zoe, however, was clearly unimpressed. When the others were further away, she stepped closer to me and crossed her arms. My breath caught in my chest when she tilted her head up and narrowed her eyes at me.

God, she was beautiful. The thought filled my mind before I could stop it. I shook it off.

"That apology was good, but you need to learn to think before you speak," she bit out, her tone as sharp as any of the knives in our kit. "I may not have worked in a professional kitchen before, but my mama raised me to know how to talk to people. I bet yours did too. You're a fucking sous chef. You should know better."

I flushed. "That's why I apologized. I knew I'd

fucked up. If I were in my own kitchen, if we had more time…" I ran a hand over my hair, grimacing at the sweat I felt in it. "I would have had a conversation about where everyone felt comfortable and coached them through what they weren't sure about."

My voice had risen a little as I spoke, just enough to catch the camera crew's attention. I cursed silently as cameras surrounded us again. Zoe glanced at one over my shoulder and cringed. It didn't stop her from speaking her mind, though.

"This competition might have a little bit more of a time crunch than you're used to, and we might not like each other, but it doesn't mean that you get to treat other professionals like children. Got it?"

I simply nodded. There was nothing else I could say. Zoe spun on her heels and walked back to her station. She arrived just as the timer went off again. I jumped, confused. I hadn't realized there was one going, but there was no time to dwell on it. Nathan stood in front of us, grinning yet again.

"Contestants, to your stations!"

———

———

Despite the issues during prep, and Zoe actively disliking me, the actual cook time began fairly smoothly.

I helped Jada fry the chicken for the first fifteen minutes, making sure each chicken thigh was an equally golden brown before sliding the full baking trays into the oven to finish cooking and stay warm until it was time to serve. When we'd completed that, I did the same for some of Fern's latkes. She moved to serve the fruit salad into the tiny short-stemmed goblets that the judges had chosen, and I left her to it.

The judges called the halfway mark, and it was now time for me to focus on the English muffins and toast that we would need for two of our main dishes. I had sliced them, buttered them, and set them on baking trays earlier, but now they needed to be toasted. There was only one way to ensure each one was perfectly done; searing them like a steak on the stovetop, then tossing them into the oven on a low temperature to finish drying out the way they needed to.

The only oven left to do that in was at the station where Zoe was stirring the blanched baby spinach into the cream mixture in one pot. The other two pots had already been combined and just needed to be left on low heat and stirred occasionally until it was time to serve.

"Mind if I borrow this half of the stove for the bread?"

She nodded, barely looking at me before going back to her spinach. I cranked up the gas on the middle front burner and tossed a sauté pan onto it to heat up.

I was glad they'd given us the professional six burner stoves I was used to working on. If they hadn't, I was pretty sure it would be almost impossible to get everything done and make sure it was at the right temperature when we served it. It would have been a lot easier to serve these order by order, but that wasn't the challenge. I wondered, as I pressed muffin after muffin into a sizzling hot pan, if that was why the judges had chosen this for the first team challenge.

I would ask Nathan, as he walked around the kitchen, but there was no time. He was watching everything we did like a hawk, touching and tasting everything we worked on, saying nothing. It was nerve-wracking, until he picked up the leftover bowl of pina colada fruit salad and started snacking. At least I could guarantee that, that tasted good, since he kept eating it as he continued his inspection of our work.

That was when it struck me. I was supposed to be in charge of the team and I hadn't tasted anything we'd cooked other than the breading for the fried chicken and the avocado mixture. Glancing over at Zoe, she was focused on her poached eggs.

"Hey, Zoe?"

"Yeah?"

I hesitated before I spoke again, taking her earlier words into consideration and wondering if I really needed to ask. But I needed to know that it would be good before it went out, and there was only one way to do that.

"The spinach smells really great. Would you mind if I have a taste of it?"

She nodded, apparently not offended. "Sure. I just added salt, so mix it in a little before you taste."

I smiled at her as I reached for one of the white plastic spoons we'd been given for tasting the food with. She stirred it herself before I made it to the pot with my spoon. Scooping out a little bit, I blew on it before letting the spoon slide into my mouth.

It was earthy and garlicky with a hint of heat from the cayenne and nutmeg, but none of the flavors overpowered any of the others because of the way it had been mixed with the cream. It was perfect.

I looked over at Zoe again and saw a self-satisfied smile on her lips. It was so unlike the scowls and frowns that I was used to that I froze for a moment. It was a smile that made me desperately want to kiss her. I blinked, shaking the thought away and focusing on her as a chef, as a competitor, rather than as a beautiful woman.

"This is the best spinach I've ever had."

Her smile widened, becoming slyer and more feline. "I know. I told you I could handle it."

"I will never doubt you again," I promised with a laugh. Before I could say anything else, the judges called the time again. Fifteen minutes remained of the challenge.

With a string of curses, I whipped around. "Jada, I'm gonna need those waffles really soon so I can start plating. Fern, you too."

"I'll bring you the first tray of chicken in thirty seconds and then start bringing you waffles in batches," Jada called back, already opening her oven. Fern echoed her and got to work.

"Sounds great! Zoe, can you…"

I didn't finish my sentence because I didn't need to. She had read my mind and was already bringing her pot of spinach up to the pass.

"You'll have the first few poached eggs in like four minutes, Amelia," she informed me, voice light.

"You are awesome," I replied. The cat-like grin came back to her face and I couldn't stop a matching one from widening on my own face. I grabbed the first tray of muffins from the oven and made my way to my station to begin plating all of our hard work.

I didn't have to ask for anything after that. Tray after tray of items came up, all perfectly cooked and crispy the way a brunch should be. When I got down to the last table, there was less than a minute left. The rest of the team had joined me, ensuring that everything got done. And it did.

When the timer went off, the lattes were properly

garnished with rose petals and each table had a tray of cream and sugar so they could adjust their drinks to their tastes. The plates looked almost like they'd come off of the pages of a magazine, and everything was perfect. There was no way we had lost this challenge, no matter what the other teams had managed to do.

———

———

I had been right. We had not lost the challenge. The crew and staff were still eating their food, but there was already a clear loser. The red team had not managed to get all of their plates filled in time, which meant that they were automatically up for elimination.

Everyone else had been sent off to the side and told to sit in the bar stools they'd provided. The stools were the only reason that several of the contestants were even visible behind the wall of holographic flames. It was good to be off of my feet and safe for one more day in the competition, especially since the crew was now arranging the kitchen. I would have killed for something to eat, though. Tasting the food during our cook time was no replacement for a real meal.

I was probably in better shape than the guys who now stood in front of the dais, though.

"Figures it was the team full of guys that couldn't get their shit together," a blonde woman from the other team said in front of me, letting her hair out of the tight bun she'd had it in for the cook time. I snorted in agreement.

"I just hope Ellis makes it through," Fern worried. "I like that old man."

That sobered me a little bit. I like him too. "Anyone know anything about the other guys on the team?"

Almost everyone shook their heads. The woman who had spoken earlier did so again. "Those two white guys were in front of me during the surprise challenge. I was honestly surprised the guy with the dreads made it through that."

"What else do you expect from a white dude with dreads, though? Appropriators like that are never as good at things as they think they are." That was from a Black woman I didn't know, but I did know that she was right.

One of the producers hushed us, pointing at the set. They had finished rearranging everything into single kitchens again and the red teams contestants had been sent to stand behind one. Each of the counters had a large, opaque black basket with the show's logo on it. The judges were starting to explain the challenge.

"For this challenge, we are going to be testing your creativity and your time management skills. And we'll be using some ingredients that will be familiar to you. Open your baskets."

The camera crew had swarmed around the other contestants, getting footage of each of them opening the lids.

"I wonder what's in the basket?" Jada murmured.

I looked back, trying to see who she was talking to. Zoe's eyes were bright as she peered at them, as if she was trying to turn on some kind of x-ray vision to find out. "I have no idea. I guess we'll find out in a minute."

The producer hushed us again and Zoe grimaced. From what I could see, the guys were looking at each other and then the contents of the basket. They started pulling out bags that looked like they were filled with pre-chopped vegetables; definitely not what I'd expected.

"In your baskets, you will see the results of your performances in yesterday's challenge. Over the next hour, you will be using them to create one dish from each of the proteins you worked with yesterday," Denise explained.

"Oh shit," I murmured. Everyone around me was saying variations of the same thing. That was a tall order, but one that would be made easier by having all of their proteins pre-portioned. At least, if they'd done a good job with yesterday's challenge.

The guy with dreadlocks was *definitely* in trouble. I guessed from the tense set of his shoulders that he already knew it. Even from here, his chicken looked like all of the bones had been chewed on, rather than cleanly cut. The fish all looked ragged, like he'd had a hard time filleting it.

After hearing how harsh the judges had been last night, I was surprised that they'd let him continue at all. Then I remembered.

This was a television show. They couldn't *just* focus on people who were great at their jobs. It wouldn't be interesting enough to keep people watching every week. Drama was what they were after, and what they would get, whether the contestants intentionally gave it to them or not.

In this case, though, there was no way he didn't know he'd mangled his proteins. Even from here, I could see that the contents of the other baskets showed much higher levels of skill. He'd have to be really creative with his dishes, if he wanted to make it through to the next episode.

We all watched as they scuttled around their kitchens,

murmuring about what they did as they swapped their dishes from stovetop to oven to cooling rack. The producers soon gave up on trying to keep us silent, but we kept our voices low as we discussed what they could possibly be making. Besides, we weren't on a mic, so the cameras wouldn't pick us up unless we started being raucous.

I wished I could hear what the judges were saying as they walked around. I assumed they were talking to them about their dishes and why they thought they deserved to stay in the competition, but there was no telling. It was the standard topic for these sorts of challenges.

When the final timer went off, most of the chefs had dishes that I wanted to taste. Some of them were messily plated, but everyone had managed to put four dishes out.

The fish they had had us work with were very versatile and the contestants were proving it. No one had made anything remotely similar, even though they all shared the same ingredients. It looked like one contestant had made what looked like monkfish curry, while another had baked his trout and vegetables en papillote. Ellis had turned his tuna into a tartare that the judges seemed to love.

In the end, they went back to the dais to continue their discussion. It looked like a fierce one. I could only see half of Denise and Bryce's face as they stood in a triangle, but their mouths moved rapidly and there was a lot of gesticulation.

The chefs cleaned their stations while they waited for the judges to finish. Ellis and a Latino man seemed to have gotten great feedback on their dishes, judging by the pleased looks on their faces as they worked. The other three contestants did not seem to have done so well.

One of the white guys, who had ridden in with me, had fury written all over his face and kept slamming cabinet doors as he tidied.

"That guy looks like he's about to throw a temper tantrum my daughter would envy," Zoe said from behind my head as I watched. She was right.

It was something I would never have accepted in my kitchen. People who couldn't control their emotions were not generally people that made a kitchen environment comfortable to work in, what with all the fire and knives. That was when her words struck me. She had a daughter?

Fern apparently realized the same thing, because she asked a series of quick questions that Zoe answered just as rapidly. Her face lit up when she told us all about Violet.

"I bet her father is having a hell of a time being the primary parent while you're here. That's gotta be hard." Jada's statement was made lightheartedly, but the joy drained out of Zoe's face.

"No," she said shortly. "She's with my mother."

The change was so abrupt that it shocked me. I wondered what the story was behind it, but it was absolutely none of my business. She didn't get a chance to say anything else, even if she'd wanted to. Nathan's booming voice got all of our attention from the dais. The judging was complete, and dreadlock guy was one of the bottom two.

He had severely overcooked his tuna to the point of inedibility. However, his offense turned out not to be the worst one. The man who had thrown the temper tantrum had served the judges nearly raw chicken. Overcooked tuna could be overlooked, but raw chicken was potentially fatal.

"Your cooking can't stand up to the heat of this kitchen. Your time here is done."

He stormed out of the room, followed by the now somewhat normal swarm of camera operators. And with that, the first full day of filming was over.

———

Chapter Fourteen

ZOE

I SLEPT MUCH BETTER THE NEXT NIGHT, LEAVING ME feeling really rested for the first time in recent memory. I was up early, like always, and the hotel floor was nearly silent around me.

It was a little weird, if I was being honest with myself. It had been a long time since I hadn't had to rush around the house making sure Violet got fed before I went to work at the diner.

Just like at home, though, I didn't let the unusual situation get in the way of the work I had to get done. I pulled the leftover teff bowl from the fridge, grabbed my laptop, and made my way down to the extra suite. Hopefully, I could find a coffee maker in there that wouldn't wake the others, because I knew that I would need all the brain power I could get to get everything done.

Settling myself into one of the plush armchairs, it didn't take long for me to fall into a familiar rhythm. I'd take a few bites of breakfast, tapping out a paragraph while I chewed, then took a glug of coffee to wash it all down while I made sure my numbers and my links were right.

After about an hour, I had nearly finished the post. All that was left to do was the search engine optimization when the door to the suite opened. It was a good thing that I was already sitting down, because I would have dropped everything in my hands at the sight of Nathan and Bryce walking in, arguing.

I must have made some sort of sound, because they both stopped talking and turned towards me with surprise written all over their faces. It was only when they took a step back that I noticed that they were standing very close to each other.

"Oh! Good morning, Mrs. Cooper! We weren't expecting anyone to be awake yet."

I smiled crookedly. "I work at a diner and usually have to wrangle a three-year-old into eating breakfast before I go. It gets you into a schedule."

"Oh, that's right! We saw your daughter's birthday cake on your blog after your audition. She's a beautiful girl."

The "we" in the statement was interesting. I wondered briefly if maybe there was more going on between the two men but shook it off. They probably just did their research on the contestants as a group after auditions.

"Thank you! She's pretty special, if I do say so myself." I winked and they laughed.

"We were just about to make some omelets for breakfast. You want one?"

"I just finished my own, unfortunately." I shook my head sadly, showing them the now-empty bowl on the side table. It pained me to refuse food from two world famous chefs, but there was no way I could eat anything else. "Would you mind if I watched you work, though?"

Nathan and Bryce exchanged a look, then shrugged almost in unison. "Not a problem. No pictures, though. We're not paparazzi ready."

I nodded and put my phone into my laptop bag. The thought hadn't even crossed my mind, but I understood why they had asked. They had to live very different lives than anything I would likely ever experience, and that was all right.

Before long, the two men were digging through the pantry and refrigerator, tossing ingredients back and forth so quickly it was like they were pro football players instead of chefs. In minutes, they had pulled together two piles of ingredients on the center island.

One pile was made up of gruyere, cremini mushrooms, chives, parsley, and a single shallot. It would be a delicious mushroom omelet. The other was decidedly sweeter than I'd expected with a jar of honey, a clamshell of raspberries, and cinnamon being the main components. I had heard of people doing sweet omelets, but I'd never cooked one for either of my favorite test subjects.

Violet was still in the phase where she didn't like her different foods to touch, and Mom had always believed that the first meal of the day should not be any more sugary than necessary. I had yet to sway her on that, despite years of arguing over it and my own preference for a sweet breakfast that I didn't have to cook every morning.

Bryce turned his back to the room and reached into the cupboard for a small blender and two small omelet pans. Nathan busied himself with getting the eggs and cream from the refrigerator. When Bryce turned back around, my curiosity got the better of me.

"Whose ingredients are whose?"

Nathan looked at the piles, then back up at me. "Who do you think?"

I blinked. I hadn't expected a question back. "Um, well…I'd guess that Bryce would want the mushroom omelet, since he's used to working off extra calories as soccer player? But you don't seem like the type to want a raspberry omelet in the morning, either."

Nathan laughed, the joy in it filling the kitchen. "You are absolutely wrong. My days of working my ass off on the field are over, so I'm eating whatever and however much I want.

"Which means eating everything sweet in the vicinity," Bryce deadpanned. I giggled, seeing the twinkle in his eyes that had nothing to do with the light glancing off of his large circular glasses.

"It's what keeps me so sweet," Nathan teased. "How else would I counteract your sour face during judging?"

Both men laughed in harmony in a way that was both practiced and effortless, telling me that there had to be something going on between them behind the scenes.

While they got to work separating their eggs and whipping the whites to soft peaks, I found myself wondering what Amelia was having for breakfast. The suite had finished off the quiche she'd made. Fern had promised to make some sort of breakfast for us all, but she'd also announced her plan to sleep as late as possible. I wasn't sure how that would turn out for them.

The door opened again to reveal the other members of my suite, as if I had summoned them with my thoughts.

"Zoe! So, *this* is where you ran off to this morning.

I'm not surprised. It looks very cozy in here." Fern stopped short in the doorway with a gasp, nearly causing a pileup with all of the other women when she saw the men in the kitchen. "Oh! Hello chefs!"

"Good morning, Fern." Bryce peered past her to see the rest of my suitemates and smiled. "Ladies. Why don't you all join us? Nathan and I were just making breakfast."

"Don't mind if we do! You cooking for a group or just for yourselves? We haven't eaten yet and I was gonna show these young things a vegan trick or two."

Nathan joined Bryce at the counter, wiping his hands on a cloth towel before tossing it over his shoulder.

"We have ourselves making omelets but it'll be all yours in just a few minutes if you don't mind hanging out."

Fern walked in confidently and plopped into the barstool on one side of me. Amelia leaned gracefully on the counter on the other with a wave of light lemony scent. She smiled at me so brightly that it made my head spin a little. My time to watch the male judges work may have been interrupted, but maybe it wouldn't be all bad.

———

———

An hour later, we all got into our chef's coats and pants.

Relief flooded through me when I saw that the set was in the same formation it had been for the elimination the previous night. The team challenge had turned out well in the end, but I really didn't want to rely on anyone else to keep moving on in the competition.

Trepidation added an edge to my thoughts as I

realized that, once again, there were opaque black baskets on all of the kitchen counters. I hoped we wouldn't all be put up to the task that had sent one of us home, then realized that was silly. Of course, they wouldn't give us the same challenge twice. That would be incredibly boring television.

I didn't have to wonder for long, though. We were shepherded into our place in the kitchen by the crew, and the judges were waiting for us on the dais.

"Today's challenge is all about your creativity. We have our first ever mystery ingredient challenge."

She went on to explain the task. We had to make one dish using at least five of the ingredients in the basket over the next hour, with the option to use items from the limited pantry they'd set up for us. Then we'd be judged, and the contestants who cooked the worst three dishes would be considered for immediate elimination.

That last part had a lump forming in my throat. What if they had given us ingredients that I've never heard of before? What if they were things that couldn't reasonably be cooked in an hour? I tamped those thoughts down and opened the basket.

The judges named each item in the basket as we pulled them out. To my relief, I knew most of them. The first was a live Dungeness crab, followed by a beautifully marbled beef tenderloin wrapped in brown paper, a small, silver tin labelled fennel pollen, a roll of goat cheese, two bars of dark chocolate, golden beets, and a couple of orange-colored fruits that were shaped like lemons.

I puzzled over them for a moment before realizing that it had to be tangelos. I'd seen them on TV shows before, and knew they were supposed to taste like a mix of oranges and grapefruits, but I'd never tried one before. Nathan gave a quick overview of the ingredients, confirming what I'd already determined.

Fennel pollen was also a new ingredient to me, but at least one I had seen in the spice aisles before. I opened the tin and was hit with an almost overwhelming scent that was sweet, tangy, and herbal all at the same time. It seemed like the kind of thing that you'd want to use sparingly.

The timer began. Looking at the ingredients on my board, my mind whirled. There was no way to use the chocolate with any five of the other ingredients in the time allotted, so I tossed it right back into the basket and focused on the others.

I could turn the crab, tangelos, and goat cheese into a warm crab salad, but only if I were able to kill, break down and cook the crab in time. I'd also have to figure something else out for two of the other ingredients. Maybe fennel pollen roasted beet chips would be good.

That wouldn't work, though. I had never worked with real crab before, let alone tried to get all of the meat from one. I couldn't risk screwing it up on a day where immediate elimination was an option, so the crab went back into the basket as well.

That left the beef as my protein of choice. I'd never worked with beef tenderloin, either. It was what filet mignons came from, and that was too expensive for us. However, it was still beef, which was a much more familiar flavor than crab.

Suddenly, I knew exactly what I wanted to do with the ingredients and there was no time to waste. I got to work, trimming the inedible silver skin and connective tissue from the top and sides, making the loin almost perfectly round. Murmuring a prayer, I cut the loin into four, two inch steaks, then chopped the rest into smaller pieces. It was easier than I'd expected to get clean cuts, though I guess that wasn't surprising given how sharp my new knives were. If I had been doing it at home, it would have been an entirely different story.

The three judges were making their way through the room, talking to each contestant the way they had the night before. By the time they made it to me, I had a piece of seasoned meat searing in a cast iron pan and was cutting the beets into bite-sized chunks.

"Good evening, Ms. Cooper," Bryce said. "It smells good! How's it going over here?"

"Well, chef! I think I've figured out the perfect meal for you." I looked up, but I didn't stop chopping. Normally, I'd have cooked them in quarters, but they would cook faster this way. Nobody wanted crunchy beets in their salad, especially in a cooking competition.

"Oh? And what is that?" Denise asked, her voice interested.

"Fennel pollen and garlic-roasted filet mignon with a beet and goat cheese salad dressed with a tangelo honey vinaigrette," I said proudly. Denise raised an eyebrow at the meat.

"You're doing filet mignon and you're already cooking the meat? Aren't you worried about overcooking it?" Her voice was nonjudgmental, but I knew a test when I heard it.

"No, ma'am, this is a test piece. I've never worked with fennel pollen or filet mignon before, so I wanted to make sure I had the balance right before I seasoned the rest of the meat."

She nodded at me in what I guessed was approval.

Nathan's face was much easier to read, as he grinned at me. "I can't wait to try it! We'll get out of your hair and let you finish cooking."

"Thank you, chefs!" I waved my empty hand at them, feeling a little silly until Bryce waved back. I smiled, tossing the chopped beets into the water and putting it onto the heat. All it needed now was a little salt, pepper, and shot of lemon juice to keep them colorful and delicious.

The two male judges kept going out of their way to be kind to all of the contestants in a way I hadn't expected. Honestly, I hadn't expected the judges to interact with us much at all. Denise was a much harder woman to get to know. We'd only been here for three days, but I'd already noticed that she held herself a lot further away from both her fellow judges and us contestants. Not that, that was necessarily a bad thing, because she was more than a little bit scary.

The scent of cooked meat dragged me back to thoughts of my meal. The test piece of beef should be just about medium rare. I pulled it out of the pan and set it on the cooling rack before making my way to the pantry. I wasn't sure what all they would have in there, but there would certainly be something to beef up this salad and make sure it was as delicious as it could be.

I almost ran to the pantry, conscious of the ticking clocks visible from every corner of the room. I needed some kind of seed or nut for a little bit of texture and some small greens for the base of the salad. Maybe arugula and some endive to add to the beet greens, if they had it.

When I got to the pantry, I wasn't the only one looking for some leafy greens. Amelia's large, bright blue chef's coat-clad form was bent over the case, rifling through the offered vegetation like she had all the time in the world. I groaned, moving over to peruse a shelf full of small, brown things. They had walnuts, pecans, and sunflower seeds, all of which would work. The sunflower seeds would fit the flavor profile a little bit better, though. They'd absorb some of the sweetness and sourness of the dressing without making it too earthy the way the others would.

Turning back to the refrigerator full of fresh greens, I saw Amelia walking away with the two ingredients I wanted for my own salad. Luckily, there was more in the refrigerator. I pulled a head of each out and dashed back to my station. I placed them on the board I'd been chopping beets on and picked up the piece of steak. It was still warm and felt like it was cooked properly, but the only way to tell was to cut it open and taste whether the seasoning was right. This would be my only chance to adjust it before I absolutely had to cook the filet mignon for the judges.

I said another prayer and sliced a triangle out of the medallion. It was a little bit overcooked, but nothing unfixable on the next cook. I blew on it to cool it, then popped it into my mouth.

It was just as delicious as I hoped it would be. The licorice-like flavor blended beautifully with the salt, pepper, and garlic to create something entirely new. Quickly, I used the same proportions of each to season each of the filet mignons, rubbing the powders gently into the tender flesh.

With deliberate slowness, I pressed the four filets into the pan one by one. The sizzle when meat met pan was thrilling, but I didn't have time to savor it. I had the rest of the meal to finish.

———

———

When the timer went off, my chest was heaving, the plate in front of me was very nearly immaculate, and the kitchen was *hot*. I lifted my arms and let my hands rest on top of my head, hoping to help myself breathe a little more deeply without looking ridiculous.

Luckily, I wasn't the only one in a weird pose. Several of the other women were leaning forward and fanning themselves. Even the judges looked like they were sweating from the front of the room.

"Everyone, bring your plates up to the front."

With trepidation, I picked up the tray with my plates and began walking toward the front of the room. This was the part that was new for me. On most of the TV shows I'd seen, you never got to see people working on more than one plate at a time. Iron Chef was the only one where I could remember seeing the contestants ensure that every plate was identical for a judge's tasting. I wondered if the editors would show this part of the competition, or if it would get left out.

"Whoa! Watch out!"

I looked up and skidded to a stop, glad I had heard the man's voice—and that the non-slip tread on my shoes had worked. I had been so deep in my thoughts that I almost ran smack into Amelia. She had stopped to let Fern out of her kitchen and I hadn't noticed. A string of loud curses flew from my mouth, ensuring that this moment, at least, would not make it onto television. Mom would have been horrified.

"Watch where you're going, would you? I swear, if you would have knocked all this onto the floor..." Amelia glared at me over her own tray, even as she left the vague threat hanging. I couldn't help but wonder how much of her attitude was a performance for the cameras and how much was just the way she was.

I raised my eyebrows at her. "What, you think I wanted to drop all of this? Don't threaten me. You're the one fucking up the flow of traffic."

She huffed and rolled her eyes. I couldn't help but follow the motion of her eyes and that was when I saw what was on her tray. Her plates would have been identical to mine if I had sliced my steak and combined it with the rest of the salad. It was like the audition all over again.

"What did you make?" I asked, my voice much quieter now. She glanced at her food, then at my tray, and groaned loudly.

"I made a steak, beet, and goat cheese salad with a tangelo and fennel pollen dressing. Yours?"

"Fennel pollen filet mignon with a beet and goat cheese salad and tangelo honey vinaigrette."

She laughed, a hard sound that echoed the frustration that had crystallized into a lump in my throat. "So much for showing off our creativity. At least the execution is slightly different?"

"There's that, I guess. And hey, maybe, one of us will have messed something up terribly and the other will shine in comparison."

A smile as thin and sharp as a blade curled her lips at my suggestion before she turned and continued walking toward the front. It was clear she didn't think she had screwed up at all. Unfortunately for her, I was fairly certain I hadn't, either.

I set my tray on the stainless steel counter and arranged my plates in a diamond. Looking at them, I was still proud of what I'd made, even if it was similar to Amelia's dish. I said one final prayer and stepped back. Everything was in the judges' hands now.

———

———

In the end, neither of us had really messed up our dishes. Amelia and I both ranked somewhere in the middle of the pack, with only a small comment about how we seemed to have similar styles of cooking.

Breonna, the Black woman who'd shared her information with the rest of us during last night's elimination, won easily with a dessert that blew the judges away. She'd made a tangelo and chocolate tart with fennel pollen-infused goat whipped cream and candied beet strings. I couldn't believe that she'd been able to get all of it done in an hour. I would never have thought quickly enough to get a tart cooked and cooled in that time frame.

Jada had come in a close second with a surf and turf dish that had used all of the ingredients except the chocolate. I could see she was disappointed to have come so close but not won, but when she joined us in congratulating Breonna, it was with all the warmth she had shown us.

Shauna found herself on the bottom three. Her food had been cooked well but lacked any kind of cohesiveness, according to the judges. Beside her was a white woman from the other suite and Christopher, a man who kept talking about how healthy his food was. Christopher had come up with a crab, goat cheese and, beet frittata that the judges had refused to eat because of how undercooked the eggs were. I thought back to this morning and how happy they had been with their own omelets. This similar dish had to be a major disappointment, even if I already knew there was no way he or Shauna would get sent home.

Brooklyn, the woman from the other suite who I hadn't gotten to know, had only managed to get four of the basket ingredients into her dish. She had explained that it was supposed to be a crab imperial that used goat cheese dressing in place of the usual mayonnaise with roasted beets covered with a fennel pollen hollandaise. Except the hollandaise had broken right before she went to serve it, so she had left it off.

That was what you were supposed to do, according to every Gordon Ramsey show I'd ever watched. But it meant she didn't have enough ingredients to fulfill the challenge. As if that hadn't been enough, the rest of her dish hadn't been good, either. The crab imperial had turned slimy because of a misjudgment in the amount of goat cheese in it. If her hollandaise had worked, she would have stood a fighting chance. She looked absolutely heartbroken when the judges called her name, and I couldn't blame her. I was pretty sure tears were streaming down her face as she left the room, followed by a bevy of cameras.

Once the double doors shut behind her, the judges—and the cameras—turned their gazes back to the remaining contestants.

"We'll have an early start tomorrow," Denise told us. "I suggest you all use any spare time you have to study and practice in the practice kitchens we had built for you all. I don't want to see anything so basic as a frittata in this competition again. In the next challenge, I want higher quality cooking and creativity than we tasted tonight."

She didn't look at Christopher, but even I could see his cheeks turned bright red from the other side of the bench. I knew my own were, simply from the embarrassment of having put up a plate so close to Amelia's.

"Yes, Chef," we chorused. I intended to take them up on that suggestion. I never wanted to perform this poorly ever again.

We filed out of the room quietly, corralled by a few members of the crew. From behind me, I could hear Shauna begin to cry as soon as the doors shut. I turned to comfort her, but found Fern was already there, wrapping an arm around her shoulders and hugging her tightly.

Instead of letting us make our way to the elevators, they led us to a room that had been set aside and kept locked until now.

Looking into the room, it was set up just like the room at the audition where we had talked about why we wanted to be on the show. Instantly, I knew that it was for the voiceover segments that helped make a finished episode flow a lot better. They must have finished going through the footage from yesterday and decided how they wanted to display it to the viewers, but we had to speak for ourselves. We weren't going to be finished for the night anytime soon.

———

Chapter Fifteen

AMELIA

The judges hadn't been kidding when they said we would have an early wake up call. Through blurry eyes, my phone read 5:15 a.m. when the crew members knocked on our doors.

I had never realized how little time was actually spent cooking while making these competition shows, or how little sleep the contestants got.

Thanks to the new filming step to finish up the previous episode, we'd had to relive the roller coaster that was the group challenge and elimination condensed into forty-three minutes.

Despite my efforts to avoid their gaze while I apologized, the cameras had caught the entire cooking process, including the apology to my teammates. It wasn't a huge focus of the episode, thanks to the implosion that was the guys' team, but it was definitely there. It was also edited to make me look a lot more asshole-y than I felt like I had been.

They'd provided us with dinner between takes, thankfully, but we had all been exhausted by the time we hit our mattresses. Given everything that had gone on the last few days, it probably wasn't surprising that my dreams had been full of anxiety. However, I couldn't dwell on it. I could only start the coffee, hop in the shower, and do my best to prepare for the day, and challenge, ahead of me.

———

When the group of us made it to the lobby, the reason for the wake-up call was still as clear as mud. The judges were standing in the center of the room, but instead of their usual suits, they were wearing work boots, jeans, short sleeved button downs, and grins that could only be called devious.

"Today, we are going to take a little road trip to learn more about how the food we cook with every day is made. There's a bus waiting out front to take all of us to Shaw's Dairy in Salem, New York, so I hope you came prepared to work."

"Yes, chef!" we chorused. There was a smile on my face as I said it. Inside, though, I was dying a little bit. I'd been to Salem a few times during culinary school and it was…an experience.

It was almost in Vermont, for one, which meant at least three hours of driving to get to the middle of nowhere. Small towns like that had always made me uncomfortable. There was a reason there were more animals than people out there, and I was pretty sure it was because farmers tended to be some of the rudest people I'd ever met.

Whatever we would be doing today, it was going to be hot and sweaty even before we got to cook. I had never minded doing hard work, but God, I did not want to spend an early August afternoon in upstate New York working in the fields or dealing with live animals. Especially after being stuck in a van with twelve other people for several hours. But I didn't have a choice. I was here to win a quarter of a million dollars, which meant that I was going to do whatever was asked of me. So, I followed the judges out the front doors of the hotel to see a large, black van with the show's branding idling in the loading zone.

Angela stood in front of the bus with a clipboard in one hand and a large coffee in the other. When she saw us coming her way, she smiled far too brightly for a morning where the sun was barely over the horizon.

"Just an FYI, everyone, there will be filming on this trip. I know that normally we do not film outside of the official set, but this is part of an episode." She slurped her coffee, waiting for us to finish groaning. When we were done, she continued. "We have a couple of go-pros set up in the bus to catch anything interesting that happens while you travel. Have fun!"

She waved her coffee mug at us and walked back into the hotel. Of course, the road trip would be fully filmed. It was silly to have thought otherwise. Basically, everything outside of our bedrooms was fair game for the camera crew. They hadn't pointed them out, but from the paperwork they'd had us sign, I was pretty sure that even the suite kitchen and living room had cameras in them.

It hadn't bothered me; honestly, we'd barely been in the suites long enough for it to catch anything thanks to the schedule they had us on. It wouldn't be the end of the world. I only wished I had my phone and a pair of headphones with me.

Without further ado, we loaded ourselves in the van.

Because I was at the front of the line, I managed to snag a seat in the first, shorter row for myself, successfully avoiding being trapped in the middle seat without enough room to breathe. Everyone else slowly seated themselves and chattered about what today might be.

Zoe was the last to get in, and there were still three seats remaining, the one next to me and one each between two of the men. She glanced at each of them, her lips pressed in a thin line, before turning to me.

"Mind if I sit with you?"

I smiled and gestured to the open space. "It's all yours. I promise I don't bite."

She snorted a laugh that made my smile grow wider. "I might, depending on what happens between us during this road trip."

"You know, we might not be friends, but this road trip might just be fun if that's the attitude you're planning to take." I raised my eyebrows and she flushed, as if she had just heard the innuendo in both of our words.

"Will y'all quit flirting and just sit down?" Ellis called from the row behind us. "The sooner we get moving, the sooner I get to take a damn nap."

Now the whole bus laughed as Zoe settled herself into the seat. We both blushed furiously, but any further chatter was cut short by the driver cranking the engine and squealing the tires as he pulled out of the parking lot like the devil himself was behind us.

Zoe fell into me from the force of changing lanes so rapidly, and my blush deepened. If he was going to drive like this the whole time, maybe this trip wouldn't be quite as long or boring as I'd expected.

———

———

After what seemed like both a year and only a few minutes, we pulled onto a road that was surrounded by bushes and tall wood and barbed wire fences. It made me feel a little claustrophobic for the first time since we'd gotten in the van, but I knew it would be over soon.

"I sure hope the cows aren't behind those," Zoe murmured. "That seems like it would be very sad."

Our driver laughed derisively, and a flush crept over her cheeks again. *Jerk.*

"No, look, you can see solar panels through the gaps." I pointed out kindly. "The cows are gonna be further in and away from the road so they don't get spooked by cars or accidentally escape."

"How did you know that?" she asked quietly, seeming to feel more than a little silly. Zoe's smile was genuine, making my heart flutter.

"I asked the same thing when I came out to one of these farms the first time during culinary school. I'd never spent much time on farms before then."

"And you do now?"

"Goodness, no," I laughed. "I like air conditioning way more than animals, thank you very much."

"Then you aren't going to like today's task," the driver pointed out knowingly.

"What do you know about what today's task is?" Christopher called from the back. "Want to give us a hint?"

"Yeah, help us out a little bit!" Fern agreed. The driver laughed again and mimed zipping his lips in the rearview mirror. I rolled my eyes. He was having way too much fun with his little bit of power.

Before we could say anything to him, he turned onto

another, wider road that opened up the entire world before us. The winding road led straight to a beautiful old fashioned farmhouse that could have been plucked right out of the early twentieth century.

It was a two-story rectangle with Carolina blue shutters surrounded by a screened in wrap-around porch. It looked like it had been recently white-washed with a sharply angled black roof bisected by a dark brick chimney that looked original to the house. The only signs of modernity around the home were the solar panels, that covered the roof, and the giant black Ford trucks parked off to the side. It honestly would have fit in well on the old farms near home, if it weren't for the rolling hills behind it.

As we pulled up in front of the house, the front door opened and five figures filed out. I was curious to see who the farm would send out to greet us. It was going to depend on what they actually did here. We'd probably meet the owner and the head of production, if no one else.

Some large farms like this had taken to running their own farm-to-table restaurants. If this one had, I would be willing to put money on meeting whoever their executive chef was.

The door to the screened in porch swung open, revealing the judges at the front of the line. Behind them were two Black women, one of whom I had never expected to see again.

My hands flew to my mouth to cover a gasp. She hadn't noticed me yet, which was probably a good thing.

"What is it? Are you okay?" The worry was clear in Zoe's voice. I could only shake my head. I didn't know what to do; what to tell her.

I tried to say something, but it came out as a murmur.

"You gotta speak up or move your hands. Are you all right?"

"I'm okay, but I'm gonna lose whatever today's challenge is. The woman who just walked out behind the judges is my ex-girlfriend from culinary school."

―――

―――

Before I could explain any further, I felt the heat of her gaze sweep over the crowd and zero in on me. When I looked up, her deep brown eyes met mine and she let out a gust of breath.

"Amelia? Is that you?" Her voice hadn't changed. It was low and almost gravelly, but still musical.

I was pretty sure that every camera in the known universe was laser focused on us.

"Hi, Corrina." My voice was small. "It's been a while."

"What is happening here?" Corrina's companion, a woman at least twenty years her senior and several shades darker, asked. It was the question everyone else was trying to answer for themselves, so all eyes were on us.

"We...went to culinary school together," Corrina tried to explain without giving any of the real details. The older woman raised her eyebrows, clearly not buying it, and Corrina ducked her head. "And we dated. We haven't spoken since."

I hadn't thought it possible, but the older woman's eyebrows raised up higher.

One of the guys wolf-whistled while the rest of the contestants oohed in chorus. On the off chance I hadn't wanted to be out to the entire world, that shot was now entirely blown.

"Can we have a few minutes to talk off camera? We'll be ready to go soon, I promise."

That question was directed at the judges, who deferred to Angela. The producer wrinkled her nose in thought, but eventually nodded. Corrina gestured off to the side of the house, and I followed her lead.

My mind spun while I walked, remembering all the time we'd spent together, and how it ended. When we were out of view of the cameras, Corrina shook her head at me.

"Of all the farms in all the world, and you walk into mine on a damn TV show."

I had to laugh a little. Casablanca had been the first movie we'd watched together.

"The world really couldn't get much smaller," I admitted ruefully. "You look like you've been doing well."

She really did. She had gained a little weight since I'd last seen her and it had done wonders for her slight figure. She looked healthier and happier than I remembered her being in school.

"I have, thank you. I'm the executive chef of our restaurant here; have been for two years."

"You've been here for two years? I thought you wanted to stay in Tennessee and do great things."

That had been a huge reason we hadn't stayed together. I had been horrified whenever she'd talked about returning to the small town she'd grown up in. It barely had a stoplight, let alone the kind of fine dining restaurant she was capable of working in.

"Mama died," her voice was quiet, but it knocked me back with the heartbreak I could hear in it.

"What? How? When?"

"It'll be three years in December. She was diagnosed with lung cancer right before graduation."

"Oh, I'm so sorry, Corrina." I almost stepped forward to comfort her, then realized what she'd said. Instead, I took a step back.

We'd been together for almost a month after graduation, and her mother never kept anything from her for more than a few days.

"That's why you moved home." The realization dawned on me, along with a rising tide of hurt. "You knew, and you never told me."

Anger flashed in her eyes. "And why would I tell you? Every time I talked to you about going with me, you made these little comments about how horrible Tennessee was. I wasn't about to ask you to go somewhere that would have made you so obviously miserable."

"You used to make the same jokes with me. I thought…" I shook my head. "Even if I would have hated Tennessee, going with you because your mom needed help is very different from going back to your hometown because you thought it's where you belonged, like you told me. I wanted you to think about the possibilities you had ahead of you outside of that tiny ass town."

"You never actually asked me what I wanted! We were together for almost three years and you never bothered asking me whether I wanted to go into fine dining, or whether I wanted to go to Raleigh with you. It was just what you thought I should do, so obviously it was the right choice!"

I was flabbergasted. "Why didn't you ever *tell* me? How was I supposed to know that? I could have…"

"What would you have done?" she snapped. "Sat with me and watched my mom die, hating every minute? I don't think so."

She took a deep breath in through her nose, her nostrils flaring, then let it out through her mouth.

"It has been the better part of a decade since any of this mattered. I'm guessing you've been doing great this whole time and now you're here to prove that you're one of the greatest cooks of all time, right?"

I flinched at the frigid tone of her voice and tried to keep my own down.

"I've never claimed to be one of the greatest of all time, Corrina. I just want to prove to myself that I've got what it takes to get to the big leagues."

"And it has nothing to do with the fact that your live-in-girlfriend left, huh?"

I bristled. "What the fuck? You don't know what you're talking about."

"We still have mutual friends. I do know what I'm talking about. You want to prove to her that you're better than she thought, that you're worth being around."

"You really don't, and I'm done talking about this. I'm not delaying everyone's competition because you want to make me feel like shit. I'm glad to see you're well and employed. If you are one of the judges today, I hope that you won't penalize me for the way we left things. And I'm really sorry about your mom."

With that, I turned my back to her and walked away. I didn't bother looking back to see if she was following me. After all, we were headed to the same place.

Maybe she had a point. Maybe I did want to prove to Janet and my parents that I was more than just a cook, that I could be more than a sous chef. That didn't mean she got to know that, though. We hadn't been together for a long time, as she'd pointed out. She didn't get to figure out why I was doing something. At least, not with my help. I had a competition to focus on.

———

Chapter Sixteen

ZOE

Amelia stormed back from her conversation with her former flame a few minutes later. I opened my mouth to say something, but snapped it shut when she turned back to me. She looked so angry; I half expected thunder clouds to form over her head and start shooting lightning.

A moment later, the other woman came back to join the judges. Her face was harder to read, but her jaw was tense when she spoke. "My apologies for the interruption, chefs. We're ready when you are."

I heard Amelia take a deep breath and nod in confirmation.

"Very well. Let's get back to business." Denise clapped her hands and the camera people swarmed into position all around us.

"Good morning, contestants, and welcome to Shaw's Dairy. This farm, owned by Mrs. Grace Shaw and her family, has been in operation for nearly 300 years and now offers a variety of organic produce, meat, and animal products. They also have their own farm-to-table restaurant, run by Ms. Corrina Carr. What better place to learn more about the way our food is grown?"

We all nodded, knowing by now that she didn't need a real answer from us at this point in her spiel.

"Today we are going to assist the farmers here with their work so that we can show a little more appreciation for the ingredients that they grow and raise here. Then, we'll be using those ingredients to create a special tasting menu for a banquet that will be held this evening. But we'll tell you more about that later. For now, we're going to break you up into pairs."

Fern was partnered with Troy, a Marine-turned-Country-Club-Chef from somewhere in the Midwest. I couldn't help but think that, that partnership was going to go up in flames very quickly. The rest of the pairs were more well suited for each other. Liam and Ronald, Ellis and Shauna, and Jada and Breonna were called out, to their apparent delight. That left only…

"Amelia and Zoe, you are our final pair."

I could feel the cameras focusing on us and resisted the urge to roll my eyes. Of course. No matter that we had begun to get along better, they still had their planned plotline.

"These are your pairs for the challenge as well, so start thinking about the possibilities for your menu while you work today. I expect great things!"

The judges walked back inside the house without another word. My gaze moved to Amelia, who simply looked resigned.

"Well, there's no point standing around here waiting to be put up for elimination. Let's get this over with."

I could already tell we were going to have a great time.

―――

―――

Every pair was assigned to a staff member and escorted to a different part of the farm to start our day's work. Some went to the restaurant, others were sent to the blueberry patches, while the rest went to the dairy.

Amelia, our camera operators, and I were entrusted to the care of possibly the oldest man I had ever met. Without a word, he took us directly to a barn that was larger than anything I could have possibly imagined.

The scent was the first thing to hit me when the doors opened. The sweet smell of hay that made up their beds mixed with the earthy, baked smell of cow dung to create an unmistakable, overwhelming atmosphere.

Amelia waved a hand in front of her face as if to protect her from it, but soon gave up.

"That is…a lot of cows," she remarked dryly. I had to laugh. Then I looked around. She was right.

There were more cows than I could count spread across the barn. Some of them were laying on the packed hay floor, while others chewed lazily on something from their feeding trough. More of them wandered in and out of the building from a back door that led to a fenced in dirt ring.

Another man walked over to us pushing a wheelbarrow with two well-used pitchforks resting in it. Of the four of us, he was the only one dressed for the work he had to do in the barn.

Finally, the man who had led us here spoke. "Grab a fork and get mucking, ladies. Let Curtis know if you have any questions. I don't want to talk to you."

He waved a hand at the other man, who smiled at us

showing off deep dimples. The old man stomped away without hesitation.

"I assume you're Curtis?"

"Yes, ma'am. You'll have to excuse Marcus. He's just like that. I'm pretty sure he hasn't cracked a smile the whole time I've worked here." His laugh was infectious, almost buoying my spirit enough to forget that we had been assigned one of the grossest duties on a farm. But then my eyes turned to Amelia, who was staring at the wheelbarrow with clear disgust.

"You have got to be kidding me," she said flatly.

I couldn't help myself. I laughed again. She looked so mortally offended by the tool that it was impossible not to. When Curtis joined my laughter, she turned her glare on me. She was ferocious and beautiful for a moment before she, too, dissolved into laughter.

Before long, all three of us were doubled over in fits of giggles. Two of the calves walked over to us, sniffing at our feet and pockets before wandering back to larger cows that I assumed were their mothers.

She snorts when she laughs, I marvelled, realizing that this was the first time I had heard her actually laugh. It was a beautiful, absolutely joyful sound that made her sound more human than she ever allowed herself to be in front of the camera.

Eventually, we all pulled ourselves together. Amelia wiped tears from her eyes and smiled at me.

"Oh, I needed that laugh. Curtis, hand me a pitchfork and show us where we're going. I'm ready to go clean out a stall and get this done."

The man did what he was told with a laugh and we followed him around the building until we found a row of stalls that looked and smelled much more used than the ones we had seen at the entrance. He led us to the very end and opened a window that I hadn't even noticed, letting a stream of blessedly fresh air waft in from the pasture outside. We both breathed a sigh of relief.

"You're gonna want to take off your chef coats. You're gonna be hot and sweaty in about five minutes, and I don't think you want to get those dirty."

That was a good idea. There was only one problem; I couldn't see anywhere to put them that was out of reach.

"Where can we put them that the cows won't get them?" Amelia asked.

Curtis reached into the wheelbarrow and pulled out two garbage bags and plastic hangers. "You can put them in here and I'll hang them out front."

Without hesitation, I began unbuttoning my jacket. A moment later, Amelia began to do the same and stripped off the coat. I couldn't help but trace her curves with my eyes. I had known she had a beautiful body in her well-cut chef's jacket, but there was a difference between seeing the outlines under two layers of clothing and seeing it through a basic black t-shirt. She was tall and broad-chested with the muscular arms that I knew only came from doing a lot of heavy lifting.

The sound of her throat clearing drew my eyes slowly back up to her face, where her lips were curved into the competitive smirk I was so familiar with.

"You lost track of what you were doing," she pointed out. I looked down at my own jacket where my hands were clenched around the second button and flushed. Forcing them to continue the work I'd abandoned, I stripped out of the jacket and hung it quickly.

Without another word, I traded my jacket for a pitchfork and walked into the stall. It was then that I realized that the stalls were not empty, as I had thought. In the back of the stall stood a brown and white cow that looked younger and smaller than many of the others we'd seen. He flattened his ears at me, a silent reproof for invading his space.

"Hi there, little guy," I said softly, as if he were one of the kids Violet played with. "Sorry for barging in on you. I didn't know you were in here. I'll leave you be."

His ears stayed flattened and his nostrils flared. Even without knowing anything about cows, I knew what that signaled. Without turning my back to him, I backed out of the stall and stepped out of the way just in time for the calf to come barreling out of the stall and back the way we'd come.

"Aw hell, I didn't know Gerald was in there. I woulda warned you. He's a little jumpy." Curtis ran a hand through his short, dark curls with a look of apology.

"Holy shit. Are you okay?" The words that echoed my own from earlier barely sounded in my ears over the sound of my racing heartbeat.

"I…I think we just startled each other. I'll be okay. " I looked up at her and found that I couldn't look away from the kindness and worry in her deep brown eyes.

As she held my gaze, I felt the tightness in my chest loosen just a little and my breaths come easier.

"You were really good with him," Curtis broke in. "Ever worked with animals before?"

I shook my head. "Only with kids. It's basically the same thing, right?"

Amelia snorted a laugh, shaking her head at me and handing me a pitchfork. Without waiting for any more distractions, Curtis showed us the best way to get the stalls cleaned; use the pitchforks to get most of the hay up, then shovel the rest.

We got to work in stalls that were parallel to each other. I kept glancing over at her through the open aluminum bars, looking away every time she looked up. It wouldn't do to be caught staring, by her or the cameras stationed on either side of us. I kept feeling like she was looking at me, too, but I never managed to prove it.

The work was hard, but it went quickly as Curtis regaled us with stories of the cow's adventures. After a while, the same cow I'd scared out of the stall earlier was peering through the doors at me. I couldn't help but smile as Curtis shooed him away with gentle persistence.

"Why is his name Gerald?" I asked. "That seems like such an old man name for such a young cow."

Curtis shrugged. "I didn't name him. Take that up with Marcus. He's in charge of naming everything here."

"No thank you," Amelia replied primly. "I think it suits him."

Gerald walked into the stall on the other side of her and snorted at us. We all laughed. When we finished, he was still standing there, watching.

"You know, I think he likes you two." Curtis checked his watch. "Y'all wanna try something a little more fun before you move to your next job?"

I looked at Amelia, who shrugged. Turning back to the farmhand, I nodded. "We might as well make ourselves useful while we're here."

He grinned. "Pick up your pitchforks and follow me."

Curtis led us out of the barn to the packed dirt ring I'd seen earlier. Setting the wheelbarrow down right outside the doors, he took the pitchforks and swapped them for what looked like short-handled, short-bristled brooms.

Confusion washed over me. "Wh...what are these for?"

"Take a guess!"

I honestly had no idea. I looked to Amelia, who looked just as perplexed.

"Are we making patterns in the dirt?" Her voice was hesitant.

Curtis snorted. "Absolutely not. That's a waste of time. You're going to brush the cows."

"Brush the cows? Do they like that?"

"Watch this."

He raised his own brush and the cows all but stampeded to surround him. They were like puppies who had seen a favorite snack, jostling each other to get closest to the hard-bristled brush. One went so far as to stretch its head around the short horns of another yearling to push its head into the brush. It was absolutely adorable.

"Y'all wanna try?"

We both nodded enthusiastically.

He showed us how to brush them, in short even strokes that knocked dirt and hay off of their backs easily. The cow he brushed nuzzled him and the tool, making sure that no spot was left uncleaned.

When we lifted our own brushes, the cows responded in much the same way. That was when I realized my mistake. The herd quickly surrounded us where we stood, pushing us back towards the wood and metal wire fencing a little at a time.

I hardly had time to notice that I was getting anxious before I felt my head begin to spin, trying to think of a way to avoid being trapped against the fence. The closer they got, the harder it got to breathe. The fence was taller than I was. I couldn't climb it.

There was nowhere to run and I was trapped and alone.

"Zoe? Are you all right?" Amelia's voice cut through the fog in my brain. I had forgotten she was there. I turned my head to look at her but she blurred in front of me. I couldn't get my eyes to focus on her; just on the cows that were getting closer with every second.

"Zoe? Zoe!" Her hand pressed down gently on my shoulder and I shrieked. My arm whipped out, backhanding her hard across the face before I could stop myself. She stumbled back with a cry, heading, back first, into the herd of cows.

That was what finally snapped me out of my panic. Lightning fast, I reached out a hand and grabbed her arm to yank her back, but I was too late. The cows had backed up, probably scared by the shouting. She landed hard on her ass with a grunt, and my body followed her before I could stop it.

Seconds later, I landed on top of her and my stomach turned over. I couldn't tell if the reaction was from the sudden flight, the fear that still tainted my every thought, or the sparks flying through me at her touch, but that didn't really matter. My brush handle smacked me in the back of the head, just to add insult to injury.

I rolled off of her and sat up, already babbling an apology. "I'm so sorry! God, I'm so, so sorry! Are you all right?"

She didn't even look at me, just raised a trembling hand to the cheek I had hit.

"What the hell is happening over there?" Curtis's voice sounded as horrified as I felt.

"I was panicking and she touched me and I freaked out and…"

"I'm okay." Amelia cut me off with soft, but firm

words. Her hand still covered most of her cheek, but I could see that it was bright red from the impact.

Curtis looked us both over, and I could only imagine how we looked. I knew I was probably as pale as a sheet, in addition to being sweaty, covered in dust, and slightly injured. Shame warmed my cheeks.

He held out a hand to Amelia after a moment, which she took gratefully. He pulled her up easily, letting her lean against the fence. As soon as she had let go of his hand, he offered it to me.

"Let's go get you some ice for that, so your face doesn't swell," he told Amelia gently. When he turned to me, his voice was much less friendly. "And for your head. You're gonna have a goose egg from the brush if we don't. Follow me."

————

Chapter Seventeen

AMELIA

THE FARMHAND LED US BACK TO THE HOUSE WHERE OUR morning had started, taking us in through the back gate.

I couldn't believe she'd hit me. Or, rather, I couldn't believe how *hard* she'd hit me. My entire face hurt like a motherfucker. More than I'd expected it to, given how small Zoe was.

One minute, she was looking like she was going to faint, and the next, I was on my ass. It was unexpected, to say the least.

Not *that* unexpected, though. I hadn't remembered it at the time, but she had mentioned during their meeting with Angela that she didn't like to be touched when things were tense for her.

Well, I'll certainly remember it next time, I thought as we walked into the house's kitchen. It looked almost as old as the house itself, though the appliances were the expensive kind of new that was designed to look old-fashioned. Curtis pulled two gingham dishcloths from a diamond-shaped rack, with hooks at each corner, and walked to the freezer.

I glanced at Zoe, whose cheeks were flaming even underneath the dust that coated most of her face. She wouldn't meet my gaze, even when I knew she could feel my focus. Behind her, our camera operators were openly staring at us through their lenses.

"Is that gonna get into the show?" I sighed; pretty sure I already knew the answer.

One of them shrugged. "We don't decide what gets into the shows. That's up to the editors and producers. We're just in charge of getting decent footage."

The other one nodded, then spoke. "Right, but if we had to guess…yeah, that's going to make it to the final cut. They wanted us to give them as much drama as possible, so…probably."

Zoe covered her face with her hands. "Jesus Christ. No one is ever going to want to work with me again."

I snorted but didn't say anything else. Curtis walked out and handed us both ice packs that had been expertly tied in the wash cloths. I pressed it to my face, relishing the pressure and cold.

"Can we get a few minutes alone to talk? Without the cameras."

The camera operators looked at each other and shrugged. "We can give you a few minutes. I really have to pee."

Curtis was a harder sell. He glanced between Zoe and I and then at the camera crew, then looked hard at me. "Are you sure that's what you want? I'm still not sure what happened out there."

I gave him what I hoped was a convincing smile. He ran a finger through his brown curls and sighed. "All right. I'll leave y'all to it. I'll be on the porch when you're finished. You do have another station to go to soon, though."

Slowly, all three of them walked out of the kitchen, leaving us alone, together. For what felt like an eternity, the only sound in the room was our breathing and the ticking of a clock on the wall.

Zoe and I stared at each other, each with an ice pack plastered to our heads. In that moment, it struck me as ridiculous and I burst into laughter. My chest heaved with each almost hysterical cackle. It made my jaw ache, but I couldn't make myself stop.

Zoe stared at me, bewilderment plain on her face. "Did I hit you harder than I thought? What's funny?"

"Just…everything!" I laughed, gesturing around me. "This entire day has just been full of things I never could have imagined and never wanted and now I'm here with you…"

To my horror, the laughter had begun to change into something entirely more embarrassing. My short breaths made my chest heave and the heat of my face spread into my eyes, which were already leaking large, hot tears. The laughs turned to sobs and I couldn't stop it.

Zoe leapt into action, coming over to me and moving to rub my back, then pulled her hand back.

"Is it okay if I touch you?"

I tried to speak but couldn't. I just nodded. Her hand rubbed circles into my back while she made soft shushing noises. Slowly, my breathing and tears slowed to the point where I felt like myself again. I swiped the hand that wasn't holding up my ice pack against my nose, clearing the snot that had made itself known, and then again against my pant leg.

When I finally looked up, Zoe withdrew her hand from my back and took a step back. Her eyes soft and pained as if she wanted to cry, herself.

"Now, I owe you a real apology, if you'll allow me to give it to you."

I nodded again, not trusting myself to speak. She took a deep breath and closed her eyes, as if it made it easier.

"I'm sorry to have added to your pain today. I did not intend to hurt you. I didn't even... I wasn't aware it was you touching me. But my intentions don't matter. I'm so incredibly sorry for hitting you."

It was clear that she meant it from the way her eyes lingered on the hurt.

"I had forgotten you said you didn't like to be touched when you were being yelled at or were otherwise highly emotional. I'm sorry for touching you without permission.

She smiled a thin-lipped smile at me. "That's true. I did say that. But it still doesn't make what I did acceptable."

I nodded, wiping a few tears from my eyes. "Thank you for the apology. I appreciate it. Really. I'm sure you've thought of hitting me before. I've been a total bitch to you since before the competition even started. I'm sure I deserved at least a little bit of what I got today."

She stared at me, confusion morphing into something more like the anger I was used to. "Amelia. No, you didn't. Tell me you don't believe that."

I shrugged, keeping my eyes on the floor. That was when I noticed there were small bees lightly embossed on each of the white floor tiles. It was sweet.

"Amelia, look at me." I couldn't resist her command. My eyes met hers and I couldn't look away from the fierceness I saw there. Everything about her thin, angular face was sincere in a way that I hadn't seen before. She searched my face, apparently finding something that concerned her.

When she spoke, her voice was firmer than I'd ever heard it. "No one deserves to be hit. No matter what they've done. No matter what the other person is feeling. There is no excuse for it, ever. I was wrong to lash out at you, even without being fully myself. Anyway, I don't want to badger you about it, but…I needed you to know I was sorry. That's all."

I nodded. I knew all of that, of course. I had been mostly joking. It was a speech that sounded like she had given it a time or two before. I couldn't help but wonder if she'd had to learn that lesson the hard way, but there was no way I could ask about that. We didn't have that sort of relationship. There was something I could ask, though I couldn't guarantee she would answer me.

"It seemed to me like you were doing fine until we got surrounded by the cows in the pen," I said slowly, trying to figure out just how to word my question. "Is there something in particular that made you panic? Is that what happened?"

Her face twisted into a pained expression and I thought she might start to cry. Instead, she took a deep, measured breath and looked down at the tile floor.

"I…I don't do well when I'm cornered. My husband…well, that doesn't matter. I didn't have an escape route, and I felt the cows closing in on me like…" She took another deep breath and squeezed her eyes shut before she continued. "It felt like I was trapped and it took me back to a bad place where the only thing I could do was wait for the worst. So, when you touched me…"

"You reacted instantly to what your body remembered in past situations, right?"

She nodded. Her free hand was clenched into a tight fist against her leg and I thought I saw a tear track on her cheek. I desperately wanted to reach out to her, to comfort her somehow, but I wasn't about to make that mistake again. It was obvious my touch would only serve to cause her more pain than she was already in.

"I won't make excuses for it, though."

Now, it was my turn to glare at her, over my ice pack. "Explaining something is not making excuses. Especially when I specifically asked you about it, Zoe. You've gotta know that."

She nodded at me, not speaking. More tears were falling from her eyes now. I could guess why she clammed up at mentions of husbands now, if he had anything to do with her reaction today.

"Do you want to talk about what you're feeling right now?" I asked, feeling like I was teetering over the line of what I could ask. "My mother swears by it."

Zoe barked a laugh. "Absolutely not. You aren't my therapist. Even if you were, we don't have that kind of time today."

Looking at the clock, I could see she was right. Our tagalong crew would be back any minute now, and we had to ready ourselves to get back on camera.

"If it happens again, is there anything I can do to help?"

She looked taken aback, then stammered a reply, as if no one had ever asked her that before. "I…um, just don't crowd me. And talk quietly. It helps."

I nodded. "Got it. Now, before we're back on camera, how does my face look? I pulled the ice pack away. Zoe grimaced, then tried to hide it by wiping her face with the backs of her hand.

"Well, the handprint is gone," she hedged. "Your

whole cheek is still pretty red, though. Maybe that'll calm down before we have to go on camera?"

"Maybe. They're gonna know you cried, though. Probably that I have too."

"Well, at least we'll look like shit together, right?"

That brought a tired smile to her face. "Right."

———

———

It was very obvious that both of us had been crying when Curtis walked back in, but he chose not to acknowledge it. I was really starting to like this man.

"Are we ready?"

The camera operators were right behind him, cameras already in position and filming. I sighed and pulled my hair out of its ponytail. It might be hotter to have my hair down, but at least I'd be able to cover my face a little bit and make myself look a little bit better.

"As ready as we're going to get," Zoe said simply. Curtis's gaze shifted to me and I nodded.

"All right then. Y'all follow me." He walked right back out the door he'd come in through, off the back porch, and in the opposite direction from the barn we'd been in before.

"Your second task of the afternoon is to pick some blueberries for tonight's dinner service."

That was much easier, and less smelly, than our first task. I used to love going to the places where you picked your own berries in the summer.

"How many do you use in a typical service?" Zoe asked.

"Well, they're in season right now, so they get used in a lot of our dishes. You'd have to ask Ms. Carr for the exact numbers, but I know whatever you pick will get used."

There was no way in hell I was asking Corrina anything, but he didn't need to know that. He was already worried about me, and even if I did think he was all right, he didn't need to worry any more. Worried men were annoying men.

"Interesting. What other kinds of produce do y'all grow here? And is it all organic?"

"Well, let's see…" Curtis held up a hand and started counting on his fingers. "Blueberries, tomatoes, green beans, bell peppers, and spinach are our main crops. We also have goats and sheep…oh, and bees! Couldn't run this place without them."

"And you do all your dairy work on the premises as well? This place has to be *huge*."

He puffed up proudly. "Our farm, grazing space, and processing facilities total a little over a thousand acres, though our pasteurization equipment is actually a little ways down the road. The only place they could have put it here was way too far from the electric grid to be reasonable."

Zoe nodded, as if that made perfect sense.

"Does your family farm, Zoe? You seem to know a lot about this stuff."

She shook her head. "No, my parents were teachers and we lived in the city limits. I used to have chickens. It's how I came up with my blog name, but…I don't anymore."

There was something she wasn't telling me there, and I thought back over everything she'd told me about herself. It wasn't much, but I knew it had to do with her husband. She obviously didn't want to talk about it, though, so I asked another, simpler question.

"Did you like having chickens?"

She smiled at me, and it was like the sun had come out from behind the clouds.

"Oh yes. They are incredibly stupid birds, but they were good company after I got married and moved away from home. Violet liked them, too, but..." She shrugged, as if it didn't matter. The small, defeated motion broke my heart a little.

"Oh, are you married?" Curtis asked, oblivious to what she wasn't saying. "You don't wear a ring. Is that a sanitation thing for y'all?"

Her eyes dropped to the grass under her feet and her smile dimmed. "I was. We're separated."

He almost tripped in his hurry to apologize. "I'm so sorry, ma'am. I didn't know."

She lifted her head and looked him directly in the eye. "That's all right. I'm not sorry we're separated. Everything is better when we're far, far away from each other."

He nodded, apparently not wanting to stick his foot any further into his mouth. That made me smile. It was the most blatant she'd been about anything in her personal life, and it still wasn't much.

I didn't know much about her relationship with her husband, but everything I did know about the man was terrible. If I ever had the chance to meet him...well, I wouldn't be nice, that's for damn certain. But for now, I'd end this awkward as hell conversation. We crested a hill, and I found the perfect way to do that.

"Are those the blueberry fields?"

The answer was obvious. There were rows and rows of green bushes dotted with clumps of blue as far as the eye could see. There was no way it was anything else. Both Curtis and Zoe were shooting me looks that told me they were grateful for the interruption.

"Yes ma'am!"

"You know you don't have to call me ma'am, Curtis," I teased, trying to lighten the mood a little. "I'm pretty sure you're the same age we are."

"Yes, ma'am," he laughed sheepishly. "It's just my habit. I hope it doesn't offend y'all."

That made us both laugh.

"Of course not! We're from the South. We know good manners when we hear them!" Zoe punctuated her statement with a wink and I could have sworn he almost tripped again. I couldn't blame him. She had a smile that would have knocked me flat on my ass as surely as her slap had, if she turned it on me.

That made me wonder, suddenly, if there was any possibility that she might. She hadn't said anything that pointed towards her being any flavor of queer, but something about her was pinging my gaydar. Not that it mattered. Before the last two challenges, I would have said she hated me. But right now,…well, I wouldn't say we were friends, but maybe she didn't hate me quite so much.

Another Black woman met us at the bottom of the hill, her hands on her ample hips. She looked remarkably like Mrs. Grace Shaw even before you looked at the expression on her face. Her eyebrow was raised at Curtis at just the same angle Grace had when she looked at Corrina. I could already tell that I was going to like her.

"You're late. You been flirting with these women, Curtis? I'm sure Mama Grace didn't tell you that was your job today."

Curtis's tan cheeks went ruddy with a blush. "No,

Kay. I've been good. We were just running a little bit behind."

"Good. Then your job here is done. Go back to your cattle. And call me when they're done filming. You're taking me out to dinner. Someplace nice."

She tossed him a saucy smile and a wink that turned him bright red. As he stammered a reply, she gestured for us to follow her. We did so, but not before Zoe gave him a quick hug.

"I'm guessing you know the general process of blueberry picking?" she asked when we had left Curtis far behind.

Zoe nodded. "Yeah, we've done this before. Is there anything in particular you're looking for?"

"Well, nothing special. We just want the ripest blueberries for our dinner tonight. And you'll want the really ripe ones, too, since these are the ones you and your fellow contestants will be using tonight."

"Oh, so there's no pressure," I laughed. She shot me a razor blade of a smile that made me nervous, but I followed her. We walked through a few rows as she told us about the farm and how they ran the organic produce operation. It was mostly for the camera's benefit, I knew, but it was really interesting. This part of farming hadn't changed that much since the farm had originally opened in the early 1900s. They even still composted their own manure and miscellaneous plant matter to make sure their fertilizer was as homegrown as possible. It was admirable, even if I found the idea of shoveling rotting cow dung and hanging onto it very gross.

Eventually, we reached the storefront area of the farm, where locals could come and harvest buckets worth of berries that they picked themselves. Those five gallon buckets were exactly what Kay was looking for.

She pushed one at each of us, barely waiting for us to catch them before waving a hand at the rows. "You ladies have fun out there! I'll be over here if you have any questions."

I knew a dismissal when I heard one, especially when she turned her back on us. I tossed a smile at Zoe.

"Ready?"

"I'm ready." She turned toward the field, then whipped back around with a furrow between her brows. "Wait; how do we know which blueberries are the ripest?"

Kay looked up and grinned wickedly. "Oh, that's easy. Just like during sex, you grab the balls and give them a light tickle. If they're really ready, they'll fall off."

Laughter bubbled up my throat before I could stop it. Zoe clapped a hand over her mouth to cover her own giggle. That was one hell of a mental image.

Kay widened her eyes in mock innocence and flapped a hand at us. "I have no clue what you two are laughing about. Now, get on and pick us some blueberries."

We continued giggling together as we made our way out into the field, buckets in hand. She took one aisle and I took the next.

The first few times I found berries that were succulent enough to drop off into my hands at the merest touch, I had to laugh some more. Judging by the shake I could see in Zoe's shoulders and the way she tucked her head into the bush, she was doing the same.

"What do you want to bet that gets cut from the footage?" I called over the bushes between us.

"Oh, one hundred percent," she laughed. "That was way too raunchy for primetime, even on cable. I loved it, though."

I grinned at her. "Me too. Even if I have no experience with that particular, ah, equipment."

"Well, I've had more than enough for the both of us," she said tartly.

I laughed and Zoe blushed. Warmth coursed through me at the realization that this was the first time she had done so out of happiness, instead of anger with me. That was when I saw the twig that had gotten caught in her hair, its two leaves brushing her cheek like a lover's caress.

"You've got bush on your face," I said without thinking, reaching forward to pluck it out. Her mouth popped open and, when I realized what I'd said, I blushed just as deep as she had and laughed.

The cameraman closest to me muttered something under his breath that sounded very much like, "Oh, for fucks sake."

My laughter turned to a snort, and I nearly dropped the bucket into the bush in my rush to cover my mouth.

"Whoa, careful there. You don't want to waste all your hard work."

I looked up to find Zoe holding the bottom of my bucket and smiling at me. My heart sped up, but before I could say anything, the purple haired camera operator behind Zoe cleared her throat.

"Ladies, can we get a moratorium on the double entendres? They're getting to be a little much and we're struggling to get footage that we can actually use."

Zoe let my bucket go and stepped back, their face going even redder. "Sorry, Portia. We'll be on our best behavior from now on."

"At least for today," I added with a smile. "We'll give you some good, wholesome, blueberry picking."

They squinted at me, and I couldn't tell if it was

because they didn't believe me, or because the sun was very bright behind me. Either way, the squint was justified. I had worked very hard in my life to avoid being seen as wholesome, despite my plump, All-American girl-like appearance. That was something I could fix, though.

Popping a few berries into my mouth, I let the juices coat my teeth before I grinned at them. Portia shuddered, but lifted their camera back into the filming position.

Reaching into the bucket again, I knew just what to do to get them some usable footage.

"Hey, Zoe, open wide."

"What?" She turned to look at me and I took aim.

"Your mouth. Open it." I held up the blueberry and tossed it at her, expecting that she'd understand what was happening.

She did, except my aim was off. Very off. Instead of catching the projectile in her open mouth, it bounced off her forehead. I laughed, then covered my mouth with my hand. She was squinting at me, as if she wasn't sure whether to be angry or not.

"Are you okay?"

She looked down at her bucket, then back up at me with a fierce glimmer in her eyes. Before I knew what was happening, I was being pelted with blueberries. I shrieked and ducked behind the bushes as much as I could.

"You can't hide from me, Amelia!" she laughed. "You're basically an amazon. These shrubs won't protect you."

She was right, of course. Even crouched down, I was head and shoulders above the greenery. Curse Mother and her tall genes. Short of literally crawling under them, there was no way I could hide. However, there was a possibility here.

There were tons of berries on the ground of varying levels of ripeness, which would make the perfect ammunition. I grabbed a handful and grinned wickedly when I caught Zoe's eye.

"Prepare to meet your doom."

———

———

By the time we made it to the restaurant for the challenge, the mark of Zoe's hand had mostly faded from my cheek, but it had been replaced by splotches of blue from the juice of about a dozen blueberries. It was hardly noticeable, except maybe through a television camera.

Angela took one look at me and ushered me right back out the door.

"Where are we going?"

"You're going to see our makeup artist. You can't be on camera looking like someone's been beating you."

I blinked in confusion. "We have a makeup artist? I just assumed we were all on our own for that."

"The judges need to look perfect for the network, as do their guests. We don't generally let you in to see them because it's unnecessary. With as much moving and heating you do, you'd sweat off almost any makeup we put on you under the lights, but in this case…" she trailed off, not needing to explain any further.

"I'm sure washing my face would go a long way just on its own. I don't really need makeup."

She gave me a look that said it didn't matter what I

thought. She knew what needed to happen and I didn't have much of a say. I sighed. Oh well. It wouldn't take long to cover the residue from the day. What harm could it do to look a little better on film?

Without ceremony, I was led to one of the vans, that had followed us, and motioned into it. What I found there was a makeshift makeup artist's studio: a rotating chair, mirrored vanity, and drawers that were full to bursting with more makeup and applicators than I had ever imagined existed. It was really impressive that they'd managed to secure all of it and make it usable, even if no one outside of a TV or movie set would probably ever need it.

I didn't have long to be impressed, though. The makeup artist, a young Indian woman, took one look at me and had to smother a gasp.

"Sit, sit. We must start work on you immediately or else you will not be able to cook." My heart sank. It was clear I had underestimated how long this would take.

———

Chapter Eighteen

ZOE

WITHIN A MINUTE OF ENTERING THE RESTAURANT, Angela whisked Amelia away, leaving me standing alone in the kitchen with a nearly full bucket in each hand. Even the camera crew had left me behind to go and swap batteries and memory cards.

The battle of the blueberries hadn't lasted long before we'd both gotten winded. I was no stranger to hard work or chasing people around, but usually I was trying to outrun a toddler, not a woman built like an Amazon. Especially after mucking out a cow's stall, having a panic attack, and accidentally slapping her. Really, it had been a roller coaster of a day. Now I was standing here like an ass, waiting for someone to tell me what to do.

"Hello? Anyone in here?" I waited but didn't hear an answer. With a sigh, I set the buckets down and looked around. There was a sink with a colander already in it, and I had blueberries that were supposed to be used tonight. I knew what I should be doing, and there was no sense wasting time that could be put to good use.

I rolled up the sleeves of my chef's coat and looked at the tools in front of me. The colander was almost the width of the deep, industrial sink, but shallow enough that it wouldn't be too heavy to lift when it was full. Hauling up one of the buckets, I got to work.

I scooped berries into the colander by the handfuls until there was enough space at the top of the bucket for me to pour them into the sink with some semblance of control. It wouldn't help anyone to throw them all over the floor on accident, especially since I hoped to use the blueberries in whatever we were supposed to for the upcoming challenge.

"Why the hell is water running in here?" a gruff, feminine voice grumbled. "I swear to God if one more pipe bursts in this place…"

I turned around to see who was speaking and found myself face-to-surprised-face with the head chef whose kitchen I had invaded.

"Oh! Corrina! I mean…Ms. Carr. I was just…"

She cut me off with a wave of her hand.

"You're the one partnered with Amelia, right? You don't have to wash these. We do have a staff here to do the work."

I looked around, pointedly searching for any hint of another living soul, and she frowned.

"Yeah, I'm not sure where they are, either. Here, at least let me help," she sighed gustily. I moved over at the sink, leaving room for her to join me in knocking the leaves, twigs, and debris into the sink.

We worked without speaking for a minute before she broke the silence. "You know my name, but I'm afraid I don't know yours. Care to enlighten me?"

"I'm Zoe Cooper." I offered a smile hesitantly.

"Nice to meet you, Zoe Cooper. Call me Corrina."

I nodded, and we lapsed back into silence. This one was a little more comfortable, though I still wasn't sure how to act around Corrina Carr. She obviously had history with Amelia, but that didn't mean that I had to be rude. Amelia and I didn't have that kind of relationship, no matter how much fun I had had with her in the blueberry field and how kind she'd been after I'd panicked.

Given that Corrina was going to be a judge tonight, it would be pretty foolish of me to antagonize the woman and not expect that to blow our chances at winning the challenge entirely. Plus, I was a people pleaser.

"So, what do you think of Shaw's?" she asked, jolting me out of my thoughts.

"Oh, it's beautiful. For some reason, I expected all of New York to be more like the city, but this is more like home than I could have imagined."

"Yeah, people always imagine the big city when they think of New York, but most of it's not like that. Where's home for you?"

"Oh, a little town outside of Raleigh. Nowhere special."

She turned her head so quickly her neck cracked. "Wait, you're from Raleigh? Did you know Amelia before the competition?"

I shook my head. "No, we met at the audition. I'd heard of her restaurant, though."

She blinked slowly as if she needed time to process what I said, even though there hadn't been anything particularly scandalous in it. Then she shook her own head and let out a small laugh. "This world is too damn small. My granny always said the world only had 5,000 people in it, but I never believed her. Maybe I should have. I might have been prepared for all of this."

She waved her hand at me and the door I'd come in. I laughed. "I'm not sure *anything* could prepare you for coming face to face with an ex you never wanted to see again. Lord knows I'd react worse than you did if mine showed up."

"It's not that I didn't want to see her again, exactly… I just thought I'd have time to prepare to see her again, you know?"

I did know. I didn't know her and I didn't know what had happened between them, but I understood needing to emotionally prepare for seeing people we'd once loved.

"There's no shame in that," I reassured her. It was the second time I'd found myself telling people things that I'd struggled to accept for myself today. It was fitting, really.

She smiled at me over the bucket of blueberries, then; a shy, quiet smile that felt more real than anything she'd presented to the camera thus far. It transformed her into even more of a beauty. "Thanks."

Just then, the back door of the restaurant flew open, banging against the side of the refrigerator. I jumped, nearly toppling the bucket I was emptying.

"Fuck! Sorry!" Amelia cried out as she tripped into the room. "I didn't mean to do that."

Corrina stiffened beside me, her arms flying to rest on her hips. "Did you just dent my fridge? That thing costs more than your car, and I just got it!"

Angela pushed past her to inspect the appliance, moving ever so slightly in a circle to peer at it from every angle before making her declaration. "Not a scratch!"

"Good," Corrina huffed. "Watch where you're going next time, please. I know you're more graceful than that, and I can't afford to replace more equipment."

"I will be." Amelia's cheeks burned with embarrassment when she replied. There was, yet again, more to this story than was being spoken out loud, but there was no time to ask for more information. The rest of the contestants were already walking in the door, chattering happily amongst themselves. It was time to focus on the challenge.

———

———

I threw up a thankful prayer when the judges explained the challenge. For once, Amelia's and my similar cooking styles would come in handy. We had an hour to come up with, prep, and cook a five course tasting menu focusing on different products that the farm produced.

My mind whirled, trying to think of all of the courses that we could cook to show off them all. A five course meal with the option for two appetizers or an appetizer and dessert left us with more creative freedom than we'd seen in any other challenge so far. It was kind of scary, honestly, but not anything that I didn't think we could handle.

When the judges revealed that this challenge would be judged anonymously, the relief that washed over Amelia's face was nearly palpable. I thought she might faint, and honestly, I couldn't blame her for it. Corrina Carr and I didn't know much about each other, but what I did know, I didn't like. I certainly didn't trust her to judge us fairly as a pair after I had argued with her just a few hours ago. Not having to worry about how she might take out her personal feelings on us was a huge weight off of both our shoulders.

When the time began, I took a deep breath. Amelia squared her shoulders and looked at me. "You ready for this?"

"Ready as I'll ever be," I smiled. "What do you think, two appetizers or an appetizer and dessert?"

"Appetizer and dessert. I want to do a blueberry goat cheese ice cream, but we'll need to start that right away and get it into the freezer. What do you think for the appetizer?"

"Oh, that sounds delicious. I had two ideas for appetizers, but I'm not attached to either of them. Let's go get those ingredients and talk at the same time."

We sped to the kitchen, talking quietly the whole time. I had been thinking of doing steamed bun, kind of like a bao with blueberry sauce, or a spinach salad with goat cheese and a blueberry balsamic vinaigrette, but neither of them spoke to Amelia.

"What about a blueberry and chive risotto? We could use vegetable stock and goat cheese as the cream in it and pump up the savory aspect. I think it would be a really striking start to the meal."

"You don't think people would balk at a purple risotto?" I asked, thoughtfully.

"Maybe, but I think it's something no one else will have the balls to do." Her eyes were fiery. "It's also a vegetarian option that'll play well with the judges because it's something very different."

Thinking about it, I realized she was right. It would also be a good way to play the savory and sweet notes in both the appetizer and the dessert. I nodded, and she beamed.

"Since we're going blueberry heavy on the app and dessert, let's keep those lighter on the entrees. For the meat entree, let's do a balsamic and goat cheese filet mignon with an herb rub."

For the chicken, we agreed on a chicken thigh roulade with brie and caramelized onions. We tossed a few ideas for the produce course while we looked around before settling on a bell pepper stuffed with potatoes, handmade paneer, onions, a few hotter peppers, carrots, and peas; and spiced with a blend of garam masala, coriander leaves, garlic, and chili powder. It was going to be delicious, even if I had never worked with the Indian spice before.

Together, we grabbed the ingredients for each course and made our way back to the actual restaurant kitchen, where we would all be collectively cooking. We got ourselves set up on one of the stovetops and started planning.

"Okay, we need to start dessert first, then the onions need to get started," I thought out loud. "I've never made ice cream before. Do you need my help with that?"

"No, you go ahead and get started on the vegetables. I just need to get this started and into the machine first thing. Then I'm gonna start the paneer, since it needs to refrigerate."

"Gotcha." I put my head down and got to work, slicing the onion as thinly as I could, then peeling and dicing the potatoes that needed to cook before they went into the peppers.

Hesitating, I looked at the space we had and thought about how best to caramelize the onions. They were notoriously finicky. Somehow, despite years of trying, I had never managed to perfect the cook time on pressure cooked caramelized onions, and I wasn't about to attempt it on an unfamiliar stove.

Ovens were more reliable and it meant we could actually use the top of the stove more effectively earlier on. So, the onions went onto a sheet tray with some salt, pepper, garlic, and oil.

Amelia was already at work on the blueberry compote and ice cream base, taking up much of the stovetop.

"I'm coming in behind you and need the oven and one burner."

She stepped to the side to allow me access to both. I quickly slid the onions into the oven and placed the pot of potatoes onto the back burner to heat, then I returned to my cutting board. It wasn't long before I heard the whir of the blender.

Next, she took the potatoes off the stove, set aside the ones for the peppers, and got to work on mashing the rest, mixing in cream and goat cheese until they were the perfect consistency. They went back in the pot to keep warm.

So far, we were working better together than I had expected, though it was still early in the challenge and we had the space to stay out of each other's way. I had to wonder how long it would last, given how much animosity we still shared.

No matter what happened later, I was glad for the calm moments now. The day we'd spent together had given us more than enough conflict to make the producers happy, but it had also helped me to see there was more to her than being a good cook and the food snob she let herself be seen as so often.

By the time I'd finished prepping the vegetables,

Amelia was pouring the ice cream base into the machine to churn.

"Doesn't the blueberry need to go in there too?"

"Nope, it gets mixed in after. Can you pour it into a sheet tray, though? It needs to go into the fridge to cool fast."

"Got it." The compote was gelatinous in the best way and smelled delicious as I poured it into the tray, with blueberry halves spread throughout. I ran it to the fridge and stuck it on the top shelf before running right back to the station.

She had already moved onto the next task; beating the snot out of the chicken thighs with a mallet.

"Remind me not to get on your bad side," I joked, and was rewarded with another of her snorting laughs while I checked on the onions. They were still softening and didn't need to get moved to the stove yet.

I pulled the brie out of the basket and chopped the rinds off of the sides and top. According to the label, it was made from milk from the cows we'd spent so much time with.

I popped a piece in my mouth, moaning at how deliciously creamy it was. It would be the perfect melted vector for keeping the chicken and onions in the right shape once we rolled them.

The onions! I remembered with a jolt of horror. *Please don't be burnt, please don't be burnt...*

I nearly sprinted to the oven, praying the whole time, only to find that the slices had melted to become beautifully soft and just starting to brown around the edges, just the way they were supposed to be. Heaving a sigh of relief, I pulled them out and set them off to the side. I needed to get a pan hot enough to finish these off.

Before I could make a run for the pantry, a stainless

steel sauté pan was thrust onto the only empty burner. I tossed a thank you over my shoulder and poured a little more olive oil into the pan, waiting for it to heat before sliding the onions into it. The sizzle was extremely rewarding, and the onions finished crisping up very quickly. I poured them into a mixing bowl and put the pan in the sink. They needed to cool just a little before we could roll them into the chicken, but it was more than enough time to get started on the next dish—the blueberry and chive risotto.

"What do we need for this risotto? Two pans, right? It's vegetable stock in one for the rice and then the blueberry butter puree in the other?"

"Right. You can use the stainless for the blueberry, since you'll need to use the immersion blender," she answered without really turning around; she had pulled the paneer back out of the fridge and was cubing it into a bowl with the other vegetables that would go into the stuffed pepper. I looked up at the clock and cursed. We only had twenty minutes left.

I poured some of the vegetable stock into the sauté pan I'd cooked the onions in. It was still hot and wouldn't contaminate the risotto because there were onions in the stock. While that heated, I grabbed the blueberries and butter and got them into a new pan on the burner behind it.

Those would need to cook low and slow for almost ten minutes before they were ready to start mixing with the rice, but that was fine, because I only needed to cook three dinner-sized portions of rice. I had just enough time to get this done, as long as I didn't screw anything up.

Risotto, like a good relationship, needed constant attention, love, and a little bit of wine in order to work well. I didn't have much in the way of good relationship experience, but I had more than enough experience cooking risotto.

Unlike regular rice, the short-grained arborio needed to be almost glue-like to be edible. That's where the wine and stock came in. Those mixed with the starches from the rice to create the creamy texture that it was famous for, helped along by the near-constant stirring that kept it from burning on the bottom of the pan.

"Coming in beside you," Amelia informed me tersely, making me jump. "The peppers need to go in and then I have to start the filet."

She put a cast iron skillet on the only open burner and poured a little oil in it. Then she spun in a circle to grab the sheet tray full of peppers and face the oven again.

I moved out of the way enough to let her open the door and slide the tray of peppers in. Even uncooked, they smelled amazing. I could only imagine how mouthwatering they would be once everything had cooked together.

Her shoulder brushed mine as she closed the door and electricity coursed through me. I stared at her, wondering if she felt it too. She wasn't looking at me, though. She only had eyes for the cast iron she'd started heating, though she rubbed her shoulder absentmindedly.

"Your oil should be just about hot now," I told her. "I can start the sear if you want to deal with finishing the ice cream."

"*Fuck*, the ice cream," she shrieked. She ran to the back where the machine was still slowly churning. I grabbed the filet and placed it in the skillet with care, rewarded with the unmistakable, delicious smell of quickly cooking meat.

Amelia dashed back past me with the bowl of ice cream as she ran to the freezer on the other side of the room. I couldn't help but be aware of her every movement as she swirled the compote into the mixture and put it in individual serving bowls.

When she came back, we talked quietly to each other, sharing what we were doing so that we made sure everything got done.

Before long, the filets had been moved into the oven to allow the cheese to melt properly. Amelia had put another pan on the stove, following a similar process with the chicken roulades, except they didn't need to go into the oven. And then I found myself adding the cream, chives, and fresh blueberries to the risotto. It was done.

I glanced up at the clock and cursed. There were only five minutes left and we hadn't plated anything but the ice cream.

"Getting plates!" I called out, dashing toward the cabinet. I took a few seconds to look at everything that was there. Plating was especially important in this challenge because whatever we did might wind up on their regular menu.

I chose a wide-rimmed plate with a shallow bowl in the center for the risotto, a round white plate for the filet, a rectangular plate for the stuffed peppers.

Grabbing a stack of trays, I laid stacks of five each on the top, one for each of the judges and one extra for the camera crew to get backup footage of, and made my way back to the station at a much slower pace than I wanted to go. It was heavy, and I didn't have time for an injury in this challenge.

Nearly everything had been pulled away from the heat, which meant we were ready.

"Thank God you're back. Set the plates down so we can get this finished."

I rolled my eyes, not caring that she could see it. She knew that was what I was doing. As soon as they had clinked on the counter, she grabbed the risotto bowls and began filling them. I started with the filet mignon plates.

The design I came up with was a simple one, but a pretty one. A scoop of mashed potatoes on one side of the plate, a spoonful of the vinaigrette spread in an artful swoop around the other, then the beautiful, circular filet in the center. On top of the filet, there was a small glob of melted goat cheese.

"Amelia, look and approve, please!"

She glanced over her shoulder at the plate. "Do a little zigzaggy drizzle of sauce over the filet and that's perfect. How's mine look?"

"Like purple risotto!" I laughed. She stuck her tongue out at me. "It looks good. Make sure each plate gets the same number of blueberries and chives, though."

"I'm already on that, and I'm gonna do the chicken next. I was gonna do a scoop of potatoes in the middle with the roulades at an angle on either side. Sound good?"

"Perfect. I'll do the peppers and then pull out the ice cream. We'll be all set."

For the next three minutes, we didn't speak another word. Our hands only stopped moving when we were walking trays to the pass. The final tray hit the pass mere seconds before the timer signaled the end of the challenge.

"Everybody, hands off your plates!"

Amelia and I looked at each other, pure joy radiating off of us both as we realized that we had made it. And we had done it well.

———

The camera crew led us all into the dining room, assuring us that our food would be well taken care of.

Two long, rectangular tables had been set up in the center of the room with five chairs spread out along it. Instead of having the table between us and the judges, like it had been for every other challenge, the chairs faced the farm-view windows of the restaurant. It was beautiful out there, but I couldn't focus on it. All I could focus on were the judges as they filed in.

Grace, Corrina, Denise, Nathan, and Bryce stood in front of their chairs, all of them presenting stoic expressions. I didn't know Grace and Corrina well enough to read them, and the judges just liked to make sure we couldn't tell what they were thinking.

"As you might have noticed, tonight's judging will be a little bit different. We will judge each menu on originality, cohesiveness, and the strength of the individual dishes. The pairings who fall short in these categories will go head to head in the elimination challenge."

I sucked in a breath, praying that Amelia and I had done well enough to make it through without having to go up against each other directly. Glancing sideways, I saw that she was looking at me and chewing her lush bottom lip. I couldn't help but wonder if she was thinking the same thing.

"Because we will be judging this without knowing who cooked what, we will not be able to see you while we taste," Denise explained. "In order to protect the anonymity of each group, you may not tell us who cooked what. If you call out at any point during the judging, you will automatically be disqualified and sent to elimination. Understood?"

We all crowed the phrase we knew better than our own names. "Yes, Chef!"

Denise grinned a wolf's grin and nodded. "Then let us begin."

———

Chapter Nineteen

AMELIA

THE JUDGES TOOK THEIR SEATS AND THE WAITERS brought out the first tray, setting a plate in front of each judge. All of us leaned forward in unison, trying to see whose food was up first.

"The first course of the first menu is a baked herb goat cheese dip served with toasted baguette slices."

Well, it wasn't us. I looked around, searching for whose it was, and my eyes settled on Fern and Troy. The former marine stood ramrod straight, as if his commanding officer had called him to attention. Fern, however, looked incredibly nervous as her eyes flitted from judge to judge while they dug in.

One problem that I quickly noticed was that, because the judges were facing away from us, it was very difficult to hear what they were saying. We also couldn't see the food that Fern and Troy had created, which made it difficult for us to have any idea what the judges might think and where we might stand.

They had chosen to go with a second appetizer for their menu, baked brie with a blueberry balsamic glaze served with gluten-free crackers. When this dish was served, I could see the judges giving each other sidelong glances. Though it would taste quite different, it was still a very similar dish to the first appetizer, which was never a good idea with such a small menu.

Their poultry focused course was one that I thought was smart, pulled chicken sliders cooked in a blueberry barbecue sauce. It smelled delicious. The meat course was also a burger, though, using the same blueberry balsamic glaze they'd used for the baked brie. The final course was produce focused. It was a goat cheese and honey salad, which was simple, but at least wasn't covered with blueberry dressing.

Only when they had finished discussing the dishes amongst themselves did the judges turn around. Fern audibly gulped at the look on the judges faces. They were not pleased.

"Whoever cooked this menu, we are very disappointed," Denise said. "This menu was cohesive, but it was also boring. Most of these dishes were very similar in color, plating, and even taste. I liked the barbecue sauce and the salad, but it doesn't feel like you used your time wisely. I would plan to take part in the elimination round, unless another pair made something worse."

Without waiting for a response, the judges turned back around in their chairs.

Fern's face crumpled, and my heart went out to her. When I looked at Troy, his expression had only stiffened into a mix of a grimace and a thousand yard stare.

I was pretty sure I could guess what had happened, what with how much arguing I'd heard from Troy during the cook time. His voice carried, even with so much already going on in the restaurant's kitchen. The good news was, though, that I was sure that Fern could cook circles around him. As long as she didn't make foolish mistakes, the competition would soon become a lot more fun.

At least, as long as any of the rest of us didn't completely fuck this up. My palms were suddenly sweaty, thinking about how we might have screwed up our meal.

I wiped them on my pant legs while the waiters brought out the next tray, only to find that my fingers tangled with Zoe's when I tried to move them again. I looked up at her in surprise, only to find that she was looking at me with the same expression. We couldn't speak, so I just waited for her to move her hand. Except...she didn't.

Maybe I needed to revise my earlier thoughts about whether we were friends or not. Or maybe we still weren't friends, but something else. Something that accounted for the sparks that crawled over me every time we touched. But whatever we were, I couldn't let the cameras see it before we had figured it out for ourselves.

I dislodged my hand from her grip, but let it hang by my side, not putting any space between them. The backs of our hands touched ever so slightly. The next two menus were more creative than the first, and several dishes were complimented, but the judges didn't say anything about choosing anything for the menu. Finally, it was our turn to be judged. My palms continued to sweat as our first tray was brought forward to muffled sounds of surprise from the judges.

I knew the risotto would be striking, I thought proudly as I grinned at Zoe. She beamed back at me, then we turned back to watch the judges pick through our plates one by one. It felt like it took them an eternity before they turned back to us.

Corrina was the one to tell us what the judges thought, because of course, she was. Fate, and perhaps this challenge, was just trying to be funny at this point.

"This was an excellent tasting menu. We admired the creativity and different variations of some very similar ingredients used throughout the different dishes. I think that Mrs. Shaw and I need to talk about the possibilities for our own menus. Feel free to chat amongst yourselves while I do so."

I let go of the breath I'd been holding since the judging began. We had made it through.

"Did you hear that? They loved our food!"

Before I could respond, Fern's voice filled the room. "I fucking told you we couldn't do two sets of dishes that were basically identical. If you can't cook anything other than burgers and hot cheese, what the fuck are you doing in this competition?"

"Oh, like your dishes were any better?" he retorted angrily. "You just did a goddamn salad and some barbecue sauce."

Zoe's smile fell from her face and she took a step back, her face falling into the carefully neutral one I had seen earlier with the cows.

"Both of which they *loved*," she pointed out, her voice shrill. "You also reused that same sauce for the baked brie after you burnt yours, so really, I did half of that dish too."

"And now we're in the elimination because what *you* did wasn't good enough." He stepped closer to her, until his face was mere inches from hers. He was almost screaming now, his fists clenching so hard that the veins in his arms were straining against his muscles. When he raised one of them towards Fern, Jada shoved her way between them.

"Enough," she said firmly. "You two are supposed to be chefs, and you sound like toddlers fighting over the best toy. Pull it together and focus on the challenge, not on your petty grudges. And Troy, I ever see you pull any shit like that again, I'm calling security. Didn't your mama ever teach you to keep your hands and feelings to yourself?"

He growled at her—*Actually* growled at her—before storming away. Idly, I wondered where he thought he was going to go, but then I realized that I didn't give a shit. I glanced back at Zoe and my heart broke.

Her wide eyes darted everywhere, as if she were waiting for something—someone—to hurt her. Her arms were stiffly crossed over her chest, but her hands shook violently under them. I renewed my desire to never meet her so-called husband if he had been the one to make her this scared.

"Hey," I called quietly, making sure not to crowd her this time. Her eyes glanced over me before moving away again, scanning as if her life depended on it. "Hey, Zoe. It's okay. The yelling is done."

I repeated those words, hoping that she heard them, until her breathing and her shaking slowed.

She looked at me, her face drained of color and mouthed, "Thank you."

I nodded at her; honestly, just glad I'd been able to help. Portia, the purple haired camera operator from earlier, brought over a glass of water and whispered something I couldn't hear. Zoe gave her a trembling smile and took a long drink. When she handed the glass back with thanks, it was nearly empty and some of the color had come back to her face. I stepped closer to her and leaned against the bar next to her, being careful not to crowd her. When she looked up, she offered me a slightly more stable smile.

"And they thought we were going to be the big enemies of the season," she murmured. "Even at our worst, we aren't that aggressive."

"Says the woman who knocked me on my ass this morning." I punctuated that with a smile, hoping she'd understand I was teasing. She wrinkled her nose at me.

"Yeah, but at least I wasn't screaming in your face. That's…it is its own thing."

I knew what she meant. There was something about someone being all up in your space like that, that was more terrifying than even getting hit could be. Especially when it was someone who was physically intimidating like Troy was.

"I hope he goes home just for that shit," I told her. "Fern deserved a better partner than him."

"Eh, I have faith in Fern, as long as the elimination isn't like…a burger challenge."

"That would be more difficult for her, but I still think she'd give him a run for his money."

Angela's voice rang out across the kitchen. "Everyone, back in place, please! We're ready to announce the results!"

Without further ado, the judges lined up in front of the table, facing us this time. Zoe and I both sucked in a breath. It was the moment of truth.

Please let them have chosen one of our dishes, I prayed silently. *Let me have this victory.*

Bryce was the one to announce the victors, and when he pointed out our menu, I couldn't hold back a shriek of delight. Without a second thought, I grabbed Zoe and spun her around.

Bryce raised his eyebrows at my antics, though he

was smiling. I set her down and cleared my throat. "Sorry."

"We really loved your entire menu," he reiterated. "Mrs. Shaw and Ms. Carr decided that they will be adding four of your dishes onto their menu; basically everything except the stuffed pepper."

I looked at Corrina and grinned. She looked like she had taken a bite out of a piece of preserved lemon. I would revel in the horror on her face if I wasn't so proud. Bryce either didn't notice the shift or didn't care. He kept talking.

"The only other dish they will be using will be from our third menu, the blueberry-glazed New York Strip with burnt onions. Who cooked that menu?"

Jada and Breonna squealed in unison, then hugged each other ferociously.

"I guess that gives us our answer," Nathan laughed. "In addition to your dishes becoming part of this season's menu, you are also all exempt from the next challenge. We've set up a spa day for the four of you, courtesy of the Roosevelt."

After a day of, literally, shoveling shit, falling on my ass, and then picking blueberries, a spa day sounded like nothing short of absolute heaven. I looked around and saw the same excitement on Jada, Breonna, and Zoe's faces. Further away, the guys looked nonplussed, but the other women looked almost heartbroken at the missed opportunity.

"You will also have the opportunity to be interviewed by others from your hometown newspapers, so make sure you're thinking of nice things to say," Bryce joked.

My eyebrows rose in surprise. How had they arranged that without knowing which of us was going to win? Not that it really mattered. Any day where I didn't have to fight for my place in the competition was a good one. One where I could get pampered would be *great.* Especially having won it from Corrina, who was approaching now.

"Congratulations on your win. I look forward to seeing how our patrons take to the new menu options." She still looked sour, but she was trying to hide it now for the camera's sake.

"Thank you. I hope they like them," I said. It surprised me to realize that I meant it. Her face congealed into something that looked more like constipation than anything else I had words for. She would hate how she looked on the screen later, which both pleased me and saddened me. She deserved better than that, even if I was still angry with her for throwing things in my face that she hadn't told me when we were together.

"I think you're missing out on not serving that stuffed pepper, though. That thing was delicious."

She shook her head. "You really are something."

I huffed a laugh. "I am a lot of things. Which thing did you mean right now?"

Now she smiled a little, the first positive emotion I'd seen from her all day. "You're ridiculous, is what you are. I have to cater my menu to my guests, and you know this town is ninety percent white and seriously old. The only way I'd get them to eat a curried pepper with paneer would be to force feed it to them. That's not what I'm working here for."

"No, you're here to serve people the food grown in the fields they're walking in. And you're doing it. Just like you always wanted."

Her mouth dropped open just enough to show me that I had surprised her. Those were almost the exact words she'd used back in college when she talked about her dreams. The ones she had told me that I had never listened to, never asked her about. She took a deep breath and then smiled for real.

"You're doing what you always wanted, too, aren't you? You always were a good chef in school and you've only gotten better. I think today proves that."

Now it was my turn to be surprised again. Today had been full of unusual twists and turns, but this was the first from Corrina that didn't feel like a punch to the gut. It was really nice to hear her. She might still be angry with me. I could allow that she had valid reasons to be, but maybe she didn't hate me as much as she had this morning. And that, to use her words, was something.

———

———

Before we had time to go too far, the producers called us back for the elimination challenge. Fern and Troy lined up at the front of the kitchen and the judges in front of them.

We were on the other side of the room with the same barstools we had used in the last elimination. Instead of being on different rows, Zoe had chosen to sit next to me. I marveled at how hard and fast the cleaning staff had worked to get the place back to sparkling after we had all used it for the initial challenge.

The judges made no bones about what they were asking them to do. Both of them had to cook the exact same meal; one they had never had before, with no recipe, in thirty minutes. The only hint the judges gave them was that it was a vegan recipe, to cater to Fern's diet.

They burst into action, taking quick bites of food from a plate. I couldn't see around the judges no matter how far I craned my neck. When they ran back to the pantry, the judges stepped away from the plate and relaxed.

"What's the recipe?" Shauna asked from the row behind me.

"If we told you, that would ruin the surprise!" Nathan chirped.

"Not to mention, it would 'ruin' the challenge for those two," Denise grumbled. "It's hardly even difficult if we tell them what it is."

I wasn't so sure about that, as I peered at the plate. It looked like some sort of pesto over gnocchi. It almost felt like they had planned it to put Troy out of the challenge. Fern was used to cooking all sorts of vegan food, while Troy was almost guaranteed to have a hard time cooking any meal that didn't revolve around a protein.

Not that I would be complaining if that was what they'd chosen. The man was a complete alphahole; the kind of man who refused to admit there was anything he couldn't do perfectly, and who thought his physical strength was a gift from God.

There was always a chance he would surprise us, though I hoped he wouldn't. I really didn't want to have to spend the entire bus ride home listening to him gloat about how great he was. Nor did I want to lose Fern's company in the suite.

The challenge flew by, thanks to the short time limit and the banter between the two of them. It was nerve wracking not to be able to really see what they were doing, though. When they brought their plates forward, I sucked in a breath. From what I could see, both of their dishes looked relatively similar to the one the judges now showed off to us.

What mattered, now, was the taste. There was a lot that could go wrong in vegetarian and vegan dishes that you wouldn't know until it was far too late to fix it. I was weirdly anxious about the results. Before I could stop myself, I found my hand drifting towards Zoe's hand where it rested on her thigh and found her fingers already questing for mine. I gave it a quick squeeze and let her go, reminding myself that the cameras were always watching, even when the judges were doing their thing.

They asked a few questions about what was in each dish and how it was made before tasting them. Eventually, they were satisfied with what they had tasted, stepping back to discuss what they thought of each.

They were arguing even faster than usual, their voices hushed and harried. I couldn't quite hear what they were saying, but the challenge must have been closer than I had thought if they had that much to say.

I caught myself reaching for Zoe again and had to clench my hands together to stop myself from getting any further. I wasn't entirely sure why it was so hard to keep myself from touching her, but I really needed to get it together. We didn't have time for this. The judges had made their decision.

"Fern, Troy, both of you made pretty good dishes," Denise announced. "However, one of these dishes was superior in its technique and its recognition of the ingredients used. One of you will be going back to the hotel tonight only long enough to pack your bags."

It felt like every single contestant was holding their breath collectively, waiting to hear the verdict.

"The dish that I created for you was a tofu gnocchi with a pistou sauce," Bryce explained. "Both of your pistous were excellently made, without the pine nuts that would have turned it into a pesto. Fern, congratulations on recognizing that the gnocchi was made with tofu and getting the consistency perfectly pillowy."

I couldn't see his expression, but I guessed he was smiling at her. Her answering smile was tremulous, but there was a spark of joy in her eyes that no one could miss.

His voice went serious as he turned ever so slightly to face Troy. The former marine's face tightened. "However, Troy, you actually made gnudi, which would be absolutely unservable for a vegan diner. Because of this, we cannot allow you to continue in this competition."

I sucked in a breath. That must have been what they were arguing about after the judging. Now, there was only one thing left for the scene. The trademark line.

"Your cooking can't stand up to the heat of this kitchen. Your time here is done."

———

———

All of our hearts were heavy when we got back into the van at the end of the night. The sun was beginning to set, and we were all exhausted. I wasn't sorry to see Troy go, but it was hard to lose another of our number.

I couldn't believe that they were having him ride back in the makeup van instead of with us, but it made sense, in its own way.

There was none of the lighthearted chatter that had

filled the morning's journey. One by one, I could hear everyone's breathing deepening and evening out as they fell asleep until Zoe and I were the only ones awake in the back of the van.

"So today was eventful," she murmured after a while. I had to hold back a snort. That was the understatement of the century.

"If it were any more eventful, I'm not sure I could have handled it," I replied, honestly. "This whole experience has just been…surreal."

She shifted in her seat so she was facing me. I could hardly see her face, because of how bright the setting sun was from the window behind her, but her silhouette was striking.

"Do you mean today? Or the whole competition?"

"Well, that's a question." She was quiet, watching me as I thought about it, pulling my bottom lip between my front teeth. "I meant today, specifically, but it's true for the whole competition, you know?"

She nodded. "Today was…so much. It was the first time it really felt real that it was a competition, especially when it looked like Fern was gonna get eliminated."

I glanced over my shoulder to see the woman in question. She was so short that the top of her head barely reached the headrest behind her, but she was fast asleep already. A small snore emitted from her open mouth. ";/.Smiling, I turned back to Zoe.

"This was the first time anyone actually decent was up for elimination," I agreed. "Neither of us really knew the guy eliminated last week, and before that everything was such a whirlwind."

She nodded, covering a yawn with her hand. "No kidding. Tonight's challenge was pretty good, though."

"We got four of our five dishes on the menu," I

pointed out. "I'd say we did a little better than 'pretty good.'"

"I'm not wild about partner or team challenges. I'm so used to working alone that I get twitchy trusting anyone else, y'know? I didn't mind working with you, though. We make a pretty good team."

Her words were simple, but they sent a rush of warmth through me. I could feel a grin spreading across my face. It took everything in me to keep myself from gasping when we took a turn and the deep reds and oranges of the sunset began to warm her face.

When I answered her, I kept my voice low but let everything I was feeling infuse into it.

"We really do. If we ever get stuck with partners for a challenge again, I wouldn't be upset if you were mine."

She smiled at me, and I couldn't tell if she had heard everything I still didn't have the words for, but it was clear she had heard more than I'd said. That would have to be enough. For now.

———

Chapter Twenty

ZOE

I WOKE UP THE NEXT MORNING WITH A SENSE OF excitement filling my chest. I couldn't remember the last time I had taken a real day off, let alone gone to a spa. Thinking back as I got dressed in a simple sundress, it had to have been before I was married. Jacob had showered me with affection and time back then, something that had stopped abruptly as soon as I had gotten pregnant.

Now, this was something I had earned for myself. Well technically, Amelia and I had earned it together. I was so proud of that, that I could burst. I was also more than a little nervous.

I'd never talked to a newspaper reporter, let alone been interviewed by one. I could count the number of times I'd even gotten a manicure anywhere but at my own kitchen table. I'd never even set foot in a spa. What if I made a fool of myself?

Shaking my head, I reminded myself that there was no way I was the first person they'd ever worked with that hadn't been there before. Besides, it couldn't be worse than yesterday's panic attack, right?

Even if I did, I wouldn't be alone. I didn't know Breonna well, but I had a good feeling about her, and Jada and Amelia were wonderful. Spending the day with them would be pretty great.

When my second alarm went off on my phone, I cursed. I needed to go. With skills I'd had years of practice at, I grabbed my things and flung the door open, only to nearly run straight into Amelia doing the same thing.

"Whoa there!" Amelia yelped, catching me by the arm to keep me from tumbling to the floor. "You really need to learn to look where you're going *before* you crash into people. This is becoming a habit."

I laughed, pleased when she joined me. "I haven't actually managed to run into anyone yet, thanks to you. Maybe you're my good luck charm."

"Maybe I am," she laughed. "You ready to go get pampered?"

"Oh, yeah. I don't know what all they offer, but there'll definitely be something great."

"For sure. I'm stiff as hell after yesterday. I think a deep tissue foot and body massage will be just the thing."

"That sounds very nice," a third voice said from down the hall. We peered around the corner to find Jada exiting her own room.

"Personally, I'm looking forward to getting a facial and a back massage," she added. "Mind if I walk with y'all?"

I shook my head. "Of course not! The more the merrier!"

We made our way out of the suite and down the hall towards the elevator.

"I'm a little upset with you two," she informed us with a twinkle in her eye as we waited. "I thought for sure Bre and I were gonna come out on top with our menu. But you had to go and do ice cream in that small time frame on top of everything else."

"Hey, you didn't do too badly yourselves," I reminded her. "That steak sounded like it was delicious."

"It was," she sighed dreamily. "I could have bathed in that sauce. Alas, I had to give the recipe away. Honestly, I may never make a sauce quite that delicious ever again, but I'm glad I did."

"I'm not sure you would have ever been able to get the smell of blueberries out of your hair if you *did* bathe in it," Amelia pointed out.

Jada waved a hand blithely. "It would have been worth it. I'm just glad I got to do this today instead of whatever hell the judges have cooked up. It's been too long since I've been taken care of the way I deserve."

"Amen to that," I murmured as the doors opened onto the palatial lobby. Portia stood there, looking hard at their phone and ignoring the people milling around them.

"You waiting on us?"

They jumped, their purple hair flopping into their startled face. I had to laugh a little when they grimaced before pulling their face into a perfect expression for customer service.

"I'm here to lead you to the spa and make sure you get to your interviews on time. For those of you who don't know me, I'm Portia. Usually, Zoe is my main priority, but today, you get to share me amongst yourselves. If you'll follow me?"

They walked away, shoving their phone into the back pocket of their tight black jeans as they went. I admired the confidence in not needing to see if we followed them, as well as the diamond pattern they had shaved into their undercut. It suited them.

They led us through a pair of frosted-glass double-doors that opened onto an indoor paradise. Portia went to talk to the receptionist, and we each went in the direction that most drew our attention.

I stood where I was and marveled. The room was warm and humid, thanks to the actual waterfall that filled an entire side of the room. It pooled in a small pond that flowed into a shallow, crystal clear river that wound around the room. Small, colorful fish darted through it, giving it a rainbow effect that was just astonishing.

I was fairly certain I had never seen anything quite so beautiful. Then I saw Amelia's face as she trailed a finger through the small pond, giggling when the koi there came to see if her fingers were food.

She looked up at me, a sparkle in her eye, and my breath caught. *She* had to be the most beautiful thing I'd ever seen.

A delicate blush creeped over her cheeks as she realized that I was staring at her with the real life equivalent of heart eyes.

"Come pet the fish," she invited me with a wave. The glimmer in her smile was irresistible, pulling at my heart like we were connected by an invisible string.

When I reached her, three koi were circling the spot where she sat, coming to the surface every so often, like they were saying little fishy hellos. For a moment, we stood there silently, just watching them. Then she took my hand gently and dipped my fingers into the water beside hers.

I gasped, though I couldn't have said whether it was

because the water was absolutely frigid or because of the way that the warmth of her touch spread to my most intimate places.

We played with the fish in silence for what felt like an eternity before either of us spoke.

"Are you okay?" Amelia asked quietly. "You seem sort of…nervous."

My heart raced in my chest, and my thoughts raced through my mind. I didn't know how to answer her. I couldn't tell her that the mere thought of being this close to her without a task at hand drove me crazy, but I didn't want to tell her that I was scared to make an ass of myself in front of the staff here. But I also couldn't lie to her.

Taking a deep breath, I answered her with the less embarrassing of the two things on my mind. The words came out in a whisper. "I've never been to a spa before."

She raised a perfectly manicured eyebrow and her mouth opened in a small oh of surprise in one smooth movement before she realized what was happening and contracted her face into an understanding expression.

"I've never been to one this fancy," she whispered back. "I don't know what I'm doing here, either, if it helps."

Strangely, it did. I knew Amelia came from money, her wardrobe and schooling alone told me that, but I could never quite tell how *much* money. Maybe there wasn't quite as much distance between us as I'd thought.

"H…How does it work?"

She thought about it, chewing on her lower lip a little. I had to keep dragging my eyes upward to avoid fixating on the beautiful sight.

"It's basically like a nail salon, if you've ever been to one. They have a selection of offerings that you can choose from, usually with different scents and upsell options like wax treatments. It's not usually very complicated."

I nodded, tucking the information away for later. Then I smiled at her, feeling shy for the first time. "Thank you. That helps."

"Usually, the people that work at places like this are super nice, so if you don't understand something, it's not out of line to ask. Or..." she hesitated, as if she wasn't sure how to word what she said next. "I could explain it to you, if I know. If that's what you want?"

I could tell she was trying extremely hard not to be as snotty as she had been in the kitchen a few nights prior. Before I could tell her how much I appreciated it, Portia poked their head around the stout tree that had hidden us from view.

"There you two are," they scowled. "Come on, they're ready for you."

———

———

The process was just as simple as Amelia had described. Except the producers had chosen what we would get: full body Swedish massages with our choice of scented lotions, manicures, and pedicures. The only caveat was that we weren't allowed to get acrylic nails, and if we polished our nails, we had to wear gloves while cooking. Those were things that shouldn't have needed saying, since we all knew that losing a nail or getting nail polish in the food would be a quick ticket out of the competition. The show liked to cover their bases, though, so we had to sign saying we understood.

Once we had done so, the attendants led us into a dimly lit, but comfortably warm room with four massage tables set up throughout. Taking a deep breath, I looked around.

One corner held what appeared to be a changing room and light instrumental music filled the space. There was no waterfall here, but some of the tropical plants had been potted and brought in and placed strategically around the room.

It made for a really relaxing atmosphere, which I guess made sense when you thought about it. It was a spa, after all. Relaxation was the whole point.

Three other women filed into the room and started telling us what to do. Their first order was to get changed into the bathrobes, embroidered with the *Heating Up the Kitchen* logo, I noticed, and then make our way to the table.

Hesitating a little, I made my way to the table furthest from the door. It would make it harder to run if I needed to, but it would also give me the greatest amount of privacy. And since I was literally bare under the bathrobe, that was more important.

Amelia chose the bed beside me, which I was grateful for.

"I'll be with you the whole time," Amelia reminded me. "It's gonna be fine."

A few days ago, I might have found the words patronizing, but instead, they warmed me to the core. It was gonna be all right.

———

———

Our trip upstairs to get changed into our chef whites—or burgundy, in Amelia's case—was a quick one. We were rushed back downstairs to get our photos taken on set, only to find the rest of the contestants just leaving and the cleaning crew getting started.

"Well, look who finally decided to show up!" Ellis hollered, turning around to watch us get set up. "You ladies look like you've had a relaxing day."

"We did! You look like you've been through hell!" Jada called back, flipping her twists over her shoulder playfully. We all laughed, but it was true.

The room was even warmer than usual, and there were bowls of various substances scattered all over every station. It smelled sweeter too. There was also at least one stand mixer at each station as well as a variety of different shaped tins. Glancing at the contestants as they passed, I could see that they were all covered in a dusting of flour and smudges of other things. As we got further into the room, it was clear that many of the bowls were full of different kinds of icing.

"Oh my god," Breonna whispered, apparently realizing it at the same time. "They made you do cakes?"

"Worse; Swiss rolls," Ellis stage whispered.

We all collectively groaned, and I found that I was more than grateful that I hadn't had to take part in this one. They couldn't have had more than three hours to do the entire challenge if they'd had a separate elimination challenge. If they hadn't, they might have had four.

Either way, I was fairly certain it would have been a quick ticket home if I had participated. One of Angela's assistants walked in and started herding everyone else out of the room.

"Out you go, we have work to do in here!" I heard her instruct them.

They all left in a hurry before I had the chance to ask how the challenge had turned out, but judging by the state of the set, I could hazard a guess.

"I wonder who went home?" Jada murmured. That was something I wanted to know, too, but it would have to wait.

Angela had just walked in with four people who had to be the reporters, based on the giant cameras that hung around their necks and the large bags they carried with other equipment that I was quite familiar with by now.

Just like that, I could feel the tension creeping back through my shoulders and neck.

What if I said something idiotic? What if she asked about Jacob or about the blog and I say something wrong? Or…

Amelia nudged me with an elbow, jolting me out of my thoughts. "Which one do you think is here for us?"

I looked at them, focusing on their appearances instead of my own nerves; a bald Black man holding a television camera, two Latina women, and a white man holding DSLRs like the one I used for my own work. There was very little information to go on, but the white man was staring at us as we spoke. That was usually a sign he was here for us.

"I would be willing to bet it's him," I sighed, waving at the man. "He looks like he belongs at the News & Observer. And he won't stop looking at us."

She turned her face away from him and wrinkled her nose. It showed off dimples that I hadn't noticed before. I loved them instantly.

"Ladies, I've brought you some admirers and their wonderful cameras! I do have to go over some ground rules for all of you, simply due to the nature and timing of the competition, but they're fairly simple."

She was right. No trash talking the competition, no giving spoilers about who had gone home and what the challenges had been past the first episode, and the article would be held until right before the competition began. They would be easy to follow. We all agreed, signed a contract to that effect, and then got into position for photographs.

I was right about which reporter was ours. The Black man worked with Jada, while the woman worked with Breonna.

We did our portrait shots in the kitchen, and it was surprisingly easy to get used to being photographed by someone other than Mama. After the reporter was pleased with the results of those, he asked us to do a few photos together.

Amelia and I were posed in a variety of different poses that all made us look a lot more competitive than we actually were: back-to-back in a facsimile of the Charlie's Angels pose, except with spatulas instead of guns; standing next to each other with our arms crossed and grim faces; even pointing spatulas at each other.

Then he took a few of us grabbing things from the pantry and pretending to cook. They were silly pictures that would probably be great for splashing across the food section of the newspaper. It'd be a good gallery to gather clicks with too.

When we were finished, one of the show's staff led us to the pantry and set up two black leather arm chairs for us.

Amelia sat in hers, grimacing a little as her freshly-lotioned arms stuck to the chair.

"It's nice to meet you both," the reporter said when

we were both situated. "I'm Paul Lancaster, and I'll be recording this conversation on video, so I'm going to need you to put these mics on."

We did so, quickly. It was almost a relief, after the spa, to be doing something I was so familiar with. I hadn't expected that.

"Are you both ready to begin?"

Amelia and I looked at each other.

"I'm ready if you are," she said hesitantly.

I smiled, grateful again for the care. "I'm ready."

The reporter turned his camera on, a blinking red on the front the only signal. Then he began to talk.

"I understand there's a little bit of a rivalry between you two on the set. Did you two know each other before you came to the competition?"

I huffed a laugh. Of course, that would be the first real question he would think to ask. Luckily, it was an easy one to answer.

"We actually met while we were standing in line to check into our hotel rooms before our audition in Atlanta," I started the now-familiar story with a cheerful smile. "I noticed her bag had an RDU tag and that her dress looked like houndstooth, but it was actually made up of teeny-tiny cat prints. So obviously I had to talk to her."

———

Chapter Twenty-One

AMELIA

As I listened to Zoe tell the reporter how we'd met, I felt a flutter begin in the base of my stomach and work its way into every part of my body.

I still couldn't believe how rude I'd been, but from everything she had said, she didn't hold it against me. She laughed, looking as comfortable as she might if she were sitting in her own living room. Lancaster laughed along with her, then turned to me.

"Is that how it happened? Or did you have your own perspective on it?"

"No, that's pretty much how it went," I told him frankly. "And then, when we actually did our auditions, we cooked nearly identical dishes! I'm honestly surprised we both managed to get into the competition, considering they were looking for creativity."

"I was worried about that too," Zoe confessed. "I'm just glad I got to be here at all."

"Is creativity something that the judges are looking for in this competition? Why don't you tell me a little bit about the competition?"

That was directed at me, so I did, telling him about the test the judges had done when we'd first arrived and the first elimination challenge.

"It seems like the judges are looking for the full package in a chef," Zoe said thoughtfully. "Someone who's creative with their food, but consistent with quality no matter what they're making."

I nodded. "Plus, we've got to keep working to get better at everything we do here in the kitchen. We can't just do the same thing every challenge and expect to succeed in this."

Paul nodded, as if he understood.

"Now, I know you can't really talk about the challenges of the competition, but I assume that you've had to work together at some point here. What's that been like, given all of your very different experience levels?"

"Interesting?" I hedged, glancing over at Zoe. She laughed and nodded, turning slightly toward me.

Only then did I realize just how close we were to each other. We had started out both facing straight toward the reporter and the camera, but somehow, both of us had turned towards each other to have the conversation.

She was nearly completely sideways in her chair facing me. It reminded me of the way she'd sit in the practice suite, with her legs flung over the arm of the chair, though she'd usually be wearing a pair of shorts and have a cookbook in her hand.

"Interesting is a good word for it," she said wryly. "For example, we learned that Amelia likes to be in charge all the time."

"Hey!" I protested, but I laughed, still looking at her. "That's not fair. I'm a head chef! Literally the whole job description is 'cook good food, be in charge.' Plus, you like to be in control of everything too."

I reached an arm out to swat her gently, and she laughed again, but there was heat in her gaze. "Yes, but I'm much better at not being in control of the whole process. I take whatever task I'm given and exert my control over it, not other people."

That was true. Even I could—and did—admit that much. Zoe had proven just last night that she was more than capable of taking charge when she needed to, but she didn't rush in like a bull to put herself there. It was probably the smarter path, but one that I never even thought to take.

"Well, I guess that's why you two are both doing well in the competition so far. Tell me, what has been your favorite part of the competition?"

"Well, without getting into too many details, I've loved being challenged to do so many different things. It really takes a different sort of mindset to come up with something unusual but delicious based on the ingredients the judges place in front of you."

"Oh, and the time restrictions!" Zoe cut in. "You have to think so quickly, otherwise you won't have time to cook everything properly. That's something I've had to get used to."

"And your least favorite?"

"The eliminations, for sure," Zoe laughed.

I nodded my agreement.

"Just watching them is so stressful. Being in them is a whole other story." Hopefully that was vague enough not to get us into trouble with the producers. If not, they could figure that out themselves.

"I guess I can understand that. We're just about out of time here, so I'm gonna wrap things up with two easy questions that all of our readers will be dying to know the answer to."

He paused, waiting expectantly. When neither of us spoke, he cleared his throat and continued. "If you win the competition, what will you do with the money?"

"Well, I love working with Chef Ian. It's been great," I replied. "However, I'd like to own my own place someday, and between the publicity of the show and the money, it would make it a whole lot more likely to actually succeed."

The reporter nodded. "Do you have plans to stay within the Triad area? I'd love to hear more about your restaurant."

I laughed. "Let's save some details for when I *actually* win this thing, Paul. I don't actually have the money yet. Besides, Zoe has just as much of a chance to win this thing as I do."

He turned to her with a charming smile. "How about you? What are your plans if you win?"

She smiled back at him; a lot shyer than before. "Well, I'm not sure I'll be the winner, but I'd like to open my own place too. I'd love to build a small catering company with a space that I could teach cooking classes in."

"Well that sounds wonderful. Are you willing to give any details of your plans, or are you going to be as tight lipped as our friend here?"

That made her laugh. "Sorry, Paul. I'll have to win to be able to tell you anymore."

He frowned at us both, but the twinkle in his eye showed he didn't mean it.

"All right, last question for real now. You two seem to be getting along really well, despite the competition.

What happens if one of you wins and the other doesn't?"

Almost in unison, we turned to look at each other. Her raised eyebrows and dropped mouth echoed the flash of worry I felt.

"It probably sounds foolish, but I hadn't thought that far ahead," I murmured, not taking my eyes off of Zoe. Specifically, the way she pursed her lips. It was attractive in a way I couldn't name, but didn't want to miss.

"I imagine we'll have to cross that bridge when we come to it. For now, I'm just happy to be here for another day."

Only when the red light turned off did I let myself take a really deep breath again. We had made it through, and really, it hadn't been as bad as I'd expected.

"Ladies, you did a great job. Thank you so much for working with me!" Paul pulled his own mic off and coiled the cord into his pocket before patting his knees. "I think this will be out in next week's edition, but don't quote me on that."

"Can you mail us a few copies when it's out?" Zoe asked, holding out her own microphone. "We're all on limited internet right now, and I'd love to have at least one for memory's sake."

"Of course. I'll have a few mailed to the producers for you here, and a few copies to your homes, if you'll give me your addresses."

He held out a notebook and pen for us to write them down. I didn't hesitate to step forward and take it from him, writing down my parents' address. They would love it. When I was done, I turned to pass it to Zoe and saw a stricken look on her face. She looked even more anxious than she had before our massages when she spoke.

"Would it be possible for someone to come and pick

up my copies? I'm not comfortable giving out our address to anyone. No offense."

He looked confused but shrugged. "I don't see why not. Give me their name and I can leave them at the front desk."

She looked relieved when she took the notebook from me, writing a name and phone number underneath my address. I took the time to uncoil my own microphone from my chef's coat. With a frown, she handed the pad back to the reporter.

"Please don't give that information out to anyone. Is there anything else you need from us?"

He thought the question over, then shook his head. "You're all set. I do think I have to be escorted out, though. The producers mentioned something about that."

Portia popped their head in, as if they had been listening the whole time. "I'm here to do that. Just follow me!"

He packed his camera into its case and did so without a backward glance. We both relaxed back into the chairs and looked at each other.

"So, what do we do now?" I asked.

She thought about it briefly before her eyes lit up. "Dinner?"

My stomach growled, as if on cue. "That sounds great. Let's go!"

Without hesitation, we jumped up and made our way off the set.

———

———

When we got up to the practice suite, we weren't the only ones there. Fern and Ellis were all sitting in the armchairs talking seriously about something I couldn't hear. The door clicked shut behind us, and they all looked up in surprise.

"Oh! You're done already!" Fern exclaimed. "We thought you'd be gone for a while. I looked up at the clock on the wall, realizing it had been just over an hour since we'd crossed paths before the interview. Somehow, it had felt much longer.

"Yeah, we're all done. It wasn't as bad as I thought it was going to be. I thought it actually wound up being kind of fun."

"It was certainly a new experience," Zoe laughed, tucking a piece of hair behind her ear. "I can't wait to see the final copy."

"Oh, and the video. Do you think the producers will let us watch it?"

"Oh god, I hope not. I hate watching myself on video."

"Don't you do video for your blog like twice a week?" I asked, and she grimaced. Everyone laughed.

"That's different," she exclaimed, blushing a little. "I'm in charge of editing that, so if I look ridiculous, I can redo something. Or cover it with a cooking video or something. This…"

"You've got no control over it," Fern finished. "I get that. I have to say, I'm not really a fan of it, either."

That was exactly it; what I'd been trying to put words to earlier. The whole competition had taken things we usually control—our ingredients, the time we spend cooking something, even who we cook with—and turned it around so that we had to work within their limits.

Now, if only I'd had this epiphany an hour ago so I could sound smart on camera, I thought, shaking my head.

"Are y'all hungry? I haven't eaten all day."

"We already ate," Fern said. "But you go on. We were just talking about the challenge today. Did anyone tell you what happened?"

I shook my head. "All we heard was what Ellis told us as he was leaving the set. What did we miss?"

Fern let out a huff. "You're gonna want some food first."

Ellis shook his head. "Well…maybe not. It's a little gross."

"How about you stop waffling about and just tell us what happened?" Zoe asked, looking exasperated.

Fern and Ellis traded glances and then Ellis shrugged. "All right then. If you're squeamish you might not want to know."

When we both just stared at them, Fern sighed. "Christopher was eliminated after he chopped off quite a bit of one of his fingers and didn't finish the challenge."

My jaw dropped.

"Holy shit. He chopped off part of his finger?" Zoe's voice rose an octave with each word, saying exactly what I was thinking. "Did he have to go to the hospital?"

"I would imagine so. He probably needed stitches," I said simply, horrified.

Ellis nodded grimly. Zoe shuddered, and I didn't blame her. Sliced open fingers were pretty common injuries in the kitchen but losing part of a finger was a pretty major one. Then a thought occurred to me.

"Wait, I thought the challenge was to do swiss rolls. What was he cutting?"

Fern shook her head. "I couldn't see."

"He was using the mandolin to slice strawberries," Ellis explained. "He set something down and went back to using it without the guard and that was it."

"Poor guy," I mused. "What a shitty way to go out of the competition. If I go, I'd much rather have it be on my own merits than on a freak accident. That's just… it sucks."

"Yeah…it was a lot. For everyone. We all got a lecture on proper food safety afterward." That got an eye roll from us all. As if any one of us had gotten where we were without knowing how to properly use a mandolin slicer.

"Who was at the bottom with Christopher?"

"Shauna and Annika. Their cakes were pretty terrible, from what the judges said."

Fern and Ellis exchanged another look, a little guiltier this time. Fern wriggled in her seat as we watched until Ellis sighed. "We overheard the judges having a conversation with them both after the elimination and… we're pretty sure Shauna won't make it past the next episode. It was not a pretty conversation."

"Poor Shauna," Zoe sighed. "She's had a rough time of it, and she knows it."

It was true. I felt bad for her. She'd been on the lower end of nearly every challenge so far, and I'd heard her crying while she video chatted with her kids and husband last night.

"Well, we'll just have to treat her as well as we can while she's here. I mean, we have no idea what's gonna happen next. Any one of us could be the next one out."

I looked at Zoe and I was nearly bowled over at the look of determination on her face. I didn't know Shauna well, and neither did she, but she was very clearly set on being as kind as she could be. I loved that about her.

I blinked, surprised at myself. I was pretty sure that, that was the first time I'd used the word love about anything other than food since Janet and I had broken up. I hadn't thought about anyone else that way in a while.

Her eyes met mine and I realized that I meant them. Even if I hadn't said them out loud, that was... something major. A good thing, to be sure, but one I wasn't sure I had the time or bandwidth to process with the competition becoming more and more real with every passing challenge.

If I wasn't careful, though, they'd grow into something more than just the crush I was starting to realize wasn't going anywhere anytime soon.

———

Chapter Twenty-Two

ZOE

FERN AND ELLIS LEFT WHEN I STARTED HUNTING through the pantry for something that struck my fancy. They'd been the two winners of today's challenge and had been rewarded with tickets to see *Hadestown* on Broadway. I would be jealous, but they had earned every second of it. Fern had been itching to get out of the hotel and go out on the town a little. This would be perfect for her to be able to do that.

As for me, I was just glad to be back on more known ground. The food-filled-walls of the pantry were wonderfully familiar, offering me so many more options than I would ever have been able to imagine back home. And with better company than I usually had too.

Amelia had followed me into the pantry to peruse the shelves of the refrigerator beside me. I was glad, because it gave me the chance to look at her without her noticing. Sometime between the interview and now, she'd pulled her honey-colored curls into a practical bun that almost managed to constrain them. Her makeup, complete with a winged eyeliner as sharp as our knives, was stunning.

She had an intense focus when it came to food that I hadn't seen anywhere else, almost as if there was nothing in the world as important to her. It was beautiful. And when she turned it on me, it made my heart stutter.

Desperate for a distraction, I opened the fridge and chose a protein at random. I needed to say something relevant so that I wouldn't blurt something out that I would regret later; something having to do with how I wanted to play with her hair.

"What do you think of some salmon? I feel like I've been eating nothing but meat-heavy dishes since I got here."

"Salmon sounds tasty. How were you thinking of making it?"

"Oh." I hadn't gotten that far. Thinking quickly, I pulled one of my go-to recipes out of my hat. "I was thinking something with a nice cream sauce. Maybe salmon piccata with roasted asparagus and fingerling potatoes?"

She nodded slowly. "It would be pretty fast *and* mean there'd be minimal clean-up, which means we'd have less work to do at the end of the night. That sounds like a plan to me."

She agreed easily. I may have pulled it out of my ass, but it sounded delicious, and I was always a fan of doing fewer dishes at the end of the night. Honestly, I probably would have agreed to eat literal garbage at that moment if it meant I got to spend more time with her. And from what I had tasted so far, she cooked well.

"What do you need? Salmon, capers, lemon, asparagus…what else?"

She started grabbing what she listed, placing it carefully in a basket, then waited for me to add to it. I pulled out a bag of fingerling potatoes and a clove of garlic and gestured towards the kitchen.

"After you, my lady." She gave me a fake curtsy and made her way back into the kitchen. I watched her go, enjoying every sway of her wide hips and round ass as she went.

———

———

As Amelia had said, the preparation process for this dish was simple. We talked about everything and nothing as we washed and halved the small potatoes, washed and trimmed the asparagus, and threw them on a sheet pan together. I drizzled olive oil over the tops and seasoned them liberally with the salt, pepper, and garlic. Now all they needed to do was bake while I seared the salmon.

At least, that had been the plan. Before I had even closed the oven door, she had put a cast iron skillet on the heat and was gently scoring the salmon skin.

I put my hands on my hips and faked a frown. "What, are you in charge now? I thought I was cooking dinner."

She looked up with surprise and her light brown eyebrows drew together with concern. "I thought I was helping. You were dealing with the potatoes, so I was going to start the salmon."

"Uh huh." I let a teasing lilt creep into my voice. "Next you'll tell me that you definitely weren't going to take over making the cream sauce too."

She set her knife down with a quiet clink. "I was, but I didn't think it'd be a problem. We're cooking together. You shouldn't have to do all the work."

My frown twisted into a smile. "That's sweet of you, but I think there's another reason behind it. Wanna tell me?"

She started pulling her bottom lip between her teeth in that way she had that said that she was thinking hard about something. In a flash, I wondered what it would feel like for her to do that with *my* bottom lip, or to pull her lip into my mouth. A shiver ran through me despite the heat of the kitchen.

When she finally spoke again, her voice was quiet and tentative, as if she wasn't sure how to feel about the words she was saying. "This is what you meant about me taking control of things, isn't it?"

I nodded, still smiling, and an apology tumbled out of her beautiful mouth before I could take another breath. The words crashed over each other, as if this was the worst thing she'd ever done until I pressed a light hand to her mouth.

"Shhhh. I'm not upset. I thought it was funny. Did you really not realize you were doing it?"

She shook her head beneath my hand and I laughed. It tickled. I pulled my hand away and found her smiling that small, self-conscious smile.

"You really are something," I told her.

"If by something, you mean an accidental control freak, then yes. I sure am something," she joked, blowing a curl out of her eyes. It was a self-conscious motion, one that drew me closer to her.

"I mean that you are beautiful and strong and an excellent chef," I told her seriously. "And a little bit of a control freak."

She laughed and the curl fell right back into her eyes. Without thinking, I tucked it back behind her ear, trailing my fingers down her silken cheek to her jaw. The motion meant there were a few mere inches between our faces. She seemed to realize it at the same time and her breath caught. I wanted to kiss her so desperately, I couldn't stop looking at her lips, the way they glistened from the way she licked them. When I finally pulled my gaze away from them, our eyes locked, only for hers to flick down to my own lips. She seemed as transfixed as I was, and it made me wonder.

Did that mean…? Did she want to kiss me too? Could I risk it?

From the way she looked at me, her pupils a little bit dilated, to the way every movement of my fingertips left slight goosebumps along her jaw, the signals were all there. I needed to risk it. If I didn't, I knew I would spend the rest of my life regretting it.

"Amelia, can I kiss you?" My voice was breathless.

Her only answer was to lean into me, pressing her lips to mine. It was sweet and gentle, until I slid my hand from her jaw to the back of her head, pulling her as close as I possibly could. She twined her arms around my waist and I melted into her, deepening the kiss. For a moment, it felt like everything was right in the world.

Her embrace filled me with the warmth that was something like the feeling a favorite cardigan mixed with the electricity of a lightning strike, sending sweet, liquid desire straight through me. It was everything that I hadn't realized I wanted, and I never wanted to let it go. I never wanted to let *her* go. And that was terrifying.

———

Chapter Twenty-Three

AMELIA

Two days and a challenge that I'd barely scraped through later, I *still* couldn't stop thinking about that kiss. The way Zoe had tasted, the sounds she'd made...I couldn't get them out of my head.

If I was being honest with myself, it was the reason I'd struggled through today's challenge. The judges had asked us to make savory pies, something that normally would have been simple. But I'd been so preoccupied with thinking about the woman standing in front of me —and watching the sway of her hips as she worked— that my dough's proportions had been completely wrong and I'd burnt the bottom crust while it baked. Having to restart everything halfway through the challenge had put me at a severe disadvantage.

The elimination had been a trio of sweet pies, and since Zoe didn't seem to have any trouble concentrating, she didn't have to take part in it. That also made it easier for me to focus on the pies and on the elimination. Denise had deemed my pies sheer perfection, and I'd been so relieved I'd almost fainted.

Shauna had been the one eliminated today, leaving the entire suite a little bit heartbroken. I'd eaten a salad for dinner quietly on my own and taken myself straight to bed hoping to sleep well. Two hours later, I still lay in the slightly too soft bed tossing and turning. Despite having had plenty of time to reflect as I stared at the popcorn ceiling, I couldn't decide what exactly was keeping me awake; thinking about the kiss and the ensuing desire that thrummed through me, the hunger that growled through my belly after a hard day's work, and not enough food, or anger at how badly I had botched the challenge.

It was probably a combination of all three making a muddle of my senses the way I'd muddled the spice blend in my vegetable curry pie.

I could hear people, probably Jada and Fern, talking in the living room, so going out to make myself something else to eat was out of the question. So was going to the hotel's gym to punch things that wouldn't get me in trouble for breaking. I couldn't stand the thought of being near other people right now. So, there was only one thing I could do to improve my mood and make it easier to sleep.

If I were at home, I'd search for something naughty to get my wheels turning, turn off the lights, and light a softly scented candle and then settle in for a good time. However, I couldn't light a candle in a hotel room and I didn't have access to the internet to find the good stuff. Luckily, I had an excellent imagination and plenty of practice to figure out what worked well for me.

I rolled over one more time so I was facing the nightstand. Pushing myself up on my elbow, I slid open the drawer with one hand and grabbed a small bottle of lube and my go-to magic wand. Laying them on the bed,

I reached over again, flipped the lights off and turned on the ocean sounds app that I had subscribed to for years. It was the perfect blend of sounds to block out just enough of the outside world and keep the rest of the world from hearing exactly what I was doing without being too loud to focus on the heat of the blood racing through my veins.

Laying back, I closed my eyes and remembered the way Zoe's body had pressed to mine, how she'd stood on her tip toes to bring her sweet, cupid's bow lips to mine. The thoughts sent a shiver of desire all the way through me. As I imagined what might have come next, I could feel my nipples press against the thin nightgown I wore.

I reached down and popped the top three buttons, releasing my breasts and allowing me to give them the attention that I dreamt Zoe might give them if she were here. A series of tugs and caresses sent even more heat to my core. I reached one hand down further, popping buttons as I went until the only thing attaching the gown to my body was the loose cap sleeves. I dipped into the wetness that had pooled between my legs, moaning as my fingers spread it to my clit. The ghost of contact felt *delicious*, and I couldn't wait for more of it. I rubbed my clit with firm, gentle fingers until it pulsed in a quiet plea for more contact, more pressure, more *everything*. And I wasn't in the practice of denying myself the pleasure I needed. Especially when I had such a glorious memory to work from.

Without hesitation, I slicked the silicon head of the wand with lube and replaced my fingers with the tool. The vibrations were almost everything I needed— almost. Dipping my other hand still lower, I plunged two fingers into my core and stroked myself to sweet, shuddering climax. The aftershocks rocked through me until finally, I was sated.

It didn't calm my nerves completely, but it did make it a lot easier for me to figure out exactly what I needed. I needed to eat something substantial and I needed to talk to Zoe. She was probably asleep by now, I realized, but it needed to happen soon. I could figure out what exactly I wanted to say to her while I made myself something to eat and then sleep on it. Easy enough, right?

———

———

Wrong. The instant I rounded the corner, I could see that all of the lights were on in the practice suite and I could already guess exactly who was in there. So much for getting time to sort through my feelings. I took a deep breath and let myself in, expecting to find her nestled into one of the chairs with a cookbook or three, taking notes so furiously that I could barely see her fingers move across her phone screen.

Instead, I found her wrists deep in some sort of sticky dough that smelled divine; nutmeg and cinnamon and maybe almonds filled the air. I watched her knead the dough as I let the door click shut behind me. She looked up and a slow, bright smile spread across her face as her gaze met mine. It very nearly stopped my heart.

"I was hoping you'd show up. I haven't been able to stop thinking about you all night." Her voice was as soft as the dough she worked, but it was like music to my ears.

"I couldn't stop, either," I admitted. That was the

truth, though she didn't need to know I'd been masturbating to the memory of her.

She waved me over with a floury hand, and a smile to match hers spread across my face. I crossed the room to reach the kitchen, inhaling the intense scents as they mixed with her gentle lavender scent. I wrapped an arm around her waist. She leaned into me and I pressed a gentle kiss to her forehead.

"What are you making? It smells amazing."

"Everybody was so sad about Shauna going home that I wanted to make something to cheer us all up. So, I'm trying to make vegan cinnamon rolls."

That explained the almond smell. Almond milk had a very distinct scent, especially when mixed with that particular blend of spices. Like the dough she turned back to, the gesture was incredibly sweet, but when I told her so, she brushed the compliment, and me, aside.

"I needed something to do," she said with a shrug. "Plus, I've been wanting to do more vegan stuff for the blog. Y'all make for pretty good guinea pigs."

"Oink, oink," I teased. It made her laugh, just as I'd intended. "Mind if I make myself something to eat? That salad didn't go very far."

"Of course, I don't mind. I'd offer you these, but, well, it wouldn't taste very good. These are about ready for their first rise anyway."

Whether vegan or standard, cinnamon buns were made of an enriched dough that needed to prove for a while in order to become the delicious, puffy things we all loved to eat. Right now, they would just taste like glop. Nothing at all like the redemption I was hoping for.

"Are you hungry? I can make enough for you too."

"Oh, no thank you. I've got mini-quiches in the oven, already, to make it warm enough to prove these."

I crouched, peering into the oven, only to see a tray of muffin-sized quiches bubbling away. I rose with a laugh. "Well, good thing I wasn't planning on doing quiche, then. I had something a little spicier in mind."

She raised a floury eyebrow at me in silent question. I didn't answer, walking into the pantry with a basket instead.

Popping open the fridge, I grabbed one of each of the herbs and vegetables I'd need, then grabbed a potato, the spices, and the olive oil.

Zoe was rolling her dough out into a long rectangle when I walked back out. She looked up as she grabbed the bowl of spiced butter and both eyebrows shot up.

"You're making vegetable curry? Again? I thought you'd want a break from it, since it went so badly this morning."

I washed everything briskly, drying them on a paper towel. She brushed the cinnamon onto the dough with a gentle motion.

"Well, usually when I make it, it's delicious. I mean, you had it when we did the stuffed peppers. When it's done well, it's the best thing in the world. This morning…it was terrible. I need to remind myself that I can actually cook it well. Even when you're distracting me."

"Me? I didn't even speak to you on set this morning. How could I have distracted you?"

"You didn't have to say anything," I told her gently. "You were working right in front of me. I'm a strong woman, but nothing in the world could have kept me from watching your hips sway. Especially after last night."

Her mouth dropped open and a gentle blush crept up her cheeks. "I didn't realize…I mean, I'm not much to look at. Not like you, with your curves and your beautiful hair."

I blinked. She couldn't be serious. Had she *seen* herself? "You're joking, right?"

She shook her head and focused on rolling her dough into the perfect bun shape. I almost couldn't believe that she believed it. Almost. I suspected this as another thought process her husband had, had a hand in corrupting. I set my knives down and stepped towards her.

"Zoe, look at me." My voice was quiet, but I poured every ounce of sincerity I had into it. She didn't, instead speaking in the quietest voice I had ever heard from her.

"There's no meat on my bones, nothing for anyone to grab hold of and enjoy. I need to be...better."

Her breath caught when I gently tugged her hands away from the pastry, and when her eyes met mine, they were wide and a little watery.

"I don't know who told you, you weren't absolutely stunning, but they clearly didn't have the taste God gave a goat."

She laughed a little, but a single tear trickled down her cheek, tracking through the flour and dripping onto our joined hands.

"I mean it. You are one of the most beautiful people I have ever met, both inside and out. Even if you don't believe me right away...I hope you'll know that I believe it."

Another tear fell, then another. "That's the kindest thing anyone's ever said to me. Thank you."

A fat, hot tear streaked down my cheek, and I realized that not every tear hitting our hands was hers. I released one of her hands and wiped tears off of my own cheeks with a shaky breath.

When had I started crying? I wondered but didn't let myself think too hard about it.

"I meant every word. And maybe someday, if you'll let me, I'll show you just how much I mean it." I pressed a kiss to her other hand and let it drop before I took a step back. From slightly further away, I let my gaze travel the length of her body, lingering on her wide hips and waist for a few seconds longer than was appropriate. Her eyes widened just a little when she saw exactly what I meant in my eyes.

A little more of my earlier desire, hot and strong, thrummed through me, just in time for the oven's timer to beep and for my stomach to growl.

Zoe let out a shaky laugh and took another step back.

"The food summons us. Let's get you something to eat."

She turned back to the oven and it was as if a spell had broken, sapping a little bit of the heat out of the room even as the oven door opened. I hoped that she'd heard my words, and that maybe someday she'd take me up on my offer.

———

Chapter Twenty-Four

ZOE

EVERYTHING ABOUT TONIGHT HAD BEEN UNEXPECTED. From Shauna being eliminated, to the way I hadn't been able to stop thinking about kissing Amelia again, to the words she'd said while she'd held my flour-covered hands.

I pulled the muffin tray out of the oven and set it off to the side before going back to my cinnamon rolls.

I wasn't sure how she could think that I was one of the most beautiful women she'd ever seen, especially when I compared myself to her tall, plump, and muscular frame with luscious honey-colored curls. She was the kind of person who drew everyone's eye the instant she walked in the room with sheer force of will. And I knew she loved it. Me? I usually did my best to keep the world's eyes off of me except when I was absolutely prepared for them.

That was part of why I'd started cooking. It gave me a reason to stay out of the line of sight for parties my parents threw and then I'd just learned that I was good at it, so I just stuck with it. That left me wondering what

Amelia's story was. I knew she'd been schooled in it, but that couldn't have been the beginning.

So, I turned and asked before I could talk myself out of it. She laughed while she finished dicing the sweet potato.

"My dad was always the cook in our house, but when I was a teenager, he kept getting asked to teach and supervise study-abroad programs. After three months of eating takeout and fast food, even my mom was willing to give cooking a shot. Except she was objectively terrible. I begged her for weeks to let me sign up for cooking classes and, after she accidentally gave us both food poisoning, she gave in. And now here I am, almost twenty years later."

I laughed with her, but I couldn't help feeling a little sad.

"That sounds like a huge responsibility for a kid. I can't imagine being in charge of making sure my whole house had something to eat at such a young age."

"I mean, it's not like I had that much on my plate," she explained with a shrug. "My parents had a woman who came in to clean twice a week, and I got to invite my friends over whenever I wanted. Plus, it brought me here and I got to meet you, so I can't complain too much."

She punctuated the last sentence with a smile that warmed me through. I smiled back, knowing I was blushing. It seemed like I was always blushing.

"I'm glad it brought you here." The words, soft and simple, slipped out before I could stop them.

"Me too. How about you? What brought you here?"

I frowned, trying to think about how much of the truth I could really tell her. Trying to decide how much I wanted to tell her.

"Well, you know that I live with my mother, right?" She nodded, and I continued. "Well, she's very persuasive."

She laughed. "Having met you, I can only imagine what your mother is like."

I stuck my tongue out at her, making her laugh harder. I told her how I'd gotten into cooking, and how Mama had talked me into trying something for myself.

"I honestly still can't believe I'm here," I admitted. "It just seems so surreal."

"I keep expecting to wake up and realize it was all a dream," Amelia agreed. "Or a nightmare, given how badly I did this morning."

I pressed a floury hand to her bare upper arm and squeezed it in a way I hoped was comforting. "Hey, you're still here and still fighting. That's what counts."

"I won't be for long if I keep cooking like that. I gotta pull it together. I need to stop letting myself get distracted. " She pressed her lips together as she stared at the onions and garlic browning in the pan in front of her. I couldn't help but feel a pang of guilt, knowing that I was the reason she'd done so poorly.

"I'm sorry," I murmured, dropping my gaze.

Amelia turned her frown on me. "For what?"

"You know…for making you do so badly this morning. For kissing you and distracting you."

"You are not responsible for my libido or my cooking," she reminded me lightly. "I made poor choices and paid for them this morning."

I dropped my hand from her arm in a flash as if it had burned me. Her words certainly had. Taking a step back, I felt tears start to well in my eyes again as thoughts raced through my mind.

She regrets the kiss. She must not have meant what she said earlier. I should have known better than to allow it to even start to sink in. I should never have put myself out there.

"Zoe? Are you okay?" Amelia's voice was soft, concerned. I didn't look up, focusing on the floral pattern on her black Crocs. "Did...did I say something snotty again?"

I tried to smile and laugh, but a sob came out instead, and suddenly she was so much closer than I'd expected.

"Zoe, what's wrong?"

"If you didn't like me, you could have just said so," I whispered through the tears. "It wouldn't have broken my heart."

My current actions belied that, though. I couldn't believe I was crying again already, especially over something so silly as being rejected kindly.

I was so focused on my own pain that it surprised me when a gentle finger touched the bottom of my chin, lifting it so that I was forced to look her in the eye. My breath caught in my throat as our eyes met. I wasn't sure if it was because of the pure sincerity on her face or because of the sobs pulling themselves from my chest.

"Zoe, that was not my way of telling you I didn't like you. I didn't mean that *you* were the poor choice. I'm so sorry. What I meant was that letting myself get super horny and fuck up my cooking was a poor choice. You are not responsible for either my libido or my cooking, ever, but especially not in a competition. You understand me?"

I tried to nod, but her finger was still holding my chin firmly in place. I took a deep breath instead, filling myself with the scent of citrus and curry. It was a surprisingly pleasant combination.

"Now, if you don't mind, I'd like to show you exactly how much I like you. May I?"

I couldn't stop my tongue from darting out to lick my lower lip as I smiled just a little bit. The finger under my chin fell away, but I barely had time to feel its loss before her strong, callused hands cupped my face and her lips gently pressed to mine.

For the second time in as many days, I felt like I had been lifted off my feet and caught in the eye of a hurricane. As she kissed me, the whole rest of the world fell away. Nothing else in the room mattered. The only thing I could focus on was her; the way she cradled me so softly but still crushing me into her, as if she couldn't get close enough to me.

The feeling was mutual. I couldn't remember ever feeling quite this wrapped up in anyone before. When we finally broke apart, we were both out of breath.

"Do you believe me now?" She didn't let go of my face, only rested her forehead against mine as our chests heaved. I nodded again, pressing a soft kiss to the inside of her palm before meeting her eyes again.

"I want you too," I murmured.

A smile burst like the sun onto her face and she kissed me again. It was less gentle this time. She moved one hand down my neck and down my body until she gripped one of my hips. The pressure was absolutely enticing and I never wanted her to stop touching me.

Something from the world outside of her body, her touch, was drawing my attention, though. I pulled away with a gasp when I realized what it was—burnt food.

"Amelia, your curry!"

She let go of me with a curse, swinging back to the oven. She let out a miserable moan and covered her face with her hands. I looked around her to find that all of the herbs, onions, and garlic in the pan had blackened.

"Not again," she moaned. "I swear I can make a decent curry!"

She looked back at me, and I tried to resist the urge to laugh. She had the biggest puppy dog eyes I'd ever seen, as if she needed me to know that she was capable of it.

"I know, honey," I reassured her, biting back a smile. "We've already made one together, remember? It was delicious."

She furrowed her brow at me, as if she was trying to remember what I was talking about. I watched as she figured it out, her face clearing like the sky after a storm. "Oh yeah, the stuffed pepper!"

I shook my head, smiling at her. "I think the curry is not meant to be today. How about a quiche instead? I've got plenty."

She took the pan off of the stove and dumped its contents into the trashcan. With a sigh, she grabbed the muffin tray and then dropped it with a cry. "Shit! Hot!"

It slammed onto the counter as I watched in horror. She rushed back to the sink and flipped the water on, letting out a string of curses.

"Oh my god! Are you okay?"

"Yeah, I'm just fucking stupid," she grumbled. "I forgot that pan had just come out of the oven."

"Here, let me see." I reached for her hand and she pulled it out from under the tap. I cradled it gently in my own smaller, equally callused hands. "It doesn't look too bad."

"Still hurts like a bitch, though."

I could imagine. A thick red line showed on her palm, but it didn't look like the skin had blistered.

"Yeah, but with some aloe you'll be all right. You got lucky." I murmured, tracing my finger in a line adjacent to the burn. Then I realized the double entendre of what I'd said and blushed. "Not like that."

That brought a smile back to her face. "If this burn was from sex with you, it would have been totally worth it. Though, I would ask you if you were trying to sabotage me."

Her tone was teasing. I pressed a kiss to her palm to hide the way my blush deepened at her words. She winced at the contact, and I pulled away.

"There's gotta be a first aid kit in here somewhere. Let's get you some aloe vera and a bandage to keep that safe."

She made a move as if to start searching herself, but I wasn't about to let her do that. "Nuh-uh. You sit your ass at the barstool and have something to eat. I can't have you fainting on me because you're starving."

"I won't faint," she objected. "I'm a big girl. I can handle myself."

"And yet you burned your hand because you picked up a tray that had been in the oven for nearly half an hour," I pointed out. "Sit down, use a spatula and get yourself a quiche."

She raised her eyebrows at me but grabbed a spatula from the countertop and levered one of the small pies from the tray before planting herself in the barstool I'd pointed out.

Across the countertop, I opened each of the drawers until I found the simple red and white plastic container in one.

"Aha! Found it!" I raised it above my head in victory.

I looked up and found Amelia looking startled, pie dough crumbles on her lips and chin. I pointed them out, trying, and failing, to keep a straight face. Laughter burst out of me while she licked the crumbs away.

I popped open the container and pulled out the travel sized bottle of aloe vera gel and a wrap bandage. Walking around the counter, I held them out.

"Give me your hand and I'll dress that for you."

"Can I finish my pie first? This is *delicious*."

I laughed again. "Of course. No rush. We've still got a while until the cinnamon buns are proved and I can go back to the room."

Sitting at the stool next to her, I grabbed a pie for myself. The chorizo, roasted red peppers, and onions inside it, created a divine aroma. When I bit into it, I realized she was right.

"Holy shit, that's good." I blurted; my mouth still full.

Amelia nodded vigorously as she ate the last bite of her quiche. "These are even better than the one I made last week. What's your recipe?"

"Oh, it's up on the blog. Not with this pie crust, though. This is an almond flour crust with some smoked paprika in it, so it's lower carb and delicious. Yay for being keto-friendly!" I did jazz hands around the pie with a laugh.

She raised an eyebrow at me, even as she frowned. "You're in this competition and doing keto? That seems... antithetical."

I realized then that I'd been cooking two things that were for specialized diets. She must think I ran a diet blog.

"Oh no. I don't do diets at all. It just makes for good blog content; everyone's googling everything all the time. My policy has always been that if it's unhealthy and tastes good, that's totally fine. If it's both somewhat healthy and tastes good, then it's all the better. And this? Is amazing."

Her brow smoothed out as I spoke. "That it is. This crust should definitely go on the blog. It's delicious. I was worried for a minute there that you were gonna be one of those diet blogs."

"What, you didn't look me up?" I put a hand to my chest, pretending to be offended. "My feelings are hurt."

She laughed. "I think you'll survive it. You hated me before we got here. Why would I look you up?"

"You didn't scope out the competition? That doesn't sound like you."

Amelia shrugged. "I figured I'd be able to learn everything I needed about everyone else when I got here. And I was right."

Now it was my turn to shrug. I stuffed the last bite into my mouth and chewed. I had looked her up. She was surprisingly easy to find online. Not that I was going to tell her that now.

"Give me your hand," I asked, changing the topic again. "You need to treat that."

For possibly the first time ever, she didn't argue with me. She laid her hand palm up on the counter and waited. The slightly raised burn mark was even redder now. I winced in sympathy.

Quickly, I opened the cap of the gel and squirted it into her palm. She flinched. "That's cold!"

"I think that's the point," I laughed. "Do you want to spread it yourself or do you want me to do it?"

"Go ahead."

With a gentle finger, I spread the gel along the burn, then wiped the excess off on the bottom of my chef jacket. Grabbing the wrap bandage, I began to loop it around her palm.

"Tell me if this is too tight," I murmured. She nodded without speaking, simply watching me work until her hand was swathed in it.

I pushed a butterfly clasp into the fabric to keep it together and pressed a kiss right on top. Pulling back, I smiled. "There you go! It'll be good as new by morning."

"Thank you," she murmured. She leaned forward, tugging me to her, and kissed me again. It was soft and sweet with just a hint of heat, like the taste of the chorizo that lingered on her lips.

I pulled back with a smile. "You're welcome."

We sat there in the quiet, smiling at each other for what felt like hours, just holding hands. It was wonderful. And then my brain kicked in, asking all kinds of questions that I had no answers to. The questions I'd been asking myself all day. I had had the guts to kiss her first and then…what now?

Aren't we here to compete? What does all of this kissing mean? It seemed so right last night, but what are we doing?

There was only one thing to do; actually have a conversation about it.

"You know, we never did talk about what this is," I pointed out, waving my free hand between us both. "Or how we want to handle whatever it is."

She looked up at me, pulling her bottom lip between her teeth. Her eyes were serious. "I was hoping for some more time to figure out what I wanted to say, but…it feels like now's the right time to talk about it. What do you *want* this to be?"

"Well, I burst into tears when I thought you didn't like me and regretted our kiss, so I think that puts my cards on the table." My tone was light, belying the tension I felt thrumming through my body.

"I really like you," she said slowly, her eyes never

leaving mine. "But I also really, *really* want to win this competition. I really don't want to jeopardize that."

I nodded. "I don't want to do anything to put us in danger here, either, but…it's been a long time since I felt this way about anyone; even longer since anyone cared for me the way you seem to. I don't want to miss out on this, either."

She was quiet, clearly thinking about what she said before it left her mouth. I was anxious. This was the most honest I'd been with anyone in a very long time. I had never felt so naked before, even when I'd actually been in the nude in front of people.

"I think…," she paused, then nodded. "I think we should just get to know each other and see where this takes us for now. I mean, we don't have to make any life-changing decisions right now, you know?"

"That sounds smart," I replied. I wasn't sure how I felt about it. Getting to know each other.

"And by get to know each other, I mean spend more time together and kissing and stuff. Cause I'd really like to do some more kissing. With you."

I bit my lip, trying to keep the smile from my face. For once, she wasn't quite sure about what she was saying. She was a little more awkward than I'd ever seen her, and I liked it. I liked *her*.

"I think I'd like that." And so, I kissed her, with no intention of stopping anytime soon.

———

———

When the cinnamon buns were finished proving and we'd pulled ourselves away from each other, we made our way back to our suite in comfortable silence, finding the shared space empty.

It felt even emptier knowing that Shauna was gone. Her door was open, showing a perfectly made bed and all of the lights off. It made sense that even though the producers made you pack all of your things in a very short amount of time, she'd leave it looking like she'd barely been here at all. Peeking in, I saw that her drawers were all closed and the trash bags were all tied up and left next to the door, leaving almost no work for the maids to do. She was just that thoughtful.

Shaking my head, I walked to the fridge and put the tray on the bottom shelf. When I closed the door and straightened, I found Amelia right behind me. I might have found her presence intimidating before, but now... it was electrifying.

"May I kiss you goodnight?" Her voice was quiet, but it rang in the stillness of the room around us. The question took my breath away. I nodded, taking one step towards her and then another. Before I knew it, I was standing on my tip toes and wrapping my arms around her neck. Her breath caught. She wrapped an arm around my waist, strong and sure. Then she kissed me and the whole world disappeared.

We could have been there for mere seconds or hours. I couldn't have said. I instantly missed the contact when we broke apart.

"Sweet dreams," she whispered, then turned and made her way towards her room. I watched her walk away, knowing that my dreams would be full of her. And I would enjoy them.

———

Chapter Twenty-Five

ZOE

THE MORNING CAME EARLY, BUT I DIDN'T CARE. FOR THE first time in this competition, I made it to the kitchen and got the cinnamon buns baking before Amelia came out to start the coffee. In fact, she was the last person to join us in the kitchen.

When I pulled the cinnamon buns out of the oven, the ensuing squeals of delight from everyone were the perfect thing to start my morning with. I was pleased with how they had turned out; light and fluffy despite it being vegan. Once again, my research had done well for me. Even Fern was impressed, which meant I was happy to call it a complete success.

Amelia tried to be subtle as she watched me from across the kitchen, but it wasn't working. No matter where I was, I could feel the heat of her gaze on my body. It warmed me to the core and caught the others' attention.

They were shooting glances between us and then at each other, as if they were trying to figure out what had changed. Honestly, if they hadn't noticed, I would be concerned about their powers of observation. It felt almost like an invisible string wrapped around me and drew me closer to her with every movement I made. I had forgotten how good this could feel, the beginning of a relationship. One thing was for sure, I wasn't going to let a minute of it go to waste.

"Good morning." I nudged her with my shoulder as I poured myself a second cup of coffee.

She rocked her hip into me with a soft smile that drew my eyes to her lush mouth. "Thank you for breakfast. You've got cinnamon on your cheek, you know. Just there."

Her eyes flicked to my lips, then back up to my eyes, waiting for me to give her permission to touch me. I could feel it like she already had, so I nodded. She reached up a gentle hand and brushed her thumb against my cheek. It took a huge effort for me not to turn my face and kiss her, especially when her thumb ghosted over my bottom lip.

A loud smack of flesh on the marble countertop jolted me out of my reverie and out of Amelia's grip. Fern's voice followed it, filling the suite with a triumphant whoop. "I knew it! I told you they were doing a little something! Didn't I tell you?"

Heat rose to my cheeks like flame from a lighter and Jada laughed quietly. "Yeah, you did. How do you want your money? Venmo or cash?"

Fern let loose the witchiest cackle I had ever heard. "You don't owe me anything, Jada girl. I just like to be right. And judging by the colors they're turning, I am extremely right."

"Wait, is that why we got cinnamon rolls this morning?" Jada asked. "Are these 'thanks for last night' cinnamon rolls? Will we survive them?"

"Oh, come on. Even if they were 'thanks for last night cinnamon rolls, you wouldn't die." Amelia rolled her eyes, then looked at me and added something. "Not that they are! They're just cinnamon rolls. Delicious ones."

She stuffed a bite into her mouth and I bit back a cackle of my own.

"I'm personally not against cinnamon rolls with a message, as long as they're vegan. And these...these are excellent," Fern declared. "You've got to give me your recipe."

"You'll have to hold that thought," Jada pointed out as all of our phones started to sound the alarm we were now very familiar with. "It's time to head downstairs for today's challenge."

———

———

I groaned when we opened the door and walked onto the set. It was set up much like our very first challenge, except there were two kitchens instead of three. It was going to be yet another team challenge.

I was worried, and I wasn't the only one. I heard worried murmurs break out among the rest of the competitors as we made our way to the front.

Judging by the shit-eating grins on the judges faces as we lined up at the front of the room, today was going to be more difficult than anything we'd done so far in the competition.

"Good evening, contestants. We have quite the challenge for you today."

———

"Today, we'd like you to come up with a four dish menu: one appetizer, two entrees, and a dessert. You get to choose what four dishes you create, but it must be a cohesive menu."

"You will be operating in two teams of four, led by the two people who won yesterday's challenge, Jada and Fern. Ladies, you will be picking your own teams today, so choose wisely."

Jada's first pick was Breonna, which I had expected. They worked well together. Fern's first pick was me, which was surprising. Jade picked Amelia next, which made my heart sink. We had been competing against each other this whole time, but every time we'd done a team or partnered competition, we'd been together. And we'd done well.

I wondered what this would mean for the competition, and what it would mean for our relationship when one of us inevitably lost to the other. I didn't have time to think too hard about it, though. Fern picked Ellis and Liam to finish out our team, putting Annika and Ronald on Jada's. We were pretty evenly matched, from what I knew of all of our cooking.

"The team captain will be in charge of the menu, so I hope you all like taking directions. You have free reign of the pantry, so you can use as many or as few ingredients as you like. That can be a blessing or a curse, so make sure to edit yourselves while you plan your menus."

They gave us half an hour to figure out the menus, shop, and learn how to cook them, if needed. Then we would have an hour to prep and cook them. We needed to make four plates of each; one for each of the judges and one for the cameras, as usual. I wondered what Fern would choose for us to cook, but it sounded fairly straightforward, even if we were likely to be cooking things that we were less familiar with.

There had to be a catch. I wasn't sure what it was going to be, but I knew there was going to be something coming back to bite us in the ass very soon.

———

Chapter Twenty-Six

AMELIA

I SHOULD HAVE KNOWN THERE WAS GOING TO BE A CATCH. Jada had worked with our skills to plan out a beautiful Cajun menu that I had been so excited about, and we'd gotten the best possible ingredients to make it delicious.

Except the instant we'd come back with our ingredients, the judges had told us what that catch was; we were cooking the menu planned out by the other team. And because Fern had planned out the menu, every single item was vegan.

We were in trouble, and we all knew it. Jada's face was pinched as she read through the short sheet of instructions we'd gotten before looking up at the rest of us.

"Okay, y'all, here's what we've got to work with."

The menu that Fern had created was a relatively sparse one, which made it that much harder. Simpler food meant there were less places for us to hide our inexperience. And we were very inexperienced when it came to vegan food.

The appetizer was a pea puree and ricotta agnolotti

served with sautéed peas and a vegan beurre blanc. The two appetizers were a whole head of cauliflower roasted in a miso glaze and a portobello stir fry, both of which would be easy enough. Finishing the menu was a coconut chocolate mousse that really sounded delicious.

The appetizer was going to be the most difficult of them all. The filling was easy enough to make, but vegan pasta dough was so much more complicated than standard pasta. If you didn't know the right proportion of olive oil to flour, or you didn't add the right amount of semolina flour, you were in trouble.

And I did not know either. Looking at the rest of the team's concerned faces, I wasn't the only one. We all sat there staring at each other, at a loss for where to start. So, I did what I do best—took charge.

"Does anyone know how to make vegan pasta?"

As everyone shook their heads, I knew that we were in for the hardest challenge we'd ever had.

———

———

When the challenge ended, the judges were pissed. I couldn't blame them for it. The plates that we had put up had been...well, disappointing was the kindest word I could think to use.

Despite our best efforts, the pasta dough was crumbly, the beurre blanc was gloopy and the cauliflower looked like shit. Literally. The portobello stir fry was so under seasoned, that Denise spit it out. At least the coconut chocolate mousse looked and tasted good. It wasn't nearly enough to save us though.

I could *smell* how perfectly Fern's team had cooked

everything on their menu from the other side of the room. The smoked oyster dip was as smooth as it could be, and they had even made their own French bread to serve with it. I hadn't even thought that was possible within the time limit, but they had done it and done it well.

It was very obvious who the winner of this challenge was, and it was not us. The judges confirmed it with little fanfare, then sent us all into the pantry so that the kitchen could be rearranged for the elimination challenge.

I could only imagine what that was going to be. It would be a wonder if I survived it, given how difficult the morning had been. I needed to get my head in the game if I was going to have a chance.

Portia was handing out water bottles to everyone when I plunked myself down in one of the barstools we usually used while we watched eliminations. They gave me a small smile when she pressed one into my hands, and it felt like they was pitying me. It stung, as did my eyes as they began to water.

In an instant, Zoe was by my side. "What's wrong? Did you hurt your burn?"

"What?" I stared at her in utter confusion before I remembered how I'd burned my hand the night before. "No, my hand's fine. It didn't even need a wrap. I'm just *pissed.*"

"You'll get through it, Amelia. You know you're one of the best chefs here. The judges know that."

Everyone was looking at me now and I hated it. The tears welling in my eyes began to roll down my face, showing just how upset I was. By the time I spoke, they were so thick that I couldn't see the sympathy on anyone's face.

"I haven't shown it the last two challenges. I'm in the bottom again, and it's all my fault. I'm not good enough." To my horror, the last words came out in a choked sob. Of course, my body would choose to do everything it could to make this moment as mortifying as physically possible. What other option could there be?

"Breathe, Amelia. It's gonna be all right." Zoe rubbed her hand in small circles on my back. It was soothing, but it didn't stop me from continuing to cry.

I hated every bit of it; the way my skin flushed in splotches, the way my eyes always itched afterward, even the sheer amount of liquid I lost from it. I could count on one hand the number of times I'd cried in the last five years and I hated that I was doing it now. As always, once I got started, it was almost impossible to make myself stop.

You're making a fool of yourself, my inner voice told me. *You're too childish to be here when you can't even show the skills the judges are looking for. Just pull it together and go out of the competition with your head held high. Do Chef Ian proud.*

I tried to fight back against that voice, reminding it that I wasn't here entirely on my own, that I was one of four people in the bottom. Just because I'd been in the elimination last time didn't mean that I would be going home this time.

I couldn't have said how long I cried. It could have been just a few minutes, it could have been thirty, but when I finally pulled myself together, everyone else had started talking amongst themselves. Except for Zoe. She had pulled a barstool up next to me and was sitting with her hand on my back. Her voice was soft as she murmured soft encouragements that sounded a lot like what I had been trying to convince myself of.

Maybe, just maybe, if she believed in me, then I had

done something right after all. If she believed in me, maybe I could handle whatever the judges threw at us next.

———

Chapter Twenty-Seven

ZOE

ANXIOUS DIDN'T BEGIN TO DESCRIBE HOW I FELT AS I watched Amelia walk back onto the set with the rest of her former team. I hadn't envied them the meal they'd had to prepare. It would have been hard for our team to complete the menu that Fern had planned, even with her help. For them to do it with almost no instruction would have been nearly impossible.

It had almost killed me to see her break down like that. She was always so confident, so in control of herself and everything around her. To see her lose that control was more difficult than I had imagined it would be.

I thought that my presence had been helpful earlier, but I wished I could do more. There was nothing I could do to help her with this challenge, though. She needed to do this on her own, to prove to herself that she was good enough to be here.

I could only pray that she would make it through to the next challenge, that she would fight through whatever was going on in her head. That would be the real battle, the way it always was for me.

But I believed in her. Even when the judges informed us all that the challenge would be one remarkably similar to the one they'd just bombed; cooking vegan food.

This time, though, they had free reign to cook whatever they wanted as long as it didn't include any animal products and it could be cooked in forty-five minutes. It made it a little bit easier for everyone, allowing them to play to their own strengths more than the other challenge had.

Hopefully, she would fare better with a little bit more creative freedom. I know I would have.

As everyone dashed past us into the pantry, I thought about what I would make if I were taking part in the challenge. Probably something that was originally intended to be vegan.

It was relatively easy to substitute in different kinds of non-dairy milk or egg substitutes and make a dish taste okay, but anyone eating it was bound to compare it to the original instead of eating it for what it was.

Besides, there were plenty of foods that had been relegated to sides in recent years. Not everything needed meat to be delicious. I turned recipes over in my head, but I kept coming back to the ones I'd learned from the Ethiopian cookbook. Most of the ones that had caught my eye were vegetarian to start with, so it would be easy to make them vegan. The breakfast bowl I'd made was already vegan, but that wasn't quite what the judges were looking for. They wanted something that would surprise them, and they wanted what they called one stunning portion.

———

All of the competitors had gone in very different directions, judging by the ingredients in their baskets. For once, the judges didn't have to shush us while they made their way back to their kitchens. Fern sat on one side of me, while Ellis and Jada sat on the other side.

Almost in unison, we craned our necks to see what everyone carried. Jada, who was closest to where we sat, had some kind of tofu, tons of seasonings, vegetables, and rice. At a guess, I'd say she was probably making a vegan stir fry, but you could never tell with her. She had a magical ability to turn the smallest batch of ingredients into something magnificent.

As she began working, I looked to Amelia. I couldn't see anything in Amelia's basket but summer vegetables, herbs, olive oil, and quinoa. My brain short circuited as I tried to figure out what she was going to make. French cooking was her go-to in all of our challenges, like the quiches we had both made since we'd arrived.

My first thought was a ratatouille, but there wasn't nearly enough time to do that well. Soups like that needed to be cooked low and slow, or in a pressure cooker. It would be easier with a smaller portion, but there was only so thin you could chop vegetables before they lost their texture. She hadn't picked out a pressure cooker, only a ring mold and some simple round white plates. I had honestly no clue what she was doing.

Ronald was making something with jackfruit, corn tortillas, and several kinds of beans. I wasn't sure what that would be either. Annika was on the far side of the bench, so it was hard to get a close look at her ingredients, but it looked like she planned to make some kind of pastry from the hopefully vegan butter, sugar, and flour I could see from my barstool.

I clasped my hands tightly in my lap, hoping that the

cameras wouldn't catch just how nervous I was about how this challenge was going to turn out. Looking around at the rest of my team, everyone else seemed to share my feelings.

Jada was repeatedly running her hands down her pants, while Ellis's knee bounced up and down faster than I'd thought possible for an old man. Fern picked determinedly at her fingernails, turning her formerly well-shaped nails into shreds in her lap as the challenge went on. At least, if the cameras did pick up on the anxiety, I wouldn't be the only one showing it. That was going to be the best I could do for now.

———

Chapter Twenty-Eight

AMELIA

I COULDN'T STOP MYSELF FROM BOUNCING ON MY TOES AS I waited for the judges to try the food we had each put in front of them.

I was proud of what I'd created, but looking at the other dishes on the bench had me worried that I hadn't done enough.

There was one plate of delicious looking jackfruit tacos with a chipotle corn salsa and guacamole from Ronald, one incredibly messy looking caramelized onion and mushroom galette from Annika, a creole tofu stir fry from Jada that had my mouth watering, and a tian with quinoa from me. The colorful summer vegetables created a veritable rainbow against the neutral beige grain, with a sprinkle of vegan "goat" cheese on the top.

I thought I might have made a better dish than Annika, but there was no telling until the judges tasted them. If I'd seasoned my dish poorly, or hers was particularly great despite its looks... I really could going home. It was all down to this one plate. But it really was an excellent plate. If I did go home, it would be because I had done my best during the challenge. That is something that I could be proud of, no matter what the outcome was.

Thinking that made it easier for me to take a deep breath. Taking a deep breath made it easier for me to think critically about what the judges were saying to the other contestants.

They were thrilled with the first dish, crediting Ronald for making every element of his dish and infusing it with flavor, even down to the tortilla. It was a complex dish and I was impressed. Their comments were a lot less kind when it came to the galette. The hand-formed pie was intended to be a little bit messy, but the onions and mushrooms were falling out the sides of the undercooked-looking pastry. If I had turned that in during culinary school, I'd have failed. And it appeared that, despite the mushrooms and onions being tasty, Annika had failed this challenge.

That helped me to breathe almost normally as they tasted Jada's stir fry beside me.

"Unusual, but delicious," Bryce declared. "I never would have put cajun seasonings in a stir fry, but it works really well here."

Denise asked her a few questions about why she had chosen particular spices, but then gave her the firm nod and small smile that made it clear she had liked the dish. Before now, only one person had been given that approval — Zoe. I desperately wanted that approval, though I couldn't say why. I wanted it almost as much as I wanted to win this competition. But then it was my turn to be judged and there was no more time to think about it.

"Well, this is certainly colorful. Why don't you tell us what you made?"

I described the dish, what I'd put into the tomato sauce that held it all together, and then fell quiet to let them eat in peace.

"What made you choose to make such a simple dish?" Denise asked while Bryce took the first bite. He made an appreciative sound, then stepped aside so she could try it.

"I wanted to make something delicious, and this was something I knew," I told them, feeling the nerves flutter in my stomach, and knowing I was about to start babbling. "Normally, I'd serve it with real goat cheese or feta for a little extra funk to offset the sweetness of the tomato, but I think the vegan cheese works well. Uh, as long as you don't have a nut allergy."

"I can assure you that neither of them do," Nathan muttered. It was almost too soft for me to hear clearly, but Denise choked on her bite of food. Bryce turned away, like he had heard something behind him, but it looked like he was trying to hide laughter. I wondered briefly what that was about, but I didn't care enough to think too hard about it. All I could think about was the food.

Denise gained her composure first, clearing her throat after she swallowed the food. Nathan stepped in to take his bite, then stepped back so they were all in line across the bench from me.

Please let it be enough, I prayed. *Let me be good enough.*

They stood there in silence for a moment, until a wide smile broke onto Denise's face. My jaw dropped. I'd never seen such a strong showing of emotion on her face.

"*That* was an excellent bite of food. You have to give me your recipe so I can try and recreate it."

I must be dreaming, I thought woozily. *There's no way this is real. My food couldn't have put that expression on her face. Could it?*

"Not a chance! I want the recipe and we can't both have it," Bryce challenged, tossing me a wink. The familiar expression was grounding, somehow. That was something I'd have to process later. I had to come up with a response right now.

"I-I would be happy to give it to you," I stammered. "Both of you?"

"I suppose we can share it," Denise said acidly, glaring at her fellow judge. "Our cooking styles are certainly different enough."

That was an understatement, but it didn't matter. The judges took a few steps towards the middle of the bench, letting the camera crew get footage of them while they discussed the dishes we'd made.

After a few minutes, they straightened and turned back to look at us. They'd made their decision. I tried to force myself to look normal, which meant a neutral expression. That was something I'd gotten used to over the years, and it had never steered me wrong.

"You all did much better on this task individually than you did in the group challenge earlier, which impressed us," Denise said crisply. "However, this is still a competition, and if you can't take the heat, you have to leave the kitchen. And there is one chef here who we believe has gone as far as they can."

I sucked in a breath when Bryce announced that Annika was the one leaving. She nodded firmly, as if she had known it was her time to go. Her fingers shook as she unpinned the logo pin from her chef's jacket, the only sign she gave of how upset she had to be. She hugged Ronald, who had been her suitemate and thanked the judges for the opportunity before walking out of the room. The gaggle of cameras followed after her like ducklings after their mother.

As soon as they were gone, my knees went weak. I had to lean on the bench for support as the realization struck me that I wasn't going to be heading back to North Carolina tonight. I got to have another chance.

That was how Zoe found me, leaning over the food the judges had asked for and trying desperately to take deep breaths.

"What on earth did you put in your food to make the judges love it so much? I can't believe they asked for your recipe! Can I try some?"

Her voice was excited, but I wasn't sure I could form words right now, so I just nodded. She pulled a tasting spoon off of the bench behind us and dug in while I tried to pull myself together. I could tell when she tasted it though, because she moaned. That sound, so guttural and pleasured, made me whip my head up to see that she had thrown hers back.

"Amelia, this is fucking *amazing*." She took another bite and moaned again. The sound sent lightning racing through my veins. It took everything in me not to pull her tight against me and kiss her until I made her make that sound and so many more.

When she pulled her head back up, her eyes locked with mine, dark and shining in the bright light of the set. God, she was beautiful. She seemed to read my feelings from the flush I could feel creeping up my neck and how I couldn't stop my lips from parting when she licked some tomato sauce off of her bottom lip.

She set her fork down and grabbed my hand

"Let's get out of here," she whispered. I had never heard a better idea in my life, so I did the only thing I could - followed her out of the room.

"Do you two want to join us for dinner in the practice suite?" Jada called as we walked past the rest of the contestants. "We were gonna make eggplant lasagna."

"No, thank you!" Zoe called over her shoulder. "We have other plans. Breakfast tomorrow, though?"

Jada shrugged. "Sounds good. See you in the morning."

And that was that. We were home free for whatever was about to happen. All we had to do was get somewhere private.

———

Chapter Twenty-Nine

ZOE

I WANTED HER SO MUCH THAT I COULD BARELY KEEP MY hands off of her. The glass walls of the elevator were the only thing keeping me from undoing the buttons on Amelia's chef one by one and running my hands over her beautiful frame. Instead, I was forced to stand a reasonable distance away from her and think. And she was the only thing on my mind.

If it were possible to fuck someone with only your eyes, I would be doing it right now. So much tension and heat filled the air that I was surprised that either of us could breathe.

I wanted her. I wanted her -needed her- to know that I wanted her, wanted to be enveloped in her scent and her arms and everything about her. I may have kissed her thinking that it was just a little bit romantic. But it was more than that. It was a thought that I had been dancing around for longer than I had realized - maybe even from that first moment in that hotel line.

Watching her cook, watching her make a dish that was so good that the judges wanted it, watching her nearly fall apart, it had crystallized something in my brain. Then taking those two bites of the tian? It had been nearly orgasmic. Literally.

When the doors opened on our floor, she took a single step out of the elevator and held out her hand. Without a second thought, I took it. She led me back to our suite, swinging the door open with her empty hand and guiding me through as if it were the most natural thing in the world. I loved that confidence.

The instant the door closed behind us, her mouth was on mine, hot and wet and insistent. It was everything I wanted - almost. We fumbled our way to her bedroom, never parting for longer than a short, sweet breath before we came back together. I couldn't get enough of her, and apparently, she couldn't get enough of me. That was sweeter than any dessert either of us could have created.

It gave me the confidence to keep her moving towards the bed, to trail kisses along the line of her jaw down towards the peter pan collar of her chef's jacket. When I reached it, I looked up, meeting her eyes for the first time since we'd stepped out of the elevator. The heat in them made my heart stutter.

"Can I see you?" I drew my finger tantalizingly down the row of buttons of her jacket. When she nodded, I teased my fingers beneath the lowest cloth button, grazing the soft gray t-shirt beneath it as I popped it free. I loved the way her rounded belly pressed into my hands more and more as I worked my way up the jacket. When all of the buttons were free, I slid my hands up her neck until I cupped her apple cheeks in my palms. I kissed her again, harder this time. She kissed me back, letting her jacket slide to the carpeted floor with a shrug.

Her t-shirt fit her perfectly, hugging her stomach and boobs like an old friend and hanging just to the edge of her black pants. I couldn't get enough of her. I wanted to see more of her, to run my hands over her bare skin, to caress her most sensitive places. So I got to work, pushing my hands under her shirt and rocking against her as I moved it up her torso. Every point of contact felt like lightning through my veins, and I still wanted more. When she pulled the shirt over her head, it revealed a bright magenta front-clasping sports bra. With a quick twist of one wrist, I unclasped it before the shirt hit the floor. It followed soon after, leaving her bare from the waist up. I couldn't leave her like this. I wanted, needed to see all of her.

Her stomach hung over the waistline of her pants, swinging a little with each heaving breath. It was mesmerizing as I freed her lower half from her pants and underwear that matched the sports bra. But what really took my breath away was the sight of her fully nude body. I had to lean back to take her in fully, and she took the opportunity to kick her clothes away, then shifted so she was slightly steadier on her feet.

"You are so beautiful," I murmured, unable to take my eyes off of her. The lights brightened her pale skin until parts of her were luminescent. No matter where I looked, she was even more stunning than I could have imagined, with stretch marks like painted ivy on her thighs and stomach culminating in a well trimmed bush in the center.

She pulled me toward her with one hand, using the other to make quick work of my own jacket and tank top until I was standing there in pants and a lavender lace bralette. A clever flick of her wrist and she'd undone the button on my pants, letting them slip down my legs.

Thank God I wore matching panties today, I thought. *At least she'll think I have my shit together.*

"Look who's talking? You look great in lace." Her voice was a growl that made the warmth racing through me pool in the lace she was such a fan of. I stepped out of them without hesitation, bringing myself chest to chest with the most beautiful woman I'd ever seen. And we were both fully nude.

I wondered if she could feel my heart pounding a hummingbird's rhythm against her chest, but then she ran her hand from my neck to my waist, caressing each breast gently as she went. It sent shivers through me until she pulled me into her with another series of kisses.

"You cannot even begin to imagine all the things I want to do to you," she murmured between kisses, taking control of the situation and guiding me towards the bed.

I pulled back when we hit the mattress, biting my lip. She paused in her attentions, looking concerned. "What is it? Is something wrong?"

There wasn't, not exactly. But a thought had been niggling at the back of my mind the whole time. I needed to say something.

"Before we go any further... there's something I should tell you," I whispered, hoping this wouldn't ruin any chance of a happy ending we might have - tonight or in the future.

She held her breath, waiting for me to continue. I closed my eyes, working up the nerve to say what I needed to.

"I've never done this - anything - with a woman before," I blurted out before I could stop myself. "I have basically no idea what I'm doing."

She let out her breath in a whoosh and I opened my eyes. I found her looking at me with eyes so soft that I almost couldn't hold them. She ran her hands up my body until she cupped my cheeks, forcing me to look at her.

"Zoe, I don't care if you've never slept with anyone. I don't care if you've slept with everybody in North Carolina. Do you want to sleep with me right now?"

I nodded, unable to make myself speak, to say *yes, more than anything*. She beamed at me, as if she could hear it anyway.

"Then that's all that matters to me." She punctuated it with one kiss that led to another that led to me crawling into her lap, desperate for more contact with her.

I straddled one of her thighs, nearly moaning when it came into contact with my slick center and my clit. I didn't hold back my sound of joy when my thigh met her core and I realized that she was just as wet as I was.

Making a woman hot was a new experience for me and one that I wanted to learn more about with her.

"Can you tell me what you like? I want to make you happy."

Her eyes darkened just a fraction. "How about I show you instead?"

I nodded again, and she flipped me onto my back in one swift movement that knocked the breath out of me. I wanted more, and when she kissed me, I arched into her until our entire body's connected. It was everything I wanted, but still I needed more.

I didnt have to wait long. She kissed her way down my jaw and neckline until she reached my breasts. Cupping each one gently, she pressed a gentle kiss to one nipple and then the other. It felt so good it was almost overwhelming.

She released one breast and snaked her hand down between my thighs, pressing a gentle finger to my clit at the same time as she sucked my nipple into her mouth. I couldn't keep myself from crying out in pleasure.

"Yeah? You like that, baby?"

She put a little more pressure on both, making me squirm under her touch. When I cried out again, she didn't give me a reprieve. Instead, she let her fingers drift toward my aching pussy and the wetness there. "I can tell how much you like it. Do you want more?"

"Yes," I panted. "Please."

She grinned wickedly and gave me exactly what I'd asked for, talking to me about exactly how she liked it, and how she was going to make me come. I had been interested in dirty talk before, but with her voice in my ear... God, it was everything I never realized I needed.

When first one and then another finger worked into my pussy and headed right for my g-spot, I couldn't stop myself from bucking into her hand. She worked my breast and my pussy, barely relenting until I came apart around her fingers with shuddering gasps. She withdrew her hand, and somehow, I felt emptier than ever before. Lifting her slick fingers to her mouth, she sucked them in. I couldn't take my eyes off of the way her mouth worked around them as she licked them clean.

"That's the way I like it when I'm on my own," she whispered roughly. "When I'm with a partner, I love it when she uses her mouth. Would you like me to show you how I like that?"

I shook my head, knowing that another orgasm like that would knock me out. I wanted to give her the gift that she'd given me, and more if she'd allow me.

"I- I would like to try it," I said when I found my voice. "Would you let me try?"

Her grin widened, showing off her pearlescent teeth. "I would love that."

"Then come sit on my face, baby. Let me make you feel good."

I slid down so that I was almost flat on the pillows, giving her space to do as I'd asked. She crawled on hands and knees, kissing her way back up my body until she reached my mouth. I could feel desire pooling in me again as I tasted the way the musk of what could only be my orgasm mixed with her mouth.

She drew away slightly, a little bit of insecurity flickering on her face. "You sure you want me on top? I'm a little heavy."

I pulled her face down to mine and kissed her, hoping I could show her how much I wanted her. "I want all of you all over me. Let me taste you. Please?"

She nodded, moving into position with a few sultry movements. I could feel the bed shake as she grabbed the rim of the headboard and pulled herself up into a sitting position. Then she lowered herself slightly so all I could see was her thighs, stomach and soaking wet pussy. I was fairly certain I'd never been happier than I was in this moment.

I pressed a wet kiss to one thigh, then the other, noticing that she was slightly tense around me.

"Does this feel good?" I asked, letting my breath wash over her most sensitive places. She moaned, and I knew it did.

"Tell me how you like it, Amelia. Please?" I had a guess at where to start - tracing my lips and tongue along her stretch marks until I reached her core. Before she answered me, she was panting above me, like what I was doing was working.

"Clit. Please." It wasn't hard to locate the bud. I swirled my tongue around it, reveling in the taste of her. I was rewarded by her pushing down into my face a little bit more. Getting the hint, I sucked it into my mouth gently to continue its treatment. She gasped and shook ever so slightly until I released her. She moaned, moving closer again. I snaked my arm around her thigh until I could reach her pussy with my fingers.

I inserted one, and then a second just like she had for me, then brought my mouth back to her clit. When I curled my fingers to find her g-spot, she rocked against my face. It felt like heaven, the way her body enveloped me. Soon, too soon, her pussy was clenching with an orgasm above me, crying my name. I didn't stop until her shudders had stilled and her muscles relaxed around me. I panted against her pussy until she shifted her leg, lifting it so that she was no longer on top of me.

When I'd caught my breath, I looked over at her, at how flushed she was from. Biting my lip, I asked the question that I'd been wondering the whole time. "Was that good for you?"

She smiled, and it was so blissful that it was like the sun shone from her face. "That was *wonderful* for me."

And when she kissed me, I had no doubt that it was true.

———

Chapter Thirty

AMELIA

THE FIRST THOUGHT I HAD WHEN I WOKE UP WAS THAT my bed was very warm. Then I remembered why.

Zoe had one of her legs curled over my hip, and the rest of her body was pressed firmly against mine, with her face nestled into my shoulder. With every breath, she came even closer in all the best places. I nuzzled into it, loving every inch of the contact and still craving more.

As if sensing my wakefulness, she yawned and stretched. She wrapped her arm around my waist and it felt more wonderful than almost anything I could imagine.

Almost. After last night, I didn't need to imagine how wonderful other things with Zoe felt. I knew exactly how good sex with her could be, but this was only the beginning.

"Good morning," she murmured. Her voice was rough with sleep, but her lips were soft and sweet when she pressed them to my bare shoulder. It left goosebumps in its wake, but not for long. She stretched gently again, pulling her arm from underneath my pillow. I hadn't even realized it was there until it was gone. She pushed herself up beside me, and I turned to look at her. The sight of her took my breath away.

The thin tank top she had slipped into before bed had shifted so that neither of her breasts were actually covered, and a soft smile tugged at her lips as she looked at me. She was beautiful.

"Good morning to you, too," I murmured, smiling as I pushed myself up on an elbow. I was suddenly intensely anxious. *Did I drool? Had I snored? What if I'd farted in my sleep?*

"That is the first good night's sleep that I've had since I left home," Zoe said with a yawn so large that her jaw creaked. "Thank you."

"No, Thank *you*," I echoed. "Last night was amazing. How do you feel?"

"I feel..." She thought about it for only a moment before she spoke again. "Perfect."

"I'm glad." With those few words, all of the nerves melted away into a warm and bubbly feeling that I never wanted to go away. There very well may have been literal stars in my eyes as I looked at her.

Leaning forward, I pressed my lips to hers and when she kissed me back, it felt like coming home.

I couldn't have said how long we stayed there, wrapped up in each other, but as usual, it wasn't long enough. Both of our alarms went off at the same time, and she sighed into my mouth.

"Do we have to get up? We don't even have a challenge today." Each word fluttered her lips against mine, like the softest butterfly's wings.

"You're the one who told Jada we would join her for breakfast," I reminded her with a laugh. "You wanna make excuses?"

Now she pulled away, pouting. "I guess not... I just don't want to lose this."

"Don't worry. You can always come back. Or I can come to you. I'm flexible."

"Yeah, you are." She waggled her eyebrows at me, giggling.

I swatted her hip playfully. "You haven't seen anything yet. Come back and see what I can do."

"Oh, I will be."

———

I watched from the bed as piece by piece, she put her clothes back on until she almost looked like she'd just walked out of last night's challenge. There was no hiding the wrinkles that came from spending a night on the floor, but I thought it added to her sex appeal.

With a few quiet steps, Zoe opened the door and poked her head out of the room. She immediately pulled it back in. "Amelia. We have a problem."

At the panicked whisper, I sat up fully. The comforter slid down my bare curves to pool at my hips. "What? What's wrong?"

"Look!" She gestured wildly at the door. I pulled the comforter away and slid out of bed, padding to the door without a word. When I looked into the hall, I saw the problem immediately.

She had to get from my room at the front of the hall near the kitchen, past Jada's room and into her own room without anyone noticing she was back in the same clothes she had worn the day before. That wouldn't normally be an issue - it was only like 15 feet total and usually, we were awake well before anyone else.

Today, however, Jada and Fern were already sitting at

the kitchen counter chattering away about their plans for the day, and they had a clear view of the hallway from where they were.

"Well, this is something I hadn't thought through," I said drily. I closed the door and leaned back against the cool wood, trying to think. I hadn't had to sneak a girl out of my bedroom since high school, and even then, it hadn't been that hard. I'd just had to distract Mother with something around the house.

But I couldn't go out there to distract them. Not yet, anyway. I desperately needed a shower, or with one sniff, they would both be able to tell exactly what we had spent the night doing. I turned away from the door and caught my reflection in the mirror with a grimace. They wouldn't even need the sniff. My normally messy curly hair had turned into a rat's nest, and I was completely naked.

"Any chance you can just make a run for it super quietly while they aren't looking?"

She shook her head. "Fern is facing straight down the hallway. She'd see me no matter how quiet I was - especially if she could tell I was trying to sneak out. She's a grandma - she's used to kids causing trouble."

Hang on, I caught myself thinking. *Why* are *we sneaking around?*

"It's not like they can do anything to us," I reminded her. We're grown adults and everything was consensual. Plus, they already figured out we were dating. Or whatever it is we're doing."

"Dating seems like a good word for it," she said with a smirk. "But I don't know that I want everyone to know exactly what we were doing all night. I'd much rather keep it just between us. At least for right now."

I could understand that. It was still really new. But it

didn't make things easy for us right now. I thought about it for a few seconds, then decided on an easy plan.

"Okay, how about this? You stay here. I'll throw on some pajamas and pretend I'm going to wake you up, let myself into your room, then grab some clothes and bring them back for you. Simple."

She stared at me as if I'd grown a second head. "You want to go and pick out an outfit for me? You don't find that weird?"

I raised an eyebrow. "This whole situation is weird. But I don't hear any other ideas. You have a better one?"

She thought it over, wrinkling her lips and moving her mouth side to side. "I guess not. Don't go snooping too hard, though. A girl's gotta have some secrets."

I laughed. "Okay. Tell me what you want to wear and I'll bring it back here."

———

I managed to get down to her room, get the clothes and get back to the room without catching Jada and Fern's notice. She probably would have gotten by on her own without an issue, but oh well. We were here now.

When I closed the door behind me, I found her sitting on the bed on a video call. She looked up at me and smiled before looking back to her phone.

"I've gotta go, Vi I've got plans for breakfast, but Grandma's gonna call me later and we'll talk then, okay?"

"Bye Mama. I love you."

"I love you, too, sweetheart… and she just dropped the phone," Zoe laughed as she pressed the phone screen to end the call. "Some things never change."

"Short attention span?" I asked.

"I feel like she's all right for a three year old," she said indulgently. "But when she's done with something, she's done and that's it. Did they see you coming back with the clothes?"

"As far as I could tell, they didn't notice me at all. I got everything you asked for." I dropped my bundle onto the bed next to her. She rifled through the bundle, double checking to make sure I had what she needed. She nodded.

"Thank you. Um, do you mind if I shower? I smell."

I grinned. "I had the same idea. Mind if I join you?"

A smile spread slowly across her face. She bit her lip and for once, it wasn't an anxious gesture. Pure lust glinted in her eyes, and I loved it.

"Mind? That is exactly what I had planned." She pushed herself off the bed and sauntered towards the shower, dropping her clothes as she went. I didn't need to be asked twice.

———

We finally made it to the kitchen for breakfast just as the first round of vegan french toast made it onto Jada's plate.

"Oh, so the lovebirds decided to join us after all," Jada teased. "We thought you two might not make it out of bed this morning. How hungry are you two?"

Zoe and I traded guilty glances. We had completely forgotten to eat last night.

"Very," I said, and she nodded her agreement.

"Good, cause we made plenty," Fern informed us. "You two get to do the dishes, though."

"That's fair," Zoe laughed. "So what did we miss last night?"

"Ronald and Ellis got into an argument about the right kind of spices to use in lasagna. Jada and I completely ignored them and made it delicious, and we all talked about the things we miss from home."

"Oh, so the usual," I laughed. Amelia shook her head. "Those two will make anything into an argument. It's just silly."

It was fun to watch the two men tease each other. Ronald and Ellis had extremely different styles of cooking and they weren't shy about debating which was better. Really, they were both excellent and they knew it. They just liked to argue for the sake of arguing.

Jada plunked a plate full of french toast in front of me, then another in front of Zoe a moment later. When Jada sat down with her own plate, we lapsed into a comfortable silence. It was only interrupted by requests to pass the powdered sugar or the blueberry syrup that Fern loved so much. Eventually, we all finished eating and Fern pointed her sticky fork at me.

"So I've got a question for you two," she said around her last mouthful, waving the fork between us. As if we needed her to make clear who she meant. "We're three quarters of the way through this thing. What are y'all gonna do when it's over for one of you, or both of you?"

The french toast suddenly didn't taste as sweet in my mouth. I looked over at Zoe, my mouth curling into a frown. Her eyebrows wrinkled in thought.

"We, uh, haven't talked about that."

I had consciously avoided bringing it up, to be specific. It was a thorny question. Everything about our relationship was so new that I hadn't wanted to spoil it with the cold, hard light of reality just yet.

Fern squinted at me like my answer was useless, then

turned her questions to Zoe. She looked like a deer in headlights under the older woman's hard stare.

"You might want to think about talking about it, and fast. This relationship could get you kicked out of the competition if the producers find out. And you two are *not* subtle."

"Now hang on just a second," I interrupted. "I feel like this is a conversation that needs to happen between the two of us. Besides, we've both been in the top of most of these challenges. They aren't gonna kick us out for having a little fun outside their purview."

"You think so?" Jada asked, sipping her coffee as if to say that she definitely didn't. "We all signed a contract that said there was to be no sexual contact between contestants. You don't think that's gonna be a problem?"

Sucking in a breath, I tried to force myself to think clearly. I remembered the meeting with Angela at the beginning of the competition where she had laid out all of the rules for us, telling us that breaking these rules would be a liability for the network. We might have just literally fucked ourselves over.

"Are you going to tell them?" A harsh tone crept into my voice. I didn't think either of them would, but maybe I had misjudged them. This was a competition, after all. A quarter of a million dollars would be good motivator for anyone to try and get the competition out on a technicality.

"No, I'm not," Jada replied. "But you two aren't exactly the most subtle. It took us, what, two days to figure out what was going on? Even if one of you two has what it takes to win this competition, only one person can win. What's that gonna do to your relationship if Amelia wins over you, Zoe? Or vice versa?"

I took another deep breath and opened my mouth to answer, but Zoe spoke first. "I came to this competition knowing I might lose. If I do, then so be it. We'll figure out the relationship from there. If one of us is $250,000 richer when it's time to do that, it'll be a nicer life for everybody."

Fern flattened her lips into a line as she looked between us. "Look, you are both adults and I'm not your mother. You're both capable of making your own choices here. I don't want to belabor the point. I just want to make sure you're thinking about the potential issues here."

Even if I hadn't been before, I certainly would be thinking about them now. And judging by the look on Zoe's face, she would be, too. I could only hope that she'd decide that we were worth it. That I was worth it.

———

Chapter Thirty-One

ZOE

I BREATHED A SIGH OF RELIEF WHEN WE WALKED IN TO find that things were in their standard single person set up. Thank God for that. I had gotten out unscathed in team challenges thus far in the competition, but it would be so nice to be moving forward on my own merits in another challenge.

My fingers itched with the desire to know exactly what we were going to be cooking today. I hoped it wouldn't be another baking challenge, because I knew my competitors would beat the pants off of me if it were. And not in the way that Amelia and I had become so good at over the last few days.

When we lined up at the front, I realized for the first time that Fern had not joined us. Instead, she made her way to the barstools, apparently free from participating in this challenge as the leader of the winning team. That would make this challenge even harder.

The judges walked onto set carrying a large bag between them that made me of Santa's toy bag.

"What on earth do you think is in there?" Jada

murmured. Ronald and Amelia both shrugged.

"Maybe our ingredients? Though they'd get awful squashed being toted around like that, wouldn't they?" Ellis wondered aloud.

"Your guess is as good as mine," I replied before being shushed by one of the camera operators. The judges had reached us and plunked the bag down on the dais.

Bryce rubbed his hands together in apparent glee.

"Good evening, contestants. Tonight, we thought we'd have a little bit of fun with how we choose the ingredients for the first challenge. Instead of having a basket full of mystery ingredients, you are going to pick your own ingredients."

No one spoke. We all knew there would be a twist. We'd been in this competition for way too long to think for even a moment they'd just let us pick whatever ingredients we wanted. Especially with the wicked grins that filled both of the male judge's faces.

"You will be limited to six ingredients from the pantry while you cook. You will also be limited in which ingredients you can choose based on what you pull out of this bag." Nathan gave the bag a light kick to punctuate his statement.

What on Earth is in that bag?

I didn't have to wonder for long, because Denise opened the bag and reached in. When her hand emerged, it held a square Scrabble-like tile with the letter R stamped on it in the show's trademark font.

"Your six ingredients must start with the six letters you pull out of this bag. It must be one dish. And it must be done in thirty minutes."

Oof. These challenges were getting harder and harder.

"Who wants to be the first victim- I mean contestant- to pick from our bag of tricks?"

We all looked at each other with nerves written all over our faces. Trepidation was making my heart flutter, but I was ready to get started. With a deep breath, I stepped forward.

"I can go first."

I didn't need to turn around to see that everyone's eyes were on me as I stepped onto the dais and pulled my first letter out of the bag. The T emblazoned on it made me feel a little bit better. There were tons of foods that started with T. That wouldn't be an issue.

I reached in again, brushing my hand against several before finding one that felt right. When I pulled it out, I groaned. It was a W, which would whittle down my choices a little further. Trying not to focus on what I would make, I kept going until I'd pulled out all

"T, W, D, H, P and R," Nathan announced. "Do you have any idea what you are going to make, Zoe?"

I shook my head, which felt like it was spinning from all of the ingredients I kept listing. I was so focused on trying to figure out what the hell I was going to cook that I didn't hear Amelia go up immediately after me and choose her own letters.

Tuna, wasabi, dandelion green, hummus, panko, rotini, hazelnut, porcini mushrooms, demarara sugar, wood ear mushrooms, duck… there were too many possibilities.

Bryce's voice interrupted my thoughts when he shared Amelia's letters - C, D, L, L, B, and T.

She walked back down to where we stood, barely looking at the cameras. I could tell she was already deep in thought by the way the laugh lines around her mouth deepened and her nose wrinkled. She was beautiful that way. For just a moment, I didn't care about the challenge. I could have stared at her for days, memorizing her every expression until I knew them as well as I knew my own daughter's.

The others chose their own letters, throwing them into a similar spiraling thought process while the judges let us have a little time to think about our dishes.

Okay, I told myself. *Decision time. Pick a protein. How about fish? Tilapia or tuna would be easy to pack flavor into… especially with a brush of dijon mustard. Oh, and a horseradish walnut crust. Maybe some parmesan?*

I counted the letters out on my fingers. That left me with the letter R, which would be easy. Rice would be the perfect base for the encrusted filet, soaking up all of the flavor from the fish without overpowering it or disappearing.

By the time the judges said go, I had the whole thing planned out in my head. Now I just had to cook it — and cook it well.

———

It was my turn to be directly behind Amelia while I cooked, and suddenly, I understood why she'd had such trouble with the challenge after our first kiss.

After learning exactly how beautiful she was in and out of her clothes, and how powerful her body was, it was incredibly difficult to focus on anything except the things we'd spent the last week doing. But I had to do a good job today. We were too far along in this competition for me to screw up my dish because a hot ass was moving around in front of me.

The first thing I had to do was get the pressure cooker heating. I had decided on rice for my 'R' food, but I was taking a risk by using arborio rice to make risotto. One of the producers had approved it, but because I didn't have any letters left to grab a box of stock, I was going to have to make my own fish stock to go with the tilapia.

Luckily, the box full of staples and seasonings that lived on every station had almost everything I needed to make a good stock for myself. It didn't have the vegetables, but that was manageable. All I had to do was season it well and put enough fish in to give it the flavor it needed.

Next, I had to focus on filleting the whole tilapia in front of me. The more I had worked on filleting things, the better I had gotten at it, but I still couldn't do it well without focusing on my cuts. I had to make sure they were as perfect as they could be as I cut the firm flesh away from the bones, and then trimmed the skin away from the other side. Then I did the same for three other fish, making sure I had the right amount for the dish.

Once that was done, I skinned the rest of the fish, tossing the head, bones and remaining flesh into the pressure cooker with a little bit of water. I added the seasonings - bay leaves, fennel, star anise, garlic, salt and pepper, and got it cooking. Five minutes at high pressure, five minutes of natural depressurization, and it would be perfectly flavored just in time to strain it and cook the risotto in the instant pot.

Please God let me have timed this right.

Then, all I would have to do was create four portions from the beautiful fish and cook it while the risotto cooked. And so I did.

With speed and precision, I brushed the tilapia with a liberal coating of dijon mustard, hoping it would counteract the naturally muddy flavor of the fish, then added salt, pepper, thyme and the crushed walnuts.

And then the judges showed up.

"There doesn't seem to be a whole lot going on here at your station," Denise noted with mild reproach. "You've only got 15 minutes left and nothing out here. Are you doing okay on time?

I would have been offended, except she was right. Aside from the cast iron pan heating the olive oil and the pressure cooker, there wasn't anything on the stove. I could see over Amelia's frame that her dish looked to be a lot more labor intensive than mine was - she had what looked like every single Asian vegetable out on her bench, and it smelled like she was cooking duck. The contrast was pretty stark.

"Well, I'm making my own stock using everything left of the fish, and I'm going to use that to make a risotto."

Denise's eyebrows raised. "You think you can make a risotto in fifteen minutes? A *good* one?"

"I think I can make a good risotto in 10 minutes, with the help of my favorite kitchen tool," I countered, turning the valve on the pressure cooker to make my point. Steam began to pour from it, surprising the judges.

"Can I try your stock?" Bryce asked, changing the topic suddenly when I'd opened the lid. I handed him a tasting spoon with a warning about the heat. He took a sip, then tossed the spoon into the sink without saying a word. Even trying to read his face was useless, the way it always was with the judges.

I'd just have to see what he thought when it came time for the judging. They certainly wouldn't hold back with their opinions. It was what they got paid for, after all. I could only hope that they'd like what they tasted.

———

Chapter Thirty-Two

AMELIA

My coconut milk and duck curry looked and smelled fucking amazing. I wanted to eat it as I waited for the judges to get to me, but that would have defeated the purpose of cooking it for them. And would get me booted from the competition very quickly.

This was the first time in a while that I hadn't felt anxious about the food I'd put up for judgement. I knew this was good. There were a few things I would have loved to add to it, but I was proud of what I'd put forward with the limit of six pantry ingredients and only half an hour.

Unfortunately, I had to wait a while because there were three other people to be judged first. Ronald was up first, and the judges were incredibly harsh with him.

Maybe I should be worried, I thought as they moved on to judge Jada's dish. But no, I knew my food was good. If this was what sent me home, then so be it. Hopefully, it wouldn't.

They were a lot nicer about Jada's food, so maybe Ronald had just had a bad challenge. They both turned to watch when it was Breonna's turn. By the sounds of things, they hated the vegan daikon stir fry that she'd made. She was almost in tears by the time they moved on to my bench.

"Okay, Amelia," Denise said with a sigh. "Tell us what your letters were and what you've made."

Taking a deep breath, I described my dish. "My letters were C, D, L, T, B, and T, and I made a coconut milk duck curry with lemongrass, lychee, broccolini and thai basil."

"Well, it looks delicious," Nathan said, digging a spoon into his still steaming portion. When it passed his lips, I could see him struggling not to moan with delight.

I didn't bother to hide my grin when the other judges tried the food. "Good, huh?"

Bryce's eyes fluttered shut as he tasted it, and Denise couldn't stop the small smile that spread on her face, either.

"That... is amazing," Bryce said. "Third time's the charm with curries for you, huh?"

"I guess so," I laughed. "I'm glad I was finally successful this time."

"The balance on this is perfect between the sweetness of the coconut milk and the sour punch of the lychee," Denise said. "Honestly, I could eat this all day. You should keep making this. We have to keep judging, but save this plate for me. I'm coming back for it."

I was smiling so hard, I thought my cheeks might fall off of my face. "Thank you, Chef. That means a lot."

They walked around my bench, coming around behind me to look at Zoe's bowls. Now that I had attention to spare for it, I looked, too.

It looked like some sort of fish fingers with risotto, which turned out to be accurate. She described it to the judges, and they tasted it with vaguely positive comments about how she'd managed her time, but they didn't have a lot to say about the actual taste of the food. That was worrying.

"We've tasted all of your food, and now, we need to discuss who the winner will be, and whose dishes have put them a little closer to the heat than they're going to be comfortable with."

They walked back to the dais, leaving us to our own devices for the first time since I'd walked onto the set. Breonna had just barely pulled herself together when Jada walked over to rub her back.

"That was tough. Not for you two," Ronald said, nodding to Jada and I, "but the rest of us. They really didn't like our dishes."

"Seriously," Zoe said. "I think they were more impressed with my time management than my actual food."

"At least they didn't completely roast your food," Breonna said, still sniffling. "I'm pretty sure I'm going home tonight."

"Maybe not," Ellis reassured her. "They didn't like Ronald's either."

"That's not comforting, old man," Ronald grumbled, making us all laugh a little.

"Places, everyone!" Angela called, interrupting our laughter. I looked up to see the judges waiting to walk onto the set. It was time for judgement - and finding out who was going home.

———

As soon as we all went back to our stations, the judges began their walk towards us. We all held our breaths as they got into their usual position on the dais.

"We've thought about it and discussed it, and we think that Jada had the best dish this week," Denise announced. "The trio of pastry-wrapped brie parcels showed us just how great she is at making pastry in a time crunch, and the flavor pairings of the jams she made were absolutely delicious."

My heart sank as Jada beamed. I had so wanted to win this challenge to make up for the last few. Especially since they had all liked it so much. The female judge didn't seem to notice, or care if she had.

"Now, unfortunately, we have to send someone home. There were three chefs who made dishes that were not quite up to the level we were expecting tonight. And, we believe that each of them knows who they are." Nathan's voice and face were grave as he looked at all of us. "If you think you belong in the bottom of this challenge, please join us at the front."

I saw Breonna's shoulders straighten as she made her way down to join Ronald. But when Zoe walked past me, I couldn't help sucking in a breath. It made sense, but surely they wouldn't send her home for a meal that was just okay?

Maybe that was just wishful thinking on my part. But, I suddenly realized that I didn't want her to go home. Not without me by her side, a trophy in one of our hands. I wanted to be in this right next to her until the very end. More than that, I didn't want this relationship to end with whatever the end of the competition was.

I was falling in love with her. The thought crystallized like a bad caramel, the only kind I had ever managed to make. And what a time for me to realize it, with the judges debating sending her home.

"Well, we appreciate you all being so forthcoming," Nathan drawled. "Everyone who came down are the ones we chose for the bottom three. What we didn't tell you before this challenge started is that two of you will be going home tonight."

All of gasped in unison. Now I was really worried.

"Zoe, please step forward," Bryce called. My heart sank like a lead balloon as she did so.

Please don't let this be the end for her, I prayed. *Let her make it at least one more round.*

Bryce licked his lips and continued speaking. "We thought it was great that you did your own stock and managed a risotto in the time frame we gave you. However, your pressure cooker did almost all of the work for you. The only thing you cooked yourself was the fish, which we didn't really love. We would have liked to have seen a little more finesse from your dish this far into the competition."

I could almost see her flinch with every sentence Bryce said to her, as if they came with a physical blow. I wanted nothing more than to grab her and reassure her, but the cameras were still focused on her.

"With that being said, the other two dishes here were significantly worse than yours. You may head back to your kitchen."

She tried to hold her head up high as she walked back to her bench, but I could see how much effort it was taking for her not to cry. I caught her gaze as she walked past me, and the sight broke my heart.

The judges were still talking to Breonna and Ronald, telling them exactly what went wrong with their dishes, but I didn't listen. My entire being was focused on Zoe, on the small sobs I could hear from my bench, on the fact that I needed to tell her how I felt before it was too late.

Breonna and Ronald made their way out, saying quick goodbyes to all of us. The cameras followed them out, and I ran to Zoe's side.

Grabbing her hands in both of mine, I pulled her tight against me and kissed her. She melted against me, kissing me back with more force than I expected, only to pull back with a gasp a moment later.

"Amelia, the cameras!" With horror flooding through me, I turned around to find that everyone in the room, from our fellow contestants to the judges to the camera people. All of their mouths hung open in abject shock.

Denise recovered first. She spoke quietly, but her clear voice rang through the silent room. "Well, *that* is something I didn't see coming!"

The room broke out into conversation as I grappled with the reality of what I had just done. The show, our relationship… I might have just destroyed everything we had built together, in one rash moment.

———

Chapter Thirty-Three

ZOE

THIS CHALLENGE HAD GONE FROM BAD TO WORSE IN A matter of minutes. My first thought was to make a run for it. Just leave the set and hide until they forgot everything they'd just seen. Show up at the next challenge like nothing at all had happened.

But I knew that wasn't a possibility. Just like Jada and Fern had warned us about, we had exposed ourselves to a whole lot of hurt with that public kiss, with all of our actions over the last few days. Before I could say anything, Angela, the judges and one of the other producers joined Amelia and I behind my bench.

"I think it's time we had a conversation," Angela said with an obviously fake sugary smile. "You two, come with us."

And so we did. No one said anything as we left the set. Our fingers were still intertwined as we followed the group of people who would decide our fate to the conference room we'd used that very first day. There was no point in letting go, and I took a little bit of comfort in the connection.

They all sat on one side of the large table, leaving Amelia and I alone on the other. The room was so quiet that I was sure that everyone could hear my heart trying to beat its way out of my chest. They stared at us. We stared at them. My mouth went dry with nerves. After what felt like hours, Angela finally broke the silence.

"Well, ladies. Is there something you two would like to talk to us about?"

I cleared my throat, trying to bring some moisture to my mouth. Amelia squeezed my leg under the table, but I couldn't tell if she was trying to comfort me or trying to stop me from answering. When I looked up, she shook her head at me, then started to speak.

"Zoe and I are in a romantic relationship. What else do you need to know?" The question was simple and unassuming. It was like she really wanted to know what they needed to know.

"Were you two together before the show began?" Angela's voice was harsh, angrier than I'd ever heard it.

"No," I answered her. "We met at the audition, then again in the airport shuttle on the way into the city. Our relationship began for real a few days ago."

"You two are aware that the contracts you both signed stipulated that there be no romantic or sexual relationship between yourself and anyone else on the set, are you not?"

"I am aware of that," Amelia said firmly. "However, I do not think that that is something that you can feasibly enforce."

I couldn't hold back a gasp at the words. Neither did the judges. Angela's eyebrows disappeared into her hairline.

"Is that something you agree with, Zoe?"

I had to think about what to say to that. I did agree

with Amelia, but I needed to be more diplomatic about it.

"I think… that we are both consenting adults and our relationship has done nothing to disrupt the filming schedule. I don't see why there should be a policy against a consensual relationship."

"That is a good point," Nathan said. "All of our filming has gone according to plan, and the other competitors have made no complaints about their conduct."

Angela shot him a look that was pure rage. "That doesn't change the fact that they signed a contract saying they wouldn't enter into any kind of non-platonic relationship while in the competition. The policy is the policy, whether they agree with it or not."

"That may be," Denise admitted. "However, you realize that Amelia and Zoe are two of the top competitors, right? If you send them home, you are absolutely changing the course of the competition - and not for the better."

At that point, the room burst into a flurry of words that I couldn't quite understand. There was too much going on for me to make out any one line of discussion. So I just looked at Amelia.

She looked back at me and smiled and a warm feeling curled all the way through me. We were in this together, whatever happened today. Whether one of us won the competition or not.

Just like that, I knew something that just might let us fix this.

"Angela, can I ask something?" My voice cut through the chaos, bringing the room back to that eerie, charged silence.

"Is the problem that you have that if something

happens between us we'll sue the network? Or are you really concerned about the fact that we're together as a queer couple?"

I wanted to say more, to continue, but I knew that if I didn't let her answer this properly, I might ruin everything. Amelia perked up, as if she realized where I was going with this.

"I have no issue with the two of you being together in a general sense," Angela said immediately. "Romantic and sexual relationships are a liability to the network, that's all. And there's the issue of the contract."

Amelia squeezed my hand and cut in with more excitement in her voice than I had heard since we'd come in.

"If there's no issue with us being together, what if we signed a liability waiver to add to the contract. The same way we did with the injury waiver. That way, if something negative happens between us, we can't sue the network."

"It *would* make great television," the other producer said. "Viewers do love a romance - especially one that started off so acrimoniously as this one did.

It was the first time they'd spoken since we'd come in, and I didn't know their name, but I was intensely grateful for them in that moment.

Angela hummed while she thought. "I would need to take it to legal, but I don't see why that wouldn't work. It's not like it's unprecedented. I just didn't expect it to happen on our very first season."

"Romance has a way of sneaking in where you don't expect it," Bryce said, glancing sidelong at the other judges. "Speaking of which… I'm gonna need one of those waivers, too. All three of us will, actually."

Now it was my turn to be shocked into silence. I wasn't the only one. Angela's jaw was almost on the floor. I'd suspected there was something going on between him and Nathan, but who could Denise be with that she would also need a form? Then Denise flushed the brightest red I'd ever seen and she smacked him.

"What ever happened to keeping this *quiet*, Bryce?" She hissed.

"Well, do you want to have *another* meeting like this? We might as well just get it over with and cover our asses." His voice was a whisper, but we all heard it.

"I thought you preferred it when we bared our asses," Nathan murmured, a wicked grin plain on his face. Denise and Bryce both groaned, and I began to realize exactly what was going on.

I thought back over the stolen moments I'd caught, and the jokes they'd made on set. Was it possible they were all sleeping together?

I exchanged a wide eyed glance with Amelia. Talk about a plot twist.

Angela just blinked at them owlishly before rubbing her eyes tiredly. "Of course you do. I'll talk to legal and set something up for everyone who needs one. Just… please, no more surprises this season? We have four episodes left. Let's just get through them, all right?"

That was something I could absolutely agree to.

————

Amelia and I didn't bother keeping our hands off of each other as we made our way back to the suite. There was no hesitation as our bodies collided with the force of all of the anxiety and the longing that had been thrumming through our veins all day. We had survived, and victory was sweet on her lips.

Unfortunately, our victory celebration was cut short when we stumbled into the suite, because all of the other contestants were standing in the kitchen having a very loud discussion. It went dead silent the instant they saw us, the same way it had when we'd kissed on set.

"Well, don't leave us hanging!" Fern nearly yelled. "What happened?"

Amelia and I grinned at each other. She raised our joined hands above our head in a victory salute. "We're in it to win it, y'all! You haven't seen the last of us yet!"

In the next instant, we were surrounded by bodies in a joyful hug. For the first time in recent memory, the press of bodies didn't give me anxiety. With Amelia's hand in mine and our friends surrounding us, it felt like coming home again.

———

Chapter Thirty-Four

ZOE AND I HAD SPENT THE ENTIRE NIGHT WRAPPED UP IN each other, celebrating the fact that we were safe. We didn't have to hide anything anymore from anyone. All we had to do was sign a couple of forms saying we wouldn't sue the show and then cook our asses off. All things we could absolutely do.

So when I walked onto the set again, I was confident that I could take on whatever the judges had to throw at me today. Even when it was clear from the layout that we would be doing some sort of group challenge. If Zoe and I worked together again, I knew that we could take the competition by storm.

"Today we have yet another new and exciting challenge for you," Bryce announced with yet another grin on his face. "This is another partner challenge, but it's going to be very different from any of the other challenges you've done so far."

"Unlike previous challenges, this will be something like a relay race," Denise explained. "Only one person from each team will be cooking at a time. Each chef will have five minutes to cook before swapping with the other person. Between the two of you, you will have just one hour to cook two completely different surf and turf dishes."

I gulped. That was the hardest task they'd set us yet. It would be a test of our creativity, communication skills and our timing.

"Jada, since you won the last challenge, you are exempt from this challenge. Head on over to the winner's corner. This is the final challenge that anyone will be exempt from, so enjoy it while you can!"

She made her way to the chair that she was getting to be very familiar with as we all watched jealously. This was going to be the hardest challenge yet. It would have been a difficult enough task with both people cooking, but with the constant back and forth, it would be harder than it looked.

"And, because we're the judges, we are going to pick your teams for you. Fern, Ellis, you are going to be our first team. Which means that our lovebirds get to be our second pair."

That was more than fine with me. Zoe and I made an excellent team, as did Fern and Ellis.

"Now that you are in your teams, you have five minutes together at the beginning of the challenge to choose your dishes and shop for your ingredients. Use it wisely. We expect delicious food from both teams with a lot of finesse. "

That was our cue. None of us wasted a second before running to the pantry to figure out what we wanted to do. This was going to be a hell of a competition, and we were ready for it.

———

We decided to go with an Asian theme for our first dish, using the sous vide machine and the pressure cooker to braise Korean short ribs in a pineapple kalbi sauce alongside a snapper ceviche that would use similar flavors without being same-y. The meal would be completed with soy-glazed potato wedges, and I was excited about it.

The second meal was a true Southern one - crispy skinned salmon and asparagus in a delicious andouille sausage cream sauce. They both had extremely different cooking techniques and times, which would hopefully show the judges the finesse they wanted with a powerful punch of flavor

We finished grabbing our ingredients just as our five minutes were up.

"Who needs to cook first?" I asked as we ran back to the kitchen. "It'll mean making the marinade and getting the sous vide going."

"You go first. I've never used one before, but I can do everything we need to prep for the potatoes and ceviche when I get in."

And that was what we did. I broke down the short ribs, seasoned them and got the marinade put together. All of them went into a large bag and into the sous vide machine just in time for the judges to call the first switch.

Zoe and I traded spots, and I got to really watch her cook at full speed for the first time since the competition had begun. Every movement was graceful and purposeful in a way that you didn't notice when she was moving slower.

She put a sauté pan on the heat with a dollop of oil before dicing the golden potatoes, salting them and sliding them into the pan to fry. While they crisped, she made the soy, garlic and fish sauce glaze that would soak into the simmering potatoes and tie the whole plate together.

"Do you want me to filet the snapper or prep the ceviche first?" She called over her shoulder

That didn't require much thought. "You don't have enough time to finish the filleting, so do the liquid for the ceviche and I'll put it in as soon as the fish is ready."

"Got it!" She moved to the pineapple, adding a few leftover chunks to the blender and blitzing it. With a sieve, she squeezed the juice out of the pineapple mush into a large glass bowl, then added the juice of several lemons and limes. It smelled divine, and I couldn't wait to get the fish into it to cook it.

Luckily for me, the switch was called out again, and I didn't have to wait. I plunked the snapper onto the cutting board, and pulled out my fish knife. With a few well placed cuts, both side of the fish were separated from the rib cage and the head. Another few slices, and the skin was off. The rest was easy. I diced all of it and submerged it in the citrus.

"Okay, what's next?" I asked, relying on her to tell me what I needed to do. We didn't have time for me to think. We only had time for me to work while I was here.

"You need to stir the potatoes and make sure those stay moist. Then just dice the onion and get it in with the fish - it needs to cook, too."

"Right, of course." I got to work, getting it all done just in time for the switch to be called again.

"God, that time goes quickly," Zoe said. "I'm just gonna finish dicing everything for the ceviche so that we can move on. Once you get in, you'll need to put the short ribs into the pressure cooker. It should be marinaded well by now."

"Got it. You remember what you need for the ceviche?"

"Yep. Cilantro, bell pepper, jalapeño, pineapple, cucumber and red onion. It's gonna take pretty much the entire time to get that done."

"No stress. Just focus on your knife skills. Ceviche's all about the good cuts."

"I know, Amelia." A hint of annoyance crept into her voice as she worked. Right. She'd ask for help when she needed it.

"Sorry, I was just trying to encourage you." That got me a smile.

"I know, and I appreciate it. I've got this, though."

And she did. She got everything done and into the bowl with seconds to spare. Just like that, a quarter of the first dish was complete. When we switched places, I put the pressure cooker on the stove to heat, then ran to the sous vide. I pulled the plastic bag out and sliced it open over the open pot, getting hit with the scent of the marinade. It smelled *amazing*.

"Happy cooking," I told the ribs as I dumped them unceremoniously into the sizzling pot. Zoe snorted a laugh, but didn't comment further.

I stirred the potatoes, making sure they were evenly coated in the simmering glaze. Those smelled delicious, too, even though they weren't anywhere near done yet. I put the lid back on the pan, and moved on. It was time to start the asparagus.

I rinsed the cutting board that Zoe had used for the ceviche ingredients, and plunked the bundle of asparagus down. I trimmed them down, making sure they were as clean as possible, before I started heating the oil in yet another skillet. As soon as it was ready, I tossed them in salt and pepper and into the pan.

In another pan, I heated oil over my final remaining burner. Simple salt and pepper went on both sides of each filet while I waited. It would need a few minutes to cook, but it needed to be done before we could start the cream sauce.

By the time we switched again, the salmon was in the pan and the potatoes were coming out. I slid them into the oven to stay warm just as time was called again.

We were in really good shape. While she got the salmon started, I peeked over at Fern and Ellis's kitchen.

Ellis was cooking, and it looked like he was struggling. There was a glossy sheen of sweat all over his bald head and he was turning back and forth in clear confusion. I couldn't help but worry about him, even as I knew we had to focus on our own food.

Before I knew it, I was back in the kitchen and working on the cream sauce. We were more than halfway through, but there was still a lot to do to get everything done.

"Zoe, when you get back in here, I want you to plate the ceviche and get that in the fridge, okay? It needs to chill before we serve it."

"Yeah, I'll work on that. You just focus on making that cream sauce unctuous and delicious."

"Listen to you and your big fancy words," I teased her with a smile. "You've been learning something from those cookbooks, haven't you?"

I looked at her and she stuck her tongue out at me. I laughed, and the judges called time.

Only fifteen minutes remained. I was confident in our flavors, but we had to get this all finished beautifully or it wouldn't matter. If we didn't, Zoe and I would be competing head to head. I wasn't sure that I could handle that, and I didn't want to find out. I wanted us to *win*.

———

By the time the judges called the final time, our plates were as perfect as we could get them. Zoe and I grinned at each other as we brought our plates up to the judges.

Fern and Ellis did not look nearly as pleased, and looking at their dishes, I could see why. One of the dishes was vegan, which was a risk in a challenge like this. Even worse, it looked *terrible*.

The "steaks" they served were lumpy and a grayish green, topped with some kind of a veganaise and mushroom salad and… were those onion rings? Surely they hadn't made onion rings for the judges. That would be ridiculous.

The second dish looked slightly better, but not by much. It looked like a whole trout had been wrapped in bacon and baked, then laid over polenta. It did not look appetizing at all.

On the other side, our plates looked bright and fresh and delicious. Our pride in our dishes was justified.

As the judges looked at all of the dishes together, I was no longer nervous that they'd be upset with our use of the sous vide and pressure cookers. Unless we had screwed something up terribly, we had made it into the semi-final.

The judges tasted our food first, complimenting us on being able to get the short rib so flavorful and tender in so short a time frame. They liked the crunch of the potatoes with the tender potatoes, and welcomed the relief of the cool ceviche after the punch of flavor that was the rest of the meal. They didn't like the second dish as much because it wasn't as creative, but thought it was well cooked.

As I expected, they were harshly critical of the dishes on the other team, and declared them the clear losers of the challenge. Zoe and I squealed with joy and held hands as we went to join Jada.

We had done it. Together, we were one step closer to one of us winning this thing, and that was a great feeling. Even if it was slightly bittersweet, since someone that we had grown to care for would be leaving by the end of the night.

"Now, the elimination challenge is the hardest one yet. You are going to have to cook with the parts of animals that are most often thrown away - offal."

I sucked in a breath. Offal wasn't just the parts that are most often thrown out. It was a catch-all term for all of an animal's internal organs. Unless someone grew up using it or went to culinary school, it was unlikely they'd know how to cook it to make it taste good. And with Fern being, well, herself... I didn't see her growing up cooking with organs.

"Wow, they weren't kidding," Jada whispered. "I am so glad I didn't have to do this one. That's just nasty."

"I'm with you on that one," Zoe said. "I think Fern is gonna puke."

It wouldn't surprise me. She hated cooking meat at the best of times, and this was nowhere near that. The timer began, and they both ran into the pantry. I wanted to be able to see into the overstocked room, to help them make dishes that would keep them in the competition. But I couldn't. All we could do was sit and wait to see what they would come up with.

They both left the pantry with full baskets, but I couldn't tell what they had planned - or even what kind of offal they had chosen to cook - until they emptied them onto the bench.

Fern had chosen some sort of brains to work with, which was a smart choice given they only had forty minutes to make their dish. Ellis, on the other hand, pulled out three different packages of meat. Two were obviously a liver and a heart, but the third was harder to identify. It looked lacy and delicate through the vacuum sealed plastic.

"Is he using caul fat?" Jada whispered, and I could have smacked my forehead. Of course it was. I should have recognized the delicate white lacy fat at once. Nothing else looked like that, and it was very common to use in offal dishes.

"What on earth is he going to do with all of that?" Zoe murmured back. "I wouldn't think they would go together very well, with the different textures."

That was when he pulled out the meat grinder, and it all clicked into place.

"Oh my God, he's going to make savoury duck," Jada gasped. "That's absolutely brilliant."

Zoe looked at her, confusion plain on her face. "What? There is no way in hell a heart that big came out of a duck."

Jada laughed and Zoe's confusion deepened. I smothered my own laugh, explaining it as simply as I could. There was no way she'd know this one.

"Savoury duck is one of those British recipes that doesn't actually have what it says it has. It's like an offal meatball wrapped in caul fat or bacon."

"That makes absolutely no sense, but what else is new?" She scoffed, throwing her hands in the air. We all turned our attention back to the chefs, watching to see if our intuitions turned out to be correct.

Sure enough, he ground up all of the liver and heart and mixed it with some herbs to create a meatball, tenderly wrapping it in the fat and placing it in a muffin tray. That was smart. In the other kitchen, Fern had heated beef stock and was braising the brains in it. It was smart - a way to infuse flavor into the tender flesh while also making it easy to remove the skin from around it. She still looked a little green, but she managed to power through it.

They both did, pulling together dishes that looked really delicious from where we sat. They even impressed the judges, who tasted each carefully before going back to their huddle to decide who would be staying in the competition.

"I feel like I'm gonna be sick," Zoe said. I understood the feeling. Fern and Ellis held hands as they waited for the judges to make their decision. They deliberated for nearly ten minutes before declaring Ellis the winner. The declaration had us all in tears as they told her why they'd chosen Ellis's meal, and how much they wanted to support her diner as soon as the competition was over.

Fern took it as well as one could, thanking them for the opportunity before walking over to us and hugging us all as tightly as she could.

"I'm so proud of all of you," she whispered as she wrapped us in her arms one by one. "You girls kick ass and take names for me, okay? And add me on Facebook when you get home. I'd like to keep in touch."

With that, she straightened her shoulders and walked off of the set with her head held high. I hoped that, if I were eliminated, I could do so with as much grace as she had.

Chapter Thirty-Five

ZOE

THE SUITE FELT EMPTY WITHOUT FERN IN IT WHEN WE got back to the suite. Unlike when Shauna had left, there were still traces of her everywhere, and I was glad for it. Her oat milk was still in the fridge, with a sticky note in her almost illegible cursive on one of the pastries. She always put them on anything with any of our allergies on it.

It felt more real, somehow, to still have these reminders that she'd been here.

I already missed the old woman, but I was so glad that both Amelia and I had made it to the semi-finals. I was even more glad that we hadn't had to see which one of us would win in a battle to the death.

"That was a hell of a day," Jada said with a sigh. "Y'all want some wine?"

"Yes, *please*. Red wine for me," Amelia said, heading straight for the cupboard where the glasses were.

"None for me. I wouldn't mind some lemonade, though."

"Got it! One lemonade and two red wines coming right up."

I sat down at the bar, kicking my shoes off with a groan while they served us all the drinks we so desperately needed after a very long day. The others settled in to the barstools on either side of me with their drinks, then passed me my glass of lemonade.

"Here's to surviving another day," Amelia said, raising her wine glass in toast. Jada and I clinked ours together, then drank deeply.

We also needed to eat, but I wasn't even sure I was hungry yet. I was just tired, and a little bit sad.

"You know what I would kill for right about now?" Jada asked.

"What?"

"A pizza."

"Oh, that sounds so good. I really don't want to cook, though. I'm all cooked out."

"I believe that. Do you think we're allowed to order in?"

Amelia answered thoughtfully. "I don't see why not, as long as we're not online to do it. The front desk has to know where's a good place to order pizza. This is New York City, for crying out loud."

"Let's try it." Jada picked up the kitchen phone and dialed the front desk with a few quick punches.

Five minutes later, we had ordered a highly recommended pizza to be delivered from a place right down the street. I was so tired that I didn't know if I'd still be awake when it got there.

Amelia swirled her wine in her glass as she thought aloud. "Does anyone else think it feels right? The competition coming down to just us three and Ellis, I mean."

Jada thought about it, then smiled wryly. "You know, it really does. I never thought I'd get this far, but... this feels good."

"I'm glad it's us," I agreed. "Whoever wins, they'll have earned the money, that's for damn sure. I don't think I could have dealt with the rage if like, Troy had won."

Jada raised her glass in acknowledgement, her smile growing. "I know that's right."

A knock on the door surprised us all. "That can't be the pizza already, can it? Who else would be knocking?"

I peered through the peephole and laughed. Ellis stood there, a bottle of whiskey in one hand and a few bags of microwave popcorn in the other. He grinned when I opened the door.

"You ladies mind if I join your party? I'm the only one left in my suite, but I came bearing gifts."

"Come on in, old man," I laughed. "We semi-finalists have to stick together."

———

The producers didn't waste time in getting us all set up and ready to go the next morning. Apparently they were in as much of a hurry as we were to get this episode started.

I was glad that Amelia and I had been placed on opposide ends of the set today. I had to focus on myself and my cooking, and if I could see her... It probably wouldn't happen. Neither of us could afford the distraction. We were here to win. That was all that mattered right now.

"Today, in honor of making it to the semifinals, we have a special treat for all of you!" Bryce crowed, clearly delighted with whatever was to come. "Your families have arrived!"

My heart leapt as the giant doors to either side of the judges' platform opened to reveal four clusters of people - one for each contestant. Was my mom back there? Was Violet? Peering through the smoke, I could see their outlines and tears began leaking from my eyes. I didn't even try to stop them.

You would have thought I'd have known this was going to happen, given how many of the other shows I'd watched in the past. Somewhere in the back of my mind, I probably had, but it was a very different thing when you were the one standing in the kitchen rather than watching on television.

It felt like it had been months since I had seen them, instead of a mere three weeks, and I was so, so grateful to the producers for making it happen.

They started walking towards us and I focused on my family. Violet had little ear plugs in, hopefully protecting her from the loud music blasting through the room, and her eyes were wide as she took in the huge room at my mother's side. Mom was beaming so hard I thought her face might split open, joy radiating from every wrinkle. I knew my expression matched hers.

The instant they reached my bench, I hugged my mother harder than I ever had before, pressing kisses to her cheek over and over again. She laughed and squeezed me tighter.

"I missed you so much," I whispered, scooping my daughter up and fluttering kisses all across her face. "I'm so happy to see you both!"

With a speed that impressed me, all of the other contestants were reunited with their loved ones. I wasn't the only one crying.

"And, we have one more surprise guest for one of our contestants!" Nathan shared. We all looked towards the door where everyone else had come in.

A lone figure walked through the smoke, faster than anyone else had, and I suddenly felt the cameras turn towards me. My spine stiffened as I realized that this figure was as familiar to me as my daughters and headed right toward me. It was Jacob.

"What's wrong?" Mom's voice was sharp in my ears, cutting through the fog that was threatening to take over my brain. "Why are you freezing up?"

"How is he here?" I whispered. I could feel her tense when she came to the same realization, but then she had stepped away from me.

In a movement I barely caught, I found myself staring at the back of my mother's head instead of my husband's advancing form. Violet had picked up on the tension, or maybe the way I was trembling while I held her. She was looking at me with wide eyes.

"Mama mad?" She asked, voice quavering.

"No baby, Mama's not mad. Mama's never mad at you," I reassured her, hating that yet again, Jacob was ruining what should have been a great moment. I hated that he was here at all. Sharing this moment with my family should have been a celebration, and now I had to worry about my daughter's safety.

He had always been great at that — making moments that were mine all about him. It was one of the first red flags that I had missed in the whirlwind of our relationship. With each step he took towards us, my breaths shortened and my chest tightened.

"Why no?" It took me a minute to realize what Violet was asking. Apparently, I had been chanting the word "no" under my breath the whole time, quietly enough that even my mother hadn't heard it.

"No. I don't want him here," I murmured. "I don't want this."

No one heard me except my family. A little bit louder, I repeated myself. I felt even more eyes on me this time. I knew that Amelia's were one of them - I could just see her out of the corner of my eye, her mouth open and eyes wide.

God, I hated that she had to see this. I hated that Violet had to see this, to see her father for the first time that she might actually remember. Most of all, I hated that the cameras would see this, would see the way that I always froze up when he looked at me with those piercing green eyes, or sneered the way he always had when I spoke up for myself. It would make great television, I was sure, but I didn't want anyone to see me like that. I was going to vomit.

———

Chapter Thirty-Six

AMELIA

I COULD NOT HAVE BEEN MORE THRILLED TO SEE MY parents. Reaching my bench in a few long strides, Mother wrapped her arms around me and rested her bony chin on top of my head. Around her, Dad grabbed one of my hands and squeezed it tightly.

"We are so proud of you, sweetheart." Dad murmured when Mother finally let me go and he got to wrap me up in his thick, warm arms. The combined scents of her perfume and his cologne melded together into a smell that brought me right back to spending days with them both as a child. I felt right at home in that moment, even under the bright studio lights and with cameras far closer to my face than was comfortable.

I could hear happy exclamations from most of the other semi-finalists. Zoe's mom and daughter had joined her in a tight huddle and had not separated. I could only imagine how happy she was to see them both.

All of us paused when the judges announcing a special guest for one of the contestants. I glanced at my parents and they shrugged. Whoever it was wasn't there for me, which was perfectly fine. There wasn't anything I wanted less than anyone else to be sharing this moment with me. I looked toward the door, curious.

That was when I noticed how ramrod straight Zoe was standing, and the way her mother had put herself between her family and the man walking towards them. Zoe's skin had turned a shade of green that was only natural for an alien, not for any of the fresh vegetables that surrounded her and certainly not for her own warm-toned skin. Something was very very wrong.

I watched her lips move, but I couldn't hear what she was saying. I took a step forward and when she repeated herself, I heard the words. "No. I don't want him here. I don't want this."

Without thinking, I took two more steps towards her and her family. Zoe didn't look at me, just stood there with her daughter in her arms, staring at the advancing figure. This had to be her husband. There was no way anyone else would have this sort of an effect on her, or on her mother, so instantaneously.

My mind kicked into overdrive. I couldn't deal with her husband for her, and there was very little else I could do to comfort her. That was very definitely not something she would appreciate. However, if I were in her place, I wouldn't want this to be happening at all. The idea of having it happen in front of a room full of other professionals, not to mention have it happen in front of studio cameras, would absolutely break her heart. That, fortunately, was something I could help with.

"What is going on?" Mom asked, her high pitched voice breathy with concern. "Why does that girl look nauseous?"

I looked at them both, my face as serious as I could

make it. "I need you both to follow my lead. That man is trouble and we need to step in."

My parents traded glances, then nodded. My father spoke for them both, his voice as serious as mine had been. "You're in charge, dear."

"We have to get them to turn off the cameras as soon as possible. I am going to go talk to the producers. I need you two to go and stand in front of Zoe and her mom and keep as many eyes on you two instead of her as we can. I don't care what you have to do, just draw their focus away from Zoe and her family. Got it?"

They both nodded. "Okay, let's go, then."

I split off from them and powered my way through the crowd of cameras around the other contestants. My elbows went into several cameras, leaving me in a bit of pain, but I didn't care. My eyes were focused on the back of the executive producer's head across the room where she was watching the angles of each camera on a huge screen.

"Angela!" I yelled. "Get the cameras off of her!"

The older white woman bristled before she turned, her shoulders rising to meet the tips of her ashy brown bob.

"Ms. Hughes," she said stiffly, enunciating each word as much as humanly possible. "What do you think that you are doing back here? You are supposed to be on set."

"What do you think you're doing, bringing Zoe's abusive husband on set as a surprise?" My voice was shrill but unwavering, drawing the attention of the assistants around her.

Angela's face drained of color, but her voice still snapped. "What are you talking about? We were informed that they had reconciled and the visit would be welcome."

"By who?" I demanded. "Just look at her through those cameras of yours. Does she look happy to see him?"

Angela turned back at the screen and I watched as one of the cameras got a close up of Zoe's gray-green face and her daughter's more normal colored one. She was still repeating the same words.

"I don't want him here."

On the screens that showed feeds from the other two cameras focused on her bench, I could see my parents' stern faces and torsos.

Unfortunately, another camera was focused on her garbage can of a husband, and I could see that he was far too close to her. Angela was frozen where she stood, her hand in front of her open mouth as she watched.

"Fucking do something, would you? Get him off of the set!"

She didn't move a muscle, so I had to take action. I shrieked, getting the attention I'd been seeking from the techs that still surrounded their boss. I looked around until I found two who I recognized.

"Portia, Franklin come with me. We're turning off those cameras."

They nodded, though they still looked shocked and more than a little confused. I knew what I had to do.

"You, Franklin. Show me to disconnect the feeds from the cameras around Zoe. Portia, go tell the judges what's going on. Tell them we'd appreciate an intervention." My tone left no room for argument, so they didn't try it.

Franklin moved to the computer and clicked a few buttons. That was all it took for the screens that had been focused on Zoe to go black. Relief flooded through me. It wasn't a total solution, but at least whatever happened next wouldn't be as easy to access for the show.

I still had to figure out how to keep that asshole away from her and Violet. Luckily, Portia was very persuasive. I could see their hands waving as they talked to the judges, whose faces shifted from confusion and concern to disgust and horror.

Without hesitation, Nathan and Bryce marched over to the man who had almost reached both my and Zoe's family.

"Sir, we're going to need you to come with us." Bryce's voice rumbled and left no room for argument, but by the way Jacob squared his shoulders, it was clear that he was going to try it anyway.

"Not until I see my wife and my daughter."

"Don't." Zoe's voice rang out like the crack of a whip. It was ragged, like she'd had to tear it free of her chest, but it was loud. "Don't come near me. Jacob, just… just go."

Every camera in the room was now pointed at the commotion. I cursed, moving faster. It shouldn't have surprised me. It should have been obvious that they wouldn't miss what was happening for long. Not when the judges and the producers were involved.

"Mr. Cooper, it's time for you to leave." Nathan was the one to insist this time, closing in on the other side of the man

"No! You aren't in charge here. They're my family and I deserve to see them."

"No, you don't. You lost that privilege a long time ago, and you need to go." This time, Zoe's mom was the one to speak. Tears were streaming down her face, too, but I could also see the same protective determination I was so familar with on her daughter's face.

I ran up behind her just in time to see Jacob sneer viciously. "No one asked you what you thought, you old bitch. Get out of my way before I make you."

"You'll have to get through more than just her if you want to get anywhere near Zoe."

"And who the hell do you think you are? Why don't any of you understand that this is between me and my wife?"

I hated the way he emphasized "my wife," as if she were his property instead of her own person. Fury burned through me as I stood beside a woman I'd never met, protecting the woman I was almost certainly falling in love with. That rage sharpened my tongue when I said possibly the stupidest thing I could have said in front of that many cameras.

"I'm her girlfriend, you jackass."

The whole room went quiet around us as everyone realized what I'd said at the same time I did. Jacob broke that silence by roaring a slew of curses, calling her and me names that definitely wouldn't make it onto television. He tried to lunge forward, but the male judges each grabbed one of his arms and held him back.

"Right. We'll have no more of that kind of language here, sir. Why don't we take this conversation somewhere a little more private?" Bryce didn't give him the option to disagree. With a nod to Nathan, they turned him around and frog marched him back the way he had come. He fought them all the way until the doors closed behind them.

Only then did I realize just how quickly my heart was racing, how hard it pounded against my ribs that ached from taking so many shallow breaths. If this was how I felt, I couldn't imagine what Zoe's family was dealing with.

I turned around, looking for Zoe and found her squatting on the floor with her head between her knees. She took deep heaving breaths that shook her whole body, breaking my heart.

Her daughter was sitting next to her, her white dress spread around her on the dark tile floor like the petals of a flower. Her face, so like her mother's, was scrunched up in concern when she looked at me.

"Mama is upset. She needs space." She pronounced those words as if she were repeating them from someone else.

Remembering what she'd said helped, I took a single step forward. Then I crouched, bringing myself closer to her eye level. It got me close enough that she could see me if she glanced up, but not close enough to make her or Violet feel crowded by my presence.

"Zoe," I said softly. "Zoe, you are safe. Violet and your mom are safe. He's gone and we're all here with you."

At first, I couldn't tell if she had heard me, or if she was processing everything I'd said. I held my position, even though my ankles creaked in protest. I repeated my promise of safety until finally, she responded.

After a few seconds, her breathing slowed down infinitesimally. A few more, and I could see her face relax just a little. Every movement felt like a victory as she pulled herself out of the nightmare that had become our reality.

Finally, she looked up and locked watery eyes on her daughter.

"Violet, are you okay?" her voice rasped, as if she'd been shouting. The girl nodded, making her tight curls bounce, then took a cautious step towards Zoe. They wrapped their arms around each other.

"Mama? Are you here?" Zoe's voice was a little stronger, but it still quavered as she looked past me.

The slight, older woman brushed past me and joined the huddle with her family. I couldn't help feeling like an intruder to their private sorrow, but I wasn't the only one there. I turned to find the whole room watching them.

"Is there any way we can get some privacy for them?" My voice was too loud, too harsh for this raw moment, but it seemed to do the trick. Jada and Ellis turned back to their families, which forced some of the camera crew to turn away. Mother and Dad still stood in front of the cameras, but they were looking at me for some kind of guidance.

Denise stepped forward and broke the silence by clearing her throat. "Why don't you all come up to the judge's suite? We've got plenty of space and it's camera free."

Zoe looked up, tears streaming down her face. "That would be nice, thank you."

I had a hard time swallowing as Denise led the trio away. I couldn't help but feel like she was taking a chunk of my heart with her.

———

Chapter Thirty-Seven

ZOE

IT TOOK EVERY BIT OF STRENGTH IN MY BODY NOT TO absolutely fall apart the instant I got into the elevator. Denise was still watching me carefully, concern written in every line of her face. I wondered if she thought I'd collapse if she took her eyes off of me for an instant. Honestly, I might have. There was no telling, after the morning I'd had.

As if she knew exactly what I was thinking, Mama slipped her hand into mine and held it tight. It was a more adult version of the way I held onto Violet with my other hand. It might have made me smile in other circumstances, but I didn't have the emotional energy to smile right now. I had to hold it together, at least until I was alone with my family. We'd made it this far. One more minute wouldn't be the end of me.

And so I walked to the judges suite, just on the other side of the practice suite where Amelia and I had spent so much time, with my head as high and my back as straight as I could make it.

When Denise opened the door to reveal a dark suite,

the relief coming off of us all was palpable. She flicked on the kitchen light and gestured for us to make ourselves comfortable.

As my eyes adjusted to the lower light than the hallway, I saw that the suite was not terribly different from the one I'd spent the last few weeks in. There were two blue cloth armchairs and a loveseat placed in a semicircle around a low walnut coffee table, with a television hidden in a matching built-in cabinet.

Violet was looking around with wide eyes as we settled onto the couch together. "This is fancy, Mama."

She was right. Everything around me was just a little more upscale than the things we had been using, and a far cry from the well-loved furniture that she was used to. The suite showed its quality in a lot of little details, like the actual marble counters instead of high quality faux granite, actual paintings instead of canvas prints. It made for a slightly classier feeling in the space, instead of the more homey space we'd been placed in. It even smelled fancier - more like a candle or room spray than the citrusy cleaning smell that filled our suite.

By the time Denise walked in with a trio of water bottles, I felt a little bit more grouned. Maybe it was the focus that finding all of those small details required, or maybe it was the fact that I was snuggled between my mother and my baby girl for the first time in what felt like forever. No matter how fancy the room around us was, I would feel at home anywhere so long as they were there with me.

The door opened again and my heart leapt, expecting Amelia to walk through the door. Instead, two large male frames filed in. My heart dropped to my stomach before I recognized them as Nathan and Bryce.

Nathan held something wrapped in cloth to his face,

and when he stepped into the light, Denise gasped. "Oh my God, what happened?"

I didn't need to hear the answer. He had a black eye and a bloody, possibly broken nose. Someone had clearly taken a swing at him and hit - hard. It was obvious exactly who had done it, too. I'd been on the receiving end of those blows a few times.

"That is a Jacob Cooper specialty," I informed them, my voice rough with emotion.

Denise sucked in a breath as she got closer and saw the extent of the damage. "Do you need to see a doctor?"

"Don't fuss, love. I'm fine. Really!" He insisted, but Denise wasn't having any of it.

"Look at your poor nose," she said mournfully, poking gently at the appendage.

"He doesn't need a doctor. He just needs to put some ice on it to get the swelling down.

"You, hush. He definitely needs to at least see the set medic. You two sit down with them. I'm calling Angela." She didn't leave room for argument, and the men meekly followed her instructions. Nathan settled into an armchair and Bryce slid to sit at his feet.

"I'm so sorry, Nathan. He's got… a bit of a temper."

Nathan and Bryce both looked at me like I'd grown three heads. "What the hell are you apologizing for? You didn't hit me."

I dropped my misty eyes to my lap, seeing the way Violet's small fingers twined with my larger ones. "Yes, but he wouldn't be here if it wasn't for me and-"

"Zoe Elizabeth Cooper!" Mama's voice cracked like a whip through the air, making the men jump. "What have I told you about blaming yourself for that man's actions?"

Tears were falling down my cheeks again. "Mama, please."

Her hand reached into my frame of vision, clasping both of our hands in hers. I looked up and found her eyes laser focused on me.

"She's right, you know." Bryce's voice was soft and kind. "I don't know what went on between you two, but this isn't your fault. None of what happened today was your fault.

A sob tore out of my chest. Violet wrapped her tiny arms tight around me, like she could hold me together if she tried hard enough.

"I'd like to know whose fault today was," Mama said acidly. "I certainly didn't tell your producers that he existed, let alone that it was a good idea to bring him here."

As if on cue, the door opened again. Once again, I looked up with excitement. And once again, I was disappointed. This time, Angela stood in the doorway. Someone in a black medic's uniform stood behind her looking worried.

"He's back here," Denise called. The medic strode past Angela, who was looking at the scene with obvious horror. "Please come in and close the door. We don't want paparazzi learning that something's wrong. If they get a picture of this, we're all screwed."

That got her moving faster than I'd ever seen her. When she reached the kitchen, she plunked herself down into a barstool.

"Well, today certainly did not go as planned," she said briskly. "This is going to set the production schedule back at least a day. Corporate is going to be so upset…"

I just stared at her as she trailed off, mouth open. She had just retraumatized me and my family, been partially responsible for what had happened to Nathan, and all she cared about was the production schedule?

Mama was the first one to find her voice. "Are you the reason that man was here?"

Angela opened her mouth as if to answer, but she seemed to think better of it and nodded.

Mama stood, letting go of me for the first time since we had been reunited. She stepped around the press of bodies easily, taking light steps until she stood toe to toe with the other woman.

"I'd like to have a private conversation with you." Her voice was made of steel in a way I'd never heard.

"Actually, I think we'd all like to be a part of that conversation," Denise corrected. Her eyes blazed.

"Violet doesn't need to be here for this," I said. My voice was quiet, but everyone heard me.

"If it's okay with you, I can take her," Bryce offered just as quietly. "Just down to the practice suite. I've got a couple of recipes I'd like to try out on some younglings before I try to feed them to my niblings."

That made me smile, just a little. It was easy to imagine the tall, buff man with children hanging off of his arms and legs.

"Violet, do you want to go help Chef Bryce cook some stuff like you do with Mama and Granny? Mama needs to talk to these people."

I hoped she'd be okay with that. I wouldn't make her go with him if she didn't want to, but I had a feeling this was going to turn into an argument. She'd had more than enough experience avoiding fights in her young life. I didn't really want her to be there for yet another one.

She looked at Bryce, then looked back up at me, then looked at Bryce again. He smiled at her, and she turned her face to me shyly.

"Do you want to go?" I asked again, trying to keep any opinion out of my voice. To my relief, she nodded, sliding her hands out of mine.

She toddled over to Bryce without a word. She put her hands on her hips and looked up at him. "What are we making?"

"Well that depends!" He replied cheerfully. "What are your favorite flavors? Do you like vanilla, chocolate or strawberry best?"

"Chocolate!" she answered predictably. I couldn't help the laugh that burbled out of me as they walked away together. Bryce listed off a bunch of chocolate recipes that I couldn't quite hear as they left the room. The medic, apparently satisfied with Nathan's treatment plan, followed soon after.

When the door clicked shut, every one of us turned to Angela with serious expressions.

"Right. I think we all need an explanation as to what the hell happened here today, Angela."

She closed her eyes and took a deep breath. "Mr. Cooper contacted the show last week and told us that you two had reconnected and were planning to renew your wedding vows. He wanted to surprise you by re-proposing. We thought that it would make for excellent, very sweet television."

I stared at her, flabbergasted.

"I've talked about my husband in your confessional booth and in the activities multiple times, which you've watched as the producer. Not to mention, I literally just told you two days ago that Amelia and I were together. You had to have us sign waivers saying that the show could use that footage and we wouldn't sue the show because of it. It didn't occur to you that maybe, just maybe, I wouldn't want my husband to be here?"

My voice rose an octave with every sentence until I was nearly shrieking.

Her face was pale. "Some people don't have a problem with multiple partners. I couldn't have known what your family situation would be like!"

I threw my hands in the air and she flinched. "You could have asked!"

"That would have spoiled the surprise!" Angela objected, and I couldn't help but scoff. As if any surprise was worth this.

"You had already contacted me," Mama cut in, her voice the calm, low counterpoint to my own. "I could have told you exactly what was going to happen if he came into our space."

Angela flinched again, her face going pale.

Denise apparently took pity on her, because she stepped in - literally putting herself between Mama and the producer. "All of us judges are also producers on this show. Any one of us could have said something at that meeting. That's on us all. However, this is definitely something that should have gone through a higher level of vetting."

"No matter whose fault this is, we have to have a discussion about what we're going to do to fix this," Nathan interjected. "Obviously, we can't undo the emotional problems we've caused here, but we have to do... something."

That was when everyone turned to look at me and I had to resist the urge to shrink back into myself.

"What do you feel would be a fitting repayment for everything that happened today?" Nathan asked.

My mind went blank except for a joke. "Uh, you could make it so I win the competition?"

They all stared at me and I waved the questions they didn't ask off.

"No, I'm kidding. Mostly. I would like to win, but I don't want to get it because I have a sob story. I want a promise that you won't use any of the footage that I know you got today. I want it *in writing* that none of this will be on the show in any way shape or form. Is that possible?"

"I'll have to talk to corporate…" Angela hesitated, looking around the room until she met Mama's steely glare. "But I think that is something we can work on."

"Talk to corporate," Mama said, folding her arms over her chest. "We'll wait."

———

Finally, what seemed like hours later, the lawyers left us behind. They had gotten me several contracts and pored over them with us until my eyes ached. Moments after they left, another knock sounded on the door.

"Who is here *now*?" Denise moaned, getting up to answer the door. She opened it to reveal Amelia and the people I assumed were her parents. She very clearly resembled them both in very different ways.

Mr. Hughes was a man who could really only be described as stout - he was roughly my height and heavyset like her. His wife was as tall as Amelia, with her high cheekbones and wide smile, but she was skinnier than I thought was possible.

She rushed in, then hesitated when she saw me sitting with Nathan and Denise. I beckoned them all over, and saw the horror set in when she took Nathan's injuries in. Her parents hesitated, as if they didn't think they belonged.

CANDACE HARPER

I smiled at them and waved them forward until they took a few, hesitant steps. The others caught the movement and turned towards the new arrivals.

"Ah, here are the real heroes of the day!" Nathan said. "You three were *amazing.* Get in here.

His voice was as warm as ever as he welcomed the Hughes family into the living room.

"It's, um, a pleasure to meet you all." Mrs. Hughes said, blushing a little bit. "I'm a big fan of all of your restaurants."

"Why, thank you!" Denise said kindly. "We're a big fan of your daughter."

That got a belly laugh from Mr. Hughes, so much like his daughters that I couldn't help but be drawn in. Amelia smiled, looking straight at me like there was no one else in the room. Everyone else's eyes fell on me, but this time I didn't care.

"Mother, Dad, there's someone I'd like you to meet." Her voice was soft and sweet. "This is Zoe, my girlfriend and the best chef I know."

Tears welled in my eyes for what felt like the millionth time today. That was the kindest thing anyone had ever said to me, and for her to say it in front of her parents… well, how could I not cry.

I stepped toward them, reaching out to grasp Amelia's hand in mine.

"It's a pleasure to meet you both. Amelia's told me a lot about you."

They exchanged glances then laughed together in perfect harmony.

"Hopefully she told you something other than the fact that I can't cook," Mrs. Hughes said. "We look forward to getting to know you a little bit better when things have calmed down."

"You, too. Oh, but you should meet my mother! Mama, come here." She wasn't far away, and she was by my side in an instant with a sincere smile on her face.

"Thank you all so much for everything you did today. You really were our heroes today."

"Oh, it was nothing," Mrs. Hughes demurred. "I'm just glad all of you are safe. That man… seemed like a piece of work."

"You got that right," Mama laughed. "I'm Alice Everett. It's nice to meet you all. I've been hearing plenty about you, missy."

That last bit was aimed at Amelia, who smiled. "And I'm looking forward to proving at least half of what she's said wrong. Now, forgive me if I'm wrong, but we're missing a part of your family. Is Violet around here somewhere?"

"She went to the practice suite with Bryce to taste test some new recipes while we discussed today's issue with Angela," I explained. "We should probably go check on them. He'll get her so hopped up on sugar that she may never sleep again."

Amelia nodded. "Would you mind if we tagged along? I wanted to show Mother the kitchen and the library."

"Mind?" I asked. "I wasn't planning on letting you go anytime soon. I can't wait for you to meet her."

————

Chapter Thirty-Eight

AMELIA

ZOE FILLED ME IN ON EVERYTHING THAT HAD HAPPENED with the judges and the lawyers as we walked. I wanted to say that I couldn't believe that her dumpster fire of a husband had actually punched Nathan, but it was entirely on par with what little she had told me about him.

Behind us, our parents talked quietly about where they were from - apparently one of Mother's colleagues had been a teacher at Mrs. Everett's elementary school before getting xir masters, which led to a long discussion about other people they all knew.

"They're getting along like a house on fire," I murmured. "At least one thing about this day is going right."

"No kidding," she laughed. "I'm just hoping Bryce hasn't given her too much sugar. She gets a little mean when she starts crashing."

"I'd imagine that's true for all of us," I said as I opened the door, holding it as each of our parents walked through.

We walked into the room and Violet ran to the door to greet us. Her face was absolutely smeared with chocolate.

"Mama! Come taste!"

Bryce grinned sheepishly. "Welcome to my laboratory, friends. May I offer you some chocolate mousse?"

Zoe groaned and I couldn't hold back a laugh. She scooped up her daughter and pressed a kiss to a clean spot on her forehead.

"Well, Chef, I would thank you for taking care of her, but I have a feeling I'm going to regret this. Can I have a wet paper towel please?"

He pulled one off the roll and rinsed it lightly before handing it to her.

"Your girl's got a great palate. She caught all of the flavors I tried to sneak past her. And she loves her chocolate."

"That she does," Zoe said proudly. "We love food in our house, don't we, Mom?"

"That we do! And we especially love chocolate. Isn't that right, Vi?"

"Chocolate!" she agreed. Everyone laughed. Zoe gently scrubbed the chocolate away from the little girl's face. I was struck by how much the girl looked like Zoe, and how little she looked like her father.

Mrs. Everett stepped up next to them, asking a question I couldn't hear. It was clear they wanted a private moment, so I turned back to my own parents, who were looking around with wonder.

"So this is where we've been spending most of our time when we aren't on set," I said, letting them have their private moment. Usually the company is sightly less distinguished, but we've been learning a lot in here.

Mother, even you could find something cookable in here."

She just stuck her tongue out at me, like I'd expected.

"I did actually make some real food, by the way." Bryce's voice was sheepish but proud. "It'll be done in about 20 minutes."

"Oh yeah? What did you make?"

"Violet helped me pick out the ingredients for a quiche."

A laugh burst out of me. When my eyes met Zoe's over her daughter's head, she was laughing, too.

"What's funny, Mama?"

"Nothing, baby. Just an inside joke between Amelia and me."

I grinned. Yet again, the feeling of rightness flooded through me as my family laughed around me, with the smell of food in the air and Zoe right in front of me.

———

By the time dinner was served, the other judges had joined us in the practice suite's dining room. It was the only place big enough for all of us to eat without sprawling on the floor.

Luckily, the quiches Bryce had made were plenty big enough for us all to eat well. There was a reason he was such a popular chef.

Nathan and Denise spent most of the meal bickering about what spices he had used until Bryce finally got tired of it and told us what he'd used. She tried to be sneaky about it, but because she was sitting next to me, I saw Zoe punch the recipe idea into her phone. When she looked up and caught my raised eyebrow, she winked before sliding her phone back into her pocket.

They excused themselves soon after we finished eating, reminding us that there was a challenge redo first thing in the morning.

Dessert was simple, thanks to the cake and pie that Bryce had made with Violet. The time was spent catching our families up on everything that had happened during the competition - specifically, how our relationship had changed so much over so little time, and for a little more information about Zoe's marriage.

It was the weirdest family dinner I'd ever been a part of, but it felt right. None of us seemed to want it to end. Like all things, it eventually had to. Violet started yawning first, then Mother caught them. The yawns were contagious, making their way around the table until we could barely speak. When the toddler almost fell asleep in her slice of pie, it was a clear sign that it was time to wrap things up.

"Where are y'all staying tonight?" I asked as we cleared the dishes. Mother rattled off the room number and I had to smile. It was the suite that had housed most of our male competitors.

"You're right next door to us!" Zoe's voice was bright. "Are all of the families staying there?"

"I believe so," Mother said. "I didn't see anyone get led elsewhere."

"That'll be quite the party crowd," I laughed, looking around the room at the sleepy group of people. Zoe had scooped up her nearly unconscious daughter like it was the easiest thing in the world. It was one of the most beautiful sights I'd ever seen.

Her mother opened the door for them and they made their way out, leaving me alone with my parents again.

I couldn't stop thinking about what Zoe had said

about her husband, and how he refused to sign the divorce papers she had served him with. Because she didn't have the money for a lawyer, she didn't have a way to make him sign them. That was his way of keeping a hold on her, even if he couldn't make her come back to him.

Suddenly, I felt an idea begin to form in my head. I knew it wouldn't work if I asked myself, but if one of my parents called for me…

"This is gonna sound like a weird request, but I need you guys to make a phone call for me. For Zoe, really. "

"Starling, out of all the requests you've made from us in the last eight hours, that is the least weird one by a far cry." Father had been quiet for most of the evening, but he had been watching everything like always.

"Tell us what you need," Mother said. And so I did.

———

Chapter Thirty-Nine

ZOE

Even though I knew that there was no way that yesterday's fiasco would be repeated, I couldn't help but be anxious as I got into position.

The judges repeated their spiel about how they had a special treat for us, opening the doors to reveal our family members. I knew exactly who would be coming out the doors and I still cried when Violet came scampering out with Mom right behind her. Everyone else reacted in much the same way, too, but I couldn't focus on them.

Violet was back in my arms and unlike yesterday, I could focus on her.

"It's so good to see you," I told her. She kissed my cheek, quick and sloppy in the way that only toddlers could, and I laughed.

Mom followed soon after with a much tidier kiss. "It's good to see you, too, honey."

With both of their arms wrapped around me, I couldn't help but know I was going to be successful at whatever the judges threw at us today.

I was right. The canned food challenge that we all competed in was a breeze for me. Amelia struggled a little bit, which made sense. She had never needed to work with canned foods, even as a kid.

What surprised me was that Ellis had completely failed to produce a cohesive dish. I had never seen him struggle so much across a challenge, and today was not the day to start struggling.

When the judges told us there was no elimination challenge, that they had already chosen who was going home, I watched the older man's shoulders slump. He knew what was going to happen. When the judges called his name, he nodded and thanked them.

He hugged each of us as he left the room with his daughter, leaving us alone with our families and the judges.

"And now, unfortunately, it's time for our families to leave us," Bryce said. They'll be seeing you all very soon, because the three of you are the first ever finalists in Heating Up The Kitchen."

I couldn't believe it, even when Mom and Violet came back to say their goodbyes.

I kissed them both on each cheek, extracting a promise from Mom to let me know as soon as they got home. And then, too soon, they were all walking off of the set.

We all looked at each other, completely bowled over. We had made it to the finale.

One of the crew members walked over and said something to Amelia as soon as we were done filming. She took a deep breath, then beckoned me over.

"I need you to come with me." The sentence was weirdly ominous, and she didn't really wait for me to accept before she started walking off the set.

"O-okay then." I did follow her, not sure what was about to happen. My heart began to beat faster when I realized that she

"There's someone I'd like you to meet." Amelia swung the door open and a petite woman walked in wearing a suit so well-tailored that Denise would have been jealous of.

She was even thinner than I was, but her presence filled the room so completely that I would never think of her as small again. I looked over at Amelia, who looked distinctly uncomfortable, but pasted a smile on her face.

"Good afternoon. I'm Janet Andrews. I understand you are in need of a divorce lawyer."

My jaw dropped. "W-what?"

Janet looked at Amelia and raised both eyebrows at me. "You didn't tell her I was coming? Amelia, really, I expected better from you."

I looked back and forth between them, realizing dawning on me like the flip of a switch. "Wait, you're Janet? Like, your almost-fiancé Janet?"

The petite woman sighed. "Yes, I am that Janet. I'm a partner at a divorce firm in Raleigh. Amelia had her parents call me and ask me to come to you to help with what they described as a particularly difficult case. Would you like my help?"

"I-I can't afford you," I stammered, heartbroken. "I'm sorry you came all the way out here, but... there's

no way I can afford an attorney right now. We'll just…
have to manage."

At that, Janet stepped closer to me, filling the air
around me with her tense presence and the scent of
bergamot.

"Money is not an issue. We take pro bono cases on a
case-by-case basis, and as a favor to Amelia and her
family, I am more than willing to take you on. So, I ask
you again. Would you like my help?"

I couldn't speak. I just nodded, feeling tears stream
down my cheeks.

"Excellent. Let's get to work then. There's a lot of
information I need to know about you and your
situation."

———

Chapter Forty

AMELIA

I slipped out of the meeting with Janet once they started getting into the details. I would learn those once I needed to know them, once she wanted to share them with me. I didn't need to hear Janet ask her thousands of questions about them.

There wasn't really time for me to process any of what had happened, though. There was too much, from Ellis going home, to us being a part of the finale, to dealing with Janet. When Portia came around the corner, their eyes lit up when they found me.

"I've been looking all over for you! The judges need to talk to you."

I glanced over my shoulder at the closed door. "Oh. Do they need Zoe? She's a little busy."

"No, we'll get her when she's free. They just finished up with Jada, so it's your turn now."

"Then I'm all yours," I declared. "Lead the way!"

They did, guiding me to the room where Zoe and I had met with Angela on that first night. There were a few more chairs now to fit the judges, and a camera operator on either side of the room to get both my face and the judges' on the screen.

"Hello, Amelia! How does it feel to be one of our finalists?"

"Honestly, I don't even know."

The judges laughed, as if they understood the feeling. "Sit down and let us tell you what the finale will entail. You will be serving a full dinner service of a three course meal to fifty people."

I sat, trying to keep my face neutral. Fifty people was a lot for one chef to cook for, even if they gave us as much prep time as we needed.

"Now, that might seem like a tall order — and it is," Denise said. "However, we're not making you do it alone. You may pick two of this season's former contestants to help you prepare, cook and serve your dishes to the restaurant."

That was a lot more manageable, and I didn't bother to hide my relief.

"Jada came first in the semifinal, so she got to have first pick of the bunch. She chose Breonna and Christopher as her teammates. You came second, so you get to pick yours next."

I thought about my former teammates. I didn't want anyone too weak, like the people who had gone out at the beginning, but I didn't want to have people who thought they should have been standing in my place arguing with me the whole time. With that in mind, it made my choice easy.

"I'd like to have Shauna and Annika on my team."

They all leaned back in their chairs with grins. "Perfect. Now let's talk about your menu and what you'll be making. Tell us some of your ideas."

———

I stumbled into the practice suite an hour later with my mind spinning. The judges and I had hashed out a couple of different menu options. Now, all I had to do was figure out which one would be doable in the time and with the chefs I'd chosen to work with - which meant I needed to get cooking.

I pulled out all of the ingredients I'd need for all three menus that we had decided were worth trying, deciding to focus on the appetizers first. They were smaller and usually the most time intense in the actual kitchen because they had to be prepared almost entirely to order.

However, there was a possibility that I could choose somethign that could be prepped ahead of time, like a potato gratin or a canape where all it would need is assembly.

I pulled out the fryer, leaning towards doing some kind of fried bread and filling it with cheese and spices. I was halfway through figuring out my recipe when Zoe came in, looking like the wheels of her mind were turning as quickly as mine had.

Her eyes lit up when she saw that I was the only one in the kitchen.

"I'm so glad I found you. Jada is cooking up a storm in our suite, and I worried you'd found somewhere else to cook. Mind if I join you?"

"I never mind if you join me. C'mon, I'm just trying to decide on a menu for the finale."

"Oh?" She arched an eyebrow at me. "I would have thought you'd have known exactly what you wanted to do the instant they gave us the challenge. I certainly did."

I raised an eyebrow right back. "What are you making then?"

"I'm not telling" she giggled. "What if we make the same thing again?"

"Oh, I don't think that'll happen," I argued. The judges would have steered you away from anything I was making."

"Ah, maybe. But I'm still not telling you. You'll just have to see it tomorrow night!" She walked into the pantry to find what she needed for whatever was on her menu.

That was when the realization hit me that the finale was *tomorrow*. Our time in these kitchens, these suites was almost up. When she came back out of the pantry with an armful of vegetables and steak.

"Tomorrow." I said, knowing that my eyes were wide and my face pale. "After tomorrow, we go back to the real world."

"I'm looking forward to it," she said blithely. "I've enjoyed being here, but I've missed working on my blog and being in my own home."

I could understand that. I turned the sentence over in my head as she dropped her produce onto the counter, trying to figure out how to say exactly what I wanted to without being too pushy.

"It's gonna be really different, not spending every night together," I finally said, after the silence had grown too wide. Now she looked at me, really looked at me.

"It doesn't have to. Well, I mean, it kind of does, because you don't want to spend every night with a toddler crawling on top of you in an already small bed. But I still want to be with you, however we can manage." She bit her lip, an uncertain gesture that made me squirm. "That is… if you want to be with me."

Tears welled in my eyes. "I want nothing more than to be with you. As long as it's you and me together, I want to figure it out. Toddler, small bed, and all."

A smile spread across her face slowly. "That's what I was hoping you would say. But first, maybe let's figure out which one of us is going to win this thing, shall we?"

I grinned back at her. "You're on, girlfriend."

———

Chapter Forty-One

ZOE

THE ACTUAL FINALE CHALLENGE HAPPENED SO QUICKLY, IT barely felt real. One moment, the judges were explaining our menus for the cameras. The next, customers were coming in the "doors" of the set restaurant and we were off to the races.

Our prep work had made it as easy as possible to be successful in the appetizers. The steaks had been marinading for nearly 24 hours, the endives were sliced and the salsa verde had been adjusted until it was as perfect as I could make it.

All we had to do now was cook as if our lives depended on it. And so they did. Fern and Ellis still made a great team, and aside from a few timing issues, the round went off pretty seamlessly. From what I could tell, our diners were happy with the food they received. At the very least, nothing got sent back.

I couldn't help but wonder how the other two teams had done. It was impossible to tell, thanks to the walls clearly separating all of our kitchens and restaurants from each other. All I could do was tidy up the kitchen and move on to the entrees.

They were a little rockier, despite our preparations. I'd known that the pork belly roulade was a risk for such a large crowd, but it was so delicious that I hoped it would be worth it. I had had the night's portions in the oven for almost two hours before the service began. It had been enough for a single portion in the tests every time, but I hadn't thought about how doing a dozen at a time would change the way they crisped up.

Smooth pork belly skin was probably one of the worst textures in the world, but it was to be expected when the juices of so many succulent roulades rose in the same oven. Luckily, Fern thought fast on her feet. We had another oven available to us, and she cranked up the broiler as high as it could go. Five minutes each in there, and the skin bubbled up perfectly without burning anything. I could have cried in relief when the last plate went out into the dining room. We had gotten through another round without anything coming back under- or over-cooked. All we had to do now was serve dessert, and we were done.

———

Chapter Forty-Two

AMELIA

CHAPTER 42

AMELIA

By the time the dessert round finished, I was exhausted. Annika and Shauna had done well for me for the most part, but my menu had been a challenging one. Maybe too challenging for the time we'd had, but we had managed it.

We'd served fifty people a full three course meal, and I was proud of what we made. The appetizer of grilled eggplant and black bean vinaigrette made for the perfect lead up to the main course of beetroot hummus and braised beef cheeks. And we'd topped that heavy meal off with the perfect tiramisu cheesecake.

As we began to clear down the kitchen, I began to wonder which dishes had gone to the judges. Was it the first plates, the ones I had checked so thoroughly that they'd almost been cold by the time I sent them out? Or the last plates, the ones I'd sent with a grin on my face?

Most likely, they got some of the plates in the middle of each course. It was for the best, really. It meant I didn't have their feedback to think about while we waited. We wouldn't get that until the very end of the night, when the diners had all gone to the room where we'd eaten our dinner the first night and they had made their decision.

It did leave me wondering how Zoe and Jada had done, though. I really, really wanted to win this, but if they won… I would be able to handle it. Eventually. I'd be upset, but I woud get over it. It was easier to lose when you knew you'd lost to a worthy opponent.

"Chef Hughes?" Portia poked their head around the wall. "The judges are ready for you."

———

"Friends, family members, guests, we are so glad to have been able to host you tonight." Bryce said into the microphone. His signature charming grin lit up the room. "Before we go any further, I'd like to introduce you to our very fine finalists: Chef Jada Andrews of Louisiana, Chef Zoe Cooper of North Carolina and Chef Amelia Hughes of North Carolina."

Each of us waved from our part of the stage at the mention of our name, turning on our brightest smiles for the audience. When the cheering died down, he continued.

"These chefs have gone through challenge after challenge, beating a dozen other chefs to have the chance to cook for you tonight, and boy, are we proud of them. There have been some highs, some lows, and some very unexpected moments throughout all of them, culminating in the meal you've all just enjoyed."

"But you didn't come here to hear us talk about the competition, did you?" Nathan interrupted. "You came here to find out who the winner is - and what they've won!"

The room burst into hoots and hollers, shouting their agreement. When they quieted, Denise started to speak into her microphone.

"As you all know, the winner of the first ever Heating Up the Kitchen competition will win $250,000. What we didn't tell you is that both of the runners up will also be winning something - a personal commitment from one of us to invest up to $50,000 in a business of theirs that gets started in the next five years."

I gasped, as did much of the audience. That was *huge*. A commitment from one of the greatest chefs in the country would make it easy for someone like us to be able to find the funding we'd need to get a business off the ground.

Zoe and Jada seemed to be floored by the announcement as well. No matter who won tonight, we would all be able to really begin our careers.

"Now, how about that winner?" Nathan called out, to more shouting. He seemed to glow under the stage lights, like a benevolent God.

He called out Jada's name, and the room erupted with cheers. She burst into tears, holding both hands in the air in a victory salute.

A single tear slid down my cheek, but before it reached my mouth, I smiled. She had earned every penny, and I was happy for her.

As if she could read my mind, Zoe grabbed my hand and pulled me to where Jada stood. We enveloped her in a giant bear hug, only to be surrounded by the judges and her family. Soon, the entire stage was full of people celebrating her loudly and joyfully - just the way she deserved.

I don't know how long we stood there embracing her, but when we finally extricated ourselves, Zoe and I looked at each other for a moment before falling into each others arms. We hadn't won, but maybe, just maybe, we'd gotten exactly what we needed anyway. We had found love.

———

Epilogue

ZOE

THE DAY WE OFFICIALLY BEGAN BUSINESS, I WAS MORE nervous than I had ever been in my entire life. My hands shook so hard that I was pretty sure they were going to fall off at the wrists, until Amelia grabbed them and squeezed them tightly.

"Relax, Zo. Everybody is going to be thrilled."

"What if I burn everything? What if the food is terrible? What if everyone thinks the concept is silly?" My voice rose an octave with each question until I was nearly squeaking.

"First of all, it's almost physically impossible for you to burn every single thing we cook. Particularly because I'm helping. Do you think that I'm someone who cooks terrible food?" Her voice was as soft and smooth as butter over toast, soothing my nerves in the way only she could.

"No..." I said, then remembered a particularly terrible meal she'd cooked a few weeks ago as an experiment. "Well, sometimes."

Amelia laughed and pressed a kiss to both of my

hands. "Okay, that's fair. But, you have several world-famous chefs acting as investors who already know that your food is great and believe in your concept. Do you think they don't know what they're talking about?"

She was right. Somewhere deep in my soul, I knew she was right. I just had to get past the anxiety and the nerves to make myself remember it. Taking a deep breath, I reminded myself what my therapist had said when we'd talked about this.

That group of people sitting out there are people who love you and believe in you. They are here because they want to see you succeed, and they want to be a part of that. Let them.

"Ladies! It's time! Are you ready?" Mrs. Hughes's high pitched voice sang through the door

I looked into Amelia's eyes and let out the breath I'd been holding. As long as we were in this together, I was pretty sure that I could handle anything.

———

AMELIA

When we cut the ribbon outside of our new restaurant, my heart —and face— glowed with happiness. With the judges and Chef Ian beside us in body and behind us financially, I had faith that everything would work out.

The final episode of Heating Up the Kitchen had aired on television yesterday, which meant that everyone around us knew that we hadn't won, but it didn't really bother me that much anymore.

Since the show ended, Cooped Up With Zoe had grown and transformed into Lemon and Lavender, restaurant and community cooking center that perfectly encapsulated everything that Zoe and I had wanted next in our careers.

It would be small at first, only serving dinners until we built up a clientele that would support more food and more services, but that was fine.

The flash of cameras reminded me that everyone we cared about —and many we didn't, through the news outlets that were covering this— watched us to see what would happen next. I grinned at Zoe and she beamed back, all nerves suddenly gone. It was time to start the real work now, and I couldn't wait.

THE END

Acknowledgments

As always, writing a book is something that is never done alone. The writing might be all mine, but it wouldn't exist without a few very key people in my life.

First and foremost, I would like to thank my spouse and my roommate, who were forced to deal with my attempts at cooking some of the recipes included in this book on top of me watching every single cooking show available on Netflix and Hulu alike for inspiration. I'm still really, *really* sorry about the quiche. And the dishes. I swear I'll pick something

I would also like to thank Lina, Chace, Amara, Abigail and X for being the ones to encourage me to keep writing this novel, to let it grow as long as it needed to be, until it became what you have just finished. Also, thank you for reminding me that the brain weasels are lying little fuckers and that no, not everyone will hate the book. I would not have been able to do this without you and words cannot express how grateful I am to each and every one of you.

My parents, as always, need to be thanked - even

though they're still not allowed to read these. Sorry I couldn't include the Swedish Chef for you in this one, Dad. Maybe the next one!

Last, but never least, I would like to thank Corey Alexander. They won't get to read this book, but they were instrumental in making it happen. They are a huge part of the reason that I am a writer and that I am who I am today. Thank you for being a part of my life. Your memory will always be a blessing to me.

Coming Up Next... Sugar, Spice and Love Struck Twice

When it comes to driving ratings, the judges of the hit cooking competition Heating Up the Kitchen know how to make fireworks--both on and off the screen and in and out of bed.

In public they're fierce professional rivals. In private they're turning up the heat into something more--and what's going on between Denise Lyons, Nathan Weston, and Bryce Jackson is spicier than anything on the menu.

It's supposed to be fun. Casual. As shallow as their television personalities and performances, a way to let off some steam with no strings attached and no feelings involved. But when Denise starts baking up a little more than buns in her oven... their easy arrangement's about to get a little more complicated.

She doesn't know if Nathan or Bryce is the father-- and she doesn't care. Denise wants this baby more than anything, and it's up to the men in her life to decide if they want to be fathers or not. Whether or not their show survives the second season, Denise is in it for the long term, and one way or another Nathan and Bryce will have to get past the wicked sparks of their animosity to fan the flames not just of chemistry...but the love that could make a family.

They're sharp. They're sweet. They're the perfect balance together, and between the three of them they could make something more. It's a mess in the kitchen, and in their lives--but if they come together just right, it could be as luscious as sugar and spice...when love strikes twice.

COMING SUMMER 2021

MRS. MIX UP

A secret crush. A mix-up in paperwork. And suddenly, a fake marriage that lands two women in one hotel room--and face to face with their denial.

After six months of simmering attraction, librarians Sofiya Anderson and Molly Andersen are ready to burst. There's a magnetism between them that threatens their commitment to professionalism, and not even a librarian's stern shushing can quiet it down. But they've managed to hold themselves in check...for now.

Until a mistake at a regional conference, a tiny oversight in spelling, makes the coordinators believe they're a married couple.

Two women. One bed. And a Mrs. Mix-Up that doesn't quite go by the books. Can they make it through four days of professional development with both their hearts and their jobs intact?

Mrs. Mix Up is a high heat, low conflict novel featuring a demiromantic lesbian and alloromantic lesbian pairing.

Available through KU on Amazon, Audible and in paperback from a bookstore near you!

About Candace Harper

Candace Harper is a queer, neurodivergent woman living with her partner, two cats and a dog in the PNW. She's known for being the overly enthusiastic about silly things and as the "mom friend." She writes queer fiction as much and in as many genres as she can manage, both under this name and as Ceillie Simkiss.

To keep up with her work, the best places to go are her newsletter and her twitter!